A surgeon by
Alex Modzel
through many
America until he finally traded his scalpel for a pen in 2006. The mysterious accents picked during his

nomadic life often appear in Modzelewski's writings, and many of his unorthodox ideas must have had originated in some far away lands.

Return to Paradise— as much as his earlier novels in the "Spun in Hawaii" series, *Woman on the Moon* and *Demon of Darien*— follow the unusual for a thriller convention where protagonists are denied any superhuman skills; they have to fight for their survival like any ordinary person would.

"What drives them?" fascinates Modzelewski. The conventional motivations, be it patriotism or love, do not get an automatic pass from this skeptic, all have to be stress-tested.

An avid kayaker and sailor, he usually lets his adventures play out on the beautiful islands and turquoise waters of his beloved Hawaii.

Alex Modzelewski's "Return to Paradise" is adult fiction at its best.

This novel is Mr. Modzelewski's revisit to the story he wrote years ago, and he returns with the firm hand of a seasoned writer. His characters are three-dimensional people who react to the cataclysm with the passion of self-preservation and unconventional but effectual logic. His protagonists become a part of the exciting experiment to find out the way to stay alive when life becomes neither ordinary nor predictable.

From the opening lines that cast his strong woman character, Cat, into a near-fatal situation, we are caught up in her story as it circles back through a flashback to the beginning of her predicament. The reader is hooked into her increasingly perilous situation, and becomes emotionally vested into the character who is as charming as she is cheeky—both brave and vulnerable due to her paraplegia.

Getting to know Cat's romantic interest, Jerry, is an adventure in itself. Tough and sensitive, intelligent and quite a bit crazy, Jerry might not be able to move mountains, but in the best tradition of heroes before him, he crosses rocky ranges and sails across the Pacific amid winter storms.

The story of Cat and Jerry is an interesting observation on influence that a strong, thinking woman may have on her partner. Jerry's desire to win back her love takes him on a risky journey where he recovers the part of himself long believed dead.

This is a very adult adventure/love story, not shoot-'em up sophomoric stuff.

The memorable characters of "Return to Paradise" appear in succeeding books by Alex Modzelewski, again amazing readers with the depth of their development, as they struggle through one crisis after another.

Gene J. Parola,
Author of "The Devil to Pay"
www.smashwords.com

Return to Paradise

by

Alex Modzelewski

Humpback Publishing
Kailua, Hawaii

Return to Paradise

All Rights Reserved
Copyright © 2011 Alex Modzelewski
V1.0
http://web.me.com/amodzelewski/Site/Welcome.html

Cover design by Alex © 2011 Humpback Publishing.

This book may not be reproduced, transmitted, or stored in whole or in part by any means, including graphic, electronic, or mechanical without the express written consent of the publisher except in the cases of brief quotations embodied in critical articles and reviews.

This is a work of fiction. Names, characters, places and events are the product of the author's imagination or are used fictiously.
Any resemblance to actual persons, living or dead, events, or locales is entirely coincidental.

Humpback Publishing,
48 Kailua Road, Kailua, Hawaii
http://www.BooksbyAlex.com

ISBN 978-0-9815183-4-3

"The natural liberty of man is to be free
from any superior power on earth,
and not to be under the will
or legislative authority of man,
but only to have the law of nature for his rule."

Samuel Adams (1722–1803)

For Ania, Ola and Maya

Chapter 1

Cat, January 8

A stiff breeze, customary for this time of year, drove clouds over a darkened beach like an old blanket shredded on thorny bushes and ridden with holes. The faint glow of the moon barely broke through the cover until a tear opened up, letting out a brief burst of colorless light. The nimbostratus glided low over the sand strip, brushed over the black mass of Kailua Park and a few lifeless streets beyond it, until the Kaiwa Range stopped it sternly with its vertical wall. Only there, it dumped the heavy load of moisture on nurseries and gardens at the foothill, pummeling roofs and leaves with big drops. The wind blowing across the beach whistled on sand, muting a low rumble of a shore break, but it was warm and humid like the air escaping through a Laundromat's open door.

Just another sweet winter night in Kailua, lovers cuddling in shallow sandpits might say; *da primo time* to share a puff of *pakalolo*, dark heads would nod, as a glowing point of Maui-wawi joint circled in the blackness from one friendly mouth to another.

But there were neither lovers nor potheads nesting in the soft sand. As the clouds broke, the beach below lit up empty and devoid of any human presence. Following a path of drifting cloud break, the moonbeam skimmed over the shoreline like a spotlight, revealing no traces of life. A few seconds later, it slid inland, bringing into sharp relief a jagged row of broken trees.

Where a stand of sturdy ironwoods grew last afternoon, faithfully protecting Kailua from the salt-laden trade winds, a field of splintered stumps lay now, some still pointing up, others displaying a black tangle of roots uncovered in final humiliation.

Then, a roofless house emerged. Reduced to stained white walls framing empty window holes, it sat crumpled in the middle of a mud puddle, but just next to it a smooth shiny plane unexpectedly lit up. A carport, once attached to the house, had its roof floating high above the ruin like a magic carpet. Its even, glowing surface was marred only by the irregular dark blot in the shape of a big ragdoll carelessly thrown on a roof. Before the darkness wiped the carport out, this black form twitched and its extensions became arms hugging the rough surface.

The creature crawled to the roof's edge and looked down gingerly. The world Cat Milewski knew ceased to exist on that eighth day of January 2011, but she survived—for now. Staring down, she saw her house transformed into a damp wreck; the whole neighborhood of Beachside—as far as she could see from her perch—had been wiped out as well.

Soaked, bruised and exposed to the wind, she shivered uncontrollably. She could not stay on her life-saving rooftop much longer. Given the magnitude of this disaster, the rescue might not arrive for days; waiting was not an option. Fifteen feet above the ground, no rope or ladder—still, she had to come down.

"I'm not dead yet, not quite …" she muttered stubbornly

Return to Paradise

between chattering teeth, creeping along the edge and dragging her lifeless legs behind. A downspout. The bent, zinc-plated pipe had been sucked away from the roof's edge by a withdrawing water mountain, but its lower brackets held and it was still attached to the carport's pillar. Cat reached for it, closed her eyes and heaved her weight off. The pipe creaked and ripped off in a slow motion, metal straps giving way one after another. She fell into the thick mud with a thud and a groan but, except for a bruise where her back landed on a loose board, she suffered no injury. The ground was evenly covered with the slick muck, hiding splintered wood, twisted metal and broken glass. To crawl in this terrain, in darkness, was asking for cuts and gashes, which—Cat had no doubts—would get infected fast.

Slowly, carefully feeling her way, she inched toward the remains of her house. A big metal chunk half-buried in the mud and smelling of gas had to be her neighbor's motorcycle. What was this big smooth surface stranded where her lawn used to be? She could not guess until a blue glaze shone in the moonlight. Ah, a roof ... a few tiles still attached. Who had blue tile on his house? She had no idea.

Sirens blared far away, but the only sounds close by were the constant whistle of wind and her strained breathing. Following the carport's foundation, then a sidewall of the house, Cat managed to slither to her kitchen with only minor scratches on her hands. The door had been blown off, but a large object in the doorway halted her further progress. Smooth metallic surface ... and ... a door and ... a stove! This was her stove stuck sideways in the doorway, standing on one of its corners like a squat clown. She squeezed through the foot-wide gap between the oven and the doorway frame, right at the floor level, and behind it she encountered her fridge, lying on its back, facing the open sky. She lifted the door and put her arm in, feeling around.

The first good news—despite the violent upheaval leveling

the whole neighborhood, her fingers detected some food inside. The wet slab turned out to be a loaf of bread, soaked and dripping salty water—inedible. But a still unopened carton of milk was intact and a package of smoked turkey in plastic bag was good. She ate as much as she could and her teeth-rattling shaking subsided. Food would be scarce in the days to come, she knew, and her supplies would spoil by tomorrow. Wet and shivering, she curled in a dark corner. At least she had time to think now.

Most likely, her wheelchair was buried under sand at the reef, and her car—if it was even still around—was nothing more than a big chunk of scrap metal. She could hear no movement around and it occurred to her that no other living soul might be left in Beachside. *I'm screwed*, she thought. Not something she was prepared to accept sniveling, but there was not much she could do until the morning. She scraped mud off her corner's floor with a piece of plastic broken off the fridge and put herself to sleep, thinking of Jerry carrying her in his arms.

Chapter 2

Cat, December 20

Nineteen days earlier, with Christmas quickly approaching, Cat was sitting barefoot, dressed in old shorts and a plain white t-shirt, at her workstation by the window. She stubbornly refused to look out toward the seductive blue water of the bay. The ocean will still be there tomorrow, she reminded herself spitefully, checking every line of her code for the third time.

The program seemed to work fine, but that was not good enough; she wanted the very last bug hunted down and fixed. This project was a biggie; the job was worth two months of her work and due for upload before the holidays. The fifteen grand it would bring was certainly welcome, but a neat little pile of greenbacks aside, Cat's future business rode on the fact that the software coming from her computer worked perfectly the very second it was installed. This was exactly the reason why people who had been exasperated by their computer programs would dump their problems onto her lap and cut her a check with joyful relief.

In other words, she was making her living due to other programmers' sloppy work and her reputation would not be dented by lure of the ocean. The last thing she needed was an irate customer grumbling about *her* blunders. The humiliation of facing up to her slipup ... apologies ... another round of debugging— no, definitely she could do without it,

thank you very much.
Cat did not relent until ten, when her snack was due. She picked slices of papaya with a fork, looking dreamily out toward Kailua Bay. The jumble of rocks in front of her house could hardly be called a beach, but the bay's water beyond was emerald and there was no end to it. A mile offshore, a dark rock in the shape of a gothic castle stuck menacingly out of the water like a bad wizard's lair in some Polynesian fairy tale. The rock had an official name but Cat could never remember it; for those who had any interest in the islet, it was the Bird Shit Rock, called so for the ubiquitous white deposits sea birds were leaving.

Shearwaters, petrels and terns had this place to themselves because the tumultuous white water surrounded it like a ring of never-ending avalanche, keeping humans out. Big waves arriving from the open ocean tumbled over the gobs of basalt at the Rock's foot, breaking, roaring and twisting in crazy, unpredictable currents. Only Kanaloa, the god of the ocean, could understand the mysterious pathways of whirlpools and sucking holes that meandered stealthily around the Rock, hunting for any breathing creature, ready to grab it and hold it underwater in sacrifice. For a mortal riding a light boat this was a treacherous site, definitely not a safe place to take a spill.

A guy in a blue kayak, who came into Cat's view during her papaya snack, paddled calmly toward the Rock but was still well away, in the safe waters. Fishing probably, she thought. Lucky man. I am not going to move my butt from here for many hours.

She put away her fork, washed her sticky fingers in a water bowl, wiped her hands in tissue and dove again into the computer, exhorting any temptations. The next time she raised her eyes from the monitor, reaching for a big glass of water sitting next to the keyboard, she stole a look at the ocean and noted that the kayaker had lost his relaxed attitude. He paddled toward the beach like hell. Either racing or scared, she concluded, observing his furious movements for a moment.

The island paddlers frequently went around the rock, carefully away from the boiling water, using it as a landmark in their practice routines. In fact, the first race of the season for Kanaka Ikaika, the club she sometimes raced with, looped

Return to Paradise

around the Rock and the Flat Island, an easy ten-mile paddle for the starters. This kayaker was no racer, she decided. And the boat ... his blue salad bowl was not designed to paddle on the open ocean; this kayak was only good enough to play by the beach with the kids.

Cat tried to concentrate on her job for another moment, but alarm bells in her head refused to calm down. She looked again; despite the kayaker's vigorous efforts his boat was not any closer to the shore and he was angling toward the whirlpool. Oh, well ... I might take a break after all, she decided. *Just as well ... I'll go out to check on him.* The disruption did not annoy her at all; it was as good an excuse to escape to the ocean as she might hope for.

Cat gleefully slid into a bright yellow kayak propped upright by profiled plastic blocks on a rough green platform of treated wood. She settled in the seat, just big enough to accommodate her rather smallish butt, and launched herself toward the water with one mighty shove, sliding along the inclined take-off pad. The hull tipped forward, slipped over props and splashed into the calm water of the canal.

Unlike the blue rental boat currently struggling by the Rock, her craft was a long and narrow surfski. Light and stiff, reinforced with carbon fibers, her boat was a proper open-ocean kayak.

She loved her "yellow ducky" for the dreamlike pleasure of gliding through quiet water, the excitement of skimming the surf like a flying fish, and for its hard-nosed attitude when an occasion arose to take the big waves and wind right on the nose. Cat's feeling of "high" was not just a metaphor; one moment, she could levitate on a wave so high that her eyes could scan the ocean for miles, and a second later she glided off the swell's backside like a barracuda. She danced with the ocean, that's how she felt, and she loved to dance. Three years had passed since this affair started, but the thrill still had not worn off.

The day she went to rescue the guy in the blue boat was unusual. The trade wind—usually blowing from the Mokolua Islands and driving waves to the shore—stopped ruffling the bay during the night, and the white surf marking the reef disappeared as well. But the breeze did not subside, as many tourists thought; it just changed its direction.

Alex Modzelewski

Now, the current of air gusted from the South Pacific. Hot and strong, it blew over Oahu, withering plants and howling over the mountain passes, until it bumped its head against the Koolau Range. This long vertical curtain of frozen lava, remnant of the great volcano that once helped to raise the island from the depths of the Pacific, stood in front of the Windward Coast, its 3,000-foot-tall wall resolutely protecting the eastern shores. The wind made a long jump over this obstacle to fall onto the water a mile or two farther away, fierce as ever.

Cat glided over the glass-smooth surface swiftly like a shearwater looking for fish in the clear water, quickly approaching the Rock and the blue kayak. A few minutes later, when she emerged from the shadow of Koolau, and the kayaker's figure separated into his white face, black hair and striped shirt, she sensed the stiff push on her back. The wind was driving her away from the island. White-crested waves suddenly whipped up from the quiet turquoise water in front of her bow.

The tourist, even further out than she was, had to fight the gusty wind shoving him away from the coast. He made a valiant effort to control his boat, but the blue kayak defiantly ignored his clumsy attempts; the poor guy had no headway to show for his desperate struggle. Like an empty bucket on deck, he wobbled this way and another, every few seconds hanging precariously on the thin edge of turning upside down. The boat kept turning sideways, exposing the paddler to powerful smacks by waves.

Apparently, this guy had no idea about sea kayaking and had no business poking around the Rock. Even worse, he seemed to have decided that the islet was his salvation and was about to enter the area of turbulence. He would be swimming in the boiling kettle pretty soon.

Cat leaned on her paddle hard and cut across the dangerous patch of violent white water in order to intercept the guy before he was hopelessly drawn into the vicious pool. Right ahead of him, the powerful whirlpool sucked the foam deep, tempting the unaware with the smooth face of circling water.

Disoriented by waves assaulting him from all directions, the man was hanging on, barely. He noticed Cat only when she

Return to Paradise

zoomed across a few yards in front of his bow. To his credit, he understood her intention instantly and caught the line she flung at him on the first try. For a moment, he was hanging in the balance on the verge of capsizing, but recovered and managed to put the loop over one of his shoulders.

Cat threw all her strength into the paddle. Her kayak was shaking like a leaf in the confused countercurrents but kept stabbing its sharp bow viciously into the wild breakers, submerging and raising it arrogantly from the flying foam. Once she towed her catch out of the frothy water a smile appeared on her face. Could be good practice for a kayak sprint, she giggled inwardly.

In the quiet water, Cat released the rope cutting into her ribs with a groan of relief, turned her "yellow ducky" around and approached the man. He had broad shoulders and strong arms but his face was pale like snow in Yosemite, and his brown eyes had the wild look of a spooked horse.

Cat felt sorry for him; not only had he been scared out of his mind, but now he was also humiliated by being saved by a woman. *And if you knew it all ...* She smiled to herself. She felt like saying something reassuring, like: You can't be good in everything, buddy ... but nothing smart or appropriate occurred to her. Instead she cut the "thank you" scene short and went home to keep grinding her project.

Chapter 3

Cat, December 20

Repeated spasms rippled through Cat's lower body the moment she flipped a toggle switch. Not the awful cramps they had been at first ... still, these contractions were not something one would be looking forward to. One, two, three—red lights flashed and she imagined the electric current shooting from electrodes into her leg muscles. Ooouch! The quads tightened like the two damned pieces of wood and Cat observed her pink toes, sticking out of the gray plastic mold, trying to take off toward her chin. The restraining shell held back her legs and five seconds later the spasm subsided. A brief break, then the controls twinkled again and electrodes delivered the punch to the back, burning the muscles in her butt and sending Cat's body into an arch like in some dumb porno movie. *Damn, that hurts!* And I'm supposed to be numb there, for God's sake! Wish I had something gentler than this cattle prod!

But Cat had no one to blame; she alone was responsible for the contraption. Many well-meaning people voiced their loud objections to her idea, but she had built this electrocution machine anyway and put it to use.

Right after the accident, she had a lot of nightmares but no ideas to speak of. But later, when her body was no longer a mere counterbalance to the weights hanging out of a traction apparatus, and when the painkillers cleared out of

Alex Modzelewski

her brain like the weed-stinking air dissipating after a party, it had dawned on her that something was not making sense. There she was—scared and bored beyond tears—day after day melting away in her hospital bed like a snowman forgotten behind a garden shed in the spring, while the rest of the world busily attended to its own business. As though nothing had happened ...

Every day a young woman physiotherapist, faking cheerful optimism, pulled back white sheets and Cat had a chance to look at the sickly white things that used to be her legs. Her limbs—always strong, tanned and looking just right, not too bony and not too fat—were being diligently bent, stretched and manipulated, but they were getting thinner and whiter and more pathetic every day. A pair of useless, ugly appendages, Cat thought, and this made her mad because no one seemed to give a damn about it. She would have to take care of her legs herself, she decided.

Volleyball, tennis and dancing—previously responsible for her limbs' shape, and so related to Cat's moral right to upset other girls by wearing a miniskirt—had unfortunately become the stuff of sad personal reminiscences and nothing more. She needed a new approach.

"So, even though you move my legs around, they will keep getting thinner and weaker unless my muscles start working," she pleasantly engaged her physio girl, who nodded. "And this is not going to happen because of my broken vertebrae and damaged spine!"

The therapist sighed. This conversation had happened every day, on every floor she worked, for the past ten years of her career. "You never know how much function you can recover with rehabilitation." That was about all she should say, a hopeful, open-ended comment concerning the hard, unpromising situation.

"But they would work—there is nothing wrong with them—if they could be stimulated by nerves ... or by a weak electric current." Cat was not going to let this conversation end until it hit a hard impenetrable wall.

"Right." The therapist suspected that her plans to complete this morning's list by eleven thirty would not work.

"So, how come Rehab doesn't have an electric machine to stimulate them?" Cat demanded. "It doesn't seem too complicated, technologically speaking." She might be a software person, but such a device looked like a high school robotics club project, and she'd taken an elective in digitally controlled industrial devices in her second year of university.

"Well, we don't." The physiotherapist shrugged. "I know that someone tried it and it didn't work too well. Why don't you ask a doctor?" She took advantage of Cat's moment of silent introspection and fled to the cafeteria by eleven twenty-five.

Cat asked a medical intern, a thin young man with dark circles under his eyes, and a resident, an anxious pale girl without a trace of makeup on her face. They both had heard of this treatment and would "check it up." But they never did, too busy. Finally, she caught the consultant, the boss man, during his rounds.

Cat presented her case for "external muscle stimulation" and volunteered to be an object of the experiment. At least she knew the proper term by then.

The man looked at her thoughtfully through his thick glasses, nodding his head slightly as though in agreement. When she finished, he waved his hands for a moment, as though he was drying wet polish on his nails, without making any sound. Then, prompted by her enquiring eyes, he sighed, "You have no idea, Cat. The FDA, the Hospital Medical Devices Committee, the budget …" He waved his hand again, clearly discouraged, and led the parade to the next bed.

It was totally up to her then. Why shouldn't it work? Cat wondered. Muscles were actually twitching on those weight-loss commercials on TV … But those were models—gorgeous, skinny individuals with no body fat. Maybe real people are too fat, and electrodes are too far from the muscles? A few inches of fat insulation under the skin could surely make a difference! Well, I'm quite thin, Cat reflected, especially on these chicken legs of mine … Or maybe people are afraid of the spasms and freak out. Or maybe they don't care, thinking—if they won't ever walk anyway, why bother? Maybe, maybe … I won't know unless I try. I can surely build something we could use.

That's when she found out that the technical design would not be her biggest problem. Is this apparatus approved by the

Alex Modzelewski

Federal Drug Administration? What about legal liability? Who is the medical doctor to supervise its use? The questions multiplied and she had no answers. Finally, she heard: Just forget it, it can't be done.

Maybe, Cat decided, as long as I am a prisoner here, but when I am out ... She called the electrical engineer friend; it was next to nothing to design an array of electrodes and a control box. Anita, her artist buddy, came two days later with a duffel bag full of plaster of Paris. Late in the evening, when the nurses finally settled in their station, Anita, bucket in hand, emerged from her hiding place in the bathroom. With lights dimmed, she made a terrific mess, but she slinked out with the mold of Cat's lower body, legs sticking out of her bag. The sturdy fiberglass shell was ready a week later and delivered to Cat's room in the guise of a sculpture.

"Modern art ..." Nurse Rose contemplatively nodded. "Whatever makes your days brighter ..."

To gain the cooperation of Eva, the woman medical resident, Cat had to swear on her parents' grave that she would never, under any circumstances, be dragged into admitting her contribution. At the end though, Eva had marked on the shell the best position for electrodes to stimulate each major muscle group. After the period of illicit activity, the device came to gather dust in Cat's apartment, awaiting her release from the hospital. Tempted as she was to test-drive her creation, Cat had had enough workouts during the later stages of her hospitalization. She got to know Ruth, and entered the phase of enthusiasm for rehabilitation, which was leaving her sore and exhausted every night.

However, on the day she rolled over her old apartment's threshold, in the evening, after the last well-wishing soul had left, Cat crawled into the contraption. She confidently dialed the low stimulus and pushed the button.

"Holy mackerel!" She groaned, as the spasm of her butt and thigh muscles shot her out of the bed onto the floor, where she twitched and arched, stupefied by the intensity of the burning pain. Cat stayed on the floor for a few minutes, resting and glaring into the dark space under her bed, before she pulled herself back. "Holy mackerel," she repeated, "that works, that really works."

The control box had to be reworked to lower the strength

of the stimuli, but she had her proof of concept. The next time, the device recalibrated, she started her experiment on the floor; the last thing she needed was another injury suffered as she fell off the bed. Velcro straps carefully adjusted so that her legs had no wiggle space in the shell, she turned the dial to the lowest current—front muscles, closed her eyes, held her breath and pressed the button. She felt the strange tingling and the fiberglass cutting into her groin; when she opened her eyes she saw her toes doing what they hadn't done in months, bending toward her face, spreading triumphantly like tiny rakes.

Many evenings went into the experimentation with her machine; she had to choose the stimuli so that they wouldn't be too painful but strong enough to give her muscles a good workout. If she erred, it would be on the harder side; she was no slacker and knew how to clench her teeth.

Three years and two machine models later, Cat still used her stimulator every night. She learned to accept the spasms just like serious athletes learn to tolerate the pain of a hard workout. In fact, it was not the pain that bothered her most but the weird sensation of crawling bugs, which overwhelmed the usual feeling of numbness with pins and needles added for extra aggravation. It followed the crease separating her thighs from buttocks, plus a few patches on her thighs, above the skin that had completely lost sensation. Sometimes, the paresthesia continued for hours following her workout, keeping her awake. Those hours of insomnia invariably took her mind to the place where she wouldn't voluntarily go during busy days, back to her hospital bed.

Kicking and struggling, she was dragged back to those moments when she had started having her first conscious, furtive peeks from behind the comfortable curtain of painkillers and sleeping pills. She again had to feel the terror and pain, which even today transformed her into a rigid ball curled under the covers.

During the first weeks after the accident, her soaring anxiety left very little mental space for rational understanding. Even on the clearest of days, the situation would make very little sense. One day she was a volleyball star, a heart-breaker for whom heads snapped wherever she went, the next day she was a cripple nailed to a metal frame like an insect in someone's collection. And what was sensible about Nick? She could still feel his hand, patting her on the back when she curled on the back seat. And now—puff? Disappeared in thin air?

Immobilized on the orthopedic frame, helpless and hopeless, Cat counted cracks on the hospital ceiling, wishing that one day she simply wouldn't wake up. But she did wake up every morning, even after a whole night spent crying. People were coming to see her, good people who wished her well, and they did not understand a thing. They tried to be positive, told her how lucky she was not to have a complete spinal transection. That she would surely get better and would dance at their weddings. And then off they went to their weddings, or to a beach, or to play soccer while she was slowly rotting away on a hospital bed.

Other people came with important papers to sign: insurance, consent for treatment, last will. "Do you understand? Would you like to ask any questions?"

"No, no questions." She signed the papers without reading. You just go, people, leave me alone, she thought. There was no meaning to all this hassle; she decided to end her life anyway. She would, as soon as she could, but for the time being, suspended in her orthopedic hardware, she was completely, utterly dependent on others. Eat, drink, take a pee—there was hardly anything she could do by herself, and it was driving her into howling madness. The only freedom she had left was in her mind, the liberty of thoughts and dreams.

What's the point of this miserable, boring life that awaits me? she thought every night. *I'm Cat!* Cat, the wing spiker! The only spikes I'll ever have now are the ones in my bones. And Nick ... We just had to go to a Latino club dancing every week. Nick wouldn't have it any other way. I would have muchachos lined around the club's floor like drooling puppies, she remembered fondly. But now Cat is gone and Nick has vanished. It's all gone. My life has run its course. An old lady in a wheelchair, that's the best I can hope for, and this is just not for me. This resolution and the furious contempt she felt for her life, and everything else connected to it, allowed her to function every day and remain sane.

She was weak when they finally took her off the frame, hardly capable of sitting up on her own. The world certainly

Return to Paradise

looked better in its customary horizontal orientation, when she could look around instead of staring into the ceiling, its tiniest imperfections burnt into her memory. She realized for the first time that she might be better off than some other patients when the rehab people helped her into a wheelchair. After a few days, with a good amount of power retained in her buttocks and abdomen, she could lift herself into her wheelchair without asking for help. She looked on with fear as her neighbors were lifted into a chair and strapped in the seat with belts. Could be me, she shuddered. So she was better off ... somewhat, but in the context of her loss, this advantage was without any significance.

She cried a lot, not only because of her loss, but also out of an indolent fury she felt at the injustice and idiocy of having her life stopped just when it was really starting. She had never made the final decision to kill herself, perhaps due to this anger, just to spite fate, to deprive the hateful providence of the satisfaction of seeing her folding in. One thing she was entirely sure about—whatever happened in the future, she would never allow herself to be dependent on others again. *Never!*

Chapter 4

Jerry, December 20

The twentieth of December, as Jerry Roberts remembered it, was an unmitigated disaster. That morning, Jerry stood knee-deep in the warm water of Kailua Bay, its smooth and still surface reflecting the white clouds above like a mirror. Weird. As a boy, he used to go to Cancun twice a year, where his parents had a timeshare, but he had never seen sea this calm. Like my life now—warm, safe and bloody boring, he thought. Not a wrinkle. The Hawaiian vacation, supposed to be a break from his annoyingly fine-tuned life, a foray into non-scheduled existence, already looked like a bowl of sweetened cereal with a handful of bran added for better bowel movement.

He shrugged with resignation and went to a kayak rental stand sprawling at the edge of a parking lot next to the beach. Two rows of sturdy, plastic, wide-hipped craft were arranged on the hot asphalt; one line, yellow, was straight like a picket fence in an expensive suburb while the blue kayaks were arranged into a rather informal lineup worthy of a run-down chicken range.

Jerry chose a blue kayak without hesitation, as the yellow, straight line impressed him as a simpleton's arrangement, miserly in data and boring in its statistical potential. He signed a page-long liability release without reading it, took a paddle and donned a much-faded life preserver. The kayak was heavy and resisted being dragged to the water's edge like a big, willful puppy facing a bath. Jerry hauled his boat around two little boys, naked but for their sun hats, who did not mind the hot and stagnant air as they threw sand at each other, squealing with delight. He smiled at the moms who ogled him appreciatively before he climbed into the kayak.

The craft felt solid and stable as he slowly paddled away. Five minutes later, Jerry glided over the reef extending from a small flat island, which looked to him like the deck of an aircraft carrier. Convoluted brown and gold shapes of brain coral passed silently under the boat's bottom, shallow enough to be touched with the paddle. Once he left the island behind, Jerry aimed for the northern end of the bay marked by a tall brown cliff rising vertically from the water.

The late morning sun was scorching his shoulders, just like ten years ago, in Somalia. The dress code is more reasonable this time, he thought with mild amusement. And that bastard Murphy's not around. But again, if not for Murph, I still might be wearing boots. Isn't that funny? A few lousy months … years ago, but it's never far from the surface. A bout of hot weather, a stupid jerk cutting me off on the road … Just about anything can send me back in a flash, like it all happened yesterday.

For years, Jerry had the unpleasant sensation of walking barefoot across a floor strewn with broken glass, every moment carrying a possibility of sudden pain, a lot of blood and unpredictable mess. And yes, bloody mess had happened, if not recently. And a hundred more times it was about to happen, even if the potential victim had no idea how close he was to an emergency room. Jerry would hate to generate such a mishap, but of course, his remorse wouldn't change anything. The poor schmuck would be in the hospital while the police were busily pulling skeletons out of Jerry's closet. His academic career would come to an end soon after.

One could call it Posttraumatic Stress Disorder and someone else a case of A-Man-Gone-Crazy; whatever the name, the important thing was to keep one's smoldering trouble in a bunker, where an explosion could be contained without major collateral damage. Jerry kept reinforcing his bunker for years, one brick to keep the public safe, another to protect his new and comfortable life, and then another brick

Return to Paradise

and another. The walls were getting higher and thicker with each year. No reportable accidents had happened for the past few years, but Jerry still could feel the heat and smell the fumes inside. Will it ever end?

Deep in his thoughts, Jerry did not notice wrinkles forming on the water and small waves appearing on the surface. A few minutes later, the slight breeze suddenly stiffened and Jerry abandoned his thoughts to look around. With certain alarm, he found himself surrounded by a lot of blue water. He was at least a mile offshore with the wind—blowing quite hard now—putting white caps on the waves around him, and driving him into the open ocean.

Not to worry, he smugly reassured himself; we'll fix the problem in no time. But the fact of the matter was that he never felt very comfortable on the open ocean. To run ten miles through a desert, or thrash all night through a jungle—backpack and all—no problem. Been there, done that. But the ocean was not something he ever trained for or had much experience with.

Jerry turned the kayak toward land and started paddling hard, but ten minutes of flat-out effort did not bring him any closer to the beach. He felt a tinge of this peculiar and unforgettable sensation one gets knowing that guys full of bad intentions lurk somewhere close in the darkness, their safety catches off.

His hard but unskilled paddling produced a lot of splashing but barely any forward motion. Even with maximum effort, he was not making any gains against the wind. A quick look around in hope of spotting a boat with a fisherman dozing off at the rudder failed to produce any prospect of assistance. The only thing sticking out of the blue—and by now quite angry—water was a jagged black rock, perhaps a mile away. The Bird Shit Rock. That's it, that's what the fellow at the kayak rental called it, Jerry remembered.

"It's the open ocean behind it, man. You don't want to go out there," the guy said. His lean muscular body and deeply tanned skin convinced Jerry that the man knew Kailua Bay firsthand.

Damn, I am almost *out there!* Paddling furiously, Jerry managed to turn the bow toward the black islet. He started making some progress now, not toward the beach, as he would prefer, but he was getting closer to that rock, as long as the kayak pointed forty-five degrees to the wind.

The water spray, or maybe it was his sweat, blinded his eyes and the boat rocked unnervingly. Buffeted every few seconds by large waves, Jerry knew he was out of his element. Neither his Army survival training nor his childhood kayaking experience on the Finger Lakes seemed to be of much value here. Determined to find shelter on the islet, he pushed the doubts out off his mind and put all his strength into paddling. Only when he got closer to the black, almost vertical rock did he realize this would not be a safe harbor. Nobody could break through the hissing surf surrounding this speck of unfriendly land.

A splash of yellow appeared in his peripheral vision, on the right side, and a moment later a long slender kayak with a small figure in the seat shot across his bow. Jerry raised his head, fully expecting it to be just an illusion of his blurred eyes, but the mirage burst into his life, cleaving the waves with its yellow bow.

A woman in the cockpit made a tossing gesture with her right hand and zoomed by on a wave within four feet of his boat. *Bloody risky*, he thought, but reached out automatically just in time to catch the rope slapping against his chest. His eyes remained fixed rigidly forward, and in a second she was out of sight, but reappeared a moment later, apparently having made a turn. She climbed the water mountain, her kayak's nose aiming into the sky, then surfed away on top of the big swell like a goddess riding her yellow horse to the rescue of a lesser creature.

The rope almost tore out of his hand when the line's slack ran out, and it yanked at him with the momentum of the fast-moving yellow kayak, almost pulling his shoulder out of its socket. He would have fallen out of the boat, but another wave mercifully slammed him from the opposite direction and brought his kayak into equilibrium.

Incredibly, the Goddess looked back without losing her balance and smiled. She belonged to this place; she had no fear. Jerry managed to slip the loop over his shoulder and started paddling with new determination. The taut line thrown by the saving angel provided the bit of extra power Jerry needed to control his bow and focus his effort. She led him out of the confused white water of the Rock and turned toward the beach.

Soon, the waves disappeared, the wind subsided and the glassy water spread all the way to the beach. The savior's light-blond ponytail was swinging rhythmically from side to side as she put in one smooth, swift stroke after another. Her back was slim, but well-defined muscles rippled it as she powered her way ahead. She could take wing over the water like a flying fish if she wanted, an unreasonable thought crossed Jerry's mind.

Fifty feet offshore, the woman turned her kayak around and the boats almost touched each other. She smiled. "These are Kona winds," she said. "A few times a year the trade winds stop and Kona starts blowing from the south and west, which means offshore on this side of the island. Visitors think there's no wind and sometimes float away from the beach, but once they get out of the island's shadow, the wind picks up and—you know what happens next."

Jerry looked at her incredulously, his mouth half-opened. The round delicate face with a small nose was deeply tanned and peppered with hundreds of freckles. But what really caught his attention was her mouth. Her full lips slightly parted, she had the most beautiful, warm smile. There was no mockery or air of superiority in her smile. She is beautiful, he thought, and gracious like a swan.

"You'll be OK now?"

"Oh, yes, thank you very much. You saved me a lot of trouble. I'll be fine now, thanks again."

"OK, good luck." She picked up her line, gracefully turned her kayak around her braced paddle, and was gone within seconds. All he could see was the swinging ponytail and her brown back crossed by pale yellow bikini straps.

It has been many years since someone saved him from harm. Back then, nobody made much of it. An appreciative nod or a slap on the back was more than adequate. After all, the helper expected the favor to be returned. But what do you say to someone who saved you on a beach? To a woman, and a beautiful one, too! He had no satisfactory answer, but was quite sure that his response was embarrassingly stupid. Had his savior been some big local guy—that would be humiliating enough. But being rescued by this beautiful, slim, young woman made him feel like the worst kind of a wimp, not a feeling Jerry was used to.

Wait, wait! He wanted to shout and opened his parched mouth, but produced no sound. What could he say? Would you like to have a drink with me? I'm a better man than a paddler? For a moment, he thought of catching up with her, but considering her kayaking skill, he just sadly shook his head. Jerry was looking at the disappearing yellow boat with the uncustomary feeling of acute sadness. A strange emotion, he reflected, slowly paddling to the beach. Not anger, not rage—something I can hardly remember.

A racing outrigger fell with a loud slap on the water next to him and a brown, muscular man deftly leaped into the seat. "Ho, Cat!" he yelled after the girl, and caught up with her with a few powerful strokes. It was at this moment that Jerry felt a sudden attack of rage, the reaction he was very familiar with, and a stab of jealousy, the emotion he found difficult to identify.

He directed the fury at himself. And why should this beautiful creature want to spend a minute of her time with me? A brick-wall man, a psychiatric case unfit for human interactions. Computer models, that's what I'm supposed to stick to! He angrily pulled the kayak halfway onto the sand and collapsed into the shallow water to cool off and rest.

When he returned the boat, Jerry answered "yes" to the question if he had had a good time. Then he went to his room where he lay down in a bathtub full of tepid water, relieved his thirst with three Heinekens and fell asleep in the tub. The soft noise of glasses shaking in the kitchen cabinet and water ripples suddenly appearing in his bathtub did not penetrate his deep slumber.

Chapter 5

Cat, December 22

Two days later, late in the afternoon, when Cat, ready to shut down the computer for the day, was saving her files to a Zip drive, three determined taps drew her surprised gaze to the doors. Hardly anyone came to visit her at home; she made a quick mental check of possible guests and drew a pathetic blank.

Through the door spy-hole she could see a six-foot-tall, rather well built man with a big bouquet of roses in his hand. He was looking at her peephole with a pleasant smile on his oval face topped with curly black hair. Astounded even more, but also eager to find out who her visitor might be, Cat turned the heavy bolt lock and opened the door.

With his flat stomach, chest bulging under his shirt's green-and-white fabric, and big hairy arms, this individual could have been one of her paddling buddies, except for the skin peeling off his pink nose flagging him as a tourist. And his outfit—the polo shirt, khaki shorts and leather sandals would make him stick out in a crowd of local guys like a tomato in a pineapple field. As he did not look familiar, she looked at him expectantly, waiting for some sort of introduction.

A moment of awkward silence followed as the visitor struggled at the doorway, searching for words. He had an intelligent face but was clearly dumbfounded. "Are you ... are you Cat?"

"Yes, I am Cat." The woman smiled. "And who are you?"

"My name is Jerry Roberts," he said then managed to close his mouth completely. "I'm the guy you helped at the Bird Shit Rock. I've come to say 'Thank you.'" He leaned forward and put the flowers on her lap because her hands were resting on wheels. He was, obviously, shocked to see her in a wheelchair but recovered quickly.

Cat was used to this kind of reaction. People she knew from telephone conversations or e-mail contacts thought she was an able-bodied person. Which in fact she was, except that her legs didn't work since the accident. At one point she accepted this limitation; everybody has one, right? Then she compensated, one might say overcompensated, for it in every way she could imagine. Unlike many people who feel crippled after winding up in a wheelchair, Cat came to the conclusion that having lost one important faculty, she still had a lot left to keep her on the good side in the ledger of abilities. Even better, she could develop some new powers to take her life by the horns. And she never found a better way to flout her independence than kayaking; as soon as she sat in her boat, she could run with the big dogs, and she did—racing kayaks. She had her life in her palm, totally.

"You saved my life; thank you." The man extended his hairy arm with a big grin.

"You're very welcome." Cat smiled back and took the hand that was warm and firm. "But let's not be that dramatic; I don't think I saved your life."

"Well, then thank you for going easy on my self-respect," he answered, keeping her hand in his.

A sharp guy and a nice smile, she thought. He reluctantly let go of her hand and followed as she wheeled to the living

Return to Paradise

room. Its open windows were partly shaded with white roll-up blinds and the breeze pleasantly flowed through the large but sparsely furnished room. A small dining table sat in the middle of a spacious dark-green ceramic tile floor, an open down-facing book and a stack of *Atlantic Monthly* on its top. Four chairs around the table and a small side-table set against the wall completed the furnishing. The only ornamental object was a shiny silver vessel on the smaller table. The light-beige walls were empty except for a crystal mirror hanging behind the table and a big poster of a flamenco dancer who, dressed in a long, fiery-red gown, contorted her voluptuous body in a provocative pose.

Cat wheeled to the table and with a gesture invited Jerry to sit. She'd made good progress with her program that day and was in a mood to celebrate. A pleasant relaxing evening with a book was what she had in mind, but this intriguing guest might be included in her private party, she decided. "Let me put these flowers in water," she said, sniffing the roses with undisguised pleasure. Roses … When did she last get roses? Local gingers or orchids maybe … but roses? That would have to be Nick.

As she rolled toward the kitchen, Jerry followed. "I happen to have some wine in the car—could I bring it?"

Just *happens* to have it! Cat thought. A rather presumptive fellow. I wonder what else he happens to have on his person. But she nodded and pulled out two wine glasses from a cupboard.

"So, how did you find me?" she asked, sniffing Petit Sirah in her glass, letting her long flaxen hair fall forward to frame her face and neck.

"Special powers," Jerry whispered slyly, leaning to Cat, his brown eyes squinting mysteriously, glued to her face. "Frankly," he smiled, straightening up, "I've just asked around who might be the best-looking kayaker in the ladies' division, and they all came up with your name."

"Good answer," she laughed. "So what do you do in your professional life—advertising agency, master salesman or other professional schmoozer?" He was not that young, she noted. A network of fine wrinkles around his eyes and a hint of sadness in the corners of his mouth belied his youthful athletic figure. Thirty-two or -three, Cat decided.

"Actually, I waste my life in front of a computer trying to model the economy. Besides, someone made this terrible mistake and made me an assistant professor, so I do some teaching, against my inclination and protestations."

"Really, they draft people to universities nowadays! How terrible!" Cat mocked Jerry with fake compassion.

"Well, it looked quite interesting at first." Jerry smiled defensively. "When I was an undergrad ... even later, while I was doing my Ph.D., it looked quite exiting. But after that—" Jerry sighed and grimaced. "Downhill all the way: inconclusive research, lazy students, long hours at the library.... I'd be better off painting houses." His tone was light but Cat sensed that his complaint was not entirely a joke.

The light outside turned into the dark gray of dusk. Cat was getting hungry but the guest showed no indications of leaving, and in fact she did not want him to leave either. She proposed to make some sandwiches and he immediately took it upon himself to cut the bread and vegetables. Easy to have around, Cat thought, watching him to dive into her fridge for tomatoes and onions.

"Jerry, help me out here." Cat's blue eyes looked at Jeremy across the plate of sandwiches with disbelief. "I only took one semester of Economics 101, but that's enough to understand that the economy is about people making their living ... or not making it. How can this be boring? Greeks made timeless tragedies out of less important stuff."

He shrugged. "You are right, but the science of bread-winning has evolved quite far from those basic concepts. I do computer modeling and, believe me, as much as I like numbers, it's hard to see actual people at work behind them." He let the words flow without much thinking because his mind was focused on her lips, full, continuously moving, sometimes stretching in a smile, and sometimes assuming the shape meant for kissing.

"I disagree!" Cat countered heatedly. "Only by numbers you can get the truth out of this meaningless soup served on TV by spin-doctors." She was close to shaking her finger at Jerry, challenging his statements.

This is one fierce interlocutor. Jerry hid his smile. Life would be so much more interesting if his undergrads in New York showed any of her excitement. And the girl did a bit of reading. In fact, even upside down, he could read the author's name on the back of the book lying on the table. Von Hayek. Old Von Hayek, the grandpa of modern libertarian fanatics.

"Let me tell you a story, Cat," Jerry offered. "A small but true anecdote to show you that numbers can be pretty deceiving."

She put her elbows on the table and cradled her face in hands, the epitome of an attentive listener.

"Imagine a small village at the edge of a desert ... poor like dirt, maybe a hundred inhabitants hang around a few dilapidated hovels, tending goats. No numbers can describe their condition because they have no money to count. Then, sometime in the seventies, some stray geologist discovers that there is actually an aquifer—you know, water underground— in their area, and a few years later the village receives a gift from the United Nations: an artesian well.

"They start growing stuff ... don't know, whatever they normally grow there. At this point, they start showing on the financial radar because they sell their produce. Tiny as this blip is, you begin having your numbers."

He smiled mysteriously at Cat who shook her head defiantly, saying, "So far so good."

"Indeed," Jerry agreed. "So they do really well; the village might have a few hundred people now. There are a few cars; kids go to school … The good folks at the UN are happy; it's heartening to have a solid success from time to time. The village's economy even starts showing in local statistics, as their cash turnover is getting bigger than a rounding error. Forward twenty years."

Cat, listening and staring at Jerry, became aware how thick and full was his black hair, the kind one would like to plunge her fingers into.

"It's a substantial, prosperous village now. Big all-wheel-drive Suburbans and F-250 trucks are parked in front of a new nice mosque at the town's square, all black for some reason. Women wrapped up to their eyeballs as ever, but jingle with their golden ornaments every step they make. A few kids sent away to universities … You look up your numbers and find there is quite a lot of wealth there. Their old friends at the UN had to be happy. And then …"

He suspended his voice.

"And then?" Cat picked up on his intonation. "Then what?"

"And then, the blip disappears from your financial screen—poof!" He sighed. "No money, no wealth, back to a tiny starving village. The miracle is over; the benefactors can't believe their bad luck."

"What happened? Did the well stop producing? The water ran out?" Cat was fascinated and demanded explanations."

"You see, the numbers don't lie, as you've said, but they don't tell the truth either. The villagers' good luck started with their artesian well, but the later explosion of wealth had quite a different base. No way they could grow enough crops to pay for all those goodies; the well was not that productive. But they were buying so much ammonia fertilizer you might think their farms were Iowa-size.

"Someone had a good look at the numbers and put one and one together. Bingo! The village turned out to be a big manufacturer of … explosives! Now those trucks and big SUVs made sense. They exported their 'produce' to places where anything more flammable than a candle caused us some serious heartburn."

"So then what happened?" Cat cried impatiently.

"We blew it up." Jerry shrugged. "The manufacturing plant, warehouses … and the well."

"We … blew it … up?" Cat asked slowly, her eyes widely opened in disbelief.

Jerry would gladly slap himself across the face. "We—like you and me; the U.S. taxpayers, who paid the guys who did it." Then hesitantly but truthfully he added, "I've never blown up anything; though I will not deny I was not far from the village. The point I am making is that although numbers don't lie, they often lead to false conclusions. As I've mentioned, I try to model the economy … I am pretty good at it, but I am more often wrong than right … and nobody is really any better. People are completely unpredictable. You can run a program to control a lathe, but people … forget it. You think you've considered all possible actions and then your jaw drops; they have some other monkey wrench to throw into your lovely model. That's why I sounded somewhat discouraged."

Cat nodded, seemingly satisfied. "I can see that, but why keep doing something that doesn't work?"

"Decision-makers love it. Most of those guys who win their jobs by expert handshaking and children kissing don't know an average from a median, but they just can't get enough of computer models. You try to explain the limitation and their eyes are glazing over. At the end the guy asks, 'Professor, just tell me: What are the chances it could be wrong? Less than one in a hundred? I'll take it!' People die and billions are wasted." Jerry made a dismissive gesture. "Why don't we talk of something more fun?"

Cat's interest in the economy was impressive, but his

attention was leaning toward the exquisite shape of her neck ... long, partly covered with exuberant light-blond hair. He tried to avoid looking directly at her ample breasts, unrestrained by a bra and stretching her white t-shirt, but an incidental glance left no doubt that she was endowed well beyond the size expected on this slim body. The shrink who once compared his emotional landscape to a brick wall had missed an important landmark; Jerry might have tried to build a wall to keep apart from the human race, but he had never lost his appreciation for female beauty.

But Cat managed to bring the conversation back to the economy, unemployment specifically, and Jerry went along for the sheer pleasure of seeing her excited and involved with him. "In my opinion, the answer is really quite simple: people mostly work if they have to. You take away the prospect of being hungry and most of your workers will find more entertaining ways of spending their time," she concluded shortly before ten.

Cat enjoyed seeing Jerry's forehead furrow and his thick eyebrows rise as he tried to absorb and counter her points. She also could not miss Jerry's efforts to look into her eyes. She liked it, and couldn't hold back her smile even as nasty phrases like "labor dispute" and "being fired" rolled off their lips. She found forgivable Jerry's somewhat excessive focus on her lips—it was not altogether unpleasant.

At ten o'clock, the guest stood up and thanked her for a lovely evening. She was astonished at how quickly the time passed and wouldn't mind him staying a bit longer. I've become a hermit, she thought, rolling to her bedroom. Human company is such an unusual treat to me. On the other hand, it's damn hard to find someone this intelligent to talk with.

"Pat, she is beautiful and smart like hell." Jerry moved the phone to his other ear. "I went to see her last night and we had a lovely evening. We joked about my rescue. She made it sound like a carnival ride. Of all the topics possible, we had a lively discussion about economics. And let me tell you, the young lady has pretty formed opinions and defends them like a bobcat."

Jerry did not call his older sister often, but after his visit with Cat, he felt a sudden urge to tell someone about the incredible transformation happening to him. Like Coke fizzing out of a bottle once the cover was cracked, his bubbling excitement couldn't be contained. Quite remarkable for an individual with a psychopathic trait and flat affect, he thought. Murph would shit his pants had he known I got off the hook before being completely and irreversibly fucked up.

His new disposition felt so foreign that it occurred to Jerry he might suffer from a split personality disorder. Suffer? Hah, if this is a split personality, I'm glad at least one of us is happy. On closer examination, however, Jerry found this new happy guy quite familiar, though much younger.

He turned off the ignition and stepped out of the car in front of a large yellow house. The initial disappointment with a hotel in Waikiki turned into a really good deal, a vacation rental in a private home. Half-price for a bright clean room a few steps away from Kailua Beach.

"I know. I haven't been so enthusiastic about anybody or anything in a long time, if ever." Jerry was luxuriating in his blissful state of mind. This girl affected him in a way no one ever had.

"But, Pat, she's handicapped. I don't know what it is, but she is in a wheelchair. It's amazing how strong her upper body has to be to make her such a good kayaker." He sniffed the air. The flowers in Hawaii were just indecent in their sensuality; a cloud of jasmine scent drifted through the backyard like a slightly pornographic flower shop float in a Valentine's Day parade. The bright red blossom of the bougainvillea, climbing over the small trellis at the entrance door, reminded him of Cat's lips.

He stopped and his eyebrows moved toward a deep frontal furrow. "Emotional problems ... Yes, I know about people with disabilities ... But I just can't believe you've said it. Of all people, I should not be the one to demand a perfect mental stability score. I might show you some of my records from the VA ..."

The female voice in the speaker spoke in soothing tones now and Jerry's face relaxed. "Anyway, she seems very confident and rational. Well, if she weren't that sweet ... I could even say slightly opinionated."

He listened for a while and shrugged. "As a matter of fact, I don't think the VA knows me anymore. Captain Murphy—colonel probably by now—was a thorough man and had good reasons to make my records disappear. That's what intelligence service is about: information management—finding info when needed and hiding when inconvenient. A basic fact they teach you in your first week."

He was standing in the middle of his room, ready to lie down on the queen-size bed and contemplate this evening. "Good to talk to you, Sis."

"Jerry, wait!" The voice in the phone rose with urgency. "You've been well ... I mean, no incidents for years, now. I know. But ... Have you told her? She has a right to know. Especially since she's handicapped. Not that it would make much difference. Jerry ... Jerry?"

He felt the wave of heat rising to his head and experienced the great urge to tell his sister to better mind her own fucking business, but a few deep breaths later he sighed into the phone: "Yeah, I will." Pam was right; Cat had the right to know. He would play it fair, let Cat sort out the bad and the good about him and make up her mind. His own mind had been already made up.

Next day he swam, walked and read—whatever might

help to fight off his desire to see Cat again as soon as possible. But his plan to stay away for at least one day, so that she wouldn't feel pressured, was crumbling by noon. At two, he reached for the phone and this time did not put it back. "Cat, I wondered … er … if you might be free later on today. I feel kind of lonely … Maybe you'd like to spend some time together? We haven't completely sorted out this welfare problem, you know."

He heard her laugh and the tense wrinkles melted on his face. "Well, Professor, you are on vacation and I am not. I have to finish my project. But if you have nothing better to do … I could put you to some useful work and then I might fix dinner for us."

Jerry put the phone down with a wide grin and looked at his face in a mirror. Well, my boy, you might not be over the hill yet. The Goddess will see us tonight, he addressed his image with satisfaction. The unshaved face in the mirror grinned back with optimism that Professor Roberts was not accustomed to.

Stepping out of the shower, dripping wet and with his head buried into a towel, he stumbled on a broken vase in the middle of his room. Apparently it fell off the shelf of its own volition.

Chapter 6

Rosen, December 23

Harry Rosen sat at his desk looking through receipts. The small, shabby room was furnished with a cheap metal desk, two folding chairs and a scratched-up gray filing cabinet. Dim yellow light radiated from a bulb barely shaded by dirty fabric. Contrasting with the drab and worn-out decor of his office was the small but exquisite sculpture of a naked girl kneeling on a pedestal, her upper body submissively resting on the ground.

Rosen was waiting, absentmindedly stroking the figurine with his finger. A local guy was to come with lobsters this evening. There was not need to wait for him, really. The manager could take care of it, but he wanted to see the boy. His principle was to make the acquaintance of some local people who could be useful in the future. You never know whom you'll need, he thought. He was looking through the receipts to kill time, thinking that life could be a real struggle if he had to depend on the income from this miserable shack.

The lobster guy, Abraham, came with a sack of lobsters at nine o'clock. The big, dark boy, with heavy muscular neck and arms, was handsome and friendly, but somehow intimidating and seemed to take up too much space in his office. The lobsters were still frisky and smelled of the ocean. That's where they were just a few hours ago, before being poached, Rosen thought. Better not to know how they got to my restaurant.

"Mr. Rosen, would you like some fresh pineapples and papayas?" Abraham pressed on with his business.

"Are you a gardener, too?" Harry asked pleasantly, although he couldn't imagine this boy digging in dirt.

"I have a friend," Abe answered, without raising his head.

Rosen nodded and two more bags appeared on the floor, filling the office with the smell of wet soil and the sweet aroma of roughly handled pineapples. Abraham's price was very good, half of what the regular supplier would ask. He grabbed the cash and was gone in a minute, did not even count the money. A big, strong guy with less than clean hands, thought Rosen. Could be useful for something other than lobsters one day. The boy came back a few minutes later. "What's up, Abe, any problems?"

"Oh no, Mr. Rosen, I just wondered if you might need a waitress. My girlfriend's looking for a job."

"Sorry, Abe, we've just hired another girl. But ... if your girlfriend is interested in light cleaning twice a week, I might use some help at home. I don't like coming back to a dump at night, and I like cleaning even less. If she's interested, tell her to come here." Rosen looked at the figurine on his desk. Some of these island girls were quite pretty—they reminded him of Consuela. That girl was a real peach—*jugosa*, they said. He smiled and gently patted the figurine with his finger.

"Abe, what do you do for fun on this island?"

The younger man squirmed uncomfortably. "What do you mean, Mr. Rosen? You can go to the movies or to a bar ..."

"I know about movies and bars, Abe. Is there anything else, anything special? What is the best fun you had last month? And I'm not asking about your girlfriend, he he he," Rosen cackled.

"Cockfighting—I like to go to cockfights." Abe did not need to think even for a moment.

"Now you're talking! Tell me about it. I've never seen a cockfight." Rosen's eyes opened wider. Maybe this dull evening would lead to something interesting, after all.

"Oh, we have great derbies here, sometimes five hundred cocks in one meeting. Great fun, if you like that kind of thing." Abe relaxed and his big shoulders dropped with relief.

Return to Paradise

He enjoyed talking about cockfights.

"So, I understand that chickens, oh well—roosters—try to peck each other's brains out. Is that really that exciting?" Rosen sounded dismissive, but the idea of creatures pecking each other to death held some excitement for him. He leaned forward and waved Abe towards the other chair.

"These are no roosters you would see in any backyard. These little devils are tough and fight like you've never seen before. They jump like … five feet in the air and fight with knives …"

"Knives? How can a chicken fight with a knife?" Rosen's hands tightly gripped the desk's edge.

"They have a small knife, like a razor, attached to the spur of the foot … and each rooster tries to jump higher than the other one. And if he gets higher, he slashes the other guy with his knife. If the cock is really good, he can finish the match in a minute. If an artery gets cut, the blood squirts all over like from a water pistol."

Harry Rosen felt excitement rising. "Do they get two knives, one for each foot?"

"No, they're like people; some are right-footed, others are better with their left. So a trainer figures out which is the better foot, and that's the one the cock gets his blade on."

"A trainer … how can you train a chicken?"

"Oh, they're all natural fighters, they know how to fight. But a trainer makes them exercise and spar for practice. Usually, an owner will have more than one hundred young chicks. If he just lets them stay together, they will fight each other like crazy. So he watches which ones come out on top. He doesn't want them too bloodied or scarred when young—that might make them wimpy. So they get something like tiny boxing gloves on their spurs. This way they can jump, fight and hit but don't get hurt."

"That sounds like a lot of trouble—just to watch them fight. Is there any money to be made in it?" Rosen tried to make some sense of this spectacle.

"There's a lot of money to be made in it, or lost. Every time you enter a cock into a derby, and you have to enter at least five, you give five hundred bucks' deposit for each one. Your opponent does the same. If you win, you get his money; if you lose, he gets yours. And, of course, the house takes its cut."

Most interesting, thought Rosen. The house ... Of course, they're the ones who make the real money. It makes them no difference who wins or whose chicken gets slashed up. Just like any other gambling, only this one sounds like more fun. Instead of drunken idiots throwing their money away, you get to see an exciting show. Harry smiled jovially. "Well, if your chickens lose, you get a very expensive dinner."

"Not even that." Abe was animated and smiled broadly. "They're so hard that you might cook them all night and still couldn't take a bite. Besides, they are full of vitamins, steroids—God knows what else. Believe me, you don't want to eat them."

"Doesn't surprise me at all," said Rosen thoughtfully. "If the stakes are high, obviously, the owners will do whatever they can to help themselves a bit. Is this legal?" The legality of the practice, any practice, was important to him only as a matter of an objective fact that needed to be addressed, but not necessarily obeyed. Besides, it's always good to know what limitations might be placed on your opponent, Rosen believed.

"That's the problem," admitted Abe with sadness, "cockfighting is illegal. You can raise them, but if they catch you running cockfights, they could send you to jail."

"Isn't that something?" Harry commiserated. "Killing chickens is legal but letting them kill each other is illegal."

Abe shrugged. "That's certainly not going to stop cockfighting, just makes it a bit more difficult."

"Do you think you could take me sometime to a derby, as you call it? Who knows, maybe we could go into a little business together."

Abe's eyes brightened up. "Are you serious? I was thinking about raising cocks from good fighting bloodlines. But, you know, it takes money to make money, and I am a bit short on cash now."

"Well, Abe ... we might be a good match. I might have some loose cash, but I don't have much interest in chicken farming. I might be interested in setting up a little establishment for fighting cocks. Let's see the show first and then—one way or another—we are going to make some money, Abe—me and you."

Abraham left the office with his heart filled with joy. He had found himself a business partner, a serious man, a restaurant owner. Now, Kalani would have to respect him for what he really was, a businessman.

Chapter 7

Jerry, December 24–26

Cat's house had white stucco walls, turning pink in the setting sun, a red clay roof and ornamental ironwork on the second-floor balcony, giving it a Spanish flavor. Located on a small peninsula projecting into Kailua Bay, it overlooked a narrow stretch of big dark-brown and black rocks slippery from the white spray of waves smashing against the shore every few seconds. However, the property had direct access to the large stream, which ran no more than fifteen feet away from the house's white wall on its way to join the bay through a shallow delta framed by boulders. The mild slope between the house and the stream was covered with short grass and punctuated by foxtail palms, beautiful trees with fronds shaped like a fox's appendage.

A classy place to live, Jerry noted, waiting for the solid oak door to open. He could hear a muffled guitar solo then a dramatic voice wailing and dry clicks of castanets. Flamenco, isn't it? The ocean creature would probably be as good a dancer as she is a kayaker, if she could walk, he thought.

Cat opened the door, a friendly smile beaming from her freckled face, and casually waved him into the living room.

Jerry walked up to the table, where last night he sat facing Cat in her wheelchair lined up along the other side. He pulled the chair out and turned it sideways, toward the room. Cat, who rolled behind him, stopped just in front of his chair and their knees almost touched when Jerry sat down. Embarrassed, he couldn't escape looking at her legs. Unlike the previous day, when she had them covered with light towel, her legs were in full view below her shorts. Brown like her face and arms, they were thin, but did not have the atrophic look of paralyzed limbs.

"Well, let's get it over with," she said, calmly watching his eye movements. "I was in a car wreck four years ago. Along with a bunch of other fractures, cuts and bruises, I had a spinal cord injury. The end result is that my legs are pretty useless, though I can move around on crutches a bit. Prefer not to—I feel much more secure in my wheelchair. Do you have a problem with that?"

"Oh, no, none whatsoever … I admire …" Jerry stuttered nervously, desperately trying to sound sincere and not too compassionate. He remembered Bill Strachan, the guy who loved to play basketball, as much—or maybe even more— after his amputations as before the world tour arranged and paid by Uncle Sam. Bill bounced all over the court on his high-tech spring-loaded prostheses like a kangaroo, tripping and falling like a drunk, as his balance was poor, but nothing could piss him off more than a hint of pity on account of his below-knee amputations.

"No need to admire, just treat me like anybody else," she cut off the topic and her full lips again stretched in a grin. "Since you expressed preference for manual labor last night …" Cat's blue eyes were squinting in a friendly smile but were undeniably tinted with sarcasm, "I wondered if you would like to see how well that suits your temperament. Are you handy with your hands, Professor? I have a little project for you. Follow me."

The living room's French doors opened onto the ocean-facing lawn, but the dirt pathway that started at the concrete patio outside the doors curved sharply left, leading across the slope to the stream. They followed it, Cat's wheelchair falling into the dark-brown ruts worn in the green turf, until they reached a wooden deck at the water's edge. A green-painted metal frame had been screwed to the weathered four-by-four planks, arching above the long yellow kayak sitting in a small cradle.

"This is the gate to my freedom," Cat announced with mock pomposity. "I can wheel myself here, then I transfer to the kayak by swinging on the frame monkey-style, push off and s-l-i-d-e into the water like an eel. No fuss, no trouble, I can do it all by myself.

But when it rains, it gets really messy and slippery. By the time I make it from my landing deck to the door, I feel like going back to the water to wash the mud off. A little ramp or boardwalk across this lawn would make my life easier. Do you think you can take on this project despite your academic pedigree?"

"Oh yes, ma'am, thank you for your order." Jerry happily accepted the challenge. Quite obviously, this was not a task for one afternoon. Now he would have a good excuse to spend time with her every night. "I'll start with building a computer model of your boardwalk." He smirked.

"*Whatevah.*" Cat was getting into Hawaiian pidgin. "I'll be busy for another hour or hour-and-a-half, so pace yourself. The tools and lumber are in the shed ... if you decide to go ahead with the non-virtual version."

Jerry made his plans and measurements at an unhurried pace, enjoying the ocean-smelling breeze, frequently stealing looks toward the window where Cat's yellow-colored hair stuck out over the computer. Her eyes appeared from behind the beige box repeatedly as well, looking out to him until she finally gave up on her work. This would not be her most productive day.

Cat certainly did not fuss over her guest. They sat at the kitchen table, eating buttery ripe avocado sandwiches prepared right there on a cutting board. They did not discuss economics anymore; she cracked open the window upon her life and Jerry looked in with fascination.

For over three years, Cat had lived by herself in this house, which doubled up as an office for her software consultancy business.

"A good way to make a living ... as long as you are not too keen on human interactions. I do almost all my work over the net or by phone. The real, paying clients want a working program, not chitchat."

"It's their loss!" Jerry offered in a teasing way, but knowing without doubt that he would like to squeeze every last minute of one-on-one time with these intelligent eyeballs, the glimmering blue of the ocean rather than the color of empty sky. Over the past two days, he'd seen these eyes filled with passion and squinting in irony, but he couldn't imagine Cat's eyes disinterested or unthinking.

With a shock, Cat felt the unexpected wave of heat rising to her face. God, I'm not blushing over this little compliment. "Thank you, but the fact of the matter is, it's much faster and easier to get an intelligent exchange through an e-mail than a conversation. People who are willing to talk about the things that interest me are not that common." She nodded slightly toward Jerry. "So, I have kayaking friends whom I meet on the ocean, but hardly see anyone else." She reflected for a moment.

"But don't think I'm some kind of antisocial hermit. I wasn't always like that. One might even say I once was a party girl." Her nose wrinkled in a naughty grin but the smile quickly disappeared. "It all ended four years ago, when Nick, my husband, drove our car into a pole. He died instantly, while I—asleep on the back seat; we were coming back from a party—woke up a few days later in a hospital, paralyzed from my waist down."

Jerry listened without interruption. If he had learned one useful thing in his Army career, it was the skill of listening.

Cat did not go into details, just stated facts for the record. "That's how I landed here, in this earthly paradise; the real one will have to wait a few more years." She smiled ironically. "I even found out that the insurance money for Nick and me could buy me this house. Three years ago, when I got into kayaking and was looking for a place with ocean access, prices in Hawaii were not that ridiculous yet. But now you tell me more about your work. Tell me about yourself," she demanded.

Jerry despised his work and, seeing her interest in the economy, it was a hard thing to admit. He had a miserable time awaiting him back in New York. Soon, the winter break would be over and he would return to class, to look into the bored faces of his undergrads. Even worse, he would have to read their moronic attempts at economics research, which—a part of the curriculum—was sacrosanct and inevitable, like death. Then he would have to write some semi-intelligent critique, just to let them know he had actually read their pitiful essays. He gave a short and unenthusiastic account of his professional life then escaped into the stories of his childhood, family travels, Cancun vacations.

At this point, he decided to leave his brief career in Army intelligence out of his resume. Supposed to remain confidential, he reminded himself, knowing well that sooner or later he would need to come clean, if this friendship was to go anywhere.

"Funny," she said, "I used to go there with my parents as well. Who knows, maybe we met at a beach in Cancun before."

"I would remember you!" he blurted out, knowing this very moment how silly he had to appear, a thirty-three-year-old man on the verge of blushing.

"I would remember you, too." She smiled and put her narrow brown hand on his.

His fine set of dating skills polished to perfection by the fifteen years of romantic experience fell off, leaving him vulnerable and awkward like a hermit crab caught while changing his shell. The wave of tenderness, very much different from a purely erotic excitement, engulfed him and Jerry allowed himself a moment of daydreaming—leave New York, quit my job ... just build the boardwalk all day, as long as I could hold her.

"Why don't you quit your job, if you despise teaching?" Cat asked as though she was reading his thoughts. "If it makes you unhappy, or even simply bores you, why not try something else?" Then she added with a crooked smile, "You could make a career of building decks and boardwalks ... as long as they are made of wood planks rather than computer code."

Encouraged, Jerry slipped back into his more socially accomplished mode, bent over the table and trapped her hand under his. Cat pulled it back but did not lean away, her lips still within his reach.

"It's a long story," Jerry said, recovering his composure. "Economics is not my first vocation ... I'll tell you sometime about the other one. But, at one point of my life, it seemed I'd do best in front of a computer monitor rather than working with people. Turned out, I had a knack for abstract thinking. When I was a student, my professor got me involved into some economics research. I did well and had some fun with it. So I kept at it and got my Ph.D."

She wouldn't like a half-truth, Jerry was sure, but that's how much he was prepared to offer at this moment. At what point do you confess having attacks of homicidal rage? How about your shrink's recommendations to stay away from people as much as possible? Jerry considered these questions briefly and ruled that the second date was not the best time for a chat about one's mental health.

"So, you got bored and disappointed ... Why not to turn to something else?" Cat was too bright to buy his explanation.

Jerry wished he could terminate this line of questioning. He stood up, went to the kitchen and got himself a glass of water. When he returned to the living room, he ambled casually toward Cat and stopped behind her wheelchair. Looking over her head into the mirror on the opposite wall, he saw her blue eyes, alert, wide-open and looking straight into his. He inhaled the warm scent of her hair, which he gently stroked with the tips of his fingers.

Cat closed her eyes and said softly, "Jerry, I'm very sensitive to touch—please, don't."

His hand withdrew and rested on her shoulder, his palm greedily absorbing the warmth of her body. Cat did not shrug, just opened her eyes wide and snapped in a very cool and clear voice, "Jerry, sit DOWN!" Like a smack with a wet towel, her command, not intended to kill or maim, carried quite a bit of weight and unpleasant coldness.

He returned to his chair and was rewarded with a synthetic polite smile and a "thank you." The rest of the evening was awkward and uncomfortable. Despite their efforts, the friendly banter had been lost and twenty minutes later Jerry thanked her for a lovely evening. He left, kicking himself for spoiling such a promising date. But there was hope as the boardwalk construction was just beginning.

On Christmas Eve, Cat and Jerry discovered they shared a lack of any religious sentiments. Wire-made reindeers grazed upon green lawns across Kailua and plastic figures of obese red-faced men baked on porches in the Hawaiian sun, but Cat's house remained unembellished. She saw no good reason to bring a fake tree into her living room, and Jerry was happy with any arrangement that consisted of Cat and him being alone. As far as he was concerned, this was to be his best Christmas ever.

On the twenty-fifth, he dug out a lot of dirt to level the pathway, sweating profusely in the afternoon heat. Still better than grading papers, he thought, grinning and looking at his blistered hands. At six, when darkness made work impossible, Jerry put the shovel and wheelbarrow away and went to the bathroom for a shower, while Cat was preparing a simple dinner. They were falling into a comfortable routine rapidly as though they have been living together for years.

He liked the intimacy of taking a shower in her bathroom. Stepping out of the stall, dripping wet and naked, he slowly dried himself with a towel, looking at her thin yellow bathrobe. Her electric toothbrush sat on the right side of the sink, and her hairbrush with a cherry wood handle, a few blond hairs tangled in its bristles, rested on the cabinet. Her very personal things, objects hidden from strangers, were within his reach. He could touch them and smell the faint aroma of her cologne. He was allowed into her private space.

To celebrate the day when the first planks were laid, Jerry brought his own toothbrush and left it next to Cat's. He was fully aware of this action's significance and carefully observed the outcome of his experiment. This test would mean nothing if the house's occupant was a male. A guy would either overlook the presence of a new object or wouldn't give it a second thought. He wants to brush his teeth, so he brought his toothbrush. Period. Not so with women, Jerry had been taught in the past. Women easily pick up on any changes in their environment and are very sensitive to their emotional significance.

"It's beyond your imagination, I suspect," Victoria used to say. She was a girlfriend with a serious educational bent, as an earnest postgraduate student might be expected. Jerry was five years out of the Army then, working on his doctoral thesis and hiding behind his emotional brick wall and a computer screen. He felt reasonably safe in his bunker—other than sex—only a guided missile could reach him there. Victoria was single, ambitious and far too busy for a real romance, not to mention a family. They were made for each other. They fulfilled one another's social obligations, stood in as "the significant other" at the university and family occasions, but mostly met in his apartment to satisfy their more private needs.

Not a great passion—Jerry remembered without any embarrassment—but a comfortable relationship based on a clear understanding and undeniable physical attraction.

Even with their relation so premeditated and rational, Jerry was not allowed to take any shortcuts. Victoria had definite ideas on the importance of proper ambiance: the right music, stimulating aromas, the thoughtfulness of small gifts and, above all, good manners. She took it upon herself to complete his development; he had the good luck any man could envy.

Having had the secrets—opaque to so many men—explained, Jerry immediately grasped the meaning of finding his toothbrush placed in the cup next to Cat's. She accepted him into her intimate world.

The same evening, Cat and Jerry shared a bowl of fettuccini Alfredo—seemingly her showcase dish—occupying the middle of a small circle of flickering, warm light. There, they could exist alone, just their faces feeling real in the space carved out by the candles, the rest of the world remaining distant, unimportant and possibly illusory.

Jerry and Cat, the two people normally filled to the brim with articulate ideas, hardly talked, afraid to break the spell. Their friendship was less than a week old; it had to be a dream, they suspected, and they would rather stay asleep. Even the scent of an unsightly jasmine bush outside the window was too sweet to fit into the rational world.

On his way home, Jerry tried to describe the magnificent sensation this evening left him with, but the appropriate terms were missing from his vocabulary. *W-40 on a really rusty screw,* he eventually sighed, wishing he could call Victoria for consultation.

Chapter 8

Kalani, December 27

Kalani's days were Mondays and Fridays. Three hours was usually enough to take care of Cat's house— clean, cook a bit, take care of the lawn—but she sometimes stayed longer if they had something particularly interesting to talk about. She worked for Cat, that was her job, but just a year younger than her employer, she was also Cat's friend. Usually she came around two o'clock, straight from Mrs. Oshiro's apartment. Having her own key to the house, she did not need to bother Cat, who worked by her window.

"Hi, Cat. How are you?" Kalani muttered from the door and Cat waved her greetings silently; she was on the phone with a client. Kalani started with the dirty dishes, her pretty face dejectedly turned to the sink.

Soon Cat wheeled into the kitchen to be met by the young Hawaiian's back. "Hi, Kalani, What's new?" Kalani had a sunny disposition on most days, but not that day. "What's wrong, Kalani? C'mon, tell me!" Cat pressed on for answer.

Kalani looked up from the sink, throwing back her long, black hair. "No new problem, always same problem—not enough money." She angrily attacked the frying pan.

"You're working at least eight hours a day, six days a week," Cat noted skeptically, "and the pay is not that bad."

Kalani shrugged. "Not enough money. I think I need to get a night job; maybe I could do some waiting on Saturday or Sunday." She was moving fast, finished the dishes and started sweeping the kitchen floor. Even while cleaning the kitchen she had the graceful, fluid movements of a hula dancer. She had practically grown up in her *halau* since she was five.

"What are you doing with the money, *wahine*?" Cat looked at her friend with suspicion. "I don't believe you spend it all on yourself. And your mother gets a government check after your father. Is Abe sponging off you?"

Kalani did not enjoy this conversation; things were bad enough without Cat rubbing it in. She stopped sweeping, put the broom away abruptly and exploded, "You just don't understand. You live here by yourself, like some *honu* in her shell, and no one wants anything from you. And what am I supposed to do? Abe comes and wants money. He's my man. If I don't give him money, he gets very angry. I'm scared when he gets angry, but I don't want to lose him either. Whatever I give him, he's done with it in a day or two."

"What does he do? Drinking, dope?"

"No, he bets on cocks. Now he decided he's going to raise his own roosters. With his buddy Jose; this *lolo buggah* never had more than a dollar in his pocket." Kalani was venting her frustration with hands on her hips. "So, Abe wants me to give him money for chicks. He'd already promised two thousand dollars! Good roosters are pricey, you know? So, if he doesn't come up with the stuff, the other guys will think he's chicken shit. I *have* to give him. Now you happy?" She let her shoulders drop in defeat and pulled out a vacuum to clean the carpet in the living room.

"So what are you going to do?" Cat just couldn't leave things unfinished.

"I have some cash in the bank, for nursing school. I'll pull it out." Kalani's voice cracked somewhat, and she wiped her nose.

"You can't do that! You are supposed to start your program in a few months!" Cat was exasperated and didn't try to hide it.

"So I won't start in a few months! Just drop it, Cat. Since when you such an expert on living with man?" Kalani went out to trim the hedge in order to escape further conversation.

Cat looked at the door for a moment, thinking: Serves me right. What do I know about living with a man? For a few years I played house with a boy, and even that was a century ago. But there is no question— this story won't end with those two thousand bucks. Kalani will have to find out on her own, I guess. She rolled back to her computer.

Kalani worked till five thirty, picked up her money from the countertop, and left in a hurry to meet Abe. On her way out, she saw a good-looking *haole* banging nails into a ramp by the canal. What do you know, looks like Cat's getting herself a boyfriend, she thought. She sent him a smile and slipped into her old Honda.

Abe was already waiting, sitting on the steps, big, dark, sending clouds of cigarette smoke, menacing like *pu'u*, a cinder cone. He jumped to his feet the moment her Honda pulled into the driveway and rushed to the car.

A tall and broad-shouldered man, but agile like a lightweight boxer, and she, a black-eyed beauty with the elegant moves of a dancer—they looked well together. Kalani's high school girlfriends stopped seeing her out of jealousy.

She and Abe had good times together once; she thought they would marry one day and have beautiful children. Boys, dark, tall and handsome like Abe, and girls, slim, soft and sweet like herself. She even had names ready for them: Maika for a boy and Lehua for a girl.

Abe laughed and joked about her dream but did not object. He was fond of the idea of having a family, too.

Besides, he liked the ending to her family dreams. He would let Kalani spin her sweet story for a few minutes, then would pick her up like a soft doll and whisper in her ear, "Well, let's start making those pretty babies. Who is going to be the first, Maika or Lehua?"

Kalani was crazy about his big hard body, smooth skin and the faint animal smell she liked to relish with her face pressed to his chest. It was like being caught in a strong riptide current—she couldn't fight against it. She didn't fight because she knew that, after much pushing and pulling and twisting of her body, it would bring her to a quiet cove filled with warm and sweet water, a place of happy dreams.

When Abe had started to change she was not sure. Maybe when his mother died, or perhaps when he stopped working on the fishing boat. He smiled less and his fuse got shorter. He still could be sweet, but was more often just irritable and snappy like an old man. He got into the habit of waking up about noon—no wonder, since he hardly ever came home before two, or at least that's what he said. Kalani was asleep by then.

She planned her day so she could come home before twelve; she needed to fix lunch. The problem was that Abe, having slept off the last night, was by then at his best mood of the day, ready to assert his manhood. She never admitted it, but it left Kalani drained and hard pressed to find energy for the remaining hours of her physical work. There was no way to persuade him to wait until evening, he had other plans—that's when he met his buddies.

Kalani looked into the rear mirror, placed a flower behind her ear, put on her best smile and stepped out of the car. Abe was smiling in the driveway and grabbed her for a long passionate hug.

"Do you have it?"

"Some ... three hundred ..."

"A lousy three hundred?" He let go of her. "What am I

supposed to do now?" His face darkened and his voice acquired a harsh quality.

"I'll have the rest tomorrow. I was late to the bank," she added hastily.

"What time tomorrow? It better be in the morning. I'll buy some drinks for the guys tonight"—he took the money from her hand—"so they will not pick on me, but tomorrow I have to have my two grand." He turned away and started walking down the gravel driveway. He stopped before turning onto the street. "By the way, I got you another job. This new guy who bought a restaurant needs some help at home. You can go and see him tonight."

"Thank you, Abe." Kalani exhaled with relief when he turned and walked away with long effortless strides. With her shoulders slumped, she entered their apartment to make dinner for herself. She was glad they hadn't rushed with Maika and Lehua; her future family looked less and less happy. She knew enough about unhappy families and would rather not make another. Kalani went to the bathroom and took a pill from the small container hidden behind a big bottle of hydrogen peroxide. She would make sure not to miss any.

Chapter 9

Jerry, December 30–31

Prompted by the guitar music flowing from the player by Cat's computer, Jerry looked at the poster on the wall where a dancer's body tried to fit her curves into the shape of a capital letter S. "A charming pose," he noted with appreciation. "You listen to flamenco a lot, don't you?"

"I love flamenco!" Cat enthused from her keyboard. She was wrapping up the day's work, impatient to join Jerry, who had left the shower a few minutes earlier. "Maybe I have some Gypsy genes I don't know about, but more likely it has something to do with my legs. It all started with a book I read, *Carmen la Coja*. Its heroine is a flamenco dancer who had polio as a child and could hardly walk without crutches. Her footwork was of course impaired, but her upper body was so expressive that she had become a top professional dancer. Have you ever seen flamenco show?"

"I did, years ago in Cancun." Jerry nodded.

"So you remember that there are two major elements to it. One is the footwork, all that stomping and strutting around. The other is the ballet of hands, arms ... the whole upper body." As the tune was ending in a fiery crescendo,

Cat raised her chin proudly, extended her long neck and stretched her arms. She made a few flowing flamenco moves. Quite obviously, she was well practiced and her gestures were graceful. The idea alone of dancing makes her happy, Jerry thought, seeing her excitement.

Cat had a refreshingly simple view on food preparation. Two pieces of fresh tuna thrown on a pan, a salad of mixed tomatoes, cucumbers, lettuce and whatever else might happen to be in the veggie compartment of her refrigerator, some bread ... Dinner appeared on the table as through a magic trick. Fifteen minutes, that's how much she was willing to spend on cooking drudgery.

"Some people love cooking," she confided. "I wish them long and enjoyable pots-and-pans pastime, but I'd rather spend my free time on the ocean." Jerry's part was even easier; he stopped at the small grocery store on his way to buy some red wine.

Cat sniffed and swished her glass of Merlot then raised it to Jerry. "To your happy new career, whatever it will be. I hope you will find your place in life."

I have found my place in life! Jerry wanted to burst out. It's here, with you! Instead he politely nodded: Thank you. The rules Professor Roberts set for this enterprise were simple: full disclosure and due diligence. Only then, if a fully informed Cat accepted him for what he was ... But he couldn't bring himself to start the dreaded conversation at this happy moment.

"Would you like to dance?" Jerry asked casually the next day, looking innocently across the bowl of fruit salad. "It's New Year's Eve, you know?"

Cat frowned, panicked as much about going out, in complete break with the past four years of her solitary lifestyle, as the humiliation of sitting in her wheelchair while everyone else hopped, skipped and boogied. "What do you mean?"

Jerry stood up without a word and went to the closet by the door. He returned with a package wrapped into glistening golden paper. "Happy New Year, Cat. We could have a party right here!"

She ripped open the paper excitedly, like a child. The thin, bright red fabric materialized into a full-length red dress richly embroidered in front. Cat held her breath and draped the gown against her front, letting it flow to the floor. She glanced at her flamenco poster. "Jerry, you are a wonderful man." Her eyes were soft and misty. "I will dance with you, Jerry, all night. Thank you!"

When Cat rolled to her bedroom to change, Jerry fetched the guitar from his car and plucked it clumsily until she made her appearance twenty minutes later.

A credit to Jerry's judgment, the dress fitted well. The shiny red fabric luxuriously spread over Cat's legs before cinching at her narrow waist. The bodice, ornately decorated with black needlework, stretched smoothly over her breasts and shrouded her cleavage with black lace. Cat's long, blond hair, tightly pulled backwards, cascaded down the red dress, like a ray of the noon sun falling through heavy window curtains. With her body proudly erect and her head held in an arrogant pose, she was sitting in the chair like a queen gracing the court with her presence.

Jerry strummed the guitar hesitantly. "I'm not much of a guitar virtuoso ... Took some lessons for a year, when I was an undergrad, but I could do a bit of rhythm thumping and stomping for you. The rest is up to the CD and your arms." He pushed the CD player's button and the dark voice, trembling with passion, vibrated the air.

"*Porque vivo a mi manera,*" cried the singer and the guitar responded with a sorrowful solo.

Jerry joined in, gently thumping his instrument and stomping his feet louder and louder as his confidence grew. The flamenco was heating up. Cat watched for a moment with approval, then the dry clicks of her castanets merged with the tune. Her hands came alive, slicing and waving through the air as though she were carving graceful objects, the magic spheres getting bigger and bigger, encouraged by Cat's fingers gently feathering their surfaces.

The haughty poise of her head sternly rejected any notion of disrespectful familiarity, while her hands, arms and breasts shamelessly threw seductive magic at Jerry.

He was happy to be charmed. When the last strum of fandango ended, Cat, breathing heavily, rolled her chair toward him. They sat facing each other, secluded alone within the narrow space defined by the gaze fixated onto the other's eyes, their thighs almost touching. The music started again with the soft tender sob of a guitar, but the tune quickened rapidly and the same dramatic female voice erupted, complaining, threatening and begging.

Jerry put away his guitar so that nothing would separate him from Cat. He perceived the air she stirred, felt her fingertips slightly brushing his hair and sensed her breath on his face. His stomping ceased; he sat captivated, his eyes riveted to Cat's mouth. Fascinated with her lips from the first day they met, he could now indulge in watching them openly, so close he could touch them with his own. She enjoyed their closeness as well, he was certain. The music stopped, and Cat put her arms around his neck. "Thank you, Jerry. This is the most wonderful dancing evening of my life." She kissed him on his mouth.

Unlike workmen who can't complete the job on time, Jerry faced the crisis of running out of work to justify his spending every day with Cat. How many days could one take to build a thirty-foot boardwalk? Jerry kept delaying completion of the project as long as he could without looking utterly incompetent.

Once all the planks were cut, fitted and assembled, he

pulled some out on pretense of certain sections needing realignment. He liberated the joists and played with the timber for a couple of hours only to put the boards together in identical position. He left the planks ready to be nailed and went inside to the restroom.

The moment he stepped out through the door, Jerry saw Cat struggling on his boardwalk. Apparently she had rolled onto the unfastened boards, which shifted under her weight. The planks and joists moved enough to trap the wheels of her chair and she was stuck like an anchor dropped on a reef.

She was heaving on her wheels angrily, repeatedly throwing her weight forward in a determined effort to escape the trap. Cat was facing away, unaware of Jerry's presence behind her. He heard her groaning with effort and breathing deeply; this struggle must have been going on for a few minutes.

He sincerely hoped she could break out on her own because he understood how much she valued her independence. His help would be considered a personal insult and humiliation. Unfortunately, the chair was stuck as firmly as though he had designed a bear trap.

Jerry approached her and said softly, "May I help you, Cat?"

The angry sun in a desert storm was the image that unexpectedly occurred to Jerry when he saw her face glowing red through the dust of brown freckles.

"You better! Hope you aren't going to build any bridges!" The pair of blue eyes attempted to burn holes into his forehead like high-powered lasers.

Standing in front of her, Jerry grabbed the arm supports and pulled. The chair did not budge. Without thinking, he moved his right hand under her legs and the left one behind her back then easily lifted her out of her wheelchair. Instinctively, she put her arms around his neck to help. He stood holding her in his arms, just like in his dreams. She was not heavy and her body had a pleasant firmness.

He wished they could stay like that forever, her arms wrapped around his neck, but after a second, she said softly, without anger, "You can put me down next to the tree and get the chair out for me, please."

Jerry carefully stepped over the loose lumber and gently lowered her next to the foxtail palm. Cat grabbed the rough trunk; she could stand on her own, clinging to the tree. The empty chair easily came out of the trap and she slid into it with a moan of relief. Cat stared at Jerry for a moment, her face still red but bearing a hint of smile, shook her head pensively and rolled away without a word, her wheelchair jumping over clumps of grass.

Although Jerry felt guilty about the circumstances of having her in his arms for the first time, this episode led them to become more physical. She liked a brief neck massage after a long spell over her computer, and he held out his head to be ruffled when they watched news on TV.

The entrapment incident made Jerry realize that—fit and independent-minded as Cat was—she was quite vulnerable and it worried him. "Cat, what would you do if you got stuck like that and I wasn't around?"

She shrugged dismissively. "I would roll out of my wheelchair and crawl uphill to the house. Done it many times."

Of course, Jerry thought, maybe I worry too much; she managed on her own for three years. But again ... I'd rather look out for her all the same.

Cat didn't wish to let this conversation end at that. "What would *you* do if you slipped in a bathtub and broke your hip or neck? You live alone, right? I knew people who had it happen to them ... shit happens." Cat was offended by the idea of needing someone to keep her safe. "You don't need to worry about me, Jerry," she snapped. "I've been doing quite well on my own; I don't need a keeper."

Chapter 10

Rosen, January 2

The restaurant's back room was small and looked like any other scruffy small business office Kalani knew. The only thing that caught her attention was the small sculpture of a naked woman on the desk. It was bright white and almost glowed in the darkened room.

Mr. Rosen, uncomfortably perched on a metal chair behind the desk, felt rather grouchy but his mood picked up when Kalani walked in. Abe has a good eye for women, he thought. Late twenties, pretty face, a bit too full in the hips—a common problem around here ... good waist, though.

He leaned forward, forced a smile, and started in a warm fatherly manner, "So, Abe tells me that you need some work, Kalani?"

"Yes, sir. I would like to work evenings, so I thought I could be a waitress. But if you could use me at home in the evening, I would like to try."

Use me in the evening ... I like the way she formulates her thoughts, Rosen smiled to himself. "I know you clean people's homes. What do they pay you?"

"Fourteen, fifteen dollars per hour."

"I will start you at twelve and maybe you will get more if I am happy with you. I will need you twice a week. Can you start tonight?"

"Yes, sir, thank you, Mr. Rosen." Kalani couldn't believe her luck. Good, regular work certainly was not that easy to come by, especially at night when everybody wanted strangers out the door. So, once in a while, Abe could do some good.

"OK then, follow my car so I can show you my home and explain your duties." Rosen went through the restaurant without paying any attention to guests and waiters, followed by Kalani who observed a girl hauling a big tray loaded with three plates and three beer bottles toward the corner table. That looked tricky; she was glad to stick to cleaning.

The old Honda could not keep up with Rosen's Mercedes and Kalani lost sight of him, but there was only one way to go to Lanikai, where he lived. Unconcerned, she drove down Kailua Street, enjoying the cool evening air flooding through the windows. Since her AC crapped out last year, driving was better after sunset, but who would care in winter anyway. Her Honda should be just fine, at least for another year. Where would she want to speed to, like Rosen? Even when she goes to her nursing school—Kalani smiled with excitement—that might save her no more than three minutes on the Pali Highway. Hardly worth the price of a new car.

Shit! Kalani stepped on her brakes, which fortunately stopped the car without locking. *Pupule!* Crazy kids! Walk off the Times parking lot to cross the street like a flock of *nene*. No looking! Not their problem, they aren't driving!

Her car stalled, of course, right at the green light, in front of Auntie's Pizza where people, having nothing better to do, made fun of her as she kept cranking her cadaveric car. What if Rosen didn't wait for her at the pillar on Mokulua Drive? People always meet there, as this is the only way to get in to Lanikai, but the *haole* might not know it. Now Kalani got angry.

But the silver Merz was sitting on the side of the road, close to the pillar, and pulled back onto the blacktop as soon as he saw her Honda wheezing, gathering speed to assault the hill ahead. They turned right into a side street and turned again, climbing up the steep incline, squeezing the last drops of life from Kalani's car.

Rosen stopped in front of a brown house at the very top. Its long driveway ran along the crest flanked by deep ravines on both sides, leaving room for no neighbors nearby.

As soon as Kalani stepped out of her car, the stiff humid breeze blowing from the ocean hit her squarely in the face and made her step back. The sky was covered with fast-shifting tattered clouds, letting the moonlight through on and off and making this place somehow spooky. She could see the lights of Kailua far below, but the deep empty shade on the sides of the driveway and the impenetrable sinister blackness of the ocean in front gave her goose bumps. Fortunately, the house had some lights on and its two-story windows glowed in the gloomy space like a castle, a refuge from the forces of darkness.

"Wow, you have a beautiful place here, Mr. Rosen, but it's a bit scary to be so alone, isn't it?" She had to shout to be heard in this wind.

"Thank you, Kalani!" Rosen yelled back. "I don't mind being alone. Come in, away from this wind."

The girl followed Rosen toward the door. He was rather short and his waist had started expanding, as often happens to middle-aged men, but he moved swiftly and lightly, like a younger person. She couldn't decide how old he might be. They entered the house—an older but elegant dwelling—through a two-story atrium leading to a living and dining room, a kitchen and a guest restroom. The house was scarcely furnished; obviously, the new owner hadn't bought new furniture yet. What would need cleaning was mostly the nice koa floor.

This is going to be a piece of cake, Kalani thought. I could do it in an hour and then relax a bit before going home. Rosen led her upstairs to show her his bedrooms. The two next to the stairway were practically empty, unless one counted a few still unpacked boxes and packages.

"This is my master bedroom," said Rosen, opening the third door. He let her slip in front of him into a large suite with expansive windows overlooking the ocean.

A large four-poster bed, covered with a carefully draped white sheet, occupied the middle of the room. A few feet from the bed stood a large, brown, strange-looking leather chair with a generously padded seat and two wooden arm supports but no backrest. In addition, there were two other, more conventional armchairs of the same color and an impressive cherry wood desk. Next to the window, in splendid isolation, sat on the floor a large white sculpture.

Kalani immediately recognized it as a larger version of the figurine sitting on Rosen's office desk. This was a large piece, almost life-size. A naked young woman, exquisitely carved in white stone, kneeled with her hands and head submissively placed on the floor in front of her, as though trying to look to the ocean over the edge of the last koa board.

Eek! Kalani scoffed. She sticks her butt up like she was asking for *moi-moi*! Abe would like it.

Rosen approached the sculpture and lovingly placed his hand on the back of the naked girl.

"I want you to take special care of this young lady. She's a great piece of art created by the greatest sculptor that ever lived. I would like you to gently dust her every day. Do you like her?"

Kalani swallowed saliva and answered, unsure of herself, "Oh, she is very pretty, sir. Just … she doesn't look very comfortable. Why does she sit like that?"

Rosen smiled slightly. "She sits as she was told, and her comfort was not an issue…." He caught himself just in time to avoid continuing with the arguments of why some women need to be uncomfortable, much more uncomfortable than the girl on her knees.

Kalani took the job, though the bedroom bothered her a bit, especially the sculpture. It looked like an easy job, something coming like a reward at the end of the day, after long hours of hard work. She took the house key and timidly drove home along the narrow, winding road to town, hoping the brakes would hold.

Harry Rosen went to the desk and, deep in his thoughts, picked up a long, black object resting on top. It had a finely sculpted ivory handle adorned with silver inlay and a foot-long, thin leather blade. He absentmindedly cut through the air; the whip gave a swishing sound and hit the padded leather with a vicious thud. Rosen waited a moment, anticipating the appearance of a dark red welt, but only living skin could do that, of course.

Another hand used to wield this instrument of ultimate power and pleasure, a hand much more skilled than his. Harry, or whatever his name was then, had stolen this object and never had a quiet night's sleep since. Many elaborate steps and cunning guises covered his tracks, but deep inside, he knew that his intellect was not a match for the awesome powers of the Master.

Chapter 11

Cat, January 2

Sometimes, insomniac after having her muscle stimulation session, the best Cat could do was to fall into a half-dream, when old scenes and conversation crawled from the dark basement of her memory, where they were supposed to stay locked in. They were not real, that much she knew, but the pain they still carried was not diluted; it was as genuine as her useless legs.

Cat sat in her hospital bed looking at the rain-streaked window, counting the ways she might kill herself with the minimum of pain, when a nurse came in, a middle-aged woman named Rose. Cat didn't like Rose, who was a rather brusque person and wouldn't waste her time on excessive nuances.

"Cat, I know that you can't talk, not to me at least, but you probably can read."

Cat did not honor her with a look. A pushy, malevolent bitch, she thought.

 "Be a sweetheart for a change, and read a bit for a nice lady who can't do it herself. You will like her. She's not like me; she loves to take shit from everyone."

Anything to get you out of my face, Cat thought. "Where is she, when should I go?" she asked unpleasantly, looking at the garbage can in the corner.

"She's in the chronic unit. You can see her anytime; she's not going anywhere. An orderly will take you there."

"I don't need an orderly; I can find her myself."

"Very well, find her yourself."

Cat wheeled herself to the chronic care unit the same day; there was not much else she had to do. She detected the faint but unmistakable odor of urine as soon as she opened the door. Unlike in her part of the hospital, the floors were hardwood and the walls were painted sunshine yellow. Halfway through the corridor, a group of white coats and blue robes milled at the nursing station. She wheeled past a male orderly pushing an empty bed and was approaching the nursing station when an old woman grabbed her sleeve with a thin, talon-like hand.

"When's Mary coming? When's she coming?" she kept asking, never giving Cat an opportunity to say that she neither knew nor cared.

Numerous patients, dressed in blue robes and long hospital shirts tied at the back, crowded the corridor and the lounge. Some sat in their chairs motionless; others nodded repeatedly, apparently in the middle of some inner conversation.

This is where I will end up. Cat shuddered. She was ready to turn around and escape to her bed, where she could relax and think some more how to end her miserable life, when the nurse caught sight of her.

"You must be Cat. You'll see how much better you feel when you talk to Ruth."

Better? I will feel even better than now? God have mercy! Cat thought, but she just mumbled, "I am supposed to read for Ruth."

The nurse pushed her chair into the room occupied by a single bed, a nightstand and two wooden chairs. An unnaturally wide head with a pale, swollen, ugly face rested on a pillow; the remainder of the body was covered with a white sheet. The pair of bright, gray eyes turned to her and the cheerful voice said, "Hi. You from the rehab unit?"

"Yes. I've come to read to you." Cat was somewhat intimidated.

"Oh, how good of you," the voice announced cheerfully. "But—before you read—can you tell me some gossip from your part of the hospital? I don't get much traffic in chitchat here and I miss it. Is Nurse Rose still there?"

"Yes. She told me to come and read to you."

"Quite a bitch, isn't she?" Ruth giggled. "But in fact, she takes care of her patients like nobody else. Things get done whether they want it or not. How about Doctor Yamashita, is he still trying to get a date?"

An hour passed and they were still trading gossip. Cat even laughed a few times, her first since the accident.

"Cat, what kind of person were you before the accident? Happy or unhappy?" The gray eyes measured her up seriously.

"Well, I was a very happy person; I had all the reasons to be happy." Cat answered indignantly. After all she had lost, someone was actually questioning the size of her tragedy.

"That's not my question," Ruth explained patiently. "Some people are happy even if their life keeps screwing them over, and some are unhappy, no matter how good they've got it. What kind were you?"

"I must say, I was mostly happy, unless something made me unhappy," Cat responded after a moment of reflection.

"Then," Ruth declared confidently, "you'll be happy again. It's a scientific fact. People return to their basic predisposition after a major event, good or bad. Happy ones are happy again while depressives go back to popping Prozac even if they win a million dollars."

Two hours passed before the nurse stuck her head in. "Enough reading for now— dinner is coming."

"Do you want to come again tomorrow? We didn't even start reading yet," Ruth asked hopefully.

Cat promised to come in the next morning and left the chronic care unit almost smiling. She spent many hours with Ruth after that first meeting, but not much reading was ever done. They became friends rapidly, and their initial light gossiping changed to some very personal subjects that Cat would never have discussed with anybody else.

Ruth had suffered from progressive paralysis for years, the last four spent in bed. She seemed to have answers to any and every question a paralyzed woman might ask. She had a lot of time for reflection. Obviously, she must have been of the sunny disposition before her disease struck because even now, paralyzed from her neck down, she was always full of good spirits.

"So what are the choices, Cat? You can decide to be happy no matter what, or you can allow yourself to be unhappy and—God knows—you will find a lot to be unhappy about. What do you think is better?" The gray eyes rolled up beatifically and closed peacefully, but in a moment they sharply shot from under the swollen eyelids. "But don't think it just happens. You need to make a clear decision and stick to it."

Cat's decision at this point was to be a happy person. She had made up her mind and stuck to it, letting a lot of dreadful stuff bounce off her skin like rain off a duck. She had also decided that the physiotherapy, which made her cry before, was not such a drag after all. That's when she concocted the idea of a muscle stimulator.

The progress she made over the next few weeks stunned even Rose, a hard-nosed hag. "Kid, you are ready to face the world," she declared. "And—I think—we should hire Ruth as a psychotherapist."

Ruth became invisible to Cat except for her eyes. Always alert, her gray eyes seemed independent of the swollen yellow face and entirely alien to the rest of her disintegrating bloated body.

"I often imagine that all I have is my brain floating in a pool that feeds and supports it." Ruth explained her own concept of her person. "The stuff they are hiding under this white sheet, the strange shape you see below my neck, is my support pool. It can't be too clean, as I can smell something disgusting whenever they lift the sheet. I hope I'll never get to see what exactly it is. A pool is a pool—what do I care about it as long as it works? I live in my brain, and you wouldn't believe how many things can hide in your brain. Sometimes it's better than real life. You can do things that you could never even try to do in the real world. I shouldn't say 'real.' Who knows what's real?"

Cat probably made a dubious face, because Ruth immediately asked, "Have you ever thought: How do I know what's real and what's not?" She let the idea sink into Cat's mind for a moment. "How do you know? Can you be sure that I am really talking to you? Maybe you'll wake up in a moment to find out that you just had a bad dream, a nightmare about being in a car crash. And then you dreamed of a freaky head talking to you. How do you know, Cat?"

The question seemed unanswerable to Cat, especially since Ruth followed through with her attack against common sense. "In fact, how can I be sure that you are real? I could easily imagine a Barbie doll like you coming every day to entertain me. And you know what? Once you give someone shape and life in your head, they become quite independent. Sometimes they amaze me with what they say or do, although I should really know—I created them."

"So that's what you do before I come, you daydream!" Cat exclaimed, excited to solve the mystery of what Ruth did all day without going crazy out of boredom.

"Daydreaming is when you entertain yourself in order to kill time." Ruth's eyes squinted and her lips turned scornfully. "What I'm doing is *creating* my reality. It may not be real to you, but it sure feels genuine to me. It's hard work and takes concentration, but it gets easier with practice. I can't claim I invented it. Athletes have used imagination to practice for years. Tennis players or skaters can have their movement patterns and strategies honed without moving a finger. You can see why, but the imagining works for runners or bikers as well. How? I have no idea, but you have to agree that what you do in your head can speed up your heart, make you sweat or puke your stomach out. Nothing unreal about it; it's a scientific fact and I am a grand master in this sport." She winked.

"What where you doing this morning, before I came?" Cat asked with curiosity.

"I was riding my horse. We're preparing for a jumping competition … a big event, a lot of competition. Spartacus is a bit wall shy, so we need a lot of practice, but he will come around in time."

"Horse jumping, eh? It must be a pretty expensive sport …"

"It is, but I am an investment banker a few afternoons a week, so we can afford it. You should try horseback riding yourself—that would be good for you."

"Thank you, Ruth, but I would rather go skiing in Utah."

"That's fine, Cat, perfect. Go skiing, but be careful … you might break your neck." They both started laughing hysterically until they ran out of giggles.

"Cat, when you were married, did you enjoy sex?"

"Ruth, I think we were obsessed. Sometimes, I think that's what we mainly did."

"Well then, you have a big hole in your life. You should try to enjoy it in your head." The gray eyes did not seem to joke at this moment.

"Do you do it?" Cat asked excitedly, her face turning pink.

"Are you kidding?" Ruth giggled. "I've had every good-looking doc in this hospital, and you wouldn't believe all the

Hollywood stars who drop in for a night! Now go back to your room and do some practice runs." Her mouth turned into a big fleshy U when Cat's face turned red like a tomato and she wheeled out of the room.

Chapter 12

Jerry, January 2

Jerry swam along the beach, keeping outside buoys to avoid other swimmers. Miniature dunes on the bottom, rippled by imperceptible currents, slid beneath his goggles unnoticed because his mind was totally preoccupied with the question: What's going on?

He was not a naïve youngster. At thirty-three, he had a lot of romantic experience. Women sought his company and he'd had many lady friends in the past, but—apart from feeding his healthy sexual appetite—none of them touched off any deeper sentimental reaction on his part for many years. *The emotional capacity of a brick wall*, the military shrink opined in his confidential report.

Confidential this document might have been for someone else, but not for a guy trained for an intelligence career. Jerry read it thoroughly, memorized its more pertinent fragments and—in the confusion reigning over that part of his life—accepted the psychiatrist's supposition for a fact, even though it made little sense. After all, the very idea of Jerry signing up for the Army stint was hatched in his father's head as a way to toughen up his overly emotional prodigy! The old college linebacker just couldn't get over his only son choosing a drama club over a football team. What's next? Ballet?

"They will make a man out of you," Daddy, the old fart, declared with great pomp, probably after having watched one too many John Wayne movies. "College can wait; you wouldn't want to play football anyway …" His voice rose slightly, hinting at a question that carried some hope, but when Jerry shrugged, he just added dejectedly, "In any case, there is no war going on, you won't get hurt."

Really! Jerry would be better off taking a bullet in one of his not-so-vital organs and being honorably discharged with a Purple Heart.

Anyway—Jerry carried on his self-examination—the first sweet love arrived on schedule, in the senior year. A psychopath I'm probably not, he decided. On the other hand, it occurred to him, the official diagnosis gave him a good cover to evade sticky emotional entanglements, which might account for his unquestioning acceptance of the label. Not nice, he admitted to himself, but perhaps for the better, as anyone trying to bond with him during those early years after the Army discharge would get hurt, for sure.

This way, while his peers were going through the exhausting rituals of meeting parents, weddings, Pampers, divorces, etc., Jerry led his barren but safe life, slowly sinking deeper and deeper into boredom and depression. And now, rather late in the mating season, his heart unexpectedly filled with tender romantic feelings.

They don't know shit! he concluded, distilling his reflections on the science of psychiatry into a concise verdict. Had I had a bullet in my head—Jerry continued his line of examination—or had my skull kicked in, they would see the problem on X-rays; I certainly had enough of those. But the tests were normal, so they started spinning theories based on the latest article to appear in some paper of high learning. And those stories, those fantasies—dressed like scientific facts in

Freudian, Jungian or whatever mumbo-jumbo language—went into my file. No hard data whatsoever. Well, that's what got me off the hook ... can't complain too much. And I was messed up pretty badly for some time, no question.

Jerry enjoyed swimming in the warm water, a perfect medium for self-analysis, way better than a couch, he thought. But later, at the VA clinic ... They just grabbed his files, undoubtedly juiced up by Captain Murphy, slapped the label on his forehead and gave him the heave-ho at the first opportunity. There are always a lot of fucked-up guys waiting for an appointment; nobody gets to stay on the active list too long.

"Try to avoid emotionally charged situations," the quack said, looking sincerely into his eyes, brimming with care for Jerry and concern for mankind. "And good luck!" Then he shook Jerry's hand and kicked him out of the VA clinic. Ah, and one for the road ... stay away from people as much as you can, for their protection—and yours.

That's when the bunker building started; the results were predictable. Except for Victoria, who kept her own head low in her foxhole, none of Jerry's girlfriends could stand his emotional desert for more than a few months. One can put a lot of month-long stints into ten years.

Now, reviewing his empty years, Jerry felt angry with himself for taking the stupid advice seriously. Actually, he considered himself to be permanently damaged goods, a violent freak best kept behind the wall for his own and others' safety. Why didn't he tell me to jump in front of a train for the common good?

But even livid, he had to admit: Well... I had my moments. But I've controlled them most of the time! God only knows what crazy urges *other* people have; as long as they keep their devils on a chain it's nobody's business. Since he had left the Army, his personal devil had jerked pretty hard on a few occasions, but the leash held.

Army. Jerry signed up not so much to please his father but because the prospect of getting away from writing essays and taking tests for a while seemed rather attractive. And since he was not sure what to study anyway ...

Boot camp and basic training felt like they were indeed making a man out of him, on the double. He didn't mind. His waist got smaller, shoulders bigger ... good buddies, poker ... lots of poker. Very quickly Jerry established himself as a star gambler in his company, admittedly not the greatest collection of talent in the game's history.

His card shark reputation was based on Jerry's observation that other guys bluffed with the regularity of a calendar. Cursed with a poor hand, Vince Corvine would fold twice; the third time around he would bluff, even with one lowly pair to show. He could be relied upon, and if Jerry had lost his count, why, he just had to ask, "Hey, Vince, you sure got a bad streak. What was it, shitty cards twice in a row?"

And if Vince confirmed it, Jerry knew for sure that the next time around he would bluff, unless his cards happened to be good, of course. You can't win every time anyway unless you want to play with a mirror. Each one of the regulars had his own pattern, carefully noted in Jerry's little file. His fame was already spreading across the barracks when Captain Murphy, the officer hardly seen on the base, called him in for a little conversation.

How Jerry came to his attention was unclear for a while. "Sit down, Roberts," Murphy barked. He kept the private fixed in his icy gaze for a good thirty seconds, saying nothing. Jerry started sweating, desperately trying to figure out which one of his transgressions might have brought him in front of the intelligence unit's chief.

Short, rather scrawny, the captain was not a model of a brawny warrior that officers were supposed to be. But what he was lacking in his physique he made up with undisguised, cold aggression.

"Yours?" he snarled, throwing a few colorful magazines on the desk, a big-assed beauty adorning the front page of the *Hustler* on top.

"Could be ..." Jerry admitted, confounded, taking the magazine in his hand for examination.

"Not the smut!" Murphy sneered. "This one!" He pulled the second periodical from underneath and Jerry blushed.

Scientific American. Some twit in the mailroom must have put it in his general mail despite Jerry's clear instruction that he would come to pick it up personally. Now Corvine and the other guys would take their sweet revenge; they would harass him forever, calling him a science freak, doctor or worse.

"I have an opening in my unit," Murphy finally said, once he noted droplets of clear fluid forming on the soldier's forehead. "This opening must be filled by a highly intelligent and patriotic man. Your commanding officer says you might fit this description. Is he wrong, Roberts?"

"Well ... sir, I ..." Jerry struggled as the captain watched him with malevolent amusement.

"That's enough, Roberts. You have a chance ... but you have to make up your mind by tomorrow, O-eight hundred. Either you report here to start your training or present yourself in your CO's office to suffer the consequences for your DUI two weeks ago. Here is the report I'm going to forward to your superior"—he suspended his menacing voice and opened the file to show a document printed on police department stationery—"unless I see you tomorrow."

Jerry traded the grueling field training for a classroom. A tape recorder and a computer had become his basic tools rather than an M16. A good deal, it appeared, especially as he could disappear from Captain Murphy's field of toxic vision a month later, when the Army sent him for off-base training.

That was interesting stuff! Jerry enjoyed learning how people think, especially since a separate module had been dedicated to some useful ways the female subjects could be manipulated. Learning about the stupid things folks do filled him with awe, and even better, he was taught how to make use of these follies for the Army's benefit. That was very actionable wisdom with great entertainment value.

Jerry's teachers, on the other hand, quickly figured out that this recruit's smarts were way above average. He was much praised, encouraged and offered additional training. A college degree in psychology and a career as a professional intelligence officer looked like Jerry's obvious future. Captain Murphy had himself a good asset and awaited him impatiently, approving requests for further training with increasing exasperation.

The payment for this interesting and stimulating education came due when Murphy wrote a big "No" on yet another application for further training. He needed his asset back and soon.

"Welcome home, Roberts," he addressed Jerry, who stood at attention in front of his desk. "It's time to see how much you've learned. We have a job to do."

Murphy raised his hand, stopping Jerry's question. "You will find out where and when like everybody else, tomorrow. But I can tell you right now, you will be in the first line of duty; there will be a lot of suspects to interrogate."

The captain leaned back on his chair, coldly studying his subordinate's face. Jerry suddenly felt nauseous. Interrogations! He felt a cold ball in his belly. I am supposed to make people talk! I just can't do that!

"I hope nobody promised you the double-O-seven job?" Murphy's thin lips curled in a contemptuous grin. "You will be doing important work that may save your colleagues' asses, so don't give me that hurt prima ballerina performance."

Captain Murphy was clearly not happy with his reaction; he sat up straight in his chair and snapped, "Don't worry, Roberts, we don't send people away for a year to study on the government's penny in order to have them swinging a bamboo stick. This talent comes cheap and needs no training. You will use your head to get what we need. Now get out and report for duty tomorrow morning."

Two weeks later Jerry found himself on a transport plane that touched down for a few hours in Ramstein, Germany, for refueling, and the same day disgorged a few soldiers wearing desert camouflage fatigues, Jerry among them, as well as a mountain of equipment on a dusty airstrip in Africa. Enemies of civilization abounded there; there was much work, and Jerry's relationship with humankind started changing rapidly.

Jerry reached the rocky finger separating Kailua Beach from Lanikai, doubled up at the boat ramp and turned his thoughts to a more pleasant subject. Then comes Cat. No, doesn't come, charges in on her yellow kayak, and ... everything changes. The bunker walls collapse and here he is ... in the open, a free man, sitting unprotected among the blooming flowers of hope that grew overnight out of the rubble. Ridiculous ... except it's more or less true.

Cat is definitely different, but why? Pretty—no question about it, but so are many others. Victoria is not a bad looker either. Intelligent, very intelligent ... and argues like a pro, but that's true of the whole university debating club, so it's hardly a unique feature. A small yellow fish, grazing on a rock, shot away when his shadow closed in. Perhaps Cat is simply my match! Supposedly, people have a one in five hundred chance of meeting their perfect match. Maybe I've just lucked out! Jerry smiled under the water.

Later that day, Jerry and Cat cuddled on the couch in front of her TV, colorful pictures flashing on the screen, talking heads nodding, smiling and grimacing. "Do you watch TV alone?" Cat asked. "I hardly ever turned my set on before you started coming over."

Jerry smiled. "I rarely watch the tube, except for news—waste of time. Even now I am not watching it. I'm just cuddling with you."

"Oh, what a waste of your time! Maybe you'd rather build some models of the economy?" Cat teased and plunged her hand into Jerry's curly hair.

"The only thing I want to build right now is an electric fence around this room, so that nobody could get in, and no one could get out." Jeremy slipped his hand under Cat's arm until warm softness filled his palm. She smiled contentedly and pressed the off button on the remote.

Chapter 13

Cat, January 4

"I think this ramp couldn't be any more perfect, Jerry." Cat, dressed in a navy-blue one-piece swimming suit, appeared on the deck unusually early, a few minutes past two. She stopped on the boardwalk short of the patch of wet paint, which Jerry—seated comfortably under a sun umbrella—was unhurriedly enlarging with the fourth coat of dark-red oil paint. "If you declare it finished, we'll go out and have some fun."

His scam was up, a development inconvenient but not unexpected. Jerry was prepared to adjust his tactics to keep those nice—and becoming ever so nicer—evenings with Cat going. But the idea of going out alarmed him. "What fun do you mean, Cat? I'm quite happy with things as they are.…"

Not quite … Since he'd held her in the entrapment episode, as they came to call it, the warm firmness of her body never left his memory. Every evening, as their bodies became more familiar with each other, Jerry craved Cat's physical love. He longed to feel her arms around his neck and imagined her breath on his face. But—to his own surprise—he was willing to wait, as long as there were only the two of them.

"I haven't gone kayaking for almost two weeks, and the ocean is calling me," Cat explained, seeing disappointment in his eyes. Now her swimsuit made sense. "I thought you would like to come with me." She observed him keenly, squinting her eyes in the sun.

Jerry had almost managed to put away the unpleasant memories of his last kayak excursion. He designated that rotten experience as the cost of meeting Cat—expensive, but worth it. He was not, however, looking forward to a repeat performance. But how could he decline her invitation? "Sorry, but I got scared and will never put my butt into a kayak again"? Jerry agreed, even faked some enthusiasm.

"Great!" Cat was thrilled and her face lit up in a big smile. "I want to make sure you don't have any fear from the last experience. The ocean is so big in my life. I love being out there in my kayak. It would mean a lot to me if you could come out with me from time to time."

She clearly wanted to include him in her life, and Jerry decided he would become a kayaker.

"The trouble you had …"—Cat was looking for encouraging words—"it was not so much your fault, you know. A lousy boat, waters you didn't know … Nothing that can't be easily fixed."

Hell, I might even try racing! Jerry thought.

"I've asked one of my kayaking friends to let us use his old boat," Cat continued, wheeling toward the canal edge along the wet boardwalk. "He dropped it off this morning. Just understand: this is a racing surfski—very fast and very unstable. You'll tip over when you first get into it, no question about it. Don't get discouraged; we all did that. For a few months, I swam every time I took my ski out. Nothing to it, just climb back in and try again. It will come. I'll be back in two hours and perhaps we'll go for a little paddle." She patted him on the arm warmly and nodded encouragingly.

Return to Paradise

"A nice shade of red," she commented on his paint job and wheeled away to her workstation, plodding through the green grass.

Jerry quickly finished the last coat of paint and changed into his swimming trunks. The long white kayak resting on the canal slope was at least nineteen feet long and no more than a foot wide in its widest portion. It had a molded indentation in the middle for a seat and two parallel deep troughs for legs. Can this pencil even stay in the water without rolling? Jerry wondered but, after all, he'd seen Cat riding confidently in a similar craft. It was not impossible then.

He picked up the amazingly light surfski and carried it, wading along the stream, to the bay. A small cove in front of Cat's house, sheltered from waves by the reef, offered a pool of calm water and Jerry floated the fragile boat gently. The warm quiet water, the clear blue sky decorated with white cumulus clouds at the horizon, the gentle breeze—nature itself wanted to encourage him.

Just like the kayaker he saw on that memorable day of meeting Cat, Jerry placed his left hand, which was also holding a paddle, on the boat's edge next to his belly and his right hand on the seat's far side. Standing in the waist-deep water, Jerry lifted himself up on his arms, balancing precariously over the narrow hull. Then v-e-r-y gently, he aimed his bottom into the seat and started transferring his weight. Without a moment of hesitation, the kayak rolled over and Jerry felt the water filling his nose and burning his sinuses.

Any hope of learning to ride this boat quickly, without much work and frustration, was lost. Jerry righted the kayak and tried again, and again, and again. Two long hours later, he could sit in it. Rigid like a plastic action figure and hardly able to move without losing his balance, Jerry finally could stay on top. Even a few puny short strokes, with his eyes nailed to the horizon, were within his capability. His progress as a surfski kayaker was modest, as the boat invariably turned upside down within seconds, but he did acquire great expertise in scrambling back on board.

Cat appeared by the boulders marking the end of her lawn shortly after four, when the sun was already hiding behind the clouds hanging over the Koolau range. Separated from the pool by the broken field of black rocks, she watched from her wheelchair for a moment as Jerry struggled, then waved for him to come ashore.

"You did extremely well, Jerry!" Cat's praise came with enthusiasm clearly disproportionate to his success. "Better than I could hope for, but … maybe you've had enough kayaking for today." In the rich copper rays of the setting sun she was looking softer and more affectionate than her customary high-spirited form, always ready for a little verbal brawl.

This change of plans seemed to Jerry a wonderful idea. He had definitely had enough of kayaking for the day, even if he wouldn't admit it. There had to be a better way to spend the evening; cuddling in front of the TV looked just fine to him.

"Why don't we have a swim instead?" Cat waited for him at the canal's edge, a picture of welcoming grace, her luscious lips parted and showing white teeth, eyes beaming good will and her hair alluringly dangling over the blue bathing suit in a thick, straw-colored braid.

My valiant efforts have been recognized, Jerry noted with satisfaction. The pool, hidden on the side of the house opposite the canal, was only four feet deep. When the quickly growing shade of the house reached it, the bright turquoise tiles of its bottom darkened and disappeared, creating an indigo-colored, bottomless, calm sanctuary. Jerry rinsed off the salt accumulated on his body during kayak training and started swimming slow, relaxing laps in the luxuriously warm water.

Cat rolled in from the front yard sporting a tiny yellow

Return to Paradise

bikini, and put the brakes on her wheelchair at the pool's entry. An inclined tiled plane, confined between a pair of metal bars, led from the pool's edge to its bottom. Like a gymnast on the parallel bars, Cat lifted herself out of the chair in one energetic heave and advanced on the railing in small forward hops until she hung above the water, her arms' muscles knotting in slender but definite outlines.

This girl finds solutions to all her problems, Jerry thought, observing Cat's slim figure going through her acrobatics. Is it even fair to call her handicapped?

She sprang forward from her bars in one big splash. As soon as her body submerged, Cat turned into a water creature, undulating through the water swiftly and with hardly a splash. The propelling wave started at her extended fingers, flowed through the arms, gathering strength in the lower torso until her hips and thighs thrust in a large, powerful stroke, leaving just her lower legs to flop limply behind.

Jerry followed her, lagging two feet behind, admiring the elegant, dolphin-like movements as she weaved through the water. To his surprise, he had to resort to a fast crawl to keep up with her. They dashed together in the dark water like they were hitched into one harness, only turns breaking their choreography.

It's a dream, Jerry suspected. He dreamt of Cat often and this swim had all the elements of his imagination going wild: Cat's almost naked body squirming within the reach of his arm, heart thumping in his ears and the surreal darkness shutting out the whole world outside. And if this was for real … He purposely mistimed his turn, bumping into Cat, and when she suddenly fell into his arms, Jerry closed them. Surprised, she quivered for a moment, but right when he expected her to break out and lead him on a joyful but even harder chase, Jerry felt arms wrapping around his neck and wet lips searching his in the darkness.

They sank to the bottom, two breathless bodies reluctant

to release the craved prize even for a moment. Clinging, they swam to the entry platform where Jerry's back found solid support.

Cat's body weighting on his chest, Jerry's hands inched down, sliding on smooth wet skin, feeling each vertebrae of her arched back. His fingers hesitated for a moment meeting the stretched fabric but dove under, urged by Cat's frantic gasping. As he pressed her even tighter to his pulsating groin, Cat moaned and slipped the top off her shoulders, releasing her breasts, so white they seemed not to belong to this deeply tanned body. Fearful but determined, she offered herself to the man who had dragged her out of her imaginary world as surely as she had pulled him out of the turbulent ocean.

The shallow, warm water let them rest, barely awake, then Cat kissed him and slowly swam away. Jerry followed her to the pool's end. "I love you, Cat, as I have never loved anyone," he whispered into her hair, wrapping his arms around her waist.

She turned to him and asked softly, "Are you for real, Jerry, or has Ruth sent you?"

Ruth, I am scared out of my mind. Your idea worked just fine until the last week. I got from the world what I could ... what I couldn't, I created in my mind, as you did. I got quite good at it, sometimes hardly could tell the difference. No complaints. I even had a reasonable love life. I never wanted a lot of men, but I had Nick visiting me quite regularly. Sometimes, I used the memories frozen on a magnetic disc, I must admit. Hope you wouldn't call it cheating; the imaginary adventures are very nice but you use what you have, right?

When we were still dating, Nick got stuck on videotaping our lovemaking and he was quite insistent. I wasn't crazy about it, but he really wanted it, and I really wanted him, so I let him make some recordings. Who thought it would be me to watch them? They came in a big box of personal stuff his mom packed for me after the accident. Hope she didn't watch them. The CDs sat under my bed for some time, but a few months after I had left the hospital, I started sorting my stuff and found the discs.

I put one into a machine and watched us making love. Didn't know whether to cry or enjoy. First I cried, then enjoyed. After all, the disc showed exactly what we were—a pair of kids crazy about each other and having a great time.

Eventually, one scene got burned into my memory. The camera must have been on the TV stand, and what I saw was his naked body between my brown half-bent knees, and his hard, small ass twitching and pumping. You know, he was a very athletic boy, a basketball player, and all that jumping gave him truly magnificent buns with gluts that felt like marble covered with soft, warm skin.

So, I watched this disc many times, and then didn't even need to watch. I would close my eyes, and his body would appear between my knees—always hungry, always crazy from desire, like then. I could climax if I wanted, all I needed to do was to put my hand under the sheet for a moment, but more often I would just burn slowly and go to sleep with a pleasant glow. You know, that was very helpful for this dreadful creepy-crawly feeling I have on my thighs after my electric treatments. As you see, I wasn't missing a lot.

Anyway, Jerry comes along. I like him and he uses every trick in the book to spend every evening with me. I got used to him and started looking at my watch about three o'clock, hoping he would soon show up at the door. We have fun together and he looks at me like a cat looks at a fish in a bowl. But that's not what I complain about.

A few days ago, after Jerry had left, I somehow felt aroused. Did my electric torture routine, took a shower and went to bed. The crawlies were bad; I felt a million ants moving all over my thighs. Well, maybe Nick will help. I closed my eyes and started thinking of Nick and his buns. I started feeling warm inside and then ... I see Jerry kneeling on the ground, making adjustment to my ramp, his behind sticking up, as if lined up just for my eyes. He has a nice body, too. The way we met puts him in a rather uncomfortable position; he feels like a wimp I had to rescue. But the fact is, though he is not very big, he has a hard, tight body, obviously takes good care of himself. Just like you, I have a special place in my imagination for the male butt, and you would score him high in this department.

I opened my eyes and thought, what's this? Wrong number, for God's sake? Well, I went along with this imposition, talked to Jerry, and he was so sweet. He told me he loved me, was gentle, we kissed ... the whole enchilada.

Now, you have to admit that Jerry had a lot of nerve to insinuate himself into my mental world and to tangle with Nick, without me ever consenting. If this is not an invasion of privacy, what is? You did mention, I remember, that the characters we create in our minds sometimes start having their own ideas at one point. Even if this idea started somewhere in the hidden place of my own brain, it gave me quite a shock to see this creature of my imagination acting on his own.

But things got worse.... The next day, Jerry came early while I still had a lot of work to do. I was a bit edgy because I disliked his invasion of my inner life; it was so well organized. You know, Nick was much better behaved; he came only when invited, but this guy just put a foot in my soul's door and keeps pushing in. You might not appreciate it, Ruth, after all those years you lived in your inner universe, but on the outside, in the physical world, you don't have that much control over others, drastically less than in our imagination. People have their own ideas and do things you would never allow in your virtual life.

So, to slow him down somewhat, and perhaps due to my prickly mood, I asked him to ride a surfski. It is really difficult at the beginning; I certainly had a hell of a time learning how to stay on it. And, considering his recent experience off the Rock, I knew it would be hard on him. You might say I was a bit sadistic, but mostly I was scared because he appeared from nowhere (actually I dragged him in myself, in a most direct way), and started moving into my life like a bulldozer.

He appears to be a well-behaved gentleman, but look what he did: Nick is not coming to see me anymore. My days are upside down; once I could work all night if I wanted and then sleep all day. Now, I start getting nervous about three and almost sit waiting for him by the door by four. I used to kayak every day, but you know the last time I was on the ocean? The day I fished Jerry out.

I am becoming dependent on him! You know damn well this is not acceptable. What if he changes his mind and goes away? Perhaps some damned ski bunny with two healthy legs saves him from an avalanche? Should I go back to Nick? Nick seems to have left my head. Back to mind-numbing medications, booze or just crash and burn? It's scary, Ruth!

Can you imagine a dog trying to get on a wooden barrel in water? That was Jerry riding a surfski. I was watching him from the window and could not help but admire his spirit. He kept climbing and falling and climbing again. He gave himself no breaks, no rest, just an unrelenting struggle. I know what a struggle is, and I respect someone with a fighting spirit. Jerry is a fighter, and giving up doesn't occur to him easily.

I digress, but it brought to my mind the observation that Nick and I were just lucky kids. We were born good-looking, smart and with natural talents for sports. We also had good families; there was no real struggle in our lives. We danced from one easy victory to another, maybe undeserved, feat. After the accident, I had my fair share of opportunities to get hurt and fight on, get knocked down and come up again. But Nick … Nick just left the ring. I'll never know what kind of a fighter he would be.

I went to see Jerry two hours later and I was ashamed of myself. He deserved better than I gave him … and he still didn't hold it against me, still had this "love me" look.

We went swimming in the pool in the darkness, just the skinny new moon shining on us. "You know my swimming pool—generally quite useless … I prefer to swim in the ocean, but sometimes I do a few laps at night, just to justify the cost of cleaning."

This swimming in darkness turned out to be somehow very intimate, and at one point we bumped into each other. His hand brushed my lower back. You know that for some reason, I have this area very sensitive to touch, almost as though it was compensating for my numb legs. When he touched me there, I felt like a jet of hot but pleasant water shot through the middle of my back all the way to my skull. Suddenly, I wanted all of my body to be enveloped by this jet and I did something I still may regret. I turned around and kissed him. Then I lost my mind.

My body staged a full-scale rebellion and it locked

up my brain in some dark and padded place, where my rational thinking could scream without being heard. I wanted Jerry so badly! I wanted to feel him with all of me. My arms, breasts, belly ... all my skin was gorging on the warmth of his body; I felt his hands plastering me against his hips and I wanted more and more of it. All those years of good, clean fun I had in my mind, this wonderful feeling of being in full control of myself ... and the rest of the world, it all splashed like a jar of strawberry jam on a white-tile kitchen floor.

Ruth, it was very, very different from the erotic romps we conjured in our heads. Remember Ronaldo, the dark, passionate and crazy man, your perfect Italian lover? Ronaldo who snuck past your three bodyguards, and stood on a window ledge for the whole day, just to spend a night with you? My point is, Ronaldo went home after this steamy affair with you and would not return until you called him back. He would go home or jump through the window any time you wished. All you needed to do was to will him. But I had no power over the events that were rushing over us. I was no longer a director. I was an actress, and my script was missing.

It was very scary, exciting and beautiful at the same time. It was even different from sex with Nick, when he was still around. With Nick it was like a ... happy game of tennis finished with a wonderful victory for both of us. Perhaps because we were healthy and innocent of suffering, our encounters were so joyful and so sweet. We could do it again and again without any fear or concern or pain.

Eventually, Jerry and I slumped on the bottom of the pool. I was still feeling "aftershocks," but my hips cramped up a bit. Maybe they cramped up before, but I wouldn't know, I was shaken to my core. This experience reduced me to the level of trembling jelly; I needed some time to reconstitute into the body I knew. I swam away to stretch my hips a bit. He followed me and said he loved me.

    Ruth, I am scared to death, I've lost control. I can't let that happen ... but I want to be with him. Will I have to depend on someone else again? I'd sworn I never would ... and I did so well, but now ... Ruth, I wish you were here. How should I protect myself?

Chapter 14

Abe, January 4

Kalani brought seventeen hundred dollars at lunchtime and Abe still had over two hundred left from the night before. That should do.

Since she came home a bit late, having stopped at the bank, there was no time to cook. Instead, she had stopped on her way at the Sloppy's to pick some local grind. The blast of sizzling hamburger smell, mixed with the sharp aroma of ketchup and hot sauce, filled the apartment the moment Kalani opened the carton container. A big honest hamburger rested on the heap of rice, soggy and brown from gravy at the bottom but still virgin-white at the top. A sunny-side-up egg perched on top, capping the mound of food like the sun rising over Haleakala, still cloaked by clouds, still enveloped into the whites.

Kalani was well aware of the fact that Abe just barely tolerated *loco moco*. Rice with gravy and hamburger patty was the taste and smell of his childhood, remembered with little fondness. Everybody seemed to have a reason, even a duty, to kick the shabby little boy who seemed to belong to no one. Only at the Marsh, where nobody could find him, had Abe felt completely safe. Then one summer, between eighth and ninth grade, he suddenly reincarnated into a lanky teenager with a bad attitude, an individual capable of inflicting serious bodily damage. The change took by surprise even his mother who—working double shifts in Honolulu—mostly saw him sleeping. That's when everybody, like on a cue, stopped picking on him. Abe found himself a job after school and broke his uneasy relationship with his mother's favorite *loco moco*.

Kalani, on the other hand, grew up with her mother cooking at home, and *loco moco* was the flavor of her teenage years spent hanging carelessly around the Café 100 in Hilo. The smell of hot grease and the tongue-burning hot sauce meant freedom from the suffocating fear at home. On that particular day, armed with a bundle of green paper in her hand, Kalani felt she could enjoy her *loco moco* no matter what Abe felt.

And she was right. He rose to the occasion and ate without complaint, trying to kill the taste and look of it with prodigious amounts of thick crimson ketchup and generous application of Tabasco. On the contrary, he complimented Kalani on her nice dress, a somewhat tight garment the color of jade patterned with huge yellow hibiscus. The dress had been her usual work outfit for at least a year, and it made her feel like crying every time she pulled it on, but once Kalani had set her mind to save money for nursing school, she could be stingy like a nun on Good Friday.

Abe was not an expert in the subject of fashion, but he couldn't miss the lovely fullness of Kalani's bottom when she bent over to wipe the gravy spilled on the floor. Unfortunately, there was just enough time for a kiss and some perfunctory kneading of her round buns.

Kalani accepted the clumsy caress without protest, although she derived no pleasure from it. That was her boyfriend's way of reaffirming his ownership rights, she realized. Not much different, really, from a dog raising his leg at a tree. Isn't it strange what happened to us? she thought. My heart used to thump when he was around, and when he touched me ... I was happy all day. And look at us now.

Abe magnanimously overlooked the shortness of their lunch encounter because his business career was awaiting a decisive step. At two, he would meet Jose and the rooster guy. Rosen ... he reflected for a moment. What would be his place in this venture? Ask him to put some money on the table right now? No, then Rosen might feel like he was buying the chicks. And this would make Abe some sort of employee. No, the chicken breeding operation, Abe's rooster enterprise, should be running first; only then would he invite the restaurateur and his money. That would make them real partners.

Happy, enjoying the cheerful consideration of his business, Abe walked toward Kawainui Marsh, where the first important deal of his budding enterprise was to take place.

The marsh was a very special place: trees, bushes, grasses, water plants, and whatever else the Good Lord created suitable for growing in this climate fought for a spot in this nine-hundred-acre valley cradled between the mountains, the ocean and the Pali Highway. It was one of those few places on Oahu where fresh water—draining from the cloud-shrouded mountains— was abundant, deep pockets of silt offered choice dirt to sink a root into and people backed off, leaving it alone as a wildlife refuge.

Banyans, monkey pod trees, spider trees, guavas, bulrush, grasses—a fierce community of plants, testing each other's strength and determination every moment of the day, crowded this water-soaked basin wrestled from the ocean over the past few centuries. Even Abe's grandfather, as a kid, could still fish for *o'opu* in the pond blanketed now by water cabbage like a thick bright-green carpet fit for a royal palace.

In a way, Abe felt like a sovereign watching his domain,

looking down from the Pali Highway. The best hours of his rotten childhood were spent here, when he lay side by side with old Pono, listening to his ancient stories. The old homeless man, fed up with the police harassment in Ala Moana Park, set up his household under an old blue tarp in the thicket, no more than two hundred yards from a *heiau*. The big pile of ancient rocks, made recognizable as an important religious site only by a small bronze plaque, had transformed back in Abe's eyes into a sacred platform. Only royalty, high priests and gods belonged here, looking from their elevation over the marsh and fields below, all the way to Kailua Bay. The lonely vagabond took the position of Abe's personal *kahuna* with great joy in his heart, and entertained the youngster with a never-ending string of tales about old Hawaiian heroes and gods.

Living on Manu-oo Street, practically next to the marsh, Abe ran to see Pono every day until the day he started working. This way, he received his spiritual training from the old Hawaiian, learning his culture within shouting range of Oahu's great shrine. The green reserve of Kawainui became his realm, backyard and playground.

He was not alone in this connection to the Marsh. Few places in Kailua, if any, could provide better protection against the prying eyes of mothers, neighbors and the law. A bottle of rum, a puff of weed, or a needle—if someone was so inclined—could be enjoyed here in the safety and tranquility of this wonderful place. Abe had never tried hard drugs, but he developed the habit of bringing his girlfriends here; even had an old mattress hidden among the aerial roots of a banyan tree, carefully wrapped in a tarp against moisture. That function became unnecessary, of course, once he got his own place.

The Marsh came to his mind immediately when Jose asked where to bring Vincent, the chicken guy. Abe turned off the Pali Highway shoulder, taking the pathway steeply descending toward and under the gray smooth trunks and branches of a big banyan then—at the bottom of the ditch—he followed the trail cutting through the thicket of fake-Koa trees. Kiawe made a solid spiky beachhead on the higher ground, fighting off the phalanx of fiddlewoods pushing from below, but being upstaged by cunning octopus trees, which—resistant to the shade thrown on invaders like a weapon by taller plants—slyly crept under their canopies. The vegetation hell-bent on survival and reproduction fiercely contested every level of the thicket, down to the ground floor of water, and below. A network of faint pathways crisscrossed this green mass, allowing anyone—who knew his way here—to come and go discreetly, or simply disappear in a blink of an eye.

The path curved sharply and twisted, seeking dry ground, but Abe felt at home. He jumped across a little stream and dove under the low-hanging thorny branch of kiawe, abandoning the path to disappear in the dense grove of giant bamboo. Once he emerged, like a magician, from the wall of green sticks, there was only a field of bulrush before him, growing on the soggy ground right to the wide expanse of grass and water cabbage behind it.

About that time, less than an hour after Abe left his home, his happy day filled with positive thoughts dissolved into a stinky, maddening mess. Two men sat on dry stumps sticking up among the weeds, waiting. Jose, a short young fellow dressed in dirty knee-length shorts and grayish sweatshirt, jumped to his feet as soon as he heard Abe trudging through the bamboo, but the other man, an older wiry guy with a brown weathered face, remained on his stump.

"Here he comes!" Jose announced proudly, stretching his acne-scar-pocked face into a wide grin. He turned with a theatrical gesture to the sitting man who nodded slightly without any shade of emotion showing on his face.

Abe rested with dignity on another stump. He allowed himself a sweet moment of being number one, slowly wiping his hot and itchy neck, removing the real and imaginary broken twigs and burs from his hair, while the other two men watched expectantly.

The older man raised his head and turned his right palm up with a silent question, but did not make any formal greeting gesture.

"There you go, Vincent." Abe finally relented and pulled from his pants pocket a thick roll of green bills bound by an elastic band. "A hundred short, but I'll give you the rest in a few days." He threw the bundle toward the older man.

Vincent caught the money with a quick swipe of his hand, removed the band and started counting loudly. "Eighteen, nineteen hundred …" He looked at Abe questioningly. "OK, that's a hundred short for chicks, but where is the money for board and feed?"

Abe's face grew dark and his shoulders rose. "You didn't say anything about board and feed."

Vincent's wrinkled Filipino face twisted in a wry grimace. "Oh, you want to keep the chicks in your apartment—good, good!" Vincent was laughing openly now. "I'm sure Kalani will be very happy; a woman can't have too many roosters!"

Now Jose started laughing too and he just had to add, "Abe, Kalani and the chickens, that will be a nice family. She always wanted chicks; one will be called Lehua and another Maika!" His whole body was shaking with nasty giggles.

Abe rose slowly to his feet and growled through his clenched teeth to Jose, "Shut your stupid mouth or I'll shut it for you!"

As for Vincent … someone would have to pay for his humiliation. "You try to cheat me, *makule*, old man? You let me believe that the chicks could run on your farm for free." He stepped toward the older man now, his hands balled into papaya-size fists. "I will pay you for board … maybe … when I feel like, and how much I think it's worth. And you'll take it, and you'll be very careful with my chicks because if any one of them goes bad, I will smash your face, just like I am going to do now."

Vincent sprang to his feet before the younger man could reach him. Abe, with his big arms raised and head lowered, closed on him like a bull terrier ready to grab a smaller dog by the neck and shake him into submission. Vincent didn't try to disappear into the green protective wall just a step behind his back, but when Abe's scowling face was within a foot of his, a skinny brown hand shot from his belt and instantly a razor blade appeared, almost touching the attacker's nose.

"You back off, boy!" Vincent hissed. "Or your mother won't know your face tonight! I could fillet you like a fish before you knew what hit you. Keep your nose clean and don't forget my hundred dollars. And it will be another hundred for feed and board, every month. Come here tomorrow with cash or forget your chicks. I will keep this as a deposit." He patted the pocket of his dirty shorts where the wad of bills had disappeared.

Abe squinted his eyes at the blade nearly touching his lip, then glanced at Jose who was standing like a wedding guest three feet away, hands on his hips, giving no indication he might want to join the fray.

"It's only fair, Abe, it's only fair ..." he blurted nervously, his head lowered and eyes stuck to the ground. The traitor just wanted a way out.

"You hear, Abe; it's only fair ..." Vincent grinned with contempt as he stepped backwards, turned around and disappeared among the bamboo.

"You brought him to me, *okole puka*, asshole"—Abe turned to Jose with a snort—"and now, when he took my money, you've backed down? You *mahu*, faggot, all you had to say was to make fun of my girlfriend?"

He took a big swing with his right hand, and when Jose ducked to avoid a right hook, Abe caught him in the belly with a hard left undercut. The skinny gray body lifted into the air from the blow, supported by Abe's great bulk, then Jose slumped on the ground barely breathing. Abe stood over him for a moment, deliberating if a few kicks should be thrown into the curled worm on the ground, but Jose was not moving, just making weak gasping sounds.

Abe spat on him, turned away and crashed through the thicket straight to the pathway leading to the highway. Uncertain what to do, he stopped by the big flat mound of rocks overgrown with lichen. *Uluo heiau,* he realized and sat on a large boulder. He'd passed the temple ruins a thousand times and sat here listening to Pono many hours, but only once had he come asking for a favor, and then it was actually his mother who'd been asking; she just dragged him along. She put a lei on a rock and asked for the boy's father to come back, but nobody saw him again after he stepped on that gangway, a new crew member on some dirty freighter.

If the gods had any power, they would help themselves first. Abe shrugged, looking over the useless rubble of the *heiau.* Anyway, his mother's prayers in church didn't do the trick either. No help was coming from this quarter. He got up and turned home.

A dark corridor led to the one-bedroom apartment Abe occupied with Kalani in the older building not far from Keolu Hills Park. He let the door slam and threw himself on the bed, a good solid-oak four-poster bed with expensive mattress. It had a firm but comfortable feel. Kalani and Abe bought it three years ago, when they decided to rent an apartment together. Money was not a big problem then; Abe worked on a fishing boat and Kalani did cleaning, like now. In fact, they were doing quite well.

To buy this new bed was like starting a new life. Kalani was excited like a kid on Christmas night, and for him … it was a good time, too. They also bought a table, chairs, and a chest of drawers, but these were secondhand, though still good. This other stuff didn't have the same meaning; it was the bed that was important. It was solid and new, like their life together.

Things changed when the skipper of his fishing boat decided he had enough of getting up at 3 AM every day. Old Nakamura had to be close to eighty and was getting clumsy and forgetful. Once they grazed a rock at the harbor channel, at the Kewalo Basin Annex where the old guy had gone in and out almost every day for the past forty or fifty years. He didn't want to leave his boat to just anyone; he wanted Abe to buy her.

"I will teach you, Abe, what you need to know. You worked with me for four years; most of it you already know." He would take the payment in installments; he trusted Abe.

Well, too late to think of it now. Nakamura's been dead for two years; the boat still sleeps in her berth at Pier 16, but someone else bosses around there. No question, Abe thought, melancholically releasing smoke from his mouth, I was happier then. And Kalani was happier, too.

But it looked like a smart thing to do: take a bit of time off … sleep in … relax a bit. Before Abe knew it, the unemployment stopped coming. Heck, he had to ask Kalani for pocket money! Odd jobs here and there: help with moving, a bit of gardening, cut a tree—all of it worthless. Sometimes he could poach a few lobsters, other times he might visit a farmer's orchard at night—hardly enough money for beer and cigarettes. Heck, Kalani keeps me, he thought unhappily.

And now, when he could start making some real money in cock fighting, of course, something had to go wrong. Really, if he had enough money, there would be no problem! A stinking two hundred and he would be in business. The stupid bitch just couldn't come up with an extra two hundred bucks!

Dirty dishes piled in the sink—Kalani had not had time to wash them—were annoying the hell out of Abe. His mother, even though she spent all her time in Honolulu, kept her house really clean. He lay on his back in bed and lit another cigarette. The ceiling was cracked and dirty. The walls, windows—all cried for a fresh coat of paint. What a dump! Someone should take care of it! I'll give the landlady hell next time I see her, he resolved angrily.

Kalani came home after six. She stopped at the door, seeing Abe sprawled on the bed, not sure what to make of the situation. He was home way too early. It couldn't be anything good.

"Oh, Abe, you're so early ... Is everything OK? How is your business?" she asked, masking her anxiety with an air of concern.

"Business would be good if you gave me all the money I needed." Abe did not move, looking grimly at the ceiling.

"But I gave you two thousand, like you asked!" Her voice was rising in anger at the injustice of his accusation.

"You can't do business without reserves; I was two hundred short." Abe was glad to find a good excuse for his failure at the last moment. This made him feel a bit better, though at the same time, it focused his attention on the fact that Kalani was responsible for his fiasco.

Kalani turned away, not wanting to show her angry face. "I gave you all you asked for, my money for the nursing school. And what about you? You couldn't make any by yourself? What are you, crippled *mahu* or something?"

That was more than Abe could stand. Vincent, Jose and now his own girlfriend—was everybody turning on him? He jumped up from the bed and harshly grabbed her by the shoulder, turning her around.

"If I need your business advice, I'll ask for it," he breathed hard into her face. "Now, clean the bloody dishes and make dinner! I am the man of this house, and you better remember it."

Kalani shook her shoulder free and stepped back. She was furious, and so she forgot the sensible rule of not being too sassy with her boyfriend. "You behave like a man of the house, and I'll respect you all right. So, Abe, when was the last time you did some decent work, like a man? You're just wasting your life and mine. You prefer to hang around with this rat-friend of yours, Jose, make dinner yourself."

A dry snap exploded in the apartment like a pistol shot when Abe's open hand connected with Kalani's right cheek. She flew across the room until the wall stopped her. She stood there without a word, holding her burning face, looking at Abe with the same paralyzing fear of her childhood. She had seen her mother standing in the same cowed posture and needed no explanation.

Abe was almost as shocked as she was. He did not even realize when his hand reached out to slap her. He certainly punched other people now and then—not that often actually as guys knew how strong he was—but it never occurred to him to hit Kalani. At her hundred and twenty pounds, she was almost half his size; he felt a sudden surge of shame and remorse. "I'm sorry, Kalani, I am sorry, I don't know why I did that. I was just very angry …"

Kalani remained leaning against the wall, pressing a hand against her stinging face. Her heart pounding in fear, she started to move slowly, sliding her back on the blue-and-white wallpaper, trying to squeeze behind the table for protection. She barely heard Abe. Only when she got the table to separate them did she regain a bit of her composure. "Just get out, Abe, just get out," she wailed softly. "I don't want you here. This is my apartment … I don't want you here!" she begged, watching fearfully for another violent outburst.

Abe stepped back to the other wall and raised his open hands in a gesture of good intentions. "OK, OK, I'll go away for a few hours, so we can cool off a bit, OK?" He tried to placate her and turned to the door.

Kalani remained silent, watching through her spread fingers until he stepped out of the room, but once he was in the corridor, Kalani moved quickly, slammed the door, turned the lock, put the chain on and yelled with hate, "If you come back here, I'll call the police! You got that? We are through—you and me—we are *pau!*"

Chapter 15

Rosen, January 4

The old man kept a lot of cash in his safe, so much that when Harry Rosen cleared him out, he needed a big leather bag to carry it away. Nothing frees the mind better than a good-sized hoard of large bills and golden coins—discreet, free of tax and paper trail. His financial matters were fine; what gnawed his mind were memories of the Master. Rosen tried to suppress all evidence of the former boss's existence in his mind, but the stooped, ascetic figure appeared behind his eyelids any time he closed his eyes, like a bad dream.

La Esperanza, named just like the nearest town, had been his home ever since he went AWOL in Panama and buried his sergeant's uniform in a deep hole. La Esperanza … The Hope, that's just the old man's wicked sense of humor. The rancho hidden at the end of a rutted trail must have been a poachers' hideaway at one time; there was nothing else around to justify anyone's presence, just miles and miles of waterlogged, dense Nicaraguan jungle. But that was before the man with the vision, will and means came and transformed it into a shrine of overpowering emotions, a sanctuary of power and beauty. Only the road remained unchanged—five hours by a jeep whining through the pitted, muddy track—for a very good reason.

Nicaragua, those were good times, he thought, but everybody needs to advance in life. I couldn't hope for anything else with the old man around, and he seemed immortal. Harry Rosen spared no expense and no trouble to make sure no tracks were left behind him. He was confident that Bonito, the Master's disciple, disappeared like a ghost from the surface of earth, and that Harry Rosen, who came into existence in Hawaii, had no traceable links to Nicaragua. Still, who would know better how crafty the old bastard was? He wasn't called El Diablo without a reason. And what would he do if he ever caught up with Bonito? Cold sweat broke on Rosen's back as he angrily ordered himself to stop thinking stupid thoughts.

The view from his window was magnificent; the deep ocean blue extending to the horizon lightened in the proximity of land and flowered into a white fringe of foam where the water touched the beach below. Two small islands were thrown in the middle of this panorama, as though a painter had decided that his composition needed more variety.

That would be almost too pretty if not actually real, Harry remarked to himself. Money well spent. But it was not the beauty of the view that caught his attention. The property's main attraction was its isolation. Splendidly situated on the summit of volcanic rock, it had no neighbors. There were, obviously, some houses down the steep narrow road, but the closest one was no less than two hundred yards away. Only frigates gliding in the sky could look into his windows, and the howling of the ever-present trade winds would drown any noise coming from his bedroom. Here, at last, he was, or rather could be, the Master.

Compare this to the view of the stinky jungle stretching for tens of miles in every direction, he thought smugly. Rosen enjoyed planning his little but absolute kingdom in great detail, more for entertainment than any immediate application. Patience. He knew well that hastiness could be fatal. Most assured assumptions fail, and problems no one could anticipate may crop up. Just look what happened to El Diablo!

Rosen's plan would be polished to perfection. Every part would be examined many times for any possible holes; all scenarios, no matter how unlikely, would be played and replayed before any concrete action would be initiated. All that takes time, but he had all the time he needed. Sooner or later all the pieces of the jigsaw would find their places.

Still, what wrong could come by the way of a little excitement, the sweet taste of memories streaming from the objects reminiscent of those times when he was Bonito, the Master's right hand? A hard hand, a fist never seen without a whip, he remembered fondly.

The black horse crop with an ivory handle, now gracing his desk, was certainly not his instrument. Much too delicate for the work Bonito did. This was a tool of an artist—to be used precisely and sparingly, an instrument of the great maestro who just got too old to perform his act. Therefore, it was up to Bonito, a.k.a. Harry Rosen, to take it from the failing hand and ensure it would keep performing.

Consuela. That ungrateful bitch Consuela was the last canvas on which the crop painted its straight lines and cubistic figures. Rosen remembered vividly the nervous twitching of her muscles in anticipation of a strike. He would wait, let the anticipation grow unbearable, and just when she started thinking that maybe, this time, for whatever reason, she would get away without a whipping, a swish of a leather-bound reed cutting through the air would send her in a panicky and futile effort to move away from pain. The crop plunged into the softness of her buttocks and a bright red line appeared immediately, slowly darkening as Rosen looked on with the satisfaction of a painter who delivered a line of perfect proportion, color and composition.

She enjoyed his art too. No way could she fake the volcanic passion that followed beatings. At first, when she appeared on the ranch, she was just a pretty girl scared into witless submission. The Master chose well. Nobody gave it a second thought when a new teacher disappeared in a village twenty miles away. A city girl ran away from her village post—happened all the time.

The Master ordered her taken to the inner yard every day, and Bonito was happy to do it. After the first few times, when she was just writhing and screaming until his culminating excitement made him drop the whip and penetrate her, she seemed to develop some taste for flogging; she used her twisting body to seduce him, which of course would shorten the whole session. Soon, she was going into an erotic frenzy the moment he tied her up to the post, which might result in only one or two strikes. Could she fake it, just to escape the whip? Bonito wondered, but that did not stop him from being more and more attached to her.

At the end, it was Consuela who talked him into cleaning out the old man and running away. "I will be your slave forever, Master." That's what did him in, "Master." She certainly knew his dreams, treacherous bitch.

Rosen was examining the leather straps attached to the wooden frame of a large armchair when the doorbell rang. Amazed, he put away the straps. Who the hell might be paying me a visit? He was flabbergasted.

"Aloha, Mr. Rosen, it's my first day to work for you." Abe's girlfriend was standing in his doorway, a thin dress stretching over her full breasts and delightful round hips.

"Kalani, I forgot about it, but please, come in and go ahead." Rosen followed the girl and only now understood why she seemed so familiar. She had some of Consuela's qualities. Her hips are a bit fuller, he thought, but Consuela lost weight with my training, nothing that couldn't be fixed.

Other than that—the same olive skin, black eyes, narrow waist.... I wonder what her temperament is like.

"Could you start with the bedroom upstairs? I will need to work there a bit later on."

"Sure, Mr. Rosen."

Rosen watched the girl dusting his nude sculpture and couldn't refrain from seeing Kalani naked, tied to the armchair, with her gorgeous ass exposed and waiting for his sort of love. Just before he started, he liked to grab Consuela's black, long hair to lift her face so that he could look into it and drink in the fear pouring from her eyes. I could do it right here, without any gags. This house is just perfect, he thought, as pressure was increasing in his pants. His excitement climbed even higher when Kalani bent over to make his bed. Who would know? I would never admit that she ever showed up for cleaning. Rosen got on his feet and started slowly moving toward Kalani.

Another bell rang. "Hell! What's this? Some kind of a bloody hotel?" Rosen turned to the entrance with a furious expression, opened the door, and his face rapidly changed into a warm smile. "Abe, do come in. Your girlfriend is here."

"Thank you, Mr. Rosen. I just wanted to talk with Kalani for a moment."

"There is nothing to talk about." The girl was standing just behind Rosen. "I've told you, we are *pau* and don't follow me. I am working now and don't bother me anymore."

How interesting, Rosen thought. Who's the suspect when a girl disappears if not a jilted boyfriend? Time brings opportunities. Thank you, Abe, for stopping me now. It would be most unfortunate and stupid of me to start this affair on the spur of the moment.

"Kalani, I just want to speak with you." Abe was not giving up. "It was such a stupid thing I did. I will make it up to you, please."

"Abe, if you follow me, I will tell the police you are stalking me. I'll press charges and get you locked up for good." Kalani was in no mood for forgiveness and shook her duster at him. Abe's humble plea eased her fear and now she allowed herself to be properly outraged.

Rosen definitely had no wish for the police to come to his house. He took Abe by his arm in a fatherly manner and led him down the driveway. "Listen, my boy, be patient. She is quite worked up now for whatever you did, but give it a day or two and try to see her again. Just stay away from the police; we don't need that." Then he went back inside, smiled kindly to Kalani, and started reading a newspaper he had bought in the morning.

Abraham walked down to the end of the driveway where his bike was hidden in the bushes. He chose a nice flat place behind some junipers and settled on the ground. The night was pleasant and no mosquitoes were buzzing around, as the wind was strong on the hilltop. He could wait. Kalani would have to pass by him.

"Sure, come over, why not? Is anything wrong, Kalani?" Cat put down the phone and thought that things with Abe and Kalani were moving faster than she could predict. Her friend was upset and sounded scared. Partner abuse in the islands was a significant problem; Cat didn't know that many people, but every woman could tell a story of a girlfriend or wife badly beaten up or murdered. This was serious; the locals could be friendly and funny one moment but vicious and hell-bent on destruction when it came to blows. And not just men; *wahine* were known to swing a machete or some other deadly object quite confidently as well.

In the not-so-remote past, Hawaiian women were not some wilting roses of European troubadour ballads but fierce fighters who often carried a war club into battles. A small and slim girl, the image of a hula dancer spread through Hollywood movies, had very little to do with tall and sturdy real Hawaiian females. They were products of fine-boned Chinese, Japanese and Filipino bloodlines grafted on the robust Hawaiian branches like sweet grapes or succulent mangoes.

But Kalani was rather small, and if she considered herself Hawaiian, it was mostly because the mix of her various ethnic identities was too complicated to be summed up in one sentence, never mind one word. Opposite Abe, a powerful hunk of a man, she certainly could not be a sparring partner in any physical scuffle.

The story of her own mother, slapped around for years before running away, came up during her second friendly chat with Cat; it was never far away from Kalani's mind. The daily terror and relief of their escape from the Big Island to Oahu were still palpable in her memory. To Cat's disbelieving ears, she sounded almost grateful for her father's alcoholism and drug problems; this was the reason he never bothered to chase down his runaway family.

So, when Kalani's car stopped at the driveway, Cat opened the door and the girl ran into it breathless. Cat shut the door and locked it with the bolt. Kalani was wearing her usual green dress and rubber sandals, but her long hair was tangled and her eyes were wide-open and wild. Cat noted redness and swelling on her right cheek.

"Just sit down and tell me what happened." She pulled Kalani to a table. "Don't worry, neither Abe nor anybody else will hurt you here."

"But I think he followed me." Kalani slumped at the table but wouldn't take her eyes off the door. Her face was ash-pale and drops of sweat were beading on her upper lip.

"No worries, I am prepared for unwelcome guests." Cat sounded confident and cool, but her heart was racing. "You don't think I have no protection, living here alone?"

"You have protection? What do you mean?" Kalani did not quite comprehend; she knew Cat lived by herself. Maybe this new man I met a few times at the door ... He wouldn't even slow down Abe, she thought. Abe was a champion wrestler in high school and had only gotten bigger and stronger since then.

"Just believe me. So what happened?" Cat pulled out cookies and a carton of milk, hoping Kalani would settle down.

"Well, I gave Abe two grand ... actually three hundred and the rest next day. He seemed pretty happy, even grateful. Then he took off. The next thing I knew, he was home when I came back at night. Very unusual. Normally, he would be hanging out somewhere with his buddy Jose until midnight. And he looked very pissed. So I asked how the business was. You know, to make him feel important. Besides, it was my two thousand bucks, for my school." She sniffed, rubbed her eyes and blew her nose. "And he really went crazy and slapped me."

"He beat you up?" Cat's eyes were sparkling with anger and her tanned hands turned into white-knuckled fists. "Has it ever happened before?"

"Not exactly beat me up ... slapped me once," Kalani corrected nervously. "Never did it before. But I saw my mother being slapped around for years, and there will be no other time with me. I told him to get out and get lost. We are *pau*." Kalani's eyes welled up with tears. Finally, she could allow herself to pour out the fear, anger and sadness. "Now I don't have a boyfriend, don't have money for school, and I am afraid to cross a parking lot to get to my car!"

Cat was sitting stiffly, her head up and eyes locked onto the black window. The trade winds were howling on the awning but nothing moved outside. This situation was new to her; she had no good and fast advice. "Whatever needs to be done, you can't go home. You are a sitting duck there. Somehow ... when I first met him ... I didn't get the impression Abe was a scoundrel, but you need to be careful. You should stay here with me until the situation clears. And Kalani, I'm proud of you. You did exactly the thing that needed to be done."

"But, I am scared now and, and ... Abe was a good man!"

The bell rang and the women shuddered. "Oh, God, it's him," Kalani whispered and shrunk in her chair. Cat wheeled to her desk and pulled out the drawer. Without saying a word, she removed a handgun and put it under the thin blanket she draped over her knees. "Just stay where you are."

Kalani's eyes were closed and she looked like she was praying. The bell sounded aggressively again and, almost immediately, once more. Cat wheeled to the door, looked through the spy hole, pulled back the bolt, moved the chair back two yards and put her right hand under the blanket. The doorknob turned, the door opened and the tall muscular man slowly walked over the threshold. He stopped in front of Cat who was blocking his way.

The slim woman looked up at the big man standing in front of her wheelchair, her face pale and grim. "What do you want, Abe? You should have called before coming." Cat's voice was cold and unwelcoming.

The man's eyes were fixed on Kalani frozen by the table. "Sorry about that; I just wanted to talk to Kalani."

Cat turned around and asked calmly, "Kalani, do you want to talk to him?" Kalani shook her head signaling "no" without looking up.

"Well, she doesn't want to talk to you. Now just leave."

"I cannot leave without talking to her." Abe moved to get around Cat, but she spun her chair quickly to block him.

"Get out of here!" she snapped in a high-pitched strained voice.

"Stop it, lady! All I want to do is talk to my woman." He put his large hand on the wheelchair's handle and immobilized it, then quickly moved around to make a step towards Kalani, who was trying to slide from her chair under the table. "I am not going to hurt you, Kalani," he added soothingly.

"Stop right there!" A sharp command and a loud metallic sound made him freeze. He slowly turned his head to look into the short barrel.

Suddenly, the rage Cat knew years ago, at the hospital, came back in all its violence, but this time with a terrible clear focus at the man who intruded into her home and did the unforgivable, tried to restrain her. Cat aimed at the middle of his chest, holding the short black handgun in her extended hand, trembling with fury. The essence of her misfortune, the invisible evil she hated with all her heart for years, finally had a face and a chest that could be ripped open with a bullet.

"No!" Kalani screamed and leaped from the table toward the man, until she was checked by Cat's hand grabbing her dress.

"Stay back and don't interfere! This is my house and nobody will push me around!" she barked hoarsely, but Kalani's movement interrupted Cat's blind rage. She exhaled and rested the shaking, weapon-holding hand on her knee.

"You want to go out and stay with him, you are free, but he's not welcome here, and he's just leaving. Right, Abraham?" The point of the barrel vaguely waved towards the door.

"I'm leaving, I'm leaving …" Abe was taking slow, deliberate steps backwards. "Just wanted to tell you, Kalani, you don't need to be afraid of me. I will never do it again. I think I was just crazy, *loco*, for a moment. I'll move out from our apartment so you can think about it, but if you see me again, you don't have to run. I love you."

Kalani stared in his eyes, moving slowly toward the door in lockstep with him, until Cat's hand still clutching her dress jerked her back. She looked back with an expression of surprise.

"Snap out of it! You look hypnotized," Cat said harshly. "I want to talk to you for a few minutes and then you can go if you want to. Can you do that for me?"

Abe stood at the door looking at the women, clearly

hoping Kalani would go with him.

"I'll stay here, with Cat," Kalani said, lowering her head, "... but, Abe, thank you."

When the door closed the big man had tears in his eyes. She wanted to protect me from the bullet; we are not *pau*, he thought. She still loves me and I can make it better. Abe walked to his bike briskly, smiling in the darkness.

"What do you think you are doing?" Cat inquired softly. "Are you ready just to go home, give him a hug and forget?"

Kalani, feeling somewhat ashamed, shrugged, and looking aside said, "But Abe is a good man, and I love him. And he is sorry. Don't you think he is sorry?"

Cat's heart was still pounding and she felt wetness in her armpits, but she could think clearly again. Pulling a gun on anyone, that was a first for her. She could be proud of her debut's dramatic impact, but neither Abe nor Kalani could guess how close to a disaster they all were. Now she was getting annoyed with Kalani.

"How many times do you think your father apologized after beating up your mother? Probably as many times as he beat her. That's why she stayed with him for years, always hoping he would change. Abe crossed the line, and crossing the line next time will only be easier for him."

Kalani slumped on the chair and hid her face in her hands. Now she remembered the mother hiding a black eye under big sunglasses, pussyfooting around her house at noon because her husband might wake up in a bad mood. She remembered slapping sounds and thuds of a body slammed against the wall in her parents' bedroom, muffled whimpers so that kids would not hear. Her body started shaking, and she broke into loud sobbing.

Cat approached her and touched her dark head. "You can stay here as long as you want, Kalani, until you figure out what to do."

"But he was a good man ..." Kalani whispered, sobbing.

"He was. I hardly know him, but you told me good things about him. But he is not anymore. He is a bum and abuser now."

Kalani raised her head. "You shouldn't call him that. He just had a stretch of bad luck." Now she was feeling a wave of irritation swelling in her as well.

"Bad luck? What's his bad luck? Perhaps he got hurt on the boat or got sick?" Cat's voice was rising in pitch and she hardly could refrain from relieving her tension by screaming. Breathing rapidly, her nostrils flaring, she could not contain the surge of adrenaline, could not step back and calmly discuss the issue at hand. Her body demanded a fight, now! "You know what his bad luck was? You—you were his bad luck!" The pair of eyes, blue and hot like the cone of a Bunsen burner, glowered in Cat's pale face now hardly tinged by her tan.

Kalani sat straight up, her eyes bulging. "Are you crazy? What are you saying? I have always loved him; I would do anything for him!"

There was no holding back now; Cat decided to dish her opinion out. "Three years ago, when I first met you, you brought him to my house once. He was a great-looking guy—happy, cheerful and in love with you. Then you destroyed him with your love. He lost his job and could have had another within a week, but you let him take it easy. Heroic Kalani could take care of her man! You worked and he fooled around with his good-for-nothing friends. You were just making sure he had enough cash for beer and cigarettes. Did you give him money for hookers as well?" Cat didn't have much sense left once the dam had been broken.

Kalani's face was purple and she appeared ready to jump at Cat, but after a moment of hesitation she just shouted with hate, "Shut up! Just shut up! You have no mercy or understanding. You are like … like your computer. Just lock yourself up with the bloody machine. You are not like the rest of us ... people!"

The silence lasted for half a minute as both women tried to get hold of themselves. Finally, Cat said softly, "I don't know the future and won't tell you what to do, but I am your friend. If you take him back now, you will end like your mother, I think. He was a good man once ... and, who knows, maybe he will be as good in the future, but now he is not. If you still want him, do yourself a favor and let him straighten up his life, all by himself. Then, maybe, you will be able to pick up where you left your happy life together, a few years ago. Now excuse me, but I need to go to sleep. You know where the guest room is."

She wheeled to her downstairs bedroom, and a few minutes later Kalani slowly dragged herself upstairs. Both women lay in their beds staring into the darkness until morning.

Chapter 16

Jerry, January 5

The ramp-building ruse no longer necessary, Jerry turned into Cat's driveway confidently, without any excuse or invitation, but in fact he was consumed by anxiety that had deepened over the past few days. The situation on the "Cat Front," as he'd code named his relationship with Cat, had bloomed into a full-blown love affair, the kind he would never have suspected himself to be capable of.

What started as a random misfortune had turned into an interesting encounter and then an exciting vacation fling. At this point the unimaginable had happened; the romantic lover—who to Jerry's surprise was hiding under his skin—forcefully demanded that a long, eternal if possible, relationship with this woman be assured. As Jerry's Hawaii escapade was inevitably coming to its end and his return trip to New York loomed, the time to take concrete steps was now.

Cat has her job and I have mine; her house is in Kailua and my apartment in New York— six time zones apart, he thought. Won't work. We need to reconcile our lives; some sacrifices will need to be made.

The lock clicked and the door opened with the usual

short delay, as Cat wheeled to it, but instead of her customary cheerful "Hi, Jerry" and the set of white teeth glistening in Cat's wide smile, he was met by tightly pursed lips and subdued greetings. Cat's skin was pale, bringing to the surface her countless freckles, and her gorgeous lips were pale pink rather than red. Jerry never saw her wearing any makeup; she usually projected the air of a "fresh-out-of-the-water" beauty with glowingly healthy skin, but that day Cat looked pasty, thin and sickly. She let him in, allowed his lips to brush against hers, but the enthusiasm and warmth which were such a central part of her personality were lacking.

Jerry had this vaguely uncomfortable sensation that he once experienced in childhood, a moment before crashing through the ice. Fortunately, they were skating on a waist-deep pond and all he had suffered was the humiliation of Pam dragging him home to change.

"What's up, Cat?" Jerry asked. "What's wrong?"

"Nothing's wrong. I just can't understand human nature and that bothers me. Apparently, I am like a computer, devoid of any human emotions," she said enigmatically.

"If you are a computer, I have to say, I love your S-drive." He tried to lighten her up, falling back on their double-speak joke, but already knowing that significant trouble was on its way.

She smiled languidly in acknowledgment of his effort, but continued, "Jerry, do you know much about spousal abuse?"

"Not really. I don't know anybody who has that problem." The cloud was still ill defined but the ominous black center was forming.

"You might be wrong, Jerry. It's not a rare thing, and if you think that abusers tend to be poor and illiterate, you are mistaken. I am pretty sure there are economists in New York who beat their wives." She was looking through the window at Kailua Beach avoiding his eyes.

"Maybe, but nobody has confided in me." Cat's irritability

was spreading to Jerry. They were very empathetic and their moods tended to synchronize within a few moments.

"That's it! Women run to their girlfriends with any problem while men remain blessedly unaware. The question that actually bothers me is not so much 'why do men do it?' What puzzles me is 'why do women take it?' I can understand that a primitive animal—and, Jerry, I am not a man hater—has a limited number of ways to communicate. So when he needs to assert his rank, he beats up on a pack member. All animals do that. Add to that poor impulse control, blah, blah, blah … I don't approve of it, but I can understand it. But why an otherwise intelligent woman, like Kalani, puts up with it, I don't get it."

"Kalani, your cleaning lady?" Jerry remembered the good-looking girl; she always gave him a sweet, friendly smile on the few occasions they met at the door, her leaving, him coming.

"Well, she cleans my house because she needs money, but I think of her as a friend, not a cleaner. I shouldn't tell you about her, but soon you will be gone so why should she care?"

"About my going away … I thought …" Jerry tried to switch the topic, but Cat continued her thought without noticing his attempt.

"First, she lets her boyfriend feed off her for a couple of years, then she gives him her college money for some bird-brain venture and then, even after he slaps her, she is all ready to make up. Does that make any sense to you?" She turned to him with a real interest to see if he had an answer. Jerry felt like a student facing an inquisitive professor.

"Maybe she still loves him and wants to keep him?" He shrugged, trying without much confidence.

"I hate to sound like Mr. Spock from the planet Vulcan, but this is not logical." Cat pounced on him immediately with an ironic glint in her eyes. "She fell in love with him when he was a fisherman. I'd met him then—charming, great-looking guy, made good money, proud of it. They were a good match. If you saw them together then, you would think they were actors from a commercial about Hawaii. But they were for real.

"That's the guy she fell in love with. Then he dropped out of the category of workingmen and has been deteriorating ever since, while she was helping him on the way down. Now, he is a despicable bum, and she can see it, although she won't admit it. He is not the guy she fell for. My question is, can he go back to being a decent, productive man?" Cat pressed for an answer impatiently with the brusque manner of a policeman interrogating a suspect.

"I have no idea, Cat. I am an economist, not a psychologist," Jerry shot back, increasingly disturbed by her assault. He knew a thing or two about psychological aggression, and the prickly sensation at the back of his neck was telling him that he was a target. His plan to fully disclose his troubled past: his work as an interrogator, his mental breakdown, his descent into emotional stupor, the psychiatric diagnosis … It all was supposed to be laid out in the open—to be seen, felt, smelled and probed by the only person whose opinion mattered. At this point, however, his instinct told him to back off; this was not the moment to expose vulnerabilities. It looked to Jerry that he was being held responsible for the fisherman's slapping his girlfriend.

Cat examined his face rather coolly and remarked, "That's the problem with you academic people: you refuse to use your brains, to think independently. If it's not in your books, not in your pigeon hole, there is no need to be concerned with it."

Enough! Jerry had seen enough of human misery and degradation, treachery and anguish to give nightmares to a hundred nice girls living in their proper houses looking out on Kailua Beach. "Refuse to use your brains …" What a rubbish! Ph.D. by the age of thirty, a good number of widely quoted articles under his belt—Jerry didn't need to take it.

And who was she to imply her superiority?

"Could you, please, elaborate on this particular statement?" he countered with exaggerated and cold politeness.

Cat knew she was taking her frustration out on the wrong person, but she arrogantly muddled through, searching for rationalization. "What I mean is that you, the academics, create unnecessarily complex systems to explain simple things, which allows you to avoid using your common sense. Perhaps I shouldn't complain because I make a living off those grandiose works."

Jerry tilted his head, signaling: What do you mean?

Cat pressed on. "A business orders a software solution but the custom program doesn't work well. The contractor provides patches, corrections, new versions and so on, but the program still sucks. At one point the manager is desperate enough to say 'to hell with it!' He calls me. I find out what it is that they *really* need, go through that malfunctioning software package and throw out all the elements that are not absolutely required to do the job. I put it together again and behold—it works. It was not so bad to start with. I made it work not because I am a software genius but because the initial project got so complex that its authors lost their way in it."

Cat relaxed a bit talking about the subject that was in her familiar territory then ploughed headlong into Jerry's field. "With your highly refined economics wisdom, what would you suggest to correct Kalani's problem? After all, it all starts with the purely economical issue: her boyfriend is not generating an income. Shall I phrase it as 'The Productivity Issue'?" She spoke with unmistakable irony and leaned back, throwing her sun-bleached hair over her shoulders.

Jerry got caught up in the argument. Obviously, the issue thrown at him was far from his field—a problem for a sociologist perhaps, certainly having nothing to do with econometrics. But he would not duck away. Miss Knows-It-All needed an adjustment in her attitude. They had had heated discussions on the economy and politics before, but those were friendly and witty. Now, Jerry could see that, apart from being a usually sweet and kind person, this Cat had a hard side to her persona and she could spring sharp claws like a real feline.

"From an economist's point of view," he carefully staked the argument, "the core problem is that the boyfriend is not working. A secondary problem is that Kalani has no money for college now."

She was listening intently. Her bright and alert eyes were glued to his, brow slightly furrowed with concentration. She was nodding her head to acknowledge his points. Still, he had the feeling that she was just watching him, waiting for him to step into a trap, and she would pounce on him the very moment the steel jaws shut.

"The first problem could be addressed," Jerry continued, sizing up the opponent across the table, "by retraining Abe to improve his chances of employment, or possibly granting him a loan for a small business. I think you have mentioned some sort of small enterprise." Now he was sure she was planning an ambush. She was smiling slightly, not her usual warm smile, more like a fox's mouth twitching before she jumps a chicken. Still, he couldn't see the trap.

"And Kalani, how could you help Kalani?" she asked sweetly.

Jerry had a premonition that a war club was being swung. "Well, Kalani could apply for a scholarship grant, get a government-guaranteed loan. Since she is, probably, in a low income bracket, she might get a free or low-interest educational loan …"

He saw Cat was moving in for the kill. She leaned forward and put her hand on his. There was no warmth coming from her palm, rather the feeling of being held, so that he could not escape at the last moment.

"You are very kind, Jerry. Now, as an economist, tell me who should pay for all these things you have just granted?"

"There are funds dedicated to these expenditures set aside in federal as well as state budgets."

"And where do governments get the money to pay for all these programs, Jerry?"

"From taxes, from people who have higher incomes, like you and me. Social solidarity, you know …" Every corporate citizen, all productive individuals, had a sacred duty—he was taught throughout his youth—to help alleviate poverty, level the playing field and reduce social tensions. The level of these obligations was disputable, no doubt, but the principle was sound and he didn't suspect Cat might attack him from this angle.

Her hand tightened as if restraining the victim before the final blow. "But Jerry, you know very well that the tax revenue doesn't cover the government's budget, by a long shot. So the money you have just distributed must be coming from other places." The trap shut with a loud clank, Jerry's foot firmly in the iron jaws. "Do you think the government might just print new money for Abe and Kalani? Would you happen to know what the current M3 is?"

Now she was just gloating, shameless in her overconfidence, her arms triumphantly crossed on her chest. M3 was a statistical measure of money in circulation, one of many indices. The government stopped publishing M3 data in 2006, raising the suspicion of trying to conceal the torrent of newly printed money flooding the country. Obviously, she knew something about economics, but how deep was her knowledge?

"Cat, why do you favor M3?" Jerry started probing innocuously, with an encouraging smile, but when she hesitated with the answer, his eyes hardened. "Of course you know the difference between M3 and … say M2, or even better the True Money Supply! We teach these basics to our first-year students."

She paused for a moment, her face darkening, but sidestepped the question like a boxer. "Well, whatever you use to measure it … you'll agree that printing money in excess of growth causes inflation, right?" She recovered her footing, ready for another assault.

"'*Whatever*' is not a term used much in economics," Jerry remarked coolly. "Anyway, there is more than one dimension to it. For God's sake, my boss, Schumacher, spent his life trying to clarify this relationship. It's complicated!" He was getting exasperated like an experienced fighter coaching a street kid who just won't quit his blind and ferocious attacks. It was not his intention to knock her down!

"That's where we disagree, Jerry." Cat had no doubts and was about to prove it. "It is, actually, quite simple. You, the academics, just make it look like it is complicated. "Imagine I have a chicken farm that produces two thousand eggs a day. You have a restaurant that needs one thousand."

Jerry had a fleeting thought this might be a way to consolidate their lives.

Cat continued, waving her arms, excited now more than upset. "I charge you a dime for each egg, which is good enough to keep your restaurant profitable, and gives me sufficient revenue to buy chicken feed as well as keep some money as profit. My other customers get an egg for a dime as well. We can go with this price forever—no inflation.

"Now, you become really smart, smart like … the government. You set up a printing shop in your basement and start printing money. Having some extra cash, you come to me and buy twelve hundred eggs, but my chickens still lay only two thousand eggs. The rest of my customers are two hundred eggs short. As you well know, demand will drive the price up. Now everybody gets stiffed with expensive eggs. That's what we call inflation, my friend, and it's caused by the excessive creation of paper money, from thin air. Nothing particularly mysterious about it."

Now she was leaning back, satisfied, her arms smugly crossed in front of her lovely breasts.

Jerry could feel the spark on his fuse zooming faster and faster. He would never want to harm this opponent, but the suffocating sensation of frustration in the face of her incessant provocation was increasing. He sincerely hoped he would not let himself blow up, just proving the shrink right. A great body of knowledge, some very sophisticated computer modeling, and the work of many bright people was being contradicted by this blundering amateur, a naïve computer geek, someone who had just learned a few terms!

He remained seated at the table in front of her, though pacing the room was what he would rather do. In a well-controlled voice, as though he was speaking to his students, Jerry said, "Your example would make sense on a tiny island, Cat. In a closed system, where inputs and outputs are easily controlled, the excessive creation of money could be linked to inflation, but—"

"Thank you, Professor," she interrupted rather rudely. "I am glad we agree that printing money causes inflation, one way or another. Going back to our example, what would you care that eggs are twelve cents at present? You could always print more paper.

"On the other hand, Abe and Kalani have to earn their living. They would have to pay the full price, and it would hurt them badly because they need every cent. Worse, even if they have managed to put a few bucks away, inflation would eat that too. So that's what you call assistance? Giving them free money by way of your programs, and then pulling cash discreetly from their pockets?" She was looking at him with cool satisfaction and arrogance he never guessed she possessed.

Jerry was sitting still, his eyes glaring. He could almost

hear his teeth gnashing, unable to control his agitation. Why is she blaming me? I am not the government. What does it have to do with me?

Apparently, she was reading his thoughts because she added, "Of course, you are not to be blamed, Jerry. You just teach others who later go on to work in the financial institutions that are robbing us all."

Fanatic, a bone-headed, blind-sided fanatic! The spark was closing on Jerry's powder keg. He jumped to his feet, violently pushing his chair away from the table. It certainly would feel good to smash it against the wall, but his anger-control mechanism still held.

"Oh, look who's talking! You mean you have never benefited from largesse of this corrupt government, Miss Righteous? Just a contributor and a benefactor?"

"Damn right, Jerry!" Cat met his eyes with her own hard hot stare. "I never took a penny I didn't earn. My parents were immigrants and didn't have this notion that someone should pay for their child's education, so they paid in full. My old folks had this funny idea that since their parents educated them for free, they owed the same to their child, a kind of intergenerational pay-forward scheme. Now, it's my obligation to pay for my kids, if I ever have any. And you can be damn sure I'll pay every red cent, with interest."

"Admirable! But this you will have to allow—there is a government here, and a certain well-established way of doing things. People who decide to live here better take orders from the authorities, whether they like them or not! At least, you could show some social solidarity, maybe a token gratitude to the nation that took your family in." Exasperated, Jerry was reaching for arguments that made him feel uncomfortable.

Cat was sitting up stiffly, thought for a moment then slowly uttered through her clenched teeth, "I am a part of this nation, Jerry. Not any less than you are, with your Mayflower ancestors. As a matter of fact, I don't have much respect for people who hide behind achievements of their forefathers. Your pride should be based on what you represent: your effort, your intelligence, your courage. In my humble opinion, people who wrap themselves into a national flag are losers who have no personal achievements to show. Being an Englishman doesn't make anyone Shakespeare. And shaking an American flag doesn't make you a patriot either, just a hypocrite hiding behind other people's glory."

Jerry stood across the table stiff like a soldier on the parade ground, glaring at her, clutching the chair and waiting for her tirade to end. He opened his mouth to respond but she raised her hand.

"One more thing, Jerry. I care very much for people like Kalani or even this bum, Abe, but not for your slavish concept of a reined-in herd that you confuse with the nation.

They don't need goose-stepping to be happy and successful. Freedom to work and security to keep the fruits of their work is what they need. Inflation, which you and your government push on them like a sweet poison, is its direct contradiction. And what Kalani and Abe certainly do *not* need is the demoralization of subsidies and free money—they are not free after all. You know as well as I do that there is no such thing as a meal without charge. So why don't you teach that to your students?"

The great declaration of hostilities was coming to an end, and Cat looked as though she was ready to roll away toward the window to wait for Jerry's counterattack, when she suddenly changed her mind and returned to the battlefield.

"I also would like to make a reading recommendation for you, Professor. When you get back to New York, Google the name Bakunin. It will come together with the word 'anarchism.' Don't be scared. Take a drink or pop a pill and read it anyway. You might discover some new, for you at least, and exotic ideas. I hope it won't hurt you to learn that some people consider a state—and I presume that would include the United States—an organization dedicated to oppressing its people. There is little good or benevolent about it—mostly nightsticks, guns and coercion to make sure a herd moves in the right direction.

Same goes for the idea of nation: your flags, hymns, holy patrons, national days—all these propaganda tools, admittedly better than batons, serve the same purpose, which is to keep folks in line. They cut down on the number of sheep dogs. Besides, isn't it more fun when a herd sings?"

Cat wouldn't wait for his response, and Jerry hardly had a coherent riposte, his thinking process encumbered by fierce anger as well as his inability to wrap his mind around the ideas so extreme and contradictory to the patriotic upbringing he had once received.

"And about my family being magnanimously allowed onto this continent …" Cat continued, agitated but clearly running out of gas. "They were young, healthy and well-educated—perfect new subjects. As a matter of fact, that's what the immigration officer told them. If you believe that was an act of compassion, you have to ask yourself this question: why is it that poor peasants from Guatemala or Honduras, or anywhere else, have to risk their lives sneaking through deserts in order to scrape a few bucks together, while being hunted like vermin?"

Jerry took a deep breath and said in a measured, grave voice, hiding his turmoil behind it, "Thank you for your reading recommendation, and I will give you some advice as well. Please, don't put your slapdash knowledge of the economy to practical use, Cat. Because if you do, whether trading stocks or playing tax games with the authorities, you will lose this lovely house as well as your cherished independence. You wouldn't like living in a government-subsidized apartment, anxiously looking forward to other handouts that this corrupt society might offer."

There was nothing else to say. He could cross swords with

any sophisticated opponent who understood the nuances of economics and parameters of discussion, but this aggressive amateur in a beautiful body wielded a rough stick. Anyway, he'd said too much already, certainly in his last sentence. The daydreams of the last few days seemed plainly ridiculous. She was a self-righteous, arrogant bitch hiding behind a sweet face.

Jerry stiffly thanked her for the pleasant evenings spent in her house during his Hawaiian vacation and silently walked out, his ability to control his temper remaining the only pitiful satisfaction. The next day he took a plane from Honolulu to Los Angeles. No one came to see him off. As he was watching the clouds over Diamond Head passing by, he already knew that something tragically stupid had happened, something that would be bitterly regretted.

Hi, Ruth, it's me again. I'm not thinking clearly ... haven't slept for two nights. This time I am done with. I know it. I've chased away the man I love and demolished the only friendship I had. What I believe, do and say ... there are just no boundaries of reason to it! I am a crazy, destructive fanatic. I don't deserve to be happy.

Cat took a pill and fell into deep, coma-like sleep that would not be interrupted even by a boulder crashing down the steep hill behind her house.

Chapter 17

Jerry, January 6–7

By the time he landed in Newark, Jerry was thoroughly depressed. A long flight and jet lag, naturally, he unsuccessfully tried to persuade himself.
But the real cause was Cat, left behind like yesterday's newspaper abandoned on an airport's bench.

They had connected so fast, so profoundly, that splitting over a single argument, one that did not even touch their personal lives, was an unbelievably stupid outcome. Two obstinate and volatile personalities might not be the best match for each other, he reflected sadly.

Cat was a strong-headed, ferocious militant for whatever she believed in—Jerry had had his proof of that—but was it necessarily a bad thing? Isn't it better to have a strong ally rather than a wishy-washy fair-weather friend? Jerry found it difficult to imagine Cat being wishy-washy in any situation.

He tried to divert his attention by reading the *New York Times*, but his eyes glided over pictures of the warships deployed in the Middle East without understanding a word of the commentary. Having experienced the warmth and happiness of being with Cat, he desperately did not want to go back behind his brick wall, but that's where he was heading.

Despite his earlier reservations, Jerry looked forward to starting classes and falling back into the bustle of teaching. His students could be counted on to keep him occupied and keep the unwelcome thoughts drowned out. They did not disappoint him. Eleven thirty on Thursday morning, right after his lecture, he found Miss Ambitious in front of his office. I can just kiss my lunch break good-bye, he thought, resigning himself to the conversation leading from nowhere to futility.

This was the sad case of diligence and ambition mismatched to the limited power of abstract thinking. Amanda attended all his lectures, sitting in the first row, eyes alert, never bored. Her assignments were always delivered on time, neat and nicely bound—no teacher could dislike her. It was just that she couldn't grasp ideas that required abstract thinking. She did fine as long as problems were solvable by the ways of arithmetic, but throw a bit more complicated abstract theory at her, and she was lost, lost, lost. How had she made it so far? Jerry wondered. This was her third year; in another year or so, Amanda could be a proud bachelor of economics. Probably no one had the heart to stop her, he concluded, just like me.

"Professor Roberts, thank you for seeing me during your lunch break," she started timidly.

Rather skinny, but with a nice round butt under tight jeans, pleasant face, dyed blond hair tied in a ponytail, not a bad-looking girl, Jerry thought. Shouldn't have any trouble getting her a boyfriend. So what's she doing at the library every time I go to do some research at night? But I am wasting my nights just like her.

"No problem, Amanda. I am not hungry at all," he lied smoothly and smiled with encouragement.

"About my research paper, how did I do?" Her voice was thin, without a trace of confidence, and her eyes locked on the backside of the photograph sitting in the middle of Jerry's desk. "The dean said that if I don't do well in your class, I will have to rethink my major."

Aw shit, now it's up to me to screw the kid over, the one student in my class making any effort to study. Is it her fault she was born without the gift for abstract thinking? Actually, someone blundered a few years ago; she should have been shoved into a subject that relies on more concrete reasoning. She could be a good administrator, so why does she need to do esoteric theories in economy? Looking at her with sympathy, he replied, "Well, you did get confused a bit in your paper."

Amanda's head dropped even lower. Jerry really hated this hatchet job.

"Amanda, can you tell me, why do you insist on graduating as an economics major? Why not business administration? You must realize you don't have a knack for highfaluting theories. At the same time, you are really good with numbers, you are well organized… Why don't you switch to something that suits your personality better?"

"My father would be very disappointed; he is an economist."

Now Jerry remembered! Of course, her father teaches economics in Chicago. There are more Nobel laureates walking the corridors in his department than many countries had in their history. This assistant professor's input into his daughter's life might not be appreciated, but who's going to help out this lost soul?

"Amanda, your father is a great economist, but you don't have to be your father. You can't be your father, whatever you do. I think the dean might be right. Your paper is really not any worse than the average for your class"—he felt charitable—"but you should think about redirecting your studies to something you will enjoy more."

She thanked him and left, no spring in her step and her head bowed.

Good advice, Professor, how about you? Cat's ironic

voice sounded in his head so clearly that it startled him. It amused rather than upset him.

You don't give up easily, Cat, do you? Hearing her voice lifted his spirits for a moment, but that gnawing feeling was back soon.

He called his sister Pam. They lived about an hour's drive from each other but met probably no more than twice a year, mostly on Thanksgiving or Christmas. With a ten-year age difference, they never had much of a chance to become friends. Recently, however, Jerry started having a need to talk to her.

If Pam were surprised, she didn't show it; they made a date for Saturday dinner. He still had Friday to be filled, or spent alone. Jerry did not feel like seeing anyone, but knew that another evening by himself meant long hours of the heart-breaking memories of Cat, and self-recriminations. So he pulled his little black book out of a drawer and went through a few pages. A prospect of romantic encounter felt, actually, horrible, but something had to be done to break the emotional bondage he found himself in.

Kelly—he zeroed in on the first candidate—a good-looking, if somewhat plump girl, had divorced a few months ago and was still quite angry about it. She was a pleasant companion and fun to be with most of the time, but turned into a viper after the second drink. And she really liked to have the second drink. Jerry moved on.

Camilla—slightly built, quiet, a bit mousy, but attractive. Could be fine, as long as animal abuse and dog rescue operations were kept out of the conversation. Jerry dialed the number only to be informed that she was engaged now, smug satisfaction palpable. One name scratched from the book.

Victoria—a fellow post-grad student, a woman of great intelligence and remarkable figure. They used to have regular unpretentious private meetings in his apartment—no great romantic passion, just good, solid sex that left them both satisfied and content. The tradition lapsed in recent months, since she started teaching on a different campus, but quite possibly could be renewed.

Call Victoria? Jerry imagined her comfortably reclining on his bed, naked and beckoning for him to come. He would sit next to her, gently run his hand starting on her brown hair, over her cheek, slide down the neck, round the breasts, linger over the stomach and submerge fingers into her curly hair. She was a good buddy and they had good times together in the past, but now, after Cat … anybody who was a real person seemed inappropriate. Once, the numbers in his notebook, and faces behind them, brought comfort to his life; now they seemed to spell "t-r-a-i-t-o-r." Jerry cursed and threw the book back into the drawer.

Oh, heck, he decided, why not toss the worries to the winds and submit to the dictates of providence? Go to a bar and see what happens. There was one nearby that he used to patronize often while writing his Ph.D. dissertation. He had no time to cultivate anything more demanding than a potted plant then and didn't feel any need for a complicated love affair either. The bar worked very well. In addition, it was close to his apartment; no need to take a cab. A romantic but reasonably short walk was appreciated by most of his new friends.

Jerry climbed down a few concrete steps from the street level and entered a large, warm room distinctly smelling of beer and chicken wings. So early in the evening, hardly past six o'clock, he had no trouble getting a strategic place at the bar. He hung his coat on the rack and sat sideways at the end of the row of high stools, his back to the wall, his left elbow comfortably resting on the bar and the room wide open for inspection on his right side.

Jerry ordered a large glass of Boston lager and was ready. The lighting was dim except for flashes of a strobe light from the empty dance floor, which he found rather annoying. The bar started filling up rapidly before he was through with his beer. People blocked his view of the scene and the noise rose to a level that forced people to yell into each other's ears. Not much chance for a conversation, intelligent or otherwise, he thought.

Jerry kept a sharp eye on the crowd. Most of the girls were young, hardly of drinking age. The guy at the gate couldn't be a very suspicious person. The platinum blond sitting next to him would be twenty-one in two or three years. A few women in their late twenties, who would be more suitable to strike up a conversation with, were rather unattractive. The only one that Jerry might consider in positive terms had an eager man on each side, both probably ten years younger than him.

What the hell am I doing here? he asked himself angrily. What did I expect—a beer commercial scene? A row of gorgeous models flashing their whitened teeth at me, just drooling at the thought I might give them my phone number? What would a good-looking, intelligent woman be doing in here, especially if she were of legal age?

He gave it another ten minutes, just in case Humphrey Bogart would show up behind the bar, asking, "So what are you up to, kid?" Then Jerry finished his beer, paid and got up. Two men leaning against the wall raced to grab his place at the bar.

The fact was, he could not fill that evening. People, or rather the women who might be available, did not seem attractive to him anymore. Places he enjoyed in the past had lost their appeal. He ended up watching the tube with a bottle of Marquis de Villard brandy within easy reach.

Serves you right, old fool—he had no mercy on himself. After thirty-three years, you've found someone who made you happy. No! A divine intervention was necessary to bring her into your life, an act of God, nothing less. And what did you do? You blew it! You pissed it for the sake of winning a discussion on the causation of inflation … against a computer programmer. Well, wait for another miracle, but even Jesus was not known to bring Lazarus from his deathbed twice.

By ten o'clock, Cat seemed to be everywhere. They argued, then they agreed; they made up and finally he had her in his arms. He finished his bottle of brandy and woke up on Saturday a few minutes short of noon with a jackhammer in his head.

At least his mind had cleared; he knew he had to get her back. Despite a horrific headache, he felt better. It took him a few hours to figure out what to say so that he wouldn't sound like he was begging for forgiveness. She's a reasonable girl, he thought. I'll make a step, she'll make a step, and we'll meet in the middle. His life held some promise again.

After a considerable amount of finger cracking, neck stretching and straightening books on the shelf—all the things he habitually did when nervous—Jerry dialed Cat's number. Her phone kept ringing but nobody picked it up and there was no answering machine. Jerry tried calling a few more times, then went to dinner with his sister's family. Maybe Pam will have something intelligent to say on how to deal with this situation, Jerry hoped.

They were different. One might even wonder how they could be children of the same couple and grow up in the same household. As a little boy, Jerry was afraid of his sister—he remembered that well. Not because she could beat him up, though she certainly could and more than once sent him reeling on the carpet. No, he was scared of her withering comments and sarcastic smiles. She was the warlord of psychological combat capable of burning her little brother into a crispy tidbit with one caustic observation. Still, he needed Pam to notice him and was desperate for her approval—both goals hard to achieve. Since Pam had left the family home early, during the remaining eight or ten years of his childhood and adolescence Jerry enjoyed the status of an only child.

Now he was knocking on her door with the old sense of anxiety. Pam opened the door and let him in. In her early forties, she was slim, strong and her dark eyes still had a menacing glint of obsidian. She ran a marathon and downed a couple of triathlons every year, in addition to working full-time in some publishing house and managing her family with a steel hand. It was always a mystery to Jeremy how she could do it all, while he had his hands full with his own career and very modest private life.

"I sleep on Sundays," she offered as an explanation, "and the kids' choice is to keep their noses clean or run a marathon with me. Since they don't like running that much, my motherly duties are not too overwhelming."

"Good to see you, Jerry." She looked him over with suspicion while he was still standing on the welcome mat. "Tell me everything's fine, or is there a problem? You don't have a habit of dropping in on me just for a little gossip."

She hadn't changed that much; the interrogation started before they got to the kitchen table.

This time, however, Jerry put his head into the guillotine voluntarily. In fact, he wanted her opinion exactly because he knew it would be a product of stern examination. Her judgment would be hard and sharp like a blade. And dear Pam could be counted on to deliver it without any sugar coating. It will hurt, Jerry thought, but I need advice made of stainless steel, and who could give it to me better than Sis? There will be no reservations or misplaced empathy.

"Where are the kids and Henry?" he asked politely.

"Kids are gone to a basketball match. Isn't it great I don't have to drive them anymore? And Henry grabbed the opportunity to go play chess. I personally can't understand how one can sit in a chair for three or four hours, staring at a chess board, but I am not Henry. So, it's just you and me. Spill it, kid!" She crossed her arms in the manner Jerry remembered only too well and turned her sinister eyes at him.

"Hmm. Remember when I called you about my little ocean adventure and about my Saving Grace?" Jerry started his case presentation.

"Sure do—you sounded like you'd fallen in love." Pam's eyes unexpectedly softened as she smiled. "As a matter of fact, I thought it was a very good idea. At your age … it crossed my mind that you might be gay. Are you, Jerry? This girl, Victoria, you brought her once … I didn't think you were really a couple."

"No, Pam, I'm not gay, and I have been enjoying a fulfilling heterosexual life." Jerry was surprised by his sister's observation. She sure picked up the vibes.

"Oh, good. My brother is a heterosexual and fell in love with a woman. So what's the problem?"

"The problem is that we had a huge fight. You won't believe it, but we argued about economics. She was stubborn and pigheaded, which made me so mad that I used some stupid arguments, even putting down her immigrant family. Pam, most of the time she is the sweetest person on earth, but she's strongheaded like a mule and her worldview comes directly from Genghis Khan."

The aroma of coffee wafted from the kitchen counter and Pam turned off the percolator absentmindedly. "You know, people get together for many different reasons—physical attraction and good sex to start with. I have nothing against it; in fact, I see no point wasting one's time on a relationship where sex is anything less than very good. It wouldn't last anyway. But this doesn't seem to be an issue with the two of you."

Jerry just nodded his head.

"After that, the very good reason to stay together is that you need someone to trust, a reliable friend. But how do you know if someone is trustworthy? You really can't know that ahead of time, but chances are good if your partner has a tough inner core, or—as you say—is pigheaded."

Pam is onto something, Jerry thought and listened without interrupting.

"Take for example Henry, a nice man with an easy smile and a soft belly. Some people look at him, thinking: weak, an easy prey. They get hurt because, despite his looks, Henry is tough like a railroad nail. He has been playing his game of chess on a board and in his life since I first met him, and people who misjudge him lose badly.

"'How can this athletic woman live with that round, fatherly Santa Claus?' strangers might ask. It takes some familiarity to discover that in our family *he* is the hard point of a spear. That's what it took to tame your sister twenty years ago. Now, do I suffer because of his inner hardness? Am I afraid of him? No and no. He is a great partner."

Jeremy noticed that Pam had developed crow's feet around her eyes, softening her sculpted features. She kept her figure, but time did not stop for her. "So how does it work, Pam? You don't quarrel like most people do, you just take orders?"

"We argue, Jerry. We don't quarrel, we argue. You can't quarrel with a chess player. If I want him to do something, I better be well prepared. He listens carefully, says little and sometimes asks a question. Then, if your argument is not reasoned like a Supreme Court decision, he will lead you down the garden path until you hang in your tangled thought process like a fly in a web. After a while, you'll feel like saying, 'Sorry for taking your time; forget my idea.' But he will never back off from a well-reasoned argument, and will not pretend that there is no point where there is one. And, Jerry, once Henry agrees, I don't have to look over my shoulder. I know he is right behind me, ready and able to push or shove or stab, if necessary."

Jerry shifted in his chair uneasily. "That's what Cat does; she is a great listener, but punches right back with her counterarguments."

"What did you argue about?" Pam abandoned her plans

to pour coffee.

"I'm not sure how we started. Basically, she said ... that people who happen to be in trouble should be left to themselves. I remember now ... her friend's boyfriend didn't work and was taking money from the girl. And she claimed that government assistance is wasteful and actually harms recipients. Rather unfeeling, don't you think?"

"I would rather say—American," Pam shrugged. "That's how America was built. Everyone had to take care of himself and his family. Know the saying about pulling oneself up by one's bootstraps?"

"Pam, you can't be serious. You are not saying that unemployed people don't deserve some help? Retraining, help with living expenses ..." Jerry was appalled; this attitude was contrary to the basic concepts of modern labor theory.

"Well," Pam reluctantly hedged her opinion, "I would first ask why is he unemployed? What's wrong with this unemployed boyfriend? Is he sick or what?"

"I'm not sure," Jerry had to admit.

"Then why do you assume he needs government help, Jerry? I'd say this should be the last thing to consider." Pam was looking at her brother with a strange expression on her face. "I like this girl more and more. And I suspect that the excess of theoretical science damaged your brain center for common sense."

Jerry felt surrounded; the people closest to him kept contradicting the very foundation of his professional beliefs.

"Pam, you were always hard on me and nothing has changed. Now you're siding with her just to put me down."

Pam did not answer for a long while, looking at him until her coffee-colored eyes lost all their hardness. "Jerry, I might have been tough on you when you were small. I thought, we all thought, you should have been hardened up. When you first came to school, you had this air of a two-day-old duckling: a soft, fuzzy, yellow ball, a perfect target for anyone with a beak. I saved you quite a lot of pecking, but I wanted you to grow and to learn how to take care of yourself. But I always loved you, my little bro, and I love you now."

Jerry found himself holding the queen of sneer in his arms, and feeling her tears on his neck. This was the moment he was longing for all his childhood, but Pam wouldn't be Pam if she tolerated it for more than a few seconds.

"Back to the subject—that's all? That's all your disagreement?"

"Well, she has this strange hostility towards the government. You should hear her accusing the government of stealing money from poor people. Sounded like Che Guevara or some other kind of anarchistic rebel."

Pam started giggling. "I don't think you remember grandfather Vito. He was a smart man, and he had built the business our father took over. Grandpa used to say that there was only one Mafia. Some families were mostly dedicated to gambling, others leaned toward prostitution and still others weighed into government. But they all did the same thing, ran a racket for profit. And he never failed to add that New York was no different from Palermo. So, I think your little friend will fit into this family very well."

Jeremy must have smiled at the idea of Cat fitting into their family, because Pam got serious and sighed.

"But you might have a hard problem on your hands, Brother. From your description, she looks deeper than you think. If she came to believe that you are an opinionated, semi-demented academic who runs away from her arguments; if she considers you a brainwashed dummy unable to think on your own, and—more than anything else—if she thinks you are a Boston cream donut inside your nicely toned body—you are toast, my friend! All intelligent women want this hard inner core in their partners; hard muscles are nice … but they are just the gravy.

"I don't know what you need to do, Jerry," she sighed.

"But I suspect that 'I am sorry, but I love you,' declared over a telephone line won't cut it." She stood up and turned to the kitchen counter. "Now, I'd like you to do a manly job. Take the mallet and pound these cutlets into submission. Henry and the kids should be back in half an hour."

Jerry liked Henry, who indeed impressed him as a rather mellow character. Now, after his sister's disclosure, Jerry looked at him in a different light. They met only a few times a year, admittedly not many opportunities to get into heated discussions, but Henry never showed any intention to draw Jerry into a serious conversation. In the society full of amateur economists, Henry was strangely indifferent to his brother-in-law's expertise, despite being a chief executive officer of a major company. Because of his company's armament contracts, the man frequently dealt with highly placed government officials, but he seemed oblivious to Jerry's background. Is he ignoring me as a harmless idiot free of any useful knowledge? Jerry wondered now.

"Henry, are there any signs of the economy mending in your line of business?"

Henry looked at him thoughtfully through his thick glasses, swallowing a piece of the meat Jerry had pounded half an hour earlier, then answered, "That depends on which economy you're referring to. Government contracts have never been better. I guess our electronics don't last very long on the battlefield. Mind you, they are pretty sturdy, almost indestructible when we test them. But, clearly, they can be blown up." He was slowly and methodically loading green peas onto a chunk of speared potato.

"How about the other, the non-governmental side of business, Henry?"

His brother-in-law looked with even more attention, chewed his mouthful slowly, swallowed, took a sip of wine and asked with a shade of surprise, "What non-government business are you asking about, Jerry? We make electronic components. Have you seen any electronic consumer goods made in the U.S.A. recently? TV sets, boom boxes, DVD players? You may see some American-sounding names, but I assure you, their manufacturers don't buy their components from us or from any of our domestic competitors."

"But don't we sell a lot of electronic goods abroad?" Jerry was positive the U.S. had a positive trade balance in high-tech goods.

"Yes, Jerry, we sell a lot of weapon systems, avionics and very advanced warships, but—to the best of my knowledge—not much more. Even our telecommunications equipment, which had practically no serious competition ten years ago, doesn't find that many buyers these days."

"This is not a healthy situation," Jeremy remarked. "Weapon sales may turn on a dime with a change in global politics. One day we might wake up with corn and soybeans as the main pillars of our economy."

"I hoped you could tell me more about that, Jerry. You are an economist. What do you tell your students?" Henry gave his brother-in-law a sincere look, begging with his expression, "please, enlighten me."

Check. Henry had put him on the defense in three moves, never losing his benevolent smile and hardly missing the tempo while cleaning his plate.

"Well, Henry, this is not really my area of expertise," Jerry carefully prepared his counterattack. "But let me tell you that as a profession, we try to figure out the conditions under which guys like you can prosper, paying taxes and providing employment while at it. Our recommendations, certainly not the only ones, go to the folks that make decisions. Whether our advice is not so good, or some other considerations warp the policy, it's hard not to notice that folks like you tend to pack up and hightail it offshore. This might explain why nobody seems to buy your components but the government."

"That's really pretty simple." Henry shrugged. "You watch

your production costs. You have to, or you go bankrupt. How long can you go on if the cost of making your product becomes higher than the price your client is willing to pay? Governments can do this kind of miracle apparently forever, but in the business where bookkeeping is honest you are dead pretty soon. Since bumping the prices up is almost impossible now, we have to go wherever the lower cost of production takes us."

How refreshing! Jerry shook his head in frustration. Someone else had recently tried to persuade him that the economy was a simple matter. "There is nothing simple about it, Henry. Your costs are determined by a thousand different factors knotted in one gigantic Gordian knot: interest rates, productivity, inflation expectations, retirement funds, labor laws—" He turned his eyes away from Henry's smiling face and noted Pam's half-open mouth and the children's glazed eyes.

"Wow," his sister remarked, "now I see what your poor girlfriend had to contend with."

"What I meant was that," Henry picked up the subject, "it's easy to understand why the industries leave. How to reverse this trend is an entirely different ballgame, and I don't even pretend I have an idea how. Quite certainly it has nothing to do with the electronics...." He smiled disarmingly.

"This cost thing might have something to do with pouring the money into rat holes," Pam needled her brother. "I'm no economist but you might ask Cat about it."

The children started shifting in their chairs. Really good kids, Jerry thought, obviously getting bored to death. Henry also noted the rebellion brewing at the table and speeded to the conclusion.

"The people we do business with are not any less intelligent than us. For the time being, they sell us their stuff and extend us new loans, pretending to believe that we'll pay them back. It's always better to be on the big guy's good side, right?

"I know that you and your sister went to regular public schools, so you must know this schoolyard racket, where the nastiest kid in the yard sells candies to the weakest youngsters. Of course, they have to pay through their noses, but that buys them the good will of the meanest bully. They pretend to enjoy the trade, and so avoid the schoolyard's unpleasant aspects, like having their noses bloodied or being thrown over a fence. It's quite an acceptable arrangement, really, if you have a bit of free cash. Did you ever know this scheme?"

"I don't think so," Pam broke in. "I used to come to his schoolyard from my high school, which was on the opposite side of the street, to kick some ass from time to time."

Now the kids started enjoying themselves. "Mom, could you come and kick some ass at our school, too? Mr. Gallant, for example?" Cecilia, the oldest one, asked sincerely.

"And Mrs. Ferraro! And Mr. Sobick!" the younger children were suggesting enthusiastically, until Henry sent them the "That's enough for now!" look.

"Our partners and neighbors do the same," Henry was wrapping up. "But imagine that the bully starts losing weight, sweats easily and coughs up blood. For some time, the racket keeps going. Nobody knows what's going on, and the consequences of bad judgment might be very unpleasant. But at one point, the truth breaks out: the big guy has tuberculosis. What do you think happens to the candy trade? But … they are still buying our candies, some at least."

Jerry went home, thinking about his unsolvable economic Gordian knot, the money pouring into a rat hole and the schoolyard racket. Was there anything more to his work than making a fairly comfortable life for himself? He tried to call Cat again, but still got no response. Falling asleep, Jerry pictured himself on a tropical beach, working with a hammer. He was smiling.

Chapter 18

Cat, January 7–8

"Cat, Cat, CAAT!" Kalani kept shaking the limp body until the eyes opened up and hands clumsily pushed her away.

"What are you doing? Why don't you leave me alone? What time it is? What day is it?" Cat was slowly regaining consciousness. Kalani let go of her shoulders.

"You've been sleeping for twenty hours. You were asleep when I was leaving in the morning, and I found you in the same position when I came back. It's seven o'clock in the evening. Are you OK? I thought that something happened to you!"

Cat sat up and pushed her legs out of the bed, dangling them down. "The fact is, my head feels like it's stuffed with old newspapers, but I feel better. I guess I needed this snooze. I took some Halcyon, and it really did a number on me. So what are you up to? Back from work?"

Kalani was wearing her "good" white-and-orange dress that Abe had bought her a few months ago in a sudden surge of romantic feelings. He had suddenly come into money, although Kalani was not aware of his getting any job.

Sometimes, it's better not to ask. She also spread a faint aroma of perfume. Obviously, she was doing something more than cleaning Ms. Oshiro's apartment.

"Have you had any problems with Abe?"

"No, not at all. Want some coffee?" Kalani looked rather perky, definitely not the way a woman would be expected to look right after a dramatic separation from the man she loved.

"Thank you, Kalani, that might help. I should check my e-mail and see how my customers are doing." Secretly, she hoped there might be some other, personal, mail but she found none. The events of the last few days came back in all their sadness, but she was better prepared to face them after a good rest.

She worked for a few hours on her software and went to sleep again. She dreamed of being safely cuddled, her head moving slowly as Jerry's muscular chest rose and fell, until the screeching brakes and the sick thud of a car crumpling against a concrete pylon woke her up. She had crashed again, she realized.

She sat barefoot in front of the computer and grimly started banging away at the keyboard. There was no chance she could fall asleep again and the work was helping. One cannot think of software bugs and her broken heart at the same time. But below the smooth flow of Cat's logical, conscious thought the ugly, dark and dangerous rock lay in wait, causing hardly a ripple on the surface, but ready to rip the tender substance of her mind without warning. She glided over this silent menace, knowing it was only a question of time before the ragged edge would tear in and plunge her again into the dark, murky misery.

Next day, she finished a few minutes after five o'clock and wheeled herself onto the ramp leading to her kayak. The boards were cut and fitted together with surgical precision.

Return to Paradise

The bright-red oil paint bridged narrow gaps between planks, giving the ramp the look of a shiny metal bridge spanning her lawn.

Jerry certainly spared no effort to smooth my ways, she smiled, getting over the spot where Jerry had rescued her from the jumble of boards and beams like a knight in shining armor. That was a long time ago; she could donate this memory to her Museum of Real Life Happenings, so that she could spin her imaginary adventures around it at some later date. Her smile faded. His arms were strong when he cuddled her like a baby. She liked the smell of his body, even after he worked for several hours in the sun. The luxurious feel of his thick hair in her fingers … tears started burning Cat's eyes.

Stop this melodrama! she rebuked herself sharply, just in time to prevent a pathetic outburst of sobbing. You will live. In fact, you'll go kayaking, right now!

But before she could turn her wheelchair around, the ground underneath bucked as if kicked from the inside by a giant foot, and Cat was thrown onto the grass. A deep, low, grinding noise surged from the earth's center and kept coming, mixing with the dry cracking of wooden boards twisted by some unimaginable power. Heavy thuds of large objects falling on the ground and the screech of torn-apart steel frames joined into the hellish symphony.

She lay on her side, grasping at the short grass in panic, desperately trying to fix herself to this particular point of earth rather than being rolled away in a direction unknown. A terrifying thought of being crushed and buried under some great mass falling from the sky seized her throat, but in a quick glimpse up she saw only the blue top shaking above like a flag in the wind. There was nothing hanging over her head to fall and squash her into the grass.

The undulating ground made her slip and roll, cutting the flow of images her retinas recorded into short clips. Now—blades of grass pushing into her face; now—the white walls of her house emitting puffs of white dust from black fissures. The disjointed pictures flooded her brain, making no sense. With unbelieving eyes, she saw red shingles falling off the roof one by one; then the whole sheet surged down to crash next to the wall in a cloud of red dust. Through the shattered front window Cat saw her desk, the computer still on it, bucking like a frightened horse until the monitor bounced to the floor.

A large segment of the second-floor wall disintegrated in a big white cloud of stucco, opening for view the upstairs bedroom, shamelessly exposing the unmade bed, Kalani's green dress and the colorful contents of the closet spilled to the floor.

Water ran down from the broken bathroom pipes, dripping from a ragged edge of the ruptured wall onto the pile of shingles below, mixing with dust into red mud. Her lawn was littered with broken furniture, underwear, computer components and other objects which—until a moment ago—constituted most of Cat's material world.

The heavy, pounding sound filled Cat with the terror of some other, yet unseen, mortal threat until she finally identified it; it was her own blood racing through arteries like a terrified herd ruled by only one desire—escape.

The fountain shooting up from the snapped PVC sprinkler pipe quickly subsided as the water lost its pressure. The ground stopped shaking soon after a short, bright flash illuminated the house's shaded interior, marking the demise of the electric system. Fortunately fire did not follow.

Cat raised her body onto her elbows and found herself looking over the canal edge. Where the water silently flowed a minute ago, gently washing her launching pad with the kayak ready to take her to the ocean like a long yellow leaf, there was only brown mud and rocks now. A small fish was thrashing in the muck, suddenly out of its element.

The ocean pulled back! But it would return very soon; a tsunami was coming. Cat learned about the murderous wave during her first year in Hawaii. The locals told stories of the wall of water slamming into the town of Hilo; the memory of this disaster was vivid even forty years later. The water withdrew from the beaches first, leaving the ocean floor littered with fish, sea cucumbers and other creatures one would never see without diving. A teacher let kids out of school to look and marvel, maybe catch a fish. But a few minutes later, a huge wave charged back, roaring, crushing and drowning everything in its way.

It wouldn't be a few minutes this time, Cat realized. The epicenter of this earthquake was somewhere close. The tsunami would come very soon, following the paths of least resistance, and her canal would be one of them.

She crawled feverishly away from the water, toward the house, clawing her fingers into grass and soft dirt, pulling her dead-weight legs behind like a caterpillar. The wheelchair, thrown somewhere by the violent earth, was nowhere to be seen. She couldn't hope to reach safe high ground. The hills of Lanikai were no more than three miles away, but with the tsunami coming fast, they wouldn't be any better destination than Colorado. All she could hope for was to reach her house and pray it could withstand the blows of the ocean.

The roar of approaching destruction reached her less than a minute later, while she was in the stairway leading to the second floor. The big wave raced up the channel, instantly flooded the lawn and crashed into the house.

Cat felt the vibration transmitted from the wooden stairs into her bones, and a moment later the house leaped as though the earthquake had hit again. The concrete walls of the ground floor resisted the water's brutal power; instead tons of brown muddy liquid gushed through the blown-in windows and doors. The currents of water swirled around, slamming into the walls and slowing somewhat in their circular motion. By the time the water reached the narrow stairway Cat was in, the flood had lost some of its smashing violence.

The water level kept rising rapidly and she found herself suddenly submerged, but a moment later the head of water shot her up the narrow passage like a human cannonball. Blinded by the brown water, tumbling up the stairway and disoriented, Cat held her breath until an unyielding wooden beam brutally met her back and halted further motion. Her head popped out of the water and a loud gasp relieved her bursting lungs.

The roof had already disintegrated, but a few remaining beams randomly spanned the space between the walls, supporting a handful of sheets of plywood. Cat grabbed onto the rafter, but the water kept pushing her up until she pivoted around the beam and found herself precariously perched on a piece of trembling, wet board.

From her perch, she could see the boiling, coffee-colored fluid raging among the beams. She broke her eyes away from the torrent and looked around. She was sitting on top of her house's slanted roof. The house—built on the slope of a small hill—had a concrete, and therefore more resistant, carport attached to it on the uphill side, their roofs touching.

Cat took a deep breath and crawled away from her life-saving plywood towards the more solid-looking carport. She already had her upper body on the carport's roof when the house finally gave in. With the final tremor the walls folded in like a house of cards and disappeared under the brown water. The roar of the torrent did not allow any sound of the dying building to intrude on its own fury. Cat clung desperately to the sturdy structure in her hands, then pulled herself up, aided by the still rising water, until her whole body rested on the carport's top.

The wave was already on its way out. She was looking down with horror as boats, cars, uprooted trees and human bodies tumbled past her vantage point, down the stream into Kailua Bay. The muddy water hissed with profuse foam; it bore no likeness to the blue and friendly element she loved and had made friends with. But it was this ugly and violent cousin that gave Cat the final push, so she could reach the place where she could live a few moments longer.

Cat stayed on her carport for three hours, knowing that the great wave might return. By nine, her intense shivering became unbearable; she had to abandon her safe spot. As she was looking down, she knew that life in this New Year would be very different from anything she had known before.

I never thought you could be such a violent individual, Cat. Ruth was flabbergasted. *The mayhem you've created in Hawaii ... All these dead bodies and mass destruction. Can't see the purpose of it! Why don't you take up parachuting or hang-gliding if you need such extreme excitement? I am kind of stuck with you, but will tell you honestly: I don't like these scenes at all. Besides, they are so realistic that I have this irrational feeling they might belong to the real world. And that makes me really uncomfortable.*

Chapter 19

Cat, January 9

Residents of Kailua emerged from the night of terror bloodied, exhausted and stunned. Thick smoke bellowing from burning houses mixed with the pungent odor of a plastic fence smoldering around the burnt-out gas station. The town resounded with cries for help, shrieks of frightened children and banging of heavy objects pulled off the collapsed houses.

Only the waterfront was silent. The tsunami had erased most of the houses, together with their occupants, on the east side of Kalaheo Street. The Beachside neighborhood, the pride of Kailua and dream of many aspiring millionaires, was no more. Single houses remained scattered along the miles of Kailua Beach, but most buildings had been shredded and dragged into the bowels of the hungry ocean.

The mud around Cat's house was baked into a hard, broken surface by ten AM, which she considered an improvement as far as traveling was concerned. She looked around for anything that could be used to help her move, but the ground was swept clean. A washing machine and the cadaver of a Harley-Davidson projected from the muddy crust of her driveway, but the wave had left behind no object light enough for her to handle.

She was increasingly thirsty, and waiting for help looked to her like a losing strategy. Besides, once before she had decided to take care of herself without looking up to anybody for help; this would be a good test of her resolve. Cat crawled out from the shade of her house and was immediately blinded by the sun. Squinting, she started creeping along her driveway toward the street. Soon her hands and elbows were bleeding, and from the waist down she was coated with a thick layer of brown dirt. Hard scabs formed on her exposed skin, drying fast except for the spots where fresh blood kept the mixture moist.

Cat stared at the small rocks embedded in the broken asphalt, wherever they emerged from under the mud cake, ten inches from her face. Thus she could measure her progress when in a painful forward surge her body left the pebbles a quarter of a yard behind, to be replaced by another short stretch of fractured pavement. She dragged herself forward with stubborn determination, knowing that soon she would be defeated. The best she could hope for was to reach the end of her driveway; there someone might find her on the street before she succumbed to thirst, heat and exhaustion.

The clear ringing of a bell sounded from out of nowhere, misplaced in this dried-mud environment like high-heel shoes in a stable. Cat raised her eyes and looked at the bike wheel in front of her face. The wheel was attached to a rickshaw, and on the rickshaw sat Abe.

"Need a taxi, ma'am?" Abe was grinning from one ear to the other. "Kalani told me to find you." Abe got off the rickshaw and picked Cat off the ground like a limp sack of papayas, placed her gently in the seat and extended the canvas roof. Looking at her with alarm, he hesitantly reached for a canteen hanging off the handle bar on a leather strap. "I've drunk from it, but … maybe you should have some."

Cat brought the open flask to her lips with both trembling

hands and drank greedily, spilling water over her face. She recovered her self-control in a moment and stretched out her hand. "I'm sorry, Abe, you need water, too."

"Oh, no worry, we have a lot of water at home. That's where we're going right now. Kalani will be so happy!" He jumped on the rickshaw and started pedaling toward Keolu Drive.

Cat slumped in the seat, closed her eyes and allowed herself not to think at all. She put her life in Abe's hands and this dependence came to her almost naturally.

Chapter 20

Jerry, January 9–10

The neighbor's blaring TV tore through the steady noise of the busy street below, hauling Jerry out of his sleep with its asinine persistence. It was only six o'clock in the morning and Jerry wished, and could afford, to snooze another thirty minutes. That's what hearing aids are for, he thought, annoyed, but got up and went to the bathroom. No point going back to bed, he decided, and turned his own set on.

"An eight-point-nine earthquake has occurred in Hawaii, at five fifteen PM local time, followed shortly thereafter by a tsunami," reported the anchor solemnly. "Casualties are not known at this time, but are expected to be high, as many buildings in Honolulu collapsed. All means of communication with Hawaii have been disrupted, except for satellite links. All airports are closed. Military observers report major damage to roads and tunnels." Jerry froze with his toothbrush in his hand.

"Cat … how is Cat?" he whispered in panic. The footage from a Katrina-ravaged New Orleans replayed in front of his eyes: handicapped people struggling and dying, trapped in a mass of able-bodied neighbors frightened into an unthinking, stampeding herd. He imagined Cat struggling in her chair against the rushing water, stuck between some boards like on the ramp he built. His instinct to protect Cat returned with overpowering force, displacing all other feelings and priorities. Without thinking, Jerry reached for the phone and called a travel agency.

"Sorry, sir, no flights are available to Hawaii. No, we have no idea when they will be. Please try again later." He put the phone away. The TV anchor was reporting on blizzards in the Midwest now. Jerry surfed through a few news channels; nobody knew anything else. There was no up-to-date footage; apparently the mainland TV stations had no reporters in Hawaii or could not get through to them. Whom to call? Henry. Maybe he'd have some connections to put me on a relief plane or a military flight, whatever flies to Hawaii.

Henry was sympathetic; apparently Pam had briefed him on the new family affairs. But the best he could do was to put Jerry in touch with a colonel in some West Coast military air transportation establishment.

Jerry called his university department head to announce he was leaving.

"Jerry, you must be kidding. You've just come back from vacation. We have a whole semester ahead of us and we're short of people. You can't go now."

"I am truly sorry, Professor, but this is a family emergency. I cannot stay. I am taking a plane tonight." It came to him very naturally to say "family emergency." Cat *was* his family, even if she didn't know it yet.

"It, it-ttt ... is a very immature attitude, it ... it's just stupid." Schumacher started stuttering as he usually did when upset. Jerry was apologetic because his boss was a decent, fair man; he drove them like dogs at work but gave his staff recognition and took care that the university promoted them as quickly as possible. But Jerry did not waver for a moment.

"Sorry, Professor, I really cannot stay."

"You are so close to tenure, Jerry. You can forget it if you leave now!"

Tenure, the ultimate academic recognition, the unassailable guarantee of employment for life … it was a carrot dangled in front of all junior professors, but suddenly it meant nothing to Jerry. "I understand," he said, without stopping for a second to consider. "I will have to quit my academic career." A bridge to his old life burnt, he had only one way open—forward. Jerry worried about Cat, but was serene about his own future.

The contact Henry had recommended was located at Edwards Air Force Base in California. Jerry managed to get a ticket for a red-eye flight to LAX the same night. He walked out into the bright sunshine a few minutes past six. He was quite tired but in high spirits. He rented a white Neon and set out for Edwards. The radio carried repetitive news and commentaries about Hawaii but no fresh assessments of the situation on the ground.

As he passed the first turnoff for Santa Clara, the Hawaiian earthquake news on the radio was pushed aside by reports of military activities around Iran. U.S. troops boarded some merchant ships in the Strait of Hormuz, Iranians protested and then shots were fired. As he was driving on the plateau toward the base, Jerry saw big transport planes landing and taking off every couple of minutes. It seemed to be a large airlift.

Colonel Kowal was a tall and somewhat stooped man of nearly Jerry's father's age. His eyes were red from lack of sleep, and dark bags under the eyes gave him the look of a sad hound.

"What can I do for you, my friend?" He was polite and friendly.

"I need to get to Hawaii," Jerry stated shortly, out of respect for the officer's time.

Kowal raised his eyebrows with curiosity. "Right now, we would love to have the means of moving people out of Hawaii, not in. What's your business there?"

"I have to take care of a family member in Hawaii," Jerry said, Cat firmly established as his family—in his mind at least.

"Out of the question," Colonel Kowal said, shrugging. "A million people on Oahu alone, they will need everything. I mean everything. Whatever supplies they have, they will be out of basic essentials in a few days. No way we are going to ferry two hundred pounds of you, when we might carry four bags of rice or a water-making machine. What's your profession? Can you honestly fit into any rescue worker category?"

"I am an economist, sir."

Kowal's shoulders dropped as he sighed. "Son, I suggest you go home and wait for further information. There is nothing I can do for you. As a matter of fact, these few long-range airlift planes I have, which could be used for Hawaii relief, have been given a different priority now."

"A different priority? What can be a higher priority than Hawaii now?" Jerry looked at the man behind the desk in disbelief.

"Do you listen to the radio or watch TV at all?" Kowal was losing patience.

"You mean," Jerry erupted, his temper flaring despite the obvious need to stay in the colonel's good grace, "you mean, killing Iranians has a higher priority than saving Americans in Hawaii?"

The officer stood up, cracked his knuckles and stretched to his full six feet. "You should go now," he said without anger. "And you need to control your emotions better. In these difficult times, you should keep certain thoughts to yourself."

"Thank you for your time, Colonel," Jerry said, suppressing his frustration, and put his hand on the doorknob.

"Jerry ..." Kowal remembered his first name. "There

will be a transport ship leaving from Coronado for Hawaii tomorrow; I cannot see how you could sneak on board with your story, but you might give it a try."

He was right. In San Diego, a few hours later, a lowly lieutenant laughed at him and threw him out of his office. "If you really, really need to get to Hawaii, the only way I can imagine that happening is by sailboat," he offered his gratuitously mocking advice. "And don't forget to take a lot of provisions; the last thing they need right now is another hungry mouth to feed." Then he yelled at his assistant; a load of the water-purification chemical was missing and the ship would certainly not wait for it.

The audience ended abruptly and less than an hour later, Jerry was walking toward downtown with nothing to show for the last two days' feverish activity. His new life, which had started with great momentum, came to a sudden stop like an express train halted by a gap in the rails ahead. He sat at a restaurant's window watching the waterfront. This would be his first meal of the day. He was very hungry, but the thought of a million people running out of food on Oahu was very disturbing. Anybody who saw TV reports of Hurricane Katrina knew that desperate people do nasty things to each other. Now Cat was in the middle of a big crowd, which would turn desperate in a few days. His fish and chips were getting stuck in his throat.

Kowal was right, Jerry thought. If the harbors and airports are badly damaged, there is no easy way to supply so many people on the islands. There will be hunger, disease and probably a crime wave as well. Only the military could do something about it, but they seem to have different priorities. I have to be there to take care of Cat. There was no doubt in his mind.

A white sailboat motored along the waterfront, its skipper nonchalantly holding the wheel with one hand, chatting with two blond girls. A quintessential California scene: one might expect Michelle Pfeiffer to lean out from the cabin, posing for a camera, or a pencil-boat roar out from behind pursued by James Bond in a small plane. A different scenery than New York in January for sure, but in a certain way, the similarity was striking. People were laughing, having lunch, drinking beer, apparently without any concern for their fellow countrymen in Hawaii or even for the war breaking out in Iran.

The waitress returned to ask if everything was OK. Young, blond, intelligent eyes—could be a student. "Would you like anything else?" she asked.

"I'm fine, thank you," Jerry said. "It's a terrible thing that's happening in Hawaii—have you heard?"

"Awful," she agreed with a smile. "Would you like another beer?"

People don't give a damn about others, unless they are very close, Jerry thought. Social solidarity! Perhaps in a small village, but across the continent or the ocean ... a propaganda tool, that's all; the Super Bowl frenzy is as far as national solidarity goes.

He paid the tab and walked along the waterfront until a forest of masts announced a small boat harbor ahead. Jerry had no sailing experience to mention, but—he wondered—how difficult could it be to sail to Hawaii? Navigation shouldn't be a problem—GPS would take care of that. Sure, there's the risk of heavy weather.... He was prepared to take a lot of risk in order to find Cat.

Jerry walked along a narrow concrete pier, boats gently swaying on both sides. Most of them were empty, sails neatly rolled and covered, hatches closed, bare teak wood dull in the setting sun. Glamorous expensive toys, he thought, used less and less as the big kids' excitement wore off. He stopped abruptly in front of a modest yacht—someone was on board. The boat's hull was dark blue, her paint moderately scratched up and peeling in some places. *Lady Luck*, the stenciled white letters announced her name. She had one mast, and hanging at the back was a box which had to be a radar unit. That was about as much as Jerry's ignorant eyes could tell.

The man on board could be sixty-five, possibly older, his face thin and wrinkled, skin worn out beyond the usual damage inflicted by age alone. He wore a thick black turtleneck sweater, gray woolen cap and oversized shorts, crumpled and wrinkled at the waist by a wide leather belt. The old sailor was reclining on a cockpit bench, reading a newspaper. Caustic smoke drifted from his cigarette and an open bottle of beer was placed within his easy reach.

The boat's deck seemed fairly messy: a bicycle leaning against the railing, laundry drying on lines in front of the mast, remnants of food on a small table in the cockpit. Unlike the other yachts in this marina, this boat was someone's home.

Jerry stood in front of the yacht looking at the man who, after a moment, raised his head, looked over his reading glasses and said, "Yes? What's the problem?" He was not too gracious but not aggressive either, mildly annoyed perhaps at this interruption of his reading.

"Sorry to bother you, sir. I was just wondering how difficult it would be to cross the Pacific to get to Hawaii," Jerry asked without any premeditated plan.

The man looked at Jerry for two seconds and shrugged, saying, "Difficult enough if you don't know what you're doing," and returned to his paper.

"I wonder how long it would take, of course providing you knew what you were doing." Jerry was not ready to end this conversation.

The old sailor sighed, put the paper down and sat up. "I sense that you definitely need to talk to me, don't you? The least you could do is bring some beer, as my supplies have just run out."

Jerry quickly walked to the little grocery store at the marina and bought a six-pack of Sam Adams. A moment later, he returned to buy chips and peanuts as well as another six-pack. This might be an interesting and long conversation.

The old-timer extended a blue awning over the cockpit to protect them from the sun and opened two bottles with an opener attached by a string to the steering wheel's base. He handed Jerry one and introduced himself. "John Browser, the skipper of this fine boat," he announced with a sweeping gesture of his hand.

"I'm Jerry Roberts. Pleased to meet you, John. I just wonder if you could tell me about a hypothetical trip to Hawaii. Are you familiar with long ocean passages?"

"I wasted most of my life making long ocean passages"—John grimaced—"so you could say I'm familiar with the subject. I was a seaman and an officer on a dozen freighters until I gave it all up a few years ago. What is it that you want to know about your hypothetical trip to Hawaii, buddy?"

He developed some interest in Jerry and studied him with keen eyes partly hidden behind heavy eyelid bags.

John's tired eyes and hands, covered in numerous liver spots, placed him somewhere closer to seventy years of age, Jerry thought. "Could you just tell me, how would you go about sailing there?" he proposed awkwardly, not knowing what would be the right questions to ask.

John took a long sip of bear. "You're not a sailor, are you?"

No, Jerry shook his head.

"Then I would start by finding myself a skipper, a captain who has all the important answers without having to ask questions."

Jerry looked for a long moment into Browser's eyes, took a deep breath and said in a deliberate manner, "It may sound a bit crazy, John, but … would you be interested in such a job?"

Browser looked him up and down. "Is this some kind of a joke? If not …" He frowned when Jerry solemnly turned his head for no.

"Man, you scare me. Are you running from something? Are you so desperate that you're ready to put your life into my hands, not even knowing if I'm a competent skipper?" He was genuinely exasperated. "Would you put a thousand dollars in my hand if you'd met me on the street? If not, how could you trust me with your life? Isn't it worth more than a thousand bucks?" After a moment, a spark of understanding flashed on his face. "You work for the government, don't you, Jerry? If that's your real name."

"Oh no," Jerry protested vehemently. "I don't work for anyone now. I was a university professor until yesterday. I'll show you my school ID." He reached to his back pocket.

The skipper waved his action away, dismissing further explanations, meaning, "If you are a spook, couldn't you have a fake ID?"

Jerry pressed on. "Good metaphor with the thousand bucks, except that on a busy street you could take the money and disappear in the crowd, while you can't vanish on the water. My only risk would be that you are, indeed, not up to the job, but then we would share the trouble. I just hope you have a healthy instinct of self-preservation."

John considered it for a moment. "True, but let's reverse the situation. Convince me that *you* are not crazy. How do I know you won't jump off the boat in the middle of the ocean, leaving me by myself; or that you won't cut my throat when I am asleep? What mentally stable person wants to sail to Hawaii in January, when the chance of running into a storm is high and some nasty weather is practically guaranteed? Besides, what's the attraction of the Islands just after the major earthquake? They must be ruined. Surely you're not a vacationer?"

He lit another exceptionally stinky cigarette, giving Jerry a few moments to decide on a further strategy. How could he provide proof of his mental stability? A lot of people, including the military shrink, Professor Schumacher and the lieutenant from Coronado, might vouch to the contrary. There was no other way—he would have to tell the truth, strange as it sounded.

"John, my wife, I mean my future wife, lives on Oahu. She is handicapped and I will do anything to get to her." Cat might be surprised to hear this explanation, considering they were not particularly friendly when Jerry was leaving Oahu, but that was another problem, to be addressed later in his battle plan.

John slowly opened another bottle and took a large gulp. "Temporary insanity, then," he stated with the air of objectivity. "You are a pup in love. That's not too bad. That guarantees that you won't try to kill yourself or me, at least until we get to Honolulu."

Chapter 21

Cat, January 12

Reuters: Violent demonstrations rock Middle East in response to US–Iran conflict. Russia concerned about escalation of fighting in Persian Gulf.

People kept busy digging out their families and neighbors, but cries for help and moaning under the rubble grew weaker with every hour. Two days later only one survivor, a baby, had been pulled out alive. Only piles of dead bodies grew in parks and empty spaces after that, until space was found for them in a few empty warehouses. Stunned survivors lifted their eyes and contemplated the damage around them.

A short walk through Kailua was enough to see that the destructive forces had affected the town in a spotty manner, without any regard for fairness. Beachside, a neighborhood of expensive houses lined up along Kailua Beach, had been almost uniformly flattened and washed away by the tidal waves. Dried mud, penetrated only by stumps of broken trees, covered the row of outsized foundations.

No living creature larger than a fly disturbed the peace of this dead zone. Even rats, that used to live in the canopies of coconut trees soaring above the residences, abandoned the strip reclaimed by the ocean. Only the waves moved in their usual gentle fashion, sweetly washing the wounded shore, covering the overturned cars, jumbled fragments of houses and other wreckage with fresh golden sand.

Further inland, where the killing water did not reach, the destruction was patchy, without any apparent pattern. Some buildings crumbled into heaps of rubble while others, next door, survived with damage no worse than broken windows. Only the loss of utilities was egalitarian—no service that required conduits survived. The violent shaking had broken water pipes, shuttered sewage ducts and ripped electrical wires.

Streets and alleys were barely passable, with wide fissures splitting the pavement in some places, and mounds of asphalt surrealistically projecting upward in others. Emergency vehicles crept slowly through the fractured roads, not even bothering to use their sirens.

The fires died out early, when the heavy rain—customary at this time of year—fell on the night of the earthquake. What struck people particularly harshly was the complete loss of communication. Landline phones and the Internet were dead, which surprised no one, but the signal disappeared from mobile phones as well. Was it due to the loss of power or damaged transmitters—who could tell? Whatever the reason, it silenced the local radio and TV stations as well.

Information, at that stage of the disaster, became the most desired commodity. Not knowing the fate of friends and family bothered people enough; the uncertainty of their own situation was even worse.

Owners of battery-operated shortwave radios turned their dials in disbelief. The local stations were no more, but the radio waves were filled with music as usual. The news broadcast from somewhere far away mentioned the earthquake in Hawaii briefly only to return to their top twenty lists. Radio hosts argued the merits of attacking Iran, but specifics about Hawaii were few and far between. Were they left to themselves? A few ham radio operators broadcast their pleas for help, but their voices went silent one by one, as battery backups failed.

Kailua learned about its isolation soon after the earthquake. The first walkers trying to reach Honolulu came back a few hours later with disturbing news.

The Pali Highway, the main artery that every day pumped thousands of cars per hour between Kailua and Honolulu, had been blocked by a collapsed tunnel. Big fallen rocks and a huge heap of rubble occupied its lower portion, leaving enough free space above only for rats and mongoose to pass. Kailua and the whole windward side of Oahu returned to its natural state—as far as transportation goes—of being separated from Honolulu by the tall and steep remnant of the ancient Koolau Volcano's slope. As in centuries past, the way to the windward led through the narrow and dangerous Pali mountain pass.

Other scouts returned from Kaleanianaole Road, a somewhat longer route winding precariously over the slope, but beloved by tourists for its unforgettable views of the ocean. The road—hacked out in the mountain halfway between the surf and the top—had a commanding view of the shore from Makapu'u Point to Waimanalo, but now its picturesque location turned deadly. In front on the Manano Island, unstable rubble spilled from the summit, covering the slope and pavement all the way to the ocean; the rockslide converted the road into a dangerous trap.

Reports from the H3 highway—connecting the windward with Pearl Harbor and the leeward side—completed the bad news: a section of elevated pavement had collapsed, leaving a breach of thirty yards high above ground. The same went for the Likelike Highway.

The sum of it all was this: a fit and brave person could

climb over the mountains, but mass transportation was impossible. The seventy thousand residents of the Windward would not find any new food supplies in grocery stores for quite some time. The ancient Hawaiians had coped with the isolation of the windward quite well, but the taro fields, guava orchards and fishponds that once fed them remained only in songs and legends.

Cat sat in a wheelchair, requisitioned by Abe from a broken health supplies store, facing a small assembly gathered around a lunch table of the Kailua police station. The brown mud had come off her body, not without vigorous scrubbing, leaving for public view the crusty abrasions covering most of her forearms and legs. Her own clothes destroyed by crawling, she wore Kalani's old shorts and a t-shirt, both ridiculously too big.

"It's Dodge City!" she said. "The quake happened only four days ago and everybody should still have a lot of supplies in their pantries, but all the grocery stores have already been cleaned out by looters. Most people just stay home, but even that is becoming dangerous. Home invasions are cropping up left and right. What's the point of locking yourself in, if a good kick breaks any door in Kailua? Our homes are certainly not castles. We have to do something!" She turned to a middle-aged man of Japanese ancestry wearing a torn and dusty police uniform.

Sergeant Yoshida opened his arms in a helpless gesture. "We have fourteen guys who can do full duties, two female dispatchers and a few walking wounded. There is no way we can respond to all the crime happening now. First, we don't even know what's happening because people have no phones. But even if we knew, we're out of gas for patrol cars." One doesn't become a police sergeant if feeling helpless is part of his mental makeup, and Yoshida did not accept defeats easily, but now he could see no way out.

"Where are these scoundrels coming from?" a thin, Asian-looking, older woman asked. "It's like with cockroaches, once you see one, it almost makes no difference if you get it; their supply is unlimited. It already feels like there must be hundreds or thousands of gangsters."

"Dr. Lim has a point," Cat interjected. "The longer this thieves' paradise lasts the more of them we will have. If this continues, the only people who survive will be thieves and gangsters."

"You've heard the man," the overweight woman in a flowery blue muu'muu said, pointing to the policeman. "They don't have the manpower and cars. What can they do but try to control the worst excesses?" As a member of the Police Board, Carol Nakamoto, a Kailua politician and a ranking member of the Democratic Party, had some understanding of the community security management.

"Not good enough." Cat was stubborn. "We cannot pretend that everything is all right, because it will only get worse, and fast. Mike, is your portable communication equipment working?"

Yoshida cleared his throat. "Well, we have a backup generator to run our station's radio, but as I said, we're almost out of gas. We've kept a few gallons for the generator, but that won't last long. We still have battery-operated radios, but if we use them routinely, we'll soon be out of any communication altogether."

"So, how did all this police business work when they had no cars and walkie-talkies?" Dr. Lim wanted to know. As the Castle Hospital's medical director, she saw firsthand what was happening in the community. She cocked her head and coolly observed the sergeant over her reading glasses.

"Foot patrols," Yoshida answered without hesitation. "In any case, most of the roads are badly broken up, so it is really back to the street beat. The problem is that with two men per patrol—and they have to sleep sometime—we will never cover the territory. Bad things will always be happening where we are not present, meaning more than ninety percent of town will be open for crime at any time."

Cat looked around the long table; she had not known any of these eight persons until this morning. No one was volunteering any ideas. "How about deputizing some people? We could make twelve or thirteen patrols—each led by a cop, with Mike and his deputy at the headquarters. They could cover a lot of territory."

The policeman looked at her with hopeful interest.

Nakamoto shifted uncomfortably. "That smells like a lot of legal problems. The deputies can get hurt and the untrained staff will break the law. We must wait for instructions from Honolulu." She made the determination with the expression of finality.

"Carol, have you had any instructions from Honolulu, Washington or anywhere else over the past few days?" Cat asked with an increasing sense of frustration. In her experience, nothing ever got better until she made it better.

The politician looked at her with scorn. "No, but there is no need to panic. I'm sure someone is working on it right now. All we need to do is wait." She wished that this pushy young person, who looked like a professional worm hunter, had not taken seriously her public invitation for this meeting.

"Mike, have you had any murder reports?" Cat again turned to the policeman, whose oriental eyes started wrinkling in the promise of a smile.

"Two likely killings on the first night, five the next night, and today I had reports of three stabbings and two gun-wound deaths, and it's only seven PM!" he reported with a stony face.

"Carol, how many dead bodies do you need to take some practical action? I don't mean writing a resolution," she added ironically, seeing Nakamoto scribbling in her yellow pad.

Carol hated to be put on the spot like that, and all her legal training was telling her: Stay away from this mess. There will be consequences. She lowered her head, pretending to take careful notes, and mumbled something difficult to interpret.

Yoshida looked at Cat and nodded with a wink.

"Well, we cannot force anybody to join, but people who would rather fight back than hide under the bed in hope that the robbers miss them should be able to defend themselves." Cat was certain now that the policeman was on her side. "I suggest that everybody present here get in touch with their friends and family. Volunteers should come here, to the police station. We'll prepare flyers, and they need to be distributed by hand. That's a lot of legwork; we need many people."

Chapter 22

Jerry, January 10–11

The skipper was a slow but steady guzzler, working through the second six-pack; however, alcohol did not seem to affect him. He had a son who lived with his mother while John plied the oceans. He did not claim much credit for his fatherly involvement, though—in his own judgment—he was not any worse than most of his shipmates. As a husband ... suffice it to say his wife had found her own way to happiness and it did not include John. With the marriage dissolved, his relationship with the boy, not strong to start with, was practically lost.

Jerry and John chatted until the sun descended low enough to become the background for the forest of masts, and wavelets raised by the dying wind smoothed into a shiny surface of glass. People started showing up on the boats and the smell of grilled meat spread throughout the marina as barbeques fired up. Jerry was getting hungry again and John gladly went along for dinner in the seaside restaurant where Jerry had had lunch.

The upsetting part of his family story occurred during the last two years. Like many single men, John retired in poor financial shape. "Can't really say what happened to my money." He shrugged helplessly. "It's not that I was lazy. I worked all my life and the wages were not that bad.... But between the child support, alimony, shore-side celebrations—I had no savings.

"That's when I discovered what a great invention is a social security check! Plus, I did some odd jobs in Long Beach, at the port—you know. I was getting by. What do I need? Beer, cheap cigarettes, a bit of food and a place to sleep—that's not a lot of money."

The young woman at the restaurant's entrance, who wore a long black skirt with a deep side split and a white long-sleeved blouse, let her eyes glide over John's old shorts and black rubber sandals with a hint of displeasure, but as he challenged her with a hard stare, she faked a smile and led them to a small table behind a pillar, not far from the toilet.

"One day—and, yes, it was the Christmas season—I get a phone call. Chris, my son, calls and invites me for dinner. I haven't seen him in ten years; thought he was lost for me. He really hated me as a teenager."

John's life ran for the next year and a half like an inspirational story about sins forgiven, love found and family life restored. Chris did well, running a small but prosperous used-car lot, and John turned out to have the gift for selling. The old mariner—accustomed to living on a really low budget—was saving money for the first time in his life. Less than two years later, he had enough money saved to fulfill his dream—he had bought the boat, *Lady Luck*.

"A nice name," Jerry snickered. "Certainly has a certain ring to it."

"If you are going to learn anything about sailing, Jerry," Browser confronted him with a stern face, "and it seems like it's your plan, the first thing you need to know is this: you need luck! No matter how smart you are and how good your boat is, with enough bad luck, the ocean will swallow you whole, without even a burp. And changing a boat's name is an invitation for bad fortune, in big red letters."

Jerry accepted the reprimand with a contrite expression on his face.

"But, Jerry," John continued, "this is the moment when the fairy tale ends. I gave my check to the boat dealer, ready to move my clutter on her during the weekend. But I didn't. On Friday, five o'clock in the morning, someone knocked on my door. Two men, dark suits, fucking 'Men in Black.'"

The skipper hung his voice for a dramatic effect and took in a long, unhurried swig. "Only they weren't funny at all. They arrested me on charges of money laundering and aiding a terror organization, put bracelets on my wrists and took me to a lockup."

He took in Jerry's disbelieving expression with appreciation.

"The next few days, I spent answering again and again questions like 'What's your name,' and 'What's your religion?' And you know, Jerry, they did not like my honest answer that I didn't subscribe to any holy church. They wanted to know if I could speak Arabic. Yes, I could: *shukram, afwan, masalama*—thank you, you are welcome, good-bye. For God's sake, I was a sailor! I can manage a few words in almost any language you ever heard of.

"Apparently, I had sold a car that the FBI, or another government organization you have never heard of, traced to some goddamned terror suspects. Their money had touched my hands so I had become a suspect myself. They kept me alone in a tiny cell for five days, their faces my only entertainment. No phone call, no lawyer ... not that I had any."

Jerry found it difficult to believe, but—on the other hand—those prisoners in Somalia were not exactly apprehended on a court order either. Same war, same tactics ... only the geography was different.

"Eventually, they let me go, making believe they were doing me a great favor, but I was sternly warned to remain in the San Diego vicinity. Apparently, something didn't check out in their theory. So I went to the bank to get some money for supplies for my boat. I was homeless, as my apartment lease had expired. The girl at the window, whom I'd known for a few years, stares into her monitor, rubs her temples and says, 'Just a moment, Mr. Browser, I'll be right back.'"

"They froze your account," Jerry moaned.

"How would you know, Jerry? Is this a normal thing that happens to everyone at least once a year?" John was getting agitated and clearly in need to spill his bile.

"The manager asks me to a back room and whispers that they cannot give me my money—by order of some government fuck empowered by the Patriot Act. Fortunately, *Lady Luck*'s check had already cleared so I had a place to sleep. Screw them. But that wasn't the worst—my son's accounts had been frozen as well."

"It's like strangling a business," Jerry sighed. "A retailer without a cash flow is dead within weeks."

"Right again." John shrugged depressively. "Other salesmen were interrogated and harassed, again and again. The money ran out quickly. A receptionist bailed out a week later and the car lot went belly up. My son never openly blamed it on me, but he stopped asking me to drop in; had enough of his own problems. Since then I basically do what you saw me doing: sit on my boat and read the old papers people leave in the marina."

Jerry and John felt comfortable with each other. The skipper did not consider Jerry crazy for his travel plans, and Jerry had already decided how to get to Hawaii. "John, here is the business proposition I want you to consider: you sell me your boat, and I hire you as a captain. Our destination will be Hawaii and your time of service 'until we touch land in Hawaii, whatever it takes.' You not too busy now?" He smiled encouragingly and his eyes were met with John's excited gaze. "We really don't know each other too well," Jerry continued, "but I have no time for extensive investigations. I'll trust you … and if you want to grill me some more, you are welcome. But I need your answer before this night ends."

John was shifting impatiently in his chair, dying to have a cigarette, their plates thoroughly cleaned up of any digestible morsels. Jerry signaled the waitress for the tab, paid and they left. John lit a cigarette right behind the door, inhaled slowly and kept the smoke in for a few seconds. "First, you will not find anyone crazy enough to sail to Hawaii in January, especially knowing that the Islands are probably flattened. So, it is either I, or you may start taking sailing classes and—if you are a hard worker—you might be ready in a year."

The skipper stuck the cigarette butt into a sand-filled ashtray and immediately lit another. "What would you offer for my boat and what would you pay me?" he asked, averting his eyes, embarrassed as though selling *Lady Luck* was a shameful act. "I … don't need this money for myself," he added hesitantly, "but I would like to repay my son, somehow."

"I have no idea what the value of your boat is, John." Jerry gripped the skipper's arm, their eyes meeting, both hoping this deal would close. "But I will offer you this—I have an apartment in New York City, nothing fancy, but it should fetch over half a million dollars. I will swap it for your boat and your services. If you agree, we'll go to a notary in the morning, and I will sign papers transferring ownership to you or your son."

"That's a lot more than my boat is worth," John said, "although it's a good boat," he added with certain haste. "You sure you want to do it?"

Jerry shrugged. "As you've said, you and your boat are the only game in town, and I am desperate. The swap is a good value to me. Besides, I won't need a New York apartment anymore." He extended his hand.

"Well, then"—Browser grasped his hand—"I will gladly take the shirt off your back, but you need to know certain facts. First, this is the storm season, and we may get into weather that will make you wish you had never left dry land. In other terms, we may die. Secondly, I am an alcoholic. I function just fine, but if you try to limit my drinking, you may have to tie me up. I wouldn't like that; neither would you. Can you put up with an old drunk for a few weeks?"

"You look to me like a very reasonable drunk, John. I won't interfere with your intake."

"As you noted, I also smoke, well over a pack a day."

"And they are a pretty stinky kind, but as long as you smoke outside, I won't complain."

"Then it's a deal." Browser shook Jerry's hand and released it to put his palm on the younger man's shoulder. "And to make our deal fairer, I will throw in something you cannot buy with money. By the time we pull into the Honolulu harbor, Jerry, you'll be a real sailor. I'll make sure."

"John, the Men in Black ... didn't they tell you to stay in San Diego? They might be unhappy."

"If I can make them unhappy, Jerry, that would be just frosting on the cake. I would love to stick it to them. In any case, there was no court order to make me stay. Besides, once we get fifty miles offshore, they can go to hell. They have no power over the open ocean, Jerry; it's the last place where you can be truly free."

They had a long night, poring until dawn over lists of provisions and supplies. The skipper made no special demands for food. He wouldn't object to dog food, probably, if this measure were necessary. Not quite sure of his water-maker, John did insist on a gallon of drinking water per day for each of them, recommending that, in the great tradition of the British Navy, a good portion of it could come in the form of beer. "Safe, healthy and keeps the crew in sweet

Return to Paradise

disposition," the captain declared.

Jerry suspected that this recommendation was not entirely unbiased but did not object. Forty cases of Heineken were added to the list, with a few bottles of tequila "for emergency."

Lady Luck was a forty-two-foot-long sloop and could carry a six-man crew, with supplies. With Jerry and John as her only occupants, they could take on some cargo. Jerry kept in mind the Coronado lieutenant's words: "The last thing they need is another hungry mouth to feed." Apart from food, Jerry wanted to take something that would be useful in Hawaii, something definitely needed. Didn't I hear about a missing load of water-purification tablets? he recalled. Had they managed to slip it onto the ship at the last moment?

"Skipper, where could we buy water-purification chemicals?"

"Bleach, it's nothing but bleach." Browser waved his hand dismissively. "You can have a ton of it for a few bucks. Just keep in mind—the heavier the boat, the slower we'll move."

When the sun broke through and the light fog settled on the oily, calm water of the port, Jerry was ready to pick up the supplies, fill the tanks and set the sail.

But John was not, making it a teaching moment. He lit one of his stinkers in the cockpit, puffed and said, "Jerry, you don't fuck with the ocean. You start cutting corners and the next thing you know, your lungs are full of water. If you want to do some good in Hawaii, first you have to get your ass over there, while it is still warm. We're taking enough risks already sailing in the winter. I need to repair a headsail and service the motor."

"How long is it going to take, Skip?" Jerry asked impatiently.

"You've got yourself a skipper *and* a mechanic, sir. I can do the engine myself, if I can find replacement parts. The sail—it shouldn't take more than a few hours to fix and reinforce it, if you pay the shop guys a bit extra."

"I'm fine with extra money, but would hate to wait for engine parts. Is it feasible to go without the motor job? We'll be crossing by sail, right?"

"Wrong," the skipper answered brusquely, shaking his head in disappointment. He put the sail in Jerry's rental car and disappeared. A few bottles of beer went with him as well.

Jerry went straight to the lawyer he had found in the Yellow Pages. He gave his sister power of attorney, signed the papers transferring the ownership of his apartment to John's son, and with a heavy heart dialed the number to Pam.

"Pam, it's Jerry."

"Jerry, what are you doing?" Pam was not waiting to exchange civil greetings, her voice hoarse.

"There is nothing I can do here in California; I am going to Hawaii by sailboat."

All he heard was irregular breathing, as if she was fighting to control sobbing. He gave her a few seconds for a question, but as none was coming, he continued. "I've found a good boat and an experienced skipper who will take me there. Don't worry, thousands of people have done it before." He did not mention that the vast majority of them did not try to cross the Pacific in winter. He also forgot to mention John's drinking problem. As to his description of *Lady Luck* as a "good boat," he might be right; they would know soon.

Pam got her breathing under control. "You've quit your job as well," she sighed.

Jerry had almost forgotten about his teaching job; it seemed a long, long time ago. "Pam, I want to ask you for a favor, there is some unfinished business…."

She easily agreed to take over all his financial affairs and didn't object to his real estate deal. Before they disconnected, she cried briefly and said, "You know, Jerry, you grew up to be the man I hoped you would. I am worried sick about you, but I am so proud of you as well. I hope you pull it off and bring

Cat to New York. I love you." Jerry had tears in his eyes; now he was ready.

He returned to the boat with Chinese take-out for John. There was no smell of tobacco on the deck, and he had a moment of terror, thinking the skipper had pulled a fast one on him. A moment later, he was ashamed of himself; the captain was lying on his belly, head in the diesel compartment, struggling to unscrew a mechanical device and wheezing with effort.

"Hey, John, there's some food up here for you. And it sounds like you need fresh air for a moment."

"Be out in a few minutes," growled the skipper from the diesel, "but not before this little fuck gives in."

He emerged ten minutes later, disdainfully displaying an old part that reminded Jerry of nothing he had ever seen. "The motor should be ready in three hours. You can pick up the sail from repair at five o'clock."

"Great." Jerry could not control his excitement. "Then I'll bring our supplies in the evening, we load the boat and we're ready to sail!"

John looked at him with a silent question.

"I went to the lawyer and made the real estate transaction; my sister will finish the deal." Jerry showed him copies of the documents. "You should mail them to your son tonight and perhaps you might write him a letter." Jerry was sorry to see John sinking into sadness every time he was reminded of his son.

"What can I tell him?" The skipper exhaled smoke noisily, lifting his eyes for a moment. "I wanted to speak with him after our defenders of freedom turned me loose. But he didn't want to see me. Never said so, but I knew. I called his house and his wife answered. When I asked to speak with him, she covered the phone for a few seconds then said he wasn't home. But he was home. I was calling from the street, just outside his house.

I hoped he would say, 'Dad, just come in, we'll talk.' Instead, I saw him sitting at the kitchen table, waving 'no' to his wife. I used to sit at that table, play with his kids, and have a beer with him. When he gets your apartment, maybe he'll see that I am not an old, worthless piece of garbage." John crushed the cigarette on a glass ashtray and cracked open a beer. Jerry didn't have anything comforting to say, just put his hand on John's thin shoulder.

They completed their last land activities at 11:30 PM, started the motor at 11:35 and slipped away twenty minutes before midnight. The forecast called for winds of ten to fifteen knots and likely showers.

Chapter 23

Cat, January 12–16

The meeting at the police station was over, but the participants lingered, talking in small groups. Kalani tugged Cat's t-shirt. "Remember, there are kids living on the streets, all alone; there is no one to care for them. Something has to be done. They are all hungry, filthy and scared to death."

"You're right, Kalani, something has to be done. You're the one who is going to do it. Hereby, I appoint you the chief of child services," Cat declared ceremoniously.

"You must be kidding!" Carol Nakamoto couldn't resist and turned away from the policeman whom she was pestering with her doubts. "This is impersonation of a public official; it's illegal."

Cat had had enough. "So where is your public official, Carol? I see no suitable official but there are hungry children. Hmm, what to do? Let's take a poll and see what the people desire. Carol, you might want to take on this problem, and we will help you, but if you would rather not then go to hell! Don't intimidate people who might actually do it!"

Nakamoto withdrew silently, her lips pursed, and walked out of the station with great dignity. Mike Yoshida watched the scene with pleasure. Carol was on the police board and had made him cringe more than once in the past. He was happy to see someone to rub her nose in the dirt, finally. "Cat, would you like to join the police force?" He broke into a wide smile.

Sergeant Yoshida was not aware of the impression he made on Cat. Six feet tall, fit and easily breaking into a wide smile, he was very different from the generally short and reserved Japanese tourists, even though his grandparents hailed from Yokohama. The Islands modify all creatures that come here, Cat thought, from *nene* to humans.

"Where am I supposed to get food for the kids? Where do I put them up?" Kalani moaned, apparently having accepted her new public responsibility. "My apartment is too small to take them all in."

"Good point," Cat remarked. "We need a house to put up the kids. Oh, I know … there is an empty one on Kailua Road. It's one of those close to the beach that survived the disaster. I did a job for the owner recently; they're on the mainland now. Decent man; won't mind if we use his property. At least nobody will break in.

"As to food, until we get some kind of supplies, you'll have to resort to guerilla tactics. Desperate times call for desperate measures. Get some volunteers and comb over the groceries. The looters must have missed something; after all, they had to work under pressure. Mike, are you willing to look the other way?"

"We're very short on staff, as you know," the sergeant replied with a crooked grin. "I don't think we'll be able to cover the Foodland and Safeway tonight."

A large black mass emerged from the darkness of Kailua Road, its two-story form blotting out the moonlight filtering through wispy clouds. Kalani paused behind Cat's wheelchair, catching her breath after maneuvering over and around innumerable cracks and holes in the pavement. The outline was unusual; its street-facing wall was distinctly round like in a medieval fortress.

"The Round House," Kalani gasped. "I always wanted to see it inside!"

Apparently, the metal gate and the solid concrete wall surrounding the house had held back the torrent of water and debris, saving the building. The front yard was covered with thick, caked mud, giving it a smooth, faintly glistening surface, easy to negotiate for the chair's wheels. The sturdy oak door was intact.

Kalani looked into the dark broken window. "Wow, it's huge, and there is not much damage." She removed pieces of shattered glass from the window frame and carefully climbed in. A moment later, the front door opened and Cat wheeled into a large hall. Its windows and the generous sunroof, set high in a cathedral ceiling, allowed enough moonlight to illuminate the interior. Dark stains marked the floor where the muddy water stood for days until it evaporated, leaving behind big rough deposits like coils of a fantastic brown dragon sleeping on the shiny sand-colored marble floor.

The women remained silent as their eyes adapted to the dim light. They saw no large cracks or any other structural damage.

"This is good," Kalani whispered, stepping carefully between shards of glass and broken pieces of terracotta sculptures, advancing with her exploration. A wide, rounded staircase led upstairs and Kalani climbed it cautiously, listening for any ominous cracks. She found three large rooms on the second floor—all free of any major damage. The windows were broken, a large crystal mirror lay splintered on the floor and a TV set was hanging off the wall, suspended on its wires. Flower vases, overturned fans and other small household items littered water-stained and wrinkled carpets, but two large beds were intact and covered with blankets. A huge sofa in front of the TV stand could easily be used as a bed as well.

"I can put eight or nine kids right here, on real beds." Kalani was happy; her task did not seem that insurmountable anymore. Her spirits lifted even more in the kitchen; the pantry was stocked with hurricane supplies.

"There you go." Cat smiled. "You can start your public career without being a thief. We'll see how long you can last."

The house was big enough to accommodate the orphanage upstairs, leaving the grand hall downstairs to become a community meeting place. If any volunteers showed up, this ballroom-size room would definitely be better than the cramped lunchroom of the police station.

"Kalani, can you go back to Mike Yoshida and tell him about our discovery? Tell him to send all volunteers here. Then you can go trolling the town for your homeless children." Cat easily slipped into the position nobody seemed to want. "I'll stay here and start preparing assignments for volunteers."

She set up her command post at a big, dark oak table at the end of the hall. Two hours after the first bunch of leaflets had been dispatched, the first volunteers showed up. Silent, depressed and exhausted people were greeted with a cup of hot soup or coffee. A camping propane burner in the backyard produced a new pot of hot liquid every few minutes. People sat against the wall, cup in hand, enjoying what was possibly their first hot drink in days, then received small but definite tasks from a skinny young woman in a wheelchair at the large table.

"Your name is John, right? John, you'll be in charge of lighting. We need a few kerosene or oil lamps, or at least a bunch of candles. Can you try to get them?"

"Leila, what did you do before the shake? Senior at the Kailua High—Excellent! You'll be our printer-in-chief. Get some kids together; you'll be handwriting notes to the public. Just remember—neat, big letters so that people can read them without glasses."

Return to Paradise

Cat looked at the pale faces, blood-soaked bandages and dirty clothes, thinking, How much can people take? We are all scared and tired ... many are injured. Then she saw backs straightening as people, offered a chance to help themselves, picked it up without hesitation. They're tough, she reflected, tougher than anyone could imagine three days ago.

The list of needs seemed to have no end. The town-sweep in search for still entrapped people—or more likely, bodies; organization of care for orphaned children; removal of dead bodies to be stored in the empty warehouse overlooking the swamp.... These would be the immediate tasks, but could the other wait?

The police department ... how could she expect the volunteers to come out from their homes onto streets controlled by criminal gangs? OK, Cat sighed, police deputies come first. There was more than enough work to occupy the few dozen volunteers filing in and out.

What even the most dedicated volunteers could not provide was food, fuel and medications, especially medications. Dr. Lee was sending desperate messages. The hospital was quickly shutting down one service after another; they were out of supplies. The operating rooms closed down first. Emergency generators hummed for forty-eight hours without a break, powering surgical lights and power-hungry equipment, as overworked and sleep-deprived surgeons tended to the crowd of wounded. Then the hum stopped, leaving the operating rooms dark but not empty. For another day, flashlights and anesthetics dripped straight on gauze masks, like a century ago, still offered some patients a chance of survival. After that no major surgery was possible.

The hospital remained open; abscesses were still drained and broken bones splinted, but the pharmacy was running out of medications. No patients were admitted; they were sent home to live or die.

A large number of Kailua's inhabitants had suffered

injuries during the quake. Now, a few days later, infections became the main worry. Septic shock claimed older people and diabetics first, but that was only the beginning. Terrified people—healthy just a week before—saw their injured skin getting hot, red and purple. Then their wounds opened like hungry mouths, draining thin scanty pus but, at this stage, the victims were not emotional anymore. They filled the emergency room feverish, despondent, and confused, watching with glassy eyes as their families begged for treatment. But there was little treatment the exhausted doctors could offer. The deadly mixture of germs found excellent breeding grounds in deep, ragged wounds inflicted by splintered wood, concrete debris and broken glass. The pile of bodies in the warehouse was growing rapidly.

The good news came first from the security front. A surprisingly large number of citizens crowded the Kailua police station, a shotgun or a pistol in hand, some craving for revenge after humiliations suffered at the hands of criminals. Sergeant Yoshida's concern was not the lack of manpower anymore. How to protect suspects—among them some innocent people—became his main worry. But these were not the times for timid measures. Yoshida ordered a curfew from ten PM till seven AM, with few exceptions granted on an individual basis. There was no ambiguity or fine-print legal subtleties in the instructions for the patrolmen: "No one's allowed to get away unchecked; shoot if you need to."

A few shots fired on the first night of the curfew brought one suspect dead and two wounded, all three in possession of stolen goods and weapons. There were no shooting incidents the next night; the cockroaches understood the change of situation and hid again. Carol Nakamoto was surprised how effective the simple measures could be.

The long table at the Round Hose easily accommodated twelve people; everyone who had any interest in the town's management could get a seat.

"How come no help is coming from Honolulu or even the mainland?" Kalani asked the question that everyone had on his mind.

"Probably Honolulu's been hit just as badly as us.... Still, they couldn't just disappear under the water like Atlantis. We keep sending radio messages on our emergency transmitter. They confirm receipt ... but don't send back any concrete orders or instruction. Just 'Hold on, folks.'" Yoshida was baffled as well.

"They have emergency warehouses ... supposed to share in a situation like this," Carol Nakamoto added. "How about the military? How about the Marines in Kaneohe?"

"That's a very strange story," Cat tried to explain. "We've sent a delegation asking for help, and they didn't even let them past the gate. A Major Stevens, their public relations officer, troubled himself to come to the gateway in order to explain that they were on the highest alert. No one is allowed on or off the base.

"They refused to share food rations or fuel with the town. Basically, they told us to get lost. They have their own problems and would rather not be bothered. Looks like they might be off to Iran shortly. Eventually, after much pleading, they agreed to provide a phone link to their headquarters. There it is, sitting on that glass table, if any of you would like to talk to Major Stevens."

"At the same time, they are flying choppers over the island, wasting fuel," remarked Yoshida gloomily.

The candle illuminating the table was almost completely burnt out, its wick flickering in a small pool of wax at the bottom of a jam jar. The meeting's participants just stared ahead; no one had anything else to say as extreme tiredness overtook their minds. Even with their eyes partly open, they ceased to function, no matter what the consequences could be.

"We're just wasting time sitting here; let's get some rest."

Yoshida stood up, took two steps towards the wall, removed a heavy volume from a bookcase, lay down with the book for a pillow and fell asleep almost immediately.

Cat closed her eyes and was about to doze off when Kalani shook her shoulder.

"You can't sleep sitting, Cat, you know it...."

Of course, she knew—with her lower body numb and immobile while she slept, she could develop necrotic skin ulcers.

"Thanks, Kalani."

Sleep went away while Kalani wheeled her to the small side office Cat appropriated as her living quarters. She eased her body out of the chair onto a small day bed. "So, how did it happen that you're with Abe again?"

Kalani felt a bit defensive. "Actually, we are not together. I love him and I want him sooo bad.... But we can't go on as we used to. We decided to start again from the beginning. Maybe we'll get it better the second time around."

Kalani kept Cat's hand as though she was pleading for understanding. "I'm not afraid of him anymore. What happened is something ... he doesn't understand. But I am sure he'll never do it again. The next day after that scene at your house, he was waiting for me on the street when I was leaving for work. I was a bit afraid, but he was very sweet and gentle.

"He wanted to come back to our apartment. But I said no. Not because I was afraid of him; I was afraid of myself. I knew that if he hugged me and kissed me, we would be in bed in no time, and then we would be back to the same old game. No—we start from scratch. He lives with his old buddy and we're dating. It's fun!" She giggled like a teenager.

"You smart woman," Cat mumbled, her eyelids drooping, "and I like this bum of yours." She fell into a heavy sleep filled with nightmares. Her hands and arms were covered with bruises and scabs, her blond hair matted into a semblance of dreadlocks, dirty and sticky. Cat's thin and pale face, colored only by a greenish tinge, was the face of the town which, hit with two mortal blows, refused to die.

Chapter 24

Cat, January 17

The sun was up, painting Kailua in bright colors. The luscious green shades of the unmowed grass thriving under the winter rains, the golden shine bouncing off cadaveric cars littering the streets like dead beetles, and the innocent blue of the clear sky confirmed the old truth: Mother Nature neither has memory nor gives a damn.

Residents emerged from their ruined homes late, still exhausted from surviving the previous day, but ready to resume the increasingly futile pursuit: looking for food. Seven days after the earthquake, personal food stores were running low. Fortunately, clean water could be collected from roofs and flat surfaces every night.

Cat scribbled on a piece of paper:

Priorities:
1. antibiotics and surgical supplies
2. food
3. fuel

She underlined the word "antibiotics." As she was mechanically adorning her note with flowering vines, she thought,There must be some emergency supplies on the

island. Someone has them. They're sitting on the provisions, use them but won't share with us. She added to her note:
Suspects:
  military
  state

Cat made a frame around the word "military." If we don't force them, they won't share—it's that simple. Doesn't look like they're going to be shamed into cooperation, she thought, picking on her left hand's itchy scab. Is there anything they might want from us? Do we have any leverage?

She threw a tennis ball toward the girl sleeping on the floor. The ball bounced and fell on the crumpled body. Leila raised her head, looking at the table.

"Leila, sorry to wake you up. Can you try to find someone who does water management at the city manager's office?"

Leila got up without a word, got on her bike and left. An hour later, a short man arrived. He had to be quite overweight once, since his pants were loosely hanging on a belt.

"Lee Kurohara, Town Hall. What can I do for you?"

Cat was continually surprised to see other people taking orders from her, almost anticipating them. After all, she was not a manager or chairman or director of anything. She was just an upstart telling people what to do, that's all.

"*Mana*, special power," Kalani declared. "You have *mana*, that's what Abe said. Some people have it and some don't. High priests and *ali'i* had *mana*, but even they had to be careful; it was granted by gods but could be stolen. He learned those things from the old guy, Pono, who lived close to *heiau*. Whoever touched you could pilfer some. And women were the worst …" She giggled. "Abe has to sleep off every time I pinch his *mana*."

Whatever the nature of her authority, Cat was prepared to carry on as long as there was someone willing to listen.

"Lee, can you tell me how the water supply works in

Kailua? We have no big problems now because it rains every night, but if the rains stopped, how could we get our water?"

"Well, we do have a lot of water in the reservoir." Kurohara shrugged. "It's actually full. But we can't pump it—no power. Then, if we actually pumped, it would all escape through broken pipes. The whole system is screwed up. It would take a lot of time to repair it, even if we had power and materials."

"Fair enough." Cat had a great temptation to tear into her left hand with her nails, but refrained. "Would you be able to reconstruct a line to some central location? Maybe close to the Times store? You know, a public watering hole so that people could come and get it."

"I'm sure we could—good idea," Kurohara agreed, surprised he didn't think of it himself. "But … we would have to pump it manually. You would have to send us some strong men."

"No problem, Lee." Cat did not want to think now how much manpower that would require. A lot of exercise … definitely. Even paddlers wouldn't like it on an empty stomach.

"One more thing—is there anybody else pumping water from our reservoir? After all, nobody gets as much rain as we do."

"There is a big pipeline to the leeward side," Kurohara answered without thinking, "but it's broken as well, and we've shut it down." He considered the question for a moment then dismissively added, "And there is a small pipeline to the Marine base, which somehow survived the shake without big damage. It leaks somewhat but pressure can be maintained. I know that because the base draws their water; they have a pumping station on their side and run it."

Cat said nothing—deep in her thoughts—until she realized the manager was still waiting for her response. "Thank you, Lee. I'll be in touch with you, probably in the next few hours."

She wheeled to the dusty glass table where a black telephone set up by the Marines rested on top. She sat there for a few minutes, staring at the apparatus and tapping her broken fingernails on the glass. What's there to lose? She sighed and reached out. "Major Stevens, please."

A few minutes later, an energetic voice sounded from the other end of the line. "Major Stevens. Whom am I talking to?"

"Major Stevens, my name is Cat. I am calling from Kailua. You spoke with our delegation a few days ago."

"I'm sorry, ma'am, I know you have a big problem on your hands, but we can't help you."

"Major, I am not calling about our problem. I am calling about your problem. Your water supply will be interrupted in thirty minutes. We have to shut it down for repairs, indefinitely."

"What kind of joke is this? And who are you?"

"As I said, my name is Cat Milewski, and I am just one of those people you refused to help. This is not a joke; your last drops are running in right now. However, we could try to help you, if you help us."

"Lady, if you are trying to blackmail the Marine Corps, you are in deep trouble!" The voice sounded surprised rather than angry. This situation was too absurd.

Cat drew a line in the dust on the table in front of her. "So what are you going to do? Drop some napalm on Kailua?" She sounded dismissively unperturbed. "You just don't understand how big our problem is, Major." Cat added some frantic whine to her performance. "We are desperate people. We are dying by the dozens every day."

Now her voice deepened, mixing in the dark pitch of threat. "We're not looking for any additional trouble, but if you don't help us, we will keep dying. We will not accept it! Either you help us or we'll do our best to make you, and the world, notice us. We are well past being afraid of what you might do to us!"

The silence on the other end of the line lasted a full twenty seconds, while Stevens tried to process the implications of this conversation. "Can I call you back? I need to speak with the commanding officer."

"May I suggest," Cat answered calmly, "that you come here in person and see for yourself. I can see your choppers flying, so obviously you do have fuel. I'm in the house at the corner of Kalaheo and Kailua Road." She gently put down the phone and stretched the rigid muscles of her arms.

They'll come … either to talk or to arrest me. Most likely I'd be better off in their dungeon. She smiled tensely.

Chapter 25

Cat, January 17

Kalani's success had become her nightmare. She collected nine stray kids camping in the streets and parks of Kailua and brought them to the Round House. They took up residence upstairs: a baby, maybe a year old, pulled from the wreckage, her parents confirmed dead; a ten-year-old girl named Ashley whose parents and brother had disappeared, their bodies probably somewhere on the reef; and seven others, between the ages of two and six, who seemingly belonged to nobody. The hungry mouths cleaned out the house pantry by day four, despite the meager rations they were limited to. From that time on, the only food available was what Kalani could beg or steal.

Both she and Cat lived on a few bites a day of whatever was available. For the most part, Abe kept them alive, making long trips into the fields of central Oahu. He climbed over the Koolau Mountains, walked many miles, hiding from gangs preying on foragers like him, to get a few pineapples, guavas or papayas. The big man lost much of his imposing bulk, eating only what had been left after the sack for Kalani was filled. But Abe was never happier in his life, except maybe for those few months when he first met Kalani. He was in love and could show his affection the way men did for thousands of years. He fed and protected his mate despite all the difficulties that fate piled up in his way.

Kalani felt the end of the rope she was hanging on ominously close and needed a moral boost. Leaving the kids in Ashley's charge, she walked down the stairway to Cat, who sat alone at her big table at the end of the cavernous hall, staring into the sunlit window.

"What's up, Cat? Any food coming from anywhere?"

"Working on it." Cat smiled mysteriously. "We can expect some military vehicles soon, carrying either supplies or the military police to get us rebels under lock and key. I hope your young delinquents will qualify for a military jail. Can you imagine all the food they would feed us?"

"Food is good … but what have you done exactly?" Kalani felt uneasy with many of Cat's ideas.

"Oh, I've just told the Marines we would cut off their water line. And, if they don't show up here in an hour, I will do just that. They must have some reserves on the base, but a lot of people live there. They can't ignore us for long. They'll be here the moment their toilets stop flushing."

Kalani's mouth opened. "You're crazy, Cat!" She stood up and nervously walked to the window.

Thirty-five minutes later, a dark-green Humvee, a mean-looking bumper in front and two tall antennas whipping above it, rumbled along the broken pavement of Kailua Road and stopped in front of the Round House, pulverizing dried mud into a cloud of brown dust. A tall, broad-shouldered officer dressed in yellow-and-brown fatigues emerged from the passenger side, and two soldiers jumped out of the back. The officer put his hat on and marched through the open gate into the big yard; the soldiers stayed with the truck.

"They're here," Kalani reported from the window, rubbing her sweaty palms against her dress.

"Do they have 'MP' on their helmets?" Cat could not hide her anxiety.

"Only one is coming, and he has no helmet, no 'MP.'"

The officer stopped in the doorway. "I am Major Stevens. I'm looking for Cat Milewski."

"I am Cat." She wheeled to the door and stopped in front of the man, defiantly looking up into his eyes. "Do you come with gifts or napalm, Major?"

Stevens stood still while his eyes adapted to the darkness of the room. What he seemed to see was a painfully thin female figure sitting in a wheelchair. How old is she, for God's sake, sixteen? Like a sixteen-year-old who ran away from home, he thought, surprised.

"You are Cat? The person who tried to shake down the Marine Corps?" Stevens could see her clearly now, and it became apparent to him that his initial plan of dealing with this nuisance was not workable. His intended tactic to break the offender with threats and verbal abuse first, before offering some modest help, would not work because he couldn't bring himself to execute it. He needed to regroup.

"You certainly have guts...." He could not hide a certain admiration for Cat's audacity. "Look—we are a military establishment. We operate by orders. It is not our decision to give away the government-issue supplies, whether we like it or not. You are trying to step on the wrong people's toes."

"Just a moment, Major. Could I ask you to go upstairs with my friend for a moment, and then we'll continue our conversation?"

Stevens followed Kalani to the second floor where she introduced him to the children, who were bunched together behind a big bed, afraid of the stranger. A litter of homeless puppies, he thought, looking into the sunken eyes cowering in the shade, faces covered with sores and crusts.

He felt relief when he could turn away and walk downstairs where the skinny person in the wheelchair awaited him. She should be in child protective custody as well, he thought.

"Do you have any children, Major?"

"Two." He extended two fingers, nodding.

"Do they look anything like that bunch upstairs?" Cat mounted an attack, without raising her voice.

The officer shrugged and averted his eyes.

"Do you think they deserve some protection from their government?"

He was under assault now, no question. The blue eyes below were angrily digging into his face, trying to intimidate him.

"Isn't there anything in your officer's code of conduct saying that the children of this country should get the most basic assistance when in dire need? I know you have the Iran problem, but that means nothing to those guys upstairs. They'll be dead before you sort out your latest adventure."

Major Stevens raised a hand like a traffic cop stopping the flow of traffic. "Hold it! Look, there's no need for any more of this." He shook her off his back like a big dog getting rid of an aggressive hissing cat. "The commander has agreed to provide you with a small amount of medical supplies and food. It comes from our standard provisions, unauthorized. He can get into a lot of trouble for that. We hope it'll get you over the hump, until FEMA wakes up. But … if we hear anything more about the water supply interruption, your town will be crawling with a lot of uniformed and very unfriendly men."

He could not resist a smile in response to the big grin on Cat's face.

"Thank you, Major Stevens. What's your first name?"

"It's Gary." Stevens seemed embarrassed.

"Thank you, Gary, and please convey our gratitude to your commander."

The two soldiers brought from the truck ten boxes of food rations, five bags of rice and five boxes marked with the Red Cross logo as Kalani watched from the upper stairway landing with a big happy grin on her face.

"On your way back, could you please drop it all off at the hospital, except for one box of food rations and one bag of rice?" Cat stole a look upstairs just in time to see the frown on Kalani's face replacing her smile.

"No problem, ma'am." The soldiers left to climb into the truck.

"Gary, can we count on some more help in the future?" She was staring straight into the major's eyes, willing him to say "yes."

"You are a remarkable woman, Cat; I would love to help you out. But short of a mutiny, the CO won't be able to give anything else without permission. But he is working on that." Stevens climbed into his truck and the Humvee kicked the brown dust storm again, jumping over the broken pavement.

"Well, we've dodged this one; we should be OK for a few days," Kalani announced from the stairway. "But it broke my heart seeing those supplies going back on the truck." She looked at Cat with accusation then shrugged with resignation. "I know, I know—the hospital is doing even worse than we do. Maybe we'll make it until something gets in from Honolulu. Anyway, I hoped they would arrest us all." She gave Cat a happy smirk and went back to her kids.

Two days later another military vehicle pulled up in front of the Round House but it did not even cut its motor. Two helmeted men in combat fatigues jumped out and pulled two large duffel bags from the back seat. Running, they brought them in and dumped the load just across the threshold. They were already on the way back when Cat intercepted them.

"Wait, wait! What's in the bags and who sends them?"

"That's from Major Stevens, ma'am. He bought out the whole cafeteria and told us to bring it here. But we have to go ..."

"Where is Major Stevens?"

"He's gone, ma'am, and we have to go, too. Bye." They

waved and left, their vehicle's roar heard for a while in the silent streets.

"Chocolate, chips, candies, fruit bars…. The kids will go ape." Kalani was digging through the bags.

"He spent his own money to get this stuff for us." Cat was gazing into space. "Good, decent man. And yet … tell me, Kalani: Why would an intelligent, honest person voluntarily give up his own judgment to anyone higher up? I don't know about you, but to me … to take orders, no questions asked, it's like being a slave. Stupid … and if you're in the business of killing people, downright immoral."

"Well, when you're with the Marines, you do what they tell you." Kalani shrugged.

"You have to be either brain-dead"—Cat looked at her angrily—"then obviously someone has to pull strings for the puppet to move, or through-and-through corrupt—then you don't care what you do. Gary Stevens is none of the above." She fell silent, thinking about the other man, an owner of a very good mind who refused to put it to good use.

"Cat, I need to hide these bags before Ashley comes back with the kids. Can we put them in your room? It's just like the night after Halloween. My mother always hid our loot bags, and we would find treats only from time to time. We felt she was robbing us!"

The duffel bags went under Cat's bed. She lay down for a short nap, trying to figure out what was the third category that Gary Stevens and Jerry Roberts could fit into: not brainless and not immoral … but ready to follow orders without having them well examined. Brainwashed? This was her best guess before she fell asleep. Somehow it made her feel better, maybe because the condition of being brainwashed is potentially reversible, unlike the two other afflictions.

Chapter 26

Cat, January 18–20

"We've got a radio conference with the governor, tomorrow, eight o'clock. You all need to come to the station." Yoshida looked around the table. The usual crowd: Cat, Kalani, Lee Kurohara, Carol, Dr. Lim and a few others who dropped in from time to time, if they had some business to attend to. Not a democratically elected government of Kailua, he realized, rather the folks who took responsibilities nobody else wanted, but they would do.

A few were town employees, like Kurohara; Carol was a career politician; and some, like Cat and Kalani, were until recently citizens so private that no journalist would report on them if they were shouting their speeches hanging upside down from a tree.

"Someone needs to speak for us," Yoshida continued, walking behind the backs of the meeting participants like a teacher. "The governor prefers an elected official. I guess that would be you, Carol?" He stopped behind Yakamoto. "You are here frequently enough to know our problems." The sergeant bated his voice, waiting for her acceptance.

"That's fine," Carol declared with a glad smile. "I'll be glad to if everyone agrees." Eventually, her patience and serenity in the face of Cat's crazy antics would pay off.

Nobody objected and the meeting moved on to the next item.

"Good news," a large man with a braid of thin, gray hair announced. "We've fixed our radio transmitter so KLBY can go back on the air. Obviously, we have no power and have to rely on a generator, so we'll broadcast only as long as someone gives us a few gallons of gas."

"That's terrific!" Carol almost clapped her hands. "People need local information almost as badly as food. We have a new panic every day, and there is no way to respond. Yesterday, there was the story of rats attacking sleeping children, but we had no such reports from the emergency room. Today, I heard that the water collected from the roofs was contaminated with radioactive fallout. Where this fallout might be coming from, and who spreads these lies, I have no idea, but people are ready to believe anything now. Someone should give a daily, short service of local news."

Nobody moved. A few long seconds later Cat sighed, "OK, I'll do it." In this way, Cat had become the voice of the lost world of Kailua.

The next morning at ten o'clock, after dealing with the first round of problems piling up overnight, Cat rode her chair toward a small building a few blocks away, where KLBY, a local radio station, had its studio. The sun-filled street felt like a different world after she emerged from the darkened cavernous hall of the Round House. Broken pavement and collapsed houses did not heal on their own, but nature was not holding off. New grass and weeds grew boldly out of the cracks and bougainvilleas assertively displayed huge red and purple bunches of flowers, taking advantage of the rainy season. A thin black cat jumped out of a bush, hoping for a handout.

Life goes on, Cat thought, trying to get her wheelchair

over a foot-wide break in the asphalt. Whatever happens to you ... is your problem. Everything and everybody minds their own business—animals, plants, and as far as people go ... some care, but only if they are close friends or family.

"Friends, this is your neighbor, Cat, speaking. I used to live by the canal, in Kaimalino." She went on with a long list of reports about the water quality, about the prospects for getting fuel, about diseases seen at the emergency room. She shared what she knew about orphaned children, about hunger—a lengthy list of evils, which would sound familiar to grandparents of her audience, but faded into the category of grim fairy tales during fat years of prosperity. Now, when the cataclysm hit, they reemerged with all the painful palpability of real-world problems, like a cancerous tumor appearing on the neck of someone who thought himself cured.

"And, since it is Friday today, I'd like to beseech you not to commit the sin of gluttony."

A wave of belly laughter and giggling rolled over the island. That's too much, too rich—overeating in Hawaii was certainly not a problem in January 2011. People needed this joke to release their tension, frustration and pain of the last days; and they loved the person who gave it to them.

A group of Kailua citizens squeezed into the police department's lunchroom where the speaker—crudely patched from the communications center—whistled somewhat, but the voice of the governor's aide came in clearly. After a brief exchange of greetings, the aide announced, "Please stand by for the governor."

Carol shifted in her chair and brought the microphone closer to her lips.

"Good morning, everyone. This is Nancy Brown," the governor spoke with the confidence of authority, her voice rich in low, warm, reassuring tones. "I am so glad that we, at last, have this opportunity to talk and share our experiences during these trying times. It is an awful, unacceptable situation that the windward side of Oahu is cut off from Honolulu so completely. We are very worried about you. Can you please give me a short assessment of your situation?"

"Good morning, Madame Governor," Carol started in a smooth, nicely modulated voice. "Thank you so much for taking the time to speak with us. We know how busy you must be. These terrible events, both the natural calamities and the geopolitical challenges our country has to meet, call for the utmost in our resolve and courage. We are certainly trying to cope."

Cat and Yoshida exchanged stupefied glances; Kalani leaned to the next person at the table and quietly whispered something, drawing a dry grin.

"Yes, yes," said the governor, "I am so glad that you understand the enormous difficulty of our position. Our resources are hardly sufficient for the population of Honolulu alone, and the relief effort from the federal government is seriously hampered by the military activities in the Middle East. By the way, whom am I talking to?"

"Oh, this is Carol Nakamoto … I'm sorry I didn't introduce myself. My apologies …" Carol was smiling her best smile and almost giggled.

"What the hell are you talking about?" Cat's shrill and unrestrained voice cut into the very civil conversation like a horsewhip. She snatched the microphone from the hands of a shocked Carol.

"Governor! We came to this conversation to find out how you can help us. We have been left to ourselves for more than ten days. We are completely out of food now; there are no emergency supplies here. We are almost completely out of fuel, even to run a generator for the police station. We have no medical supplies; people are dying every day from simple infections. What are you going to do about it? We cannot cope by ourselves anymore!"

The silence on the air stretched for many seconds before a question came. "Who is this?"

"My name is Cat Milewski. I coordinate some of the work we're doing in Kailua. And what's the importance of my name? I would like to know why we haven't received any emergency supplies yet. I know that the roads are closed, but how about airdrops? How about supplies by boat? To the best of my knowledge, the sky didn't fall and Kailua Beach is still open!"

Brown recovered somewhat, and answered in a stern but not unfriendly voice, "Cat, I understand that you are desperate, but so are we. I don't have any helicopters or transport planes at my disposal, and we are running on the last drops of fuel ourselves. We do have some food reserves, but I also have close to a million people to feed. The truth is, I cannot promise you any significant relief."

"How about the National Guard, aren't they supposed to help in such circumstances? How about the military? We see them flying over our heads, wasting fuel. What's with the federal government, the rest of the country? Ten days is not enough to send some help?"

"The National Guard had been committed somewhere else. The military cannot provide any assistance because of the Middle East events. I can assure you that the helicopters you see flying do so for very good reasons. We do receive some modest relief from the federal government, but the port facilities are mostly ruined."

"Does that mean you are going to leave us here to die because our government is too busy? That we keep all these military bases in Hawaii for someone else's benefit? Hell, what's the use of being a part of the glorious Union? Maybe we should start looking for new tenants for Pearl Harbor!"

"Cat, you are talking treason now. I suggest you calm down and give the microphone back to Carol!" The voice was cold, containing an unveiled threat.

"Just one more thing, Governor! I want you, and your buddies in Washington, to know that some of us will survive, and this conversation will be remembered. If you abandon us now, don't expect our loyalty in the future. We are not traitors; you are! Our loyalty will be to our families and neighbors, people who helped us as we helped them. Today, we've found out that the promises you made for years are empty. You can go to hell!"

Cat threw the microphone on Carol's lap, backed away from the table and furiously wheeled out, followed by Kalani.

New York Times: Cat to Governor, "Go to Hell!"

International Tribune: "Hawaii to U.S.—Traitors"

London Times: "Your promises are empty,
 our loyalty is not for you."

The transcript of a conversation recorded in a Washington restaurant by an unnamed security service:

Voice 1: The whole conversation was over the open airways. Anybody with a scanner could hear and record it. And, believe me, there are a lot of scanners in and around Hawaii. Reuters made the transcripts available through their feeds within two hours. I'm sure there were transcripts with URGENT stamped all over them on some very important desks within a few hours.

Voice 2: So what can they do about it?

Voice 1: Basically, two choices: either have this Cat person arrested and sweep her under the rug, or make her a Very Important Person in a Very Important Government Office.

Voice 2: They can't hide her now; she is already a celebrity.

That would cause an unending open season on the prez. She would come up at every press conference.

Voice 1: Then she has to be promoted until she shuts her face up.

Chapter 27

Jerry, January 12–15

By dawn, *Lady Luck* was forty miles off the California coast, laying a white trail behind her stern as she gracefully heeled in the fifteen-knot wind. Jerry and John had slept little during the past two days, but the skipper was wide-awake and cheerful like a robin on a spring day. It seemed to Jerry, who felt queasy, that the old buzzard might break into a loud triumphant song. He turned on a wind vane, a wind-driven autopilot, to take over the steering duties and climbed down below the deck.

Jerry remained in the cockpit, where—although cold—he was a tad less nauseous as well as closer to the boat's side, in case his stomach proved to be stronger than his will not to vomit. He heard a pan banging on the burner and the crackling of eggs on hot metal. The skipper was making breakfast, humming and thumping a spoon on a cutting board in the rhythm of a fast mambo.

A steaming cup of coffee emerged from the companionway followed by John's balding head.

"Take your coffee, Jerry. Eggs will be ready in a moment."

"What is it with you, John?" Jerry grumbled as he reached

down to take the mug. "Are you high on drugs now? I didn't know you were such a fun-loving reveler." The smell of fried eggs filling the companionway turned his head away.

"Ho, ho, there is no happier moment for a sailor than the first morning on the sea." Browser's grinning face appeared under another coffee mug. "Well, perhaps, except for the first morning after landfall. Are you feeling sick, Jerry?"

"Maybe not really sick," Jerry hedged his admission, "but I surely don't feel like eating anything … least of all the greasy eggs you've made. I forgot to take Dramamine."

"I have news for you, my boy." The rest of John's figure came into view as he emerged from below with a frying pan in his hand. He placed the eggs on the table to free his hand, and his right index jabbed the air in Jerry's direction. "You'll get worse as we pick up more wind; this balmy weather will not last. But then you will get better. None of this Dramamine nonsense. Do you know that Admiral Nelson got seasick every time they left port? Nobody saw him on deck on the first day of a journey—puking in his cabin probably … and look how well he did afterwards!

"You have it so much better without all the pressure he had to take! Be my guest and lean over the lee railing anytime you feel like, no shame. Enjoy the fresh air and this wonderful view! As for Dramamine … maybe on a cruise ship … even then you would have to be careful with booze, so what's the point? But on a boat like ours—you might get drowsy, fall overboard, and that's where your trip would end. Better get used to it. But you have to eat, very important …"

Jerry waved his eggs away with disgust but had some black coffee and felt marginally better. When the nausea subsided completely he could not say, because the skipper started his sailing school immediately, leaving no time for introspection.

Anyone observing *Lady Luck* would have to conclude that her crew fell to some mental disorder, perhaps due to spoiled food or an excess of fermented hop and barley. The boat tacked, jibed and drifted; her floppy sails bulging with the wind like bed sheets drying on a line, only to be tightened a moment later into flat planes rigid like sheet metal. *Lady Luck* gracefully ran with the wind, ferociously crashed into the waves and stood her place, restrained, shaking like in a fit of malaria. The sails came down and went up; the sea anchors were deployed and picked up, while she made big irregular circles amidst the open ocean stretching in all directions.

The skipper wished to take advantage of the gentle weather, suitable for training, despite Jerry's concerns about delaying their arrival to Hawaii.

"This is not a highway," Browser countered. "You take advantage of whatever is offered to you. We have the right conditions to train, we train. Don't worry about wasting good wind— I'm pretty sure we'll have more than we need pretty soon."

Jerry cleaned fuel filters, tied knots and trimmed sails, feeling like a young cadet on a man o' war. As he barely coped with the steep learning curve John dictated, the skipper annoyed him with his strange attachment to old technologies, like sextant readings every time the sun showed its face above the water. Only then was Jerry allowed to read the boat's latitude from one of the two GPS instruments on board.

"Do you have any guarantee the GPS will be on the next time you want to check your position?" Browser was asking stubbornly. "What if some space junk blows the satellites off? What if the U.S. government decides to turn them off, just to piss off the Iranians? What—"

"What if we get struck by a meteorite, John?" Jerry interrupted, annoyed to see his measurements indicating their position off the coast of Oregon.

The old man looked at the figures and remarked snidely, "Good progress, my boy. Yesterday, I was concerned about the shoals off Alaska. Now, we—I mean you—have to check if the wind vane works properly."

"I know, Skipper, you can't fuck with the ocean." Jerry was resigned to the fact that his work would not be over until John started snoring in his berth.

"Right on."

The twenty-knot northwester, which propelled them some comfortable four hundred miles during the first three days, started changing a few hours after Jerry had noticed the barometric pressure falling. He didn't need the skipper to tell him; they were moving into a low-pressure system and conditions would change for worse.

The boat heeled sharply as gusts of wind pounced on her, only to straighten up a moment later like a tree accustomed to dealing with the blustery weather.

Browser watched the doubly reefed mainsail for a minute, checked the trim of the jib, meditated for a moment and went below deck, snapping in the passage, "Watch it, Jerry!"

As the night fell, the wind singing in the shrouds increased into an obnoxious loud whistling. Jerry watched the white trail—barely visible in the darkness—of *Lady Luck* as she plowed through the waves like a motorboat. Ten knots—he was pleased to see the number on display; they were coming to Hawaii in a hurry.

The waves pounded the boat, emerging from the night like black mountains, invisible until a second before exploding on the deck in white foam. Jerry, enthralled with the speed, yelled for John to wake up only when *Lady Luck*'s railing started disappearing under the white waves, taking longer and longer to come out of the boiling water.

The old man climbed on deck in his yellow rough-weather suit and a fisherman's hat. "Fuck, we're carrying way too much sail. You should have got me up a long time ago. We have to take down the jib."

"OK, Skipper." Jerry started scrambling out of the cockpit.

"Get down here!" The yellow-clad figure impatiently waved at Jerry. "Hold the wheel. I'll do it!"

The waves blasted the shuddering hull every few seconds, bursting in white explosions and flooding the deck with cascades of surging water. The wind speed was increasing very rapidly now. The vibrating deck tilted steeply, and patches of foam flew through the air. A trip to the bow was a risky undertaking for anyone under these conditions, more so for the old man.

"John, I will—"

"Just shut up and hold the wheel! Turn into the wind when you see me at the bow. It's no time to—"

"I know ... fuck with the ocean," Jerry muttered.

Overruled, he watched from the steering wheel as the yellow figure crawled along the railing through the sheets of rain. John stopped next to the mast, gestured toward Jerry, and when the boat's bow pointed into the wind, he lurched at the halyard, disappearing behind the furiously flapping white mass of the mainsail. A long anxious moment later, Jerry saw the flash of the yellow figure, which seemed to swim, waving his arms vigorously in the white pool of the fabric until the jib fell down on him from the invisible height of the mast.

The boat got up off her side and the deck's tilt decreased immediately. John fought the rebellious sail for a few minutes, until he wrestled it down completely and tied it to the railing. Then he inched his way back, and slid into the cockpit. He was smiling widely. "That's the life for us, Jerry, isn't it?"

Jerry looked at the skipper with newfound respect. This was no fragile old-timer at sea; he was Captain Hook. The boat still heeled, but her railing stayed above the water. The winds diminished at dawn, and only then could Jerry fully appreciate the ocean's condition. *Lady Luck* was surrounded by thousands of big waves crowned with angry-looking whitecaps. Streaks of foam still flew with the wind, and long patterns of wrinkles whipped up by the gusts marked the water between breakers.

"What do you think the wind speed is?" The wind meter

had quit working on the second day at sea.

"Forty knots maybe," John answered nonchalantly.

"What do we do if the wind picks up to fifty knots?" Jerry wanted to know.

"We drop the main and deploy a sea anchor."

"And what if it's even stronger?"

"Then, Jerry, we could start saying Hail Mary or open this emergency tequila bottle you've bought. I'm for the bottle."

AP flash news: A Panama-flagged tanker carrying 80,000 tons of crude oil sank after being struck by a land-to-ship missile in the Straits of Hormuz. The crew of 21 is missing.

Reuters' flash update: U.S. carrier-based warplanes and cruise missiles destroy Iranian coastal missile installations.

Chapter 28

Jerry, January 16–19

Once at sea, there was no question who the boss was, but John treated the younger man more like his son than a crew member or even an employer. He never missed an opportunity to teach Jerry something about sailing.

The stinking smoke of his cigarettes stayed outside the cabin even if it rained, and beer flowed at a rate ensuring the happy combination of a good mood and an alert mind. Browser seemed to have visited every obscure harbor of the world in his merchant marine career, and he had a story to tell about most of them.

"But at the end, they are all alike," he concluded. "Your crew gets drunk, local women just want your money and the police treat you like shit. You are really better off out there, at sea. But then, after a week or two, you again want to see concrete piers, trees, bars and some female forms, no matter if they wear dresses, pants or *burkas*."

"John, I have a confession to make…." Jerry felt distinctly uncomfortable, holding back the revelations of his past. Time to come clean, he decided, and the skipper turned to him with an encouraging gesture.

"The Men in Black ... I was their colleague ... for a while, not long. Only I was on the Army payroll."

All semblance of warmth left Browser's face. "You know, I had this feeling when we first met, and you said you didn't work for the government." John looked at the younger man sharply, with no hint of good humor.

"I didn't lie." Jerry met his eyes. "I was indeed with the university for over ten years. But before that ... I had a stint with Army intelligence, which ended in a rather unpleasant way. So, you might say I was a failure as a Man in Black, or if you prefer, a spook redeemed."

"Tell me about it, Jerry." John's shoulders fell as he relaxed somewhat, and his right fist opened to pull a cigarette out of a box. "I would like to hear about that failed spook. Ah, sit on the starboard bench; you should have the sun shining in your eyes." He grinned slightly.

"I wasn't even twenty, and green like a cucumber, when I signed up with the Army. They decided I could be more useful collecting information than blasting enemies to hell." Jerry accepted the offer of a beer and they both gulped in silence. "You realize that every army needs intelligence, so that's what I was trained to do."

John watched Jerry keenly, without interruption.

"People think that you basically beat the information out of prisoners, and I am not saying that it never happens—though I was never a part of it—but it's not true. What you could squeeze out of your captive this way is really not that useful, and has a very short shelf life. Simple information—an address, a name, a phone number—yes, you could have them, but those things change very rapidly. Your information becomes worthless within days or hours, as soon as the news about detention gets out. Often it's worse than worthless; a prisoner can send you on a goose chase. You waste your time and resources while the bad guys are preparing some unpleasant surprise.

"What you really need is the cooperation of your subject. You want him to volunteer information that is more permanent and meaningful, to tell you the structure of their organization, how it operates. Why would he do that? The art of interrogation lies in giving him the reasons. In a sense, you want him to help you for his own selfish reasons. If he comes to believe that your success is to his advantage, you've got yourself a well that never dries up. Even if he really has nothing more to tell, he can still help you to understand those disconnected scraps of info coming your way from other sources—a cryptic note in someone's calendar, an offhand and apparently innocent comment on the phone, a name without face and background information ... this kind of stuff."

"Sounds pretty benign so far," John remarked. "Almost hard to believe."

"Well, it's not benign, John. This approach is quite easy with common criminals; public prosecutors cut deals of this nature all the time. But criminals are not particularly well known for high ethic standards and loyalty. They sell their comrades for a lighter sentence without scruples.

"It's a completely different story with extremists, terrorists, rebels and whomever else the Army needs to deal with. Those are committed people; they actually believe in their causes and often don't give a damn about their lives. You can call them any ugly name you prefer, but they are strong believers, no matter how misguided. Otherwise, they wouldn't be there in the first place."

John nodded with understanding but raised his hand to stop Jerry. He walked to a winch to adjust the mainsail, which had started wrinkling and fluttering, then returned to his seat. "You were saying ..."

"I was saying that in order to bring those people over to your side, you have to destroy their beliefs, honor and self-respect. You have to kill their soul. It can be done—not always, but even an occasional success is a big breakthrough. They are exposed to relentless pressure, anxiety, fear and sleep deprivation—until they crack. The object is to turn them into stinky, shaking goo, whose only desire is to be left alone or get some small favor, like a warm blanket for a night. Once they start talking, they have no way back. Their every attempt to resist is countered by the threat that their earlier deeds of cooperation will be leaked to their former comrades."

"A soul killer. Congratulations, Jerry." Browser's mouth was set in an angry grimace, and his irony contained no hint of good-humored ribbing. "You better tell me quickly how you failed in your work. I feel tempted to take the dinghy and part ways with you, leaving you and the boat you've bought."

"The problem with this business, John, is that soul killing is a very dangerous job. Every time the screw tightens on your client, it does something strange to you, too. In effect, it kills you both, at least if you were a normal person to start with. There are people who seem to be particularly well suited for this line of work, but you wouldn't like them in your preferred circle of friends. In fact, some of them enjoy this work so much that they get kicked out on the grounds of committing torture crimes. My unit had a guy who deserted some years ago in Panama the very day an investigation had been launched into his methods. More often interrogators just break down, like I did. That's why the Army always needs new blood."

"I'm glad to hear you broke down, Jerry." John's eyes lost their metallic look. "How did you get out of this mess?"

"We were in Somalia. I inherited a turncoat Arab who used to be an officer with the insurgents—a tall, handsome man, member of a respected local family. He had been worked on for two months before I got him, and started giving some valuable insights. His handler had to be sent home and he fell into my lap.

"I did a terrible thing, John: I developed some sympathy for him. I knew all about his life. I saw pictures from when he was a boy at school. I knew more about his wife than about my sister. I was thoroughly familiar with his kids … He was a menace to our troops, no question, but I saw him also as a brave, upright man, a guy you would want as your neighbor.

"Under my mismanagement, this man bounced back from the bottom, and started having second thoughts. Those were not any coherent ideas—he was anything but a rational human being at this stage—but he knew that his only escape from the nightmare was to die. My job was to put a jackhammer to this newly found self-respect and remorse. I tried, John, and I failed miserably. His chance to go back to his previous life had been irrevocably annihilated by his cooperation, but he begged for the opportunity just to stop his existence."

"What did you do, Jerry?" The skipper held his breath.

"I couldn't let him go free, of course. I couldn't let him touch my weapon either. The only thing I could do for him was to shoot him myself. That day, he knew I was going to kill him; he looked into my eyes with deep gratitude, love almost. Well, I failed even at that. The interpreter who was in the room knocked me down the moment I reached for my side arm. Apparently, Captain Murphy, my commander, had some suspicions about me; the interpreter had been ordered to knock me on the head the moment I reached for my weapon."

"And they let you get away with it?" John clearly was not convinced.

"Well, just lucky coincidence." Jerry shrugged. "I was under arrest, awaiting my superior's decision what to do with me. You know, court martial or whatever he might come up with … and he was not a nice man. No belt, no shoelaces—standard procedure. Then, the commanding general appeared suddenly for an unannounced inspection. When I heard the general was visiting, I thought he might want to see the rotten bottom of the barrel as well, the miscreants under arrest. You have to understand, John, I was pretty crazy then, just a notch above my Somali. I had no hopes for a normal life. Heck, I'd lost the concept of normal life, living there at the edge of the desert—sleeping, interrogating, writing reports and getting drunk so I could sleep.

"No laces—no shoes; no belt—no pants, I thought. When the general entered my cell I was standing at attention in my jacket and nothing else. The old man looked at me for a moment, said nothing to me, then turned to Murphy who was standing behind him. 'I see why your reports read like someone crazy wrote them, Murphy. I want this man sent back home immediately.'"

"So they just sent you back to the U.S.?"

"I was on a plane next day, but that was certainly not the end of it. The shrink on the base talked to me a few times and, eventually, I got discharged on the grounds of being unfit to serve. I did exaggerate my mental problems a bit, of course. But the fact was, John, I was really screwed up big time."

"I can't blame you." John shrugged. "I'd be disappointed if you weren't."

"The shrink wrote a report that got me off the hook. He said that I had a psychopathic trait, and had the emotional capacity of a brick wall, although I was quite normal until my overseas adventure. Whatever. It did the trick; they kicked me out. I think Murphy wanted to get rid of me with minimal damage to his career and added his own little insight about my mental fitness."

"So what happened next?" John was fascinated, like he was watching a spy movie. "Did you go back to your family, your old place?"

"I tried, John, but it didn't work out. I felt that my father had given me bad advice that screwed up my life; I didn't want to see him. I realize he meant well, but I still can't bear to see him. I agreed with the psychiatrist that I should stay away from the public as much as I could. I had lost the ability to treat people as persons. We had been trained to see humans as objects—to be intimidated, manipulated and exploited. I hated this new personality of mine, but couldn't shake it off. I was a very lonely man after the discharge.

"Women ... they wanted me a lot, but wouldn't stay with me; my turnover was mind-boggling. They often didn't understand what the problem was ... There was a lot of crying, but in the end nobody could connect with me. In a way I was a brick wall; no roots could penetrate beneath the stucco. It was even worse with men: I had these attacks of aggression, was close to killing a few guys over really minor stuff."

"And you say you were a professor, you taught kids?" John turned his head, amazed.

"The Army knows how to keep their secrets, John. I don't think my professor ever got his hands on my medical file. In any case, I enrolled into economics, and found out that I could find peace working in front of a computer monitor.

I breezed through my undergrad years and did a Ph.D. in econometrics. I was good at it and had more time on my hands than other guys. You see, I knew all the emotional buttons to push to get sex, and I didn't want or need anything else from girls. So, I spent a lot of nights at the library, while my fellow postgraduates entertained their girlfriends or wasted time visiting their parents. Not that it made me happy, but I learned that it just didn't matter. I was simply not interested in them as people, and they would figure that out sooner rather than later."

"So what the hell are we doing here, in the middle of the Pacific?" John raised his arms to the heavens. "I thought you were a puppy in love. Now what, a squid in love?" He was perplexed and growing impatient.

"A miracle happened, John." Jerry took his sunglasses off. "I met a girl in Hawaii who simply tugged on my old, stiff, uncomfortable skin and it fell off, like from a shedding snake."

"Hallelujah! I hoped there would be a happy end to this story, Jerry." The skipper went downstairs to bring up a new beer pack.

> Reuters' news flash: Price of crude shoots to 180 dollars a barrel today. The Department of Energy announces release of strategic reserves to counteract shortages.

John was not optimistic about the current conditions of life in Hawaii; he did not hold humankind in high esteem. "People look after themselves, Jerry. When there is plenty of everything and the weather is fine, you can see a lot of nice folks, charity and so on. But when food gets scarce or a disaster of some sort strikes—watch out! There are no nice folks anymore, just mobs of guys ready to steal your last piece of bread or kill you for it.

"I saw it in Pakistan, saw it in Kenya and I am sure you saw it in Somalia. I don't think we would be any different in the U.S. It's just that nobody has been really hungry in America for a long time, so we forgot how it feels. We better be very careful when we get to Hawaii. A boat like this, with supplies, would be a great target for anyone who can get to her."

On the morning of the tenth day after their departure from San Diego, a mountain appeared on the horizon. "Mauna Kea, Big Island," the skipper declared. John knew Hilo, a town on the island, since he worked on a cruise ship calling at this port regularly.

"If you want to see a place where people get along fairly well, and someone's skin color or shape of face is not that important, this is it. You'll see it tomorrow. That's how God meant for people to behave."

This piqued Jerry's interest because, as a New Yorker, he always believed that the Big Apple was a model—even if an imperfect one—of interracial integration. Wave after wave of immigrants, speaking hundreds of languages, descended on the city and somehow sank into its big body, although they differed in appearance just as much as Collies and Dobermans.

John just waved his hand dismissively. "That's your upper-middle-class experience talking, Jerry. Yes, if you have enough money, you can have some nice black or brown or yellow neighbors in your expensive condominium. They will have some serious moolah as well and you will get along just fine. But were you challenged in the cash department, you would find very quickly that your waves of immigrants didn't peacefully dissolve into New York's big body. I like your metaphor though; the Big Apple is more like a big, fat whore: you can sink in her and get lost there.

"Africans, Mexicans, Puerto Ricans—they all stick to their own and hate all the others. Even small nations—take El Salvadorians—make their own gangs and try to beat the brains out of the other guys. No, Jerry, there is no brotherly love and understanding on the streets of New York, perhaps except at a few addresses where folks like you live."

A faraway mountain grew within the next few hours, dominating the view on the port side. It had a coal-black top, which turned to yellow and sickly green at the midsection, deepening into lush emerald at its base. Rivers of frozen lava spilled from the lifeless apex like the long hairy legs of a tarantula, cutting deep into the green slopes, reaching for the vibrant vegetation below.

The sun was quickly diving behind the volcano by the time the Big Island's northern shore opened to their eyes. A long, uninterrupted chain of hostile black rocks was shrouded in the fine water spray produced by the pounding surf. This coast did not look like a friendly sanctuary, but further down, along the harsh cliffs, lay Hilo, one the few harbors on this island.

The skipper was back to his musings about racial

integration in Hawaii. "Hilo is a completely different story. There is no big money there; heck—there isn't much medium-size money there. So these guys cannot buy a cocoon around them. Maybe there are some gated communities there, but I've never heard of any.

"They actually learned to tolerate each other. Sure, they aren't blind—they can see your skin color and know which way your eyes are slanting. They tease each other, but where it counts, they don't seem to care much for all those superficial differences.

"Tomorrow in Hilo, you'll see so many interracial couples you'll believe me. Youngsters try to get into each other's pants, no matter what the ass's color, and then they have kids. Let me tell you, Jerry, you can't hate your grandchildren. In fact, most of them, islanders, are so racially mixed up that you could never guess what's in the mix. They say this enlightened attitude goes back to the ancient Hawaiians, a spirit of Aloha. It could be; I've never seen anything like it anywhere else."

According to the pilot book, Hilo had a large harbor protected by a reef and a wave break, which the skipper knew well from his cruise ship times, and a small connected area called Radio Bay, where a sailboat could drop anchor. John planned to stop there to find out what the situation in the Islands was, but by the time they approached the harbor's entrance, the sun was down. With the sky overcast, the night was pitch black and there were no lighted buoys marking the watercourse.

Not willing to risk an encounter with a rock, Browser guided *Lady Luck*, motoring with the speed of a snail, until he could see the breaker's head, faintly distinguishable because of the white spray of waves smashing into the stonewall. He slipped past it and turned into the black space where he hoped the harbor's channel was. Jerry read the depth gauge continuously, expecting the shudder of touching a rock at any moment, while the skipper kept his white-knuckled hand on the lever, ready to roar the engine into reverse instantly. Soon the wind calmed down and the boat stopped wobbling on the waves; they had to be in the protected area. They dropped anchor in eighteen feet of calm water without incident.

"That's good enough—we're protected from the wind and waves." John shut down the motor with relief. "We'll sleep now. At daybreak, we'll take a dinghy to the harbor office and find out about Oahu." Even in the harbor, they were not receiving any regular Hawaii radio stations; just scraps of conversations came through sounding like the communications of a police or fire department.

They opened a bottle of tequila, the first one of the passage, raised a toast to Neptune and went to sleep.

Chapter 29

Rosen, January 21

Reuters: Chinese Navy battle group steams toward Taiwan. State Department requests an urgent meeting with Chinese ambassador. Routine exercises scheduled six months ago, Beijing insists.

Harry Rosen sat in his restaurant, all the doors locked and chained from inside. The windows were broken, but they wouldn't hold back looters anyway. That's why he was sitting in the corner, reclining on two chairs as comfortably as possible, with the food cellar door in clear view and his handgun at his side. The building had not suffered much damage, mostly windows shattered, glass covering the floor now. Rosen found it useful, though—no one could sneak by, taking advantage of him closing his eyes, without a lot of crunching noise.

He was tired from lack of sleep, and his butt was sore from camping in the corner, but otherwise he felt quite well. The storage room was full of canned goods, so even though the refrigerated food had spoiled, he did not fear hunger. The thought of selling food, for a very nice profit, occurred to him for a moment, but he realized that a crowd at his door—a certainty— would be impossible to control. Better wait. For now, his survival was all that counted.

Eventually, the inevitable occurred; his eyes, closed for a moment of rest, did not open as he had planned. He fell asleep.

A piece of glass broke under someone's foot like an alarm bell in the quiet room. Even before Rosen's eyes opened, his right hand closed on the gun handle.

A slim figure was standing just inside of the window. The thief stood motionless, frightened by the crack of glass. Rosen grinned with malice; this one had to be the fifth intruder that day. In a second, he would see the robber flying through the broken window in a great hurry. The figure turned sideways and the silhouette of female breasts came into his view clearly outlined.

Rosen held his breath. The situation one patiently waits for eventually happens. But when it happens, one has to be prepared to grab it. He raised the gun, clicked the pistol's safety catch menacingly and said sternly:

"Over here, come over here with your hands on your head." The shocked intruder jumped like a startled rabbit then meekly advanced a few steps toward his corner, her hands obediently placed on her head.

"Kalani! Are you a robber now?" Rosen was most amused—this situation was getting even better than he could have planned. He put away the gun.

Kalani lowered her hands with a gasp. "Oh … Mr. Rosen, it's not what you think. I take care of nine kids, and we're completely out of food." Her voice was breaking into sobs as her fear started mixing with relief now. "I thought I would borrow some from you until we get some assistance."

"Borrow, eh?" Rosen laughed loudly. "But Kalani, I'd be happy to share my food with you. I understand how difficult it must be to survive these days. Look, I have a lot of good stuff; it will be only fair if I give some to you and your kids." He opened his arms as though he was going to hug the girl.

"Oh, Mr. Rosen, you're such a wonderful man." Kalani's eyes filled with tears of joy. "God will bless you. We're in such a terrible situation ... You're like an angel sent to deliver us from starvation." She looked ready to cry, which really did not fit into Harry's plans.

"Now, now, my girl, have courage. We must be strong. It's not time to be fainthearted." Rosen gave a hearty pat on Kalani's back. "I will give you food, as much as you need, but you must help me take a load of supplies from here to my place first. Then you can take from the storage as much as you can carry. Whatever ... I have all kinds of cans, salami, cheese, Spam—things that will never go bad without a fridge."

Excited, Kalani was ready to start packing immediately, but Harry thought it prudent to wait until dark. The streets were mostly empty, but no one could know who was gawking through darkened windows. After sunset, with no streetlights working, they could move through the town like ghosts. There would be enough time to complete the task before curfew.

With a warm, pleasant sensation filling his pelvis, Rosen was confident and happy with himself. A clear objective and the unflinching patience of a hunter waiting in his blind— any illiterate village boy could come up with these, he thought. But execution ... the flawless execution, built on his uncompromising and thorough planning, that would be the mark of a master.

He felt goose bumps forming on his arms. Now he would carry it out—methodically, without haste, taking all the time necessary for his plan to develop to its fullest, blossom into the art form conjured by his fertile imagination. It would be the long-awaited feast. A bit of delay would just whet his appetite.

"Come on, Kalani, we're not going to do all this heavy

hauling on an empty stomach. Let's have a little snack before we go." Unhurriedly, he opened a restaurant-size can of cooked ham and slowly cut an old and crusty French baguette into smaller pieces, which he buttered carefully, stopping often to pick up dry crumbs.

Kalani watched, drowning in her saliva, feeling her insides churning and twisting in anticipation.

Rosen placed thick slices of ham on the bread, precisely cut thin wedges of pickle then looked at the sandwich critically and finally pushed it toward her. "There you go."

She swallowed it in five seconds, hardly chewing the rock-hard bread, scratching her gums and throat in a great rush to deliver the food to her frantic stomach.

Harry watched her with a smile. She had lost a lot of weight. Now, she looked more and more like Consuela ... same big black eyes, thin waist and her hips still very, very nice.

"Would you like another one, dear?"

"Yes, please."

He enjoyed the hungry expression in her eyes, which followed his every move. *She'll be a gem, a gem I'll polish to perfection.* Rosen taunted Kalani, creating the second sandwich even more slowly before he let her snap it up. The game was already wonderful. *A little appetizer before the main course,* he thought.

After dark, they packed a big, wheeled suitcase with Spam, canned meats, jams and other victuals until it was too heavy to be lifted off the ground. A rolling duffel bag and two jammed backpacks completed the cargo. *Going up my driveway will be quite a trip,* he sighed. Alas, someone had drained the gas from his Mercedes a few days earlier.

Kalani was anxious about getting home late, but the prospect of bringing the mountain of food she saw in the storeroom overweighed any other consideration. This would be more than Abe could collect in weeks of his long expeditions.

Trudging through the broken and dark streets, Kalani and Rosen reached the lower end of his driveway an hour later, exhausted and panting. It was still another thirty minutes of hauling the heavy cargo up the steep hill before they passed the heavy entrance doors. Rosen locked the doors securely as soon as they went in.

"We can drop the bags here, next to the kitchen." He pointed at the open door.

They faced each other, both worn-out and breathing heavily, but smiling happily. Kalani was thirty minutes away from grabbing her treasure trove; Rosen was barely seconds away from achieving his elaborate goal.

"Before you go … I'd like to give you something for the kids," he said warmly. "We need to get it from my room upstairs."

In gentlemanly fashion, he let the girl walk in front of him, led her into his bedroom and lit a kerosene lamp. "Over there—" he gently directed her to the nightstand next to his large bed.

When she stopped in front of it, a forceful shove threw her forward. Falling, she stretched her arms instinctively to protect her face, and at that exact moment Rosen jumped at her back, squashing her flat into the mattress. He slammed handcuffs on her extended wrists with the expertise acquired by a thousand dry runs carried out in the patient anticipation of this glorious moment.

That's it. She's my property. There's nothing that she can do now! Rosen was triumphant. It was easier than in his daydreams; it was unbelievably easy for someone who prepared well! He clipped the handcuffs to the chain running through a block over the bed and pulled it tight.

Kalani was sitting now on the bed, her arms stretched up and terror in her eyes. She did not scream or talk, but her breathing increased to a fast whine. Rosen stared into her fear-crazed eyes and listened to her high-pitched whimpers as he sat comfortably in the armchair by the bed, a lamp glowing steadily on the desk. Consuela had had the same wild expression when he was taking her to the courtyard. But this time he was no longer Bonito, an instrument of the Master. He was the Master.

That's how intelligence, courage, diligence and patience bring dreams to fruition, he congratulated himself. The timing was perfect; the whole town was in disarray. Nobody had any idea she might be in his house; no one would come here to disturb him. He had ample supplies of food and he could stay at home for many days, living his daydreams and enjoying the fruits of his clever scheme.

Rosen picked up the black crop with the ivory handle. For a moment, with great satisfaction, he watched Kalani squirming in fear then he started an introduction.

"From now on, you are my slave, Kalani, and I am your master. You don't understand this relationship yet. How could you? You've never been instructed. But I will spare no effort to educate you." He slowly brushed her face and neck with the crop. She recoiled with terror.

"This is a tool. I like to use it, but it's only a tool. The objective is for you to submit the last little bit of your free will to me. You will do what I tell you; you will guess what I would like you to do, without questioning, without any resistance. And it will make you happy. It will take us a long time and a lot of discipline to get there, but I am more than willing to contribute. Are you, my little darling?"

Kalani's body, suspended at the end of the chain, trembled; she closed her eyes and did not answer.

"Well, you refuse to answer. Disobedience, in the very first moment of our relationship! We'll try to remedy that right away."

He released the chain and her hands fell down. Rosen pushed the girl on her face, put his knee across her shoulder blades and raised the crop. A loud swish was followed by a thud as the blade cut across her buttocks covered with thin fabric. Kalani screamed, and her body tensed, only to fall limp a moment later.

Rosen controlled his desire to see the effects of the whip on her skin. The time will come. I will proceed slowly, enjoying every moment, he persuaded himself.

For now, he was giving her instructions, speaking slowly like a teacher to a dim-witted student. "This was just to get your attention. I am going to let you up now and you will undress. Then you'll have a good look at my sculpture and you'll assume a position exactly like her. You'll remain in this position until I tell you otherwise. Her name is Anaïd. She is your role model. Learn from her, and that may spare you a lot of pain. Now, get moving."

He removed his knee from her back, moved a kerosene lamp next to the sculpture and walked out of the room, leaving Kalani handcuffed, at the end of a long, loose chain. He watched from the dark doorway as she moved slowly from the bed. Obviously, she was smarting badly. "That must be quite a cut," he chuckled to himself. We'll see later.

Kalani slowly wiggled out of her dress and pushed it up the chain as far as the handcuffs allowed. Then she slipped off her underwear and went up to Anaïd, studied her for a moment and kneeled on the floor with her hips raised. She lowered her face to the floor and turned it somewhat to the left side, exactly like the sculpture. Then she became motionless.

This girl is a canvas worthy of the great masters, thought Rosen, watching the naked girl with admiration. Let's have her wait for me a bit and contemplate her situation.

Harry Rosen went to the kitchen to make himself a roast beef sandwich, richly garnished with pickles and baby artichokes. After a moment of deliberation, he added a slice of Swiss cheese and a bit of red paprika. Perfect. He chewed slowly in the flickering light of a candle and washed the food down with a glass of Castillo del Diablo. Not a bad wine by itself, he thought, but he really got his kicks from its name.

Then he went upstairs to continue the first lesson of submission, slowly at first but increasing the pace as his excitement overcame his intellectual satisfaction.

Kalani knelt with her face to the floor, rigid like marble, exactly like Anaïd. Very pleasing. He looked at the sculpture, then again at Kalani.

Well, Monsieur Rodin, or shall I call you Auguste? I like my creation even better than yours, he chortled with delight. He was exuberant. Even from the doorway, in the lamp's poor light, he could see the bright red line crossing the top of Kalani's buttocks. What a beautiful beginning for the piece of fine art I am going to create today. He felt inspired.

Rosen came closer and Kalani raised her hips in the gesture of sexual offering that any male mammal would understand.

Just like Consuela, only you figured it out faster, he thought, amused. But he himself had learned quite a bit since then as well. He put his right hand on the girl's arched back and slowly moved it into the crease between her buttocks, following it down and forward.

A little cheat, he chuckled. She was not aroused at all. That didn't bother him. It was not her pleasure that he was seeking. In fact, he figured out years ago, had she enjoyed whipping, what would be the point of it? The slave should be scared out of her mind, again and again, until she lost any mental resistance. Only then could she be considered a real slave, and this, certainly, wouldn't happen overnight.

Rosen squeezed the buttock hard until the skin paled, except for the red line of the whip mark. She did not react, which annoyed him slightly. It was supposed to hurt! He desired to see pain in her eyes. Harry walked to the front, grabbed Kalani's black hair close to the scalp and harshly lifted her head. The large dark eyes were not filled with the fear he expected but were spewing out hatred. He appreciated this discovery too late.

Two hands, joined together and wrapped with the metal chain hidden in the green fabric of Kalani's dress, shot from below and hit him in the middle of his face.

His head bounced back simultaneously with the sickening sound of broken bones he felt rather than heard. His eyes filled with blinding tears. A second later another blow—to his right temple. Then, just as he was falling, yet another vicious knock on top of his head sent his face crashing into the floor.

Rosen was stunned but not unconscious. He felt a hand searching his pockets, but didn't even twitch. His terror centered on the kerosene lamp sitting on the floor within Kalani's reach. She could easily crash it on his head, setting him ablaze. He stayed still, pretending to be knocked out.

The hand found the key then the chain fell clinking onto the floor. A minute later, he felt a kick—soft, delivered with a naked foot—into his right flank and then the door downstairs slammed.

Barefoot, Kalani flew down the dark road to Kalama Park and along Kalaheo Street to the Round House. She did not slow down until she had passed the gate and saw the open door, beaming yellow light into the dark yard. She stopped in the doorway. Her hair tangled and face twisted in feral fear, she was gasping for air.

Cat was talking with Mike Yoshida, his deputy and a town manager at the glass table. Leila and her crew of writers sat at the big table, copying yet another proclamation. Abe dozed, sitting on the floor with his back against the wall, waiting for Kalani. All heads turned to the door and conversations stopped. Kalani was pale as a ghost, and her bare feet were bleeding.

"What happened to you?" Cat gasped.

"I've been kidnapped ..." Kalani cried and broke into nervous sobbing.

As she was telling her story in confused fragments and blubbers, separated by attacks of sobbing, she became aware of the strange looks her audience exchanged among themselves.

She abruptly stopped and challenged Yoshida angrily. "You don't believe me, do you? Crazy Kalani invented a story to get attention! Well, how about this?" She turned around and lifted her dress for everyone to see the red line crossing her bottom. "You think I did it myself?" She was enraged.

Yoshida gave a soft whistle. "Sorry, Kalani, I've never heard a story like that. Have you, Ben?" He turned to his deputy who made a grimace meaning "never!" "This crazy bastard is going to kill someone. I don't think you have finished him. We better pick him up right away. His cover is blown—he won't hold back now." The sergeant stood up.

"He has a gun, Mike. You better take someone with you." Kalani looked around. "Where's Abe? He was sitting here a moment ago."

Abe was gone. "He went after Rosen, and Rosen has a gun! He's going to shoot Abe...." Now Kalani broke down again. "Mike, please hurry! Help him!"

The policemen ran out. When Yoshida and his deputy reached Rosen's house, twenty minutes later, Abe was sitting on the front steps.

"He's gone, just a pool of blood in the bedroom. The bastard ran away, but I'll finish the job Kalani started."

Chapter 30

Jerry, January 22

A quiet but persistent, rhythmic banging penetrated the thick cover of sleep and Jerry opened his eyes. The sun was not up yet and the cabin was dark, but the ink of night was fading into the light gray of dawn.

He climbed the companionway and, sticking his head above the deck, noticed a long blue outrigger bouncing at the starboard side. So, that's what's banging—we have company, he thought. Suddenly, a hand clasped over his mouth and a sharp metallic object firmly dug into his neck. Jerry shuddered; the hand pressed his head against someone's muscular chest and the pressure on his neck increased.

"You move, you die," he heard a strangely accented whisper and stopped struggling. His captor led him up the last few steps of the stairway, then to the aft end of the cockpit where he pushed Jerry onto the bench. Two more men stood on the foredeck, not visible from the stairs. One was a young man, under thirty, a tall and powerfully built individual with the heavy arms and big chest of a paddler. The other intruder, older by perhaps ten years, was short and wiry.

Seeing Jerry immobilized, they quietly moved on their

bare feet toward the cabin's entrance. But before they could look inside, John's balding head appeared above deck, and almost simultaneously, a fishing spear shot from the companionway, striking the man who was holding the knife to Jerry's neck. The projectile slid under his raised left arm and entered the chest.

The knife fell, and the intruder's other hand slid away from Jerry's mouth. The prowler stumbled backwards and crashed on the bench, the shaft of the metal spear jutting out of his chest below the armpit. He burst into a spasm of violent coughing, spewing copious amounts of blood from his mouth.

His two companions pounced toward the stairway. The skinny man was faster and he reached it first, crashed into John and they both went tumbling down the stairs. The second attacker could not get into the narrow space blocked by four kicking feet; he hesitated, waiting for the stairway to clear.

He had just managed to put his foot into the companionway when Jerry leaped over the body flailing in the cockpit and grabbed a boat hook. This was not a modern, light aluminum tool; John kept on deck a six-foot-long, heavy wooden shaft fitted with a solid piece of brass. Jerry's big swing ended with the hardware landing just below the base of the invader's skull. Instantly, the big man crumpled like a rag doll and slid down the companionway, his head bouncing on the steps.

Jerry dropped the boat hook and rushed down the stairs. There was little movement in the cabin, just soft groaning and gurgling sounds mixed with harsh respiration coming from the jumble of limbs and backs. The body of the intruder Jerry had hit rested on top of the pile, his head grotesquely twisted sideways on his crushed neck. He was dead; Jerry pulled the slippery cadaver off by his belt. Then he saw a white object, barely recognizable in the deep shade—John's face protruding from under the body of the older prowler. The skipper's eyes were open and his lips moved a few times without making any sound.

Jerry grabbed the second, unconscious, intruder by the arm and flipped him on his back, away from John. A jet of blood spurted rhythmically from the robber's neck wound, and a mass of pink froth was pouring out of his mouth with every breath, burying the face beneath.

John lay flat on the cabin floor, strangely quiet and composed. Only a small puncture wound above his left nipple, discharging a thin stream of bright red blood, told the story of his struggle. He tried to smile, squeezed Jerry's hand, moved his bluish lips again, but a few seconds later his eyes rolled up and his head turned aside limply. He was dead. The gurgling sounds behind Jerry, who was still holding John's hand, were becoming less and less frequent and soon stopped as well.

Four men had died in the span of a minute, and Jerry had lost his friend and mentor. *Welcome to Paradise* was the absurd thought that came to his head. But grief had to wait. He was acutely aware that he had to leave this place immediately. His future on the Big Island would consist—under the best of circumstances—of either jail or never-ending explanations. A quick stab delivered by the killed men's kin was another likely outcome.

Whatever might delay his arrival on Oahu, Jerry would not accept it. His mission was to find Cat; whatever interfered with it would be sidestepped or overcome. The diesel started on the first crank and Jerry stepped on the winch button, rattling the quiet harbor with the noise of the winding anchor chain.

The colorless dawn was quickly changing into a bright new day. Now he could clearly see the full length of the breakwater and the town of Hilo across the bay. He saw no boats on the water, but a few brightly colored outriggers sat on the black beach. There were no buoys, but the way out of the harbor was obvious. Jerry engaged the diesel and slowly motored out into the open ocean. He set his course to the northwest and turned on the autopilot.

John's death seemed so absurd that Jerry could barely absorb it. The old guy was snoring on his berth two feet away only an hour ago, and then in a violent flash he was gone. Right again—Jerry thought, looking over the intruders' bodies—John was right; people can't be trusted. These individuals did not even look emaciated; they were not hungry, desperate people but predators thriving on others' misery.

He pushed the intruders' bodies off the boat some twenty miles offshore. The physical act of removing the heavy cadavers from the cabin, pulling them up the narrow and steep companionway, was a challenge. Eventually, he rigged a block and hoisted them one by one with a rope looped under their arms. The three corpses slipped off *Lady Luck* with gentle splashes and stayed behind, floating in single-file formation, surrounded by a cloud of blood.

I hope the sharks get you, Jerry thought, without a trace of regret about their death. They soon disappeared among the waves, left behind by the fast-moving boat.

John was a slightly built man and Jerry could easily carry him up in his arms. He put the body on the blood-splattered cockpit bench, where the old man used to lounge with his newspaper. You kept your word, Skipper, he thought. You brought me to Hawaii. He watched over the body for a few minutes as the truth sank in: John was no more. He gently eased the body overboard and did not look back.

There were many things to do, as Jerry was the crew and captain of *Lady Luck* now. He wiped the cockpit benches and washed the pools of blood from the cabin floor again and again, disturbed by the sickly sweet smell that seemed to hang persistently under the deck.

He gave up eventually and returned to the deck to hoist the sails. There was nobody to give him a hand, offer advice

Return to Paradise

or just keep him company. He graduated from Skipper John's sailing school earlier than intended and there were no remedial classes. He could sail or sink; dropping the class was just not an option.

He turned off the motor and set the wind vane. The trade winds blew steadily, and a few hours later *Lady Luck* entered the Alenuihaha Channel, the body of water separating the Big Island from Maui. The channel, much feared by sailors for its violent weather, greeted him with just a fresh breeze. It gave the beginner a chance.

> AP News Flash: Nationwide, temporary rationing of fuel is in effect. Administration promises unrestricted supplies shortly.

Jerry kept dozing off in the cockpit, raising his head and checking the horizon every ten or fifteen minutes. He tried not to go down into the cabin; the smell of blood still hung in the air. At daybreak, the round cupola of Koko Head volcano, and soon after the sharp multifaceted mass of Diamond Head, came into view. He was within a couple hours of sailing into Honolulu harbor.

The VHF radio was still silent. The boat's regular stereo picked up some music and programs in foreign languages. Eventually, he found some English-language news. A real, shooting war in Iran, casualties in Iraq, movements of the Chinese navy ... nothing about Hawaii.

Jerry was surprised to see the lighthouse on Makapu'u Point flashing and then a buoy off Diamond Head was on the water. Finally, someone was alive and doing his job!

Like any tourist, Jerry knew the Honolulu waterfront from the land. He was not a great fan of Waikiki, but he had walked the beat a few times. Now looking at it from the offshore perspective, the landmarks were difficult to identify. A line of white breakers clearly marked the reef; as long as he stayed well outside the surf, he should be safe.

A large pink hotel on the beach looked undamaged, not counting the broken and blackened windows. The towers—which Jerry remembered reflecting the glory of the Hawaiian afternoon in their gold-colored glass when his plane was leaving—were still standing. But this time, they appeared like zombies in a horror movie, cadavers that had lost their skin. The acres of gleaming sheets were fractured and splintered, exposing big patches of gray bleak flanks.

Finally, he got through to the Honolulu Coast Guard on Channel 16. "Ala Wai Marina is out of service. Wrecks are blocking the access channel," a young voice advised him. The commercial Honolulu port was absolutely off-limits, except by special permit, which a private sailboat certainly would not obtain.

"How about Pearl Harbor?" Jerry asked, half in jest, half in hope for the special circumstances to work to his advantage.

"I hope you are joking, sir." The voice on VHS was not amused at all.

"So, where can I stop? I have been at sea for two weeks."

"Sir, your best bet is Keehi small boat harbor. It's only three miles downwind Ala Wai. You still have two hours of daylight; you should easily make it before sunset. You must be careful, though! There are major navigational hazards right at the mouth of the channel. Don't try to enter after dark."

"You think they'll have space available for me? Can I call them?"

"There's no one to call there; the harbor master's office has been wiped out, but I wouldn't be worried about berths. There are very few boats left in Hawaii, and you will easily find a spot in the lagoon to drop a hook."

As *Lady Luck* continued sailing along the south shore of Oahu, Jerry for the first time observed some human activity. Not far from the Aloha Tower a yellow crane was moving; a big black shape dangled off it, slowly sailing through the air.

Return to Paradise

A few other pieces of the port's machinery seemed strangely disfigured and frozen in bizarre positions.

They must be unloading supplies; some emergency stuff is reaching Hawaii, Jerry thought with relief.

The superstructure of a large ship appeared directly on *Lady Luck*'s course a few minutes later, bringing Jerry's stomach to his throat. It had no business being so close to the shore. But the mystery revealed itself before an alarmed Jerry started the hasty maneuver to get off the big bully's course, running into the open ocean. Carried by the tsunami, the unfortunate ship had landed on a reef, where she hung now, a few hundred yards offshore, immobile and listing sharply toward the land.

Half a mile short of the dead freighter, Jerry noticed a tangled mass of sunken boats, right at the mouth of the port channel. Between the low, mangrove-covered island and the end of the reef marked by white surf, a mass of bows and sterns protruded from the water at dramatic angles, and multiple masts stuck out in all directions like needles on a porcupine. These were the boats that had been mooring in the lagoon when the tsunami hit. Yanked loose from their anchorage by the big wave, they had been trashed against the concrete piers, swamped and then sucked out by the enormous current of water exiting the basin when the flow reversed. All movable objects, regardless of size, had been snatched by this gigantic vacuum cleaner and dumped into the deeper water, where they sank.

Jerry aimed the bow into the narrow space between this menacing mass of projecting points and the edge of brown reef visible under two feet of water. Her diesel humming unobtrusively, *Lady Luck* slowly inched through the narrow passage, leaving the tangled wreckage behind.

The Keehi lagoon turned out to be a long body of water enclosed between the concrete-hardened shore and a confused jumble of low islands, tiny coves and mangrove swamps forming its outer border. It used to be a safe home for hundreds of small boats, but now their wrecked bodies were submerged under the water or heaped one on top of another. Patches of impenetrable thickets of twisted plastic and metal formed along the piers, and smaller clumps of wreckage erupted among the green mangroves like necrotic sores.

Not a single boat looked usable. The harbor had returned to the state of wilderness, rimmed by a surrealistic jungle of steel, aluminum and fiberglass.

Since the disastrous invasion at Hilo, Jerry was acutely aware of his precarious security situation. A working boat would be a great trophy for any gang, both for its supplies and the craft itself. It was also his only material asset, one he would dearly need in his search for Cat. But how could he defend it? He had to sleep, and he would have to leave the boat unprotected when he went ashore to search for Cat. *Lady Luck* had to be hidden.

Jerry motored slowly along the convoluted outer rim of the lagoon. He passed coves choked by greenery and deep blue channels cutting in between islets. Finally, he came upon a tangle of three boats blocking access to the narrow but clear-water channel ending in a mangrove. There seemed to be twelve feet of space between the red-painted keel of the dead boat, resting on her side, and the green branches of a bush perched at the channel's rocky edge.

He coasted forward dead-slow, in neutral, until the bow touched the submerged boat, then he jumped on the wreck with a bowline in his hand. For the next few hours, he pulled, pushed and cajoled *Lady Luck* into the cove in order to hide her behind the mass of overturned wrecks.

These were already stripped of their ropes, instruments and everything holding any value. The looters considered this area already done with, Jerry hoped. Before night descended on the lagoon, *Lady Luck* was hidden from a casual look cast from the land and Jerry felt almost safe. Exhausted, he dropped on the cockpit bench and fell asleep; the cabin still smelled of blood.

Chapter 31

Jerry, January 24-25

Jerry's jaw dropped when he turned the radio on that morning and heard the closing sentences of the broadcast. The woman's voice on the radio told people to join the motorcycle rally, which would parade through Kaneohe and Kailua and proceed along the Pali Highway to Honolulu. It would end with the ceremony of lei presented to the governor in recognition of loving care extended to the Windward citizens.

At first, he was not sure if this was Cat's voice, though it had her low timbre and the characteristic inflection that left listeners wondering if she was making a statement, asking a question or making a disguised joke. But, certainly, it was her wicked sense of humor. That was his crazy Cat.

He finished camouflaging his boat; lines removed, sails taken down under the deck, large pieces of broken metal and fiberglass heaped on the deck—*Lady Luck* looked like all other boats in Keehi, a broken, rusty wreck unworthy of a second look. But she held a treasure: enough food to last a few weeks, if used sparingly, the remaining fifteen gallons of diesel fuel, fishing gear and some other useful stuff, including bleach.

Jerry lowered the dinghy and rowed towards the shore, meandering along the reef, taking cover behind obstructions, in case someone was spying from the shore. Once on shore, he dragged a large piece of half-rotten plywood to cover the dinghy, and threw a few pieces of deadwood on top to complete the masquerade.

The wooden slips of the marina were completely ripped out, and only the concrete foundation slab marked the site of a building which had to be the harbormaster's office. A distinct chemical smell permeated the air despite a breeze.

Jerry walked inland, following an asphalt road behind the harbor. The broken pavement was covered with a thick slick of oil slowly leaking from the one large storage tank still standing upright. Two other tanks were knocked off their foundations, and lay on their sides where the tidal waves had left them, contents long gone.

A thin middle-aged man passed him on a bike. The man kept a safe ten-foot distance when Jerry stopped him, but provided useful information.

From Keehi one could walk along Nimitz Highway to the east, where food was being distributed in Honolulu, but big crowds waited for relief packages day and night, fighting for supplies tooth and nail.

Turning west would take a traveler over the broken—but passable on foot—freeway intersection, past the deserted industrial parks and the paralyzed, empty airport. Eventually, past Pearl Harbor, there was another residential area, but that part of the island saw hardly any government presence. No food distribution centers could be found there, but the locals seemed to cope by themselves well enough.

The man did not know much about Kailua, as the town seemed to be cut off, but he had heard of some guys from the leeward crossing over the mountains along the Likelike or H3 Highway.

Jerry went west. Carrying a small backpack with enough food for a day, fishing hooks for trading and a box of bleach, he trudged along the blistering highway. He saw no people among the warehouses, shops and car lots; the industrial area had no occupants. He walked along the Navy base, quiet, protected by high walls, barbed wire and armed sentries, and a few hours later—dog-tired from the walking he was not accustomed to—Jerry finally reached the residential district.

He stopped in front of the first house, a run-down white bungalow nestling among waist-high weeds. His mouth was parched and he felt dried out like a November leaf. Having drained the last drops from his water bottle four hours ago, Jerry hoped to get a drink. He had not urinated for a few hours, and the last time he did, his pee was the color of orange juice.

The front yard was tiny and consisted mostly of a gravel driveway occupied by an old, blue pickup. A man stood on a ladder leaning against the house, closing a window with a sheet of old weathered plywood. Jerry walked up to the ladder and cleared the thick sticky mucous from his throat. When the worker looked at him from above, Jerry asked for a glass of water.

Unexpectedly, the man just shrugged and went back to banging nails into the plywood. Jerry was too thirsty to accept this unreasonable denial. "C'mon, man, you're not going to refuse me a drink of water!"

The guy stopped nailing and considered the unwelcome visitor, weighing a hammer in his hand. "Just move along, buddy. You know I don't have any good water to share with you. It's either you, or me and my family. You want water, help yourself." He pointed his hammer towards a puddle filled with murky fluid. "Fresh—there was a bit of rain last night; it'll be gone by the evening."

Jeremy went to the puddle, plunged in his hand and brought wet fingers to his lips. At least the water was not salty. It was brown with dirt but tasted fresh. He took out his empty water bottle, put a bit of bleach in it and topped it with the water, carefully skimming the puddle's surface. Then he sat in the shade of the house with a groan of relief and started shaking the bottle. A few minutes later, he tasted the water, it smelled like a swimming pool, but to his dry mouth it was the best drink of his life.

The worker watched him with interest. "You think you'll be all right? People get pretty sick drinking dirty water, you know."

"Oh, I'll be fine," Jeremy answered with great confidence. "This is good water—as long as you have the proper purification chemicals."

The man put his hammer away and sat beside Jerry. "You have the purification stuff?"

"A lot. I could make a lot of clean water … but I could use some help myself."

Jerry's new friend, Ekualo, lived with his wife and two kids in the white house. Someone tried to break in early that morning, so he decided to board the kitchen windows. Thieves … not looking for money but for food and water—especially water.

People were getting desperate. It rained little on the leeward side, even though it was January. One couldn't count on rainwater. Ekualo, known also as Ed, built a small water still from a garbage can, but it produced just a glass or two a day, hardly enough for his family. Some people drank water from the stream uphill, but it was clearly polluted, as a lot of them got sick. Young children in particular were falling ill in large numbers. The remaining option was to trek ten or fifteen miles to Honolulu.

"How many cans of water can you carry?" Ekualo complained.

Jerry didn't blame him for refusing a drink of water to a stranger.

Ekualo's family, just like his neighbors, lived off the land. Remnants of taro or pineapples forgotten in the fields in good times, garden bananas, wild guava fruit picked in the mountains—these were the new meager staples, occasionally augmented by fish caught off the ocean-side rocks or a feral pig shot in the bush.

The Hawaiian *ohana*, a big family organization including all related people, proved its worth, ensuring that the food shortage in the leeward was not too severe; everyone was hungry but no one was really starving. The real big issue was the shortage of clean water.

Ekualo took Jerry down the narrow street to meet a community elder, a man called Kawika. They walked between the old bungalows, painted in fading yellow, pink and blue tones, decorated with white plastic lattice to hide crawl spaces, until they stopped in front of yet another inconspicuous plantation-style house.

Clad in pale-yellow vinyl siding, it had a small porch in front bearing remnants of a plastic wraparound screen. The warped door was unlocked and moved indolently with the feeble wind. Ekualo knocked on it hard. A moment later a big face appeared behind the door's upper glass panel almost a foot above Jerry's eyes.

The man looked over his visitor carefully then, seeing Ekualo behind him, pushed the door open and walked out onto the porch. He was an individual of imposing size. His ugly brownish shorts, ending just above his massive knees, and faded blue t-shirt were definitely shabby and yet he projected an air of noble dignity. He invited them to sit on the steps with a royal gesture and looked questioningly at Ekualo.

"Water!" the younger man exploded. "He has chemicals to make water good!"

Kawika listened intently to the visitor's boast about his water-purification chemicals; thought for a moment then asked a few pointed questions, looking sharply into Jerry's eyes.

"How do we know it's good? How much water can you treat? Where do you get the chemicals?" His dark eyes expressed a keen interest as well as a hint of a threat, in case the *haole* was less than sincere.

"Are they good? You'll see by tomorrow. Ekualo saw me drinking a whole bottle of muddy water I treated with my stuff." The witness enthusiastically nodded. He felt that credit was due to him for finding Jerry and his bleach.

Jerry could not disclose *Lady Luck*'s existence; she was his only asset in this dealing. "I have a warehouse where my chemicals are stored, and I will provide them as necessary. You need to find a large tank or a reservoir where I can treat water in large quantities; that would be more economical," Jerry added with the confidence of a water-treatment plant manager.

Kawika closed his eyes, considering Jerry's words. "You stay with me." His eyes opened, intelligent and alert but friendly now. "I keep eye on you. You OK in the morning, we give it a try. Maybe in a swimming pool? I know this guy who has a small pool in his backyard ... might be cracked now, but that can be fixed." He suspended his voice, waiting for Jerry's reaction.

"Sounds good." Jerry grimaced. "Let's do it."

"This, my friend, will be a great thing!" The big man slammed Jerry's back with his shovel-size hand, his initial reservation forgotten. "I'll have people fill the pool with the water from streams and ponds. It should be ready by tomorrow."

Jerry, usually indifferent about religion, was begging for divine intervention that afternoon when he developed belly cramps. But, whatever the reason, he did not get sick even though he continued to drink his concoction mixed in a big cooking pot in Kawika's kitchen.

Return to Paradise

Inspection of the empty pool, a small and shallow concrete hole hidden among tall weeds, showed a long crack starting at one side and extending along half of the bottom. "No problem." Kawika shrugged. By the next morning the fissure was patched and dry, a gray streak across the faded blue paint.

At daybreak, people started filing in with buckets, canisters and jars in their hands, dumping water into the makeshift filter Jerry had fashioned out of a sand-filled bucket. Every drop falling into the pool had to seep through the drainage holes at the bucket's bottom.

The pool was half-full at ten o'clock when Kawika proudly, in a ceremonious procession, brought Jerry to it.

The biological tests had gone well—Jerry was alive and apparently healthy. To his joy, the house owner had an old kit for testing pool water. Keeping the water's pH within the range appropriate for swimming was the key, Jerry figured. It should make the water safe enough to drink while no one would get his guts burned.

He poured in half of his bleach container, mixed it thoroughly with a long pool pole and took a rest in the shade of the house, ignoring the expectant crowd outside. He emerged thirty minutes later, used the testing kit, poured in some more bleach, mixed, and went back home....

The great performance of water preparation went on for two hours, while people patiently stood around the pool in ever increasing numbers. Even as the sun reached its zenith, the spectators looked on with interest, without a sound of protest. Eventually, Jerry filled the water bottle and solemnly brought it up against the sun to examine its contents. The water appeared clean. He raised it in a formal toast to the crowd, and greedily drank it all. It was noon and he was thirsty.

All heads turned to Kawika who, after a theatrical pause, gave a solemn go-ahead nod, triggering a rush to the pool.

People first sated their immediate thirst then began filling their buckets and canisters. The silent crowd suddenly turned into a block party. Women thronged around the pool, chatting and laughing as they filled their water containers, while men carefully tasted from glasses and cups as though they had a new and exotic beer to savor.

The pride Jerry unexpectedly experienced at that moment shocked him; he'd never felt this much satisfaction, even when he received his doctoral diploma in front of his family and many colleagues.

Kawika pushed to him through the unruly crowd. "Thank you, Jerry." He put a hand on Jerry's arm. "You did a great thing for us. What can we do for you? Ah, wait …" he interrupted just when Jerry opened his mouth. "We go celebrate now. You tell me at home."

Jerry's story sounded like a fancy movie script; as a viewer he would dismiss it as too far-fetched. But there he was—with the load of bleach and *Lady Luck* hiding in the Keehi Lagoon, the undeniable evidence of his truth telling.

Kawika, his body sprawling from an extra-large solid oak chair onto the kitchen table, listened without interruption, leaning more and more toward Jerry.

"I would like to have a friend like you," he declared, looking him straight in the eyes. "Things …" He struggled for words. "Mean … we don't care much for things … Friends, good friends, make us rich. We'll give you a hand."

As the big Hawaiian got to his feet and left, searching for someone in the crowd, Jerry knew he was much closer to finding Cat.

Kawika returned accompanied by two young men, whom he sat at the table with a gesture. "This lady friend of yours …" He suspended his voice while returning to his oak throne. "You say you heard her on the radio yesterday. If she's the one broadcasting from Kailua, you got yourself a famous woman. The whole island listens to her. She is a spunky girl and funny, too. She'll take good care of you, ha ha ha," he roared, smacking Jerry on the arm.

The two young men were the guides Kawika appointed to take Jerry over the mountains to Kailua. Alika, the taller one, had trekked to the Windward a week earlier to check on his sister. "Long walk." He shrugged glibly. "We go tomorrow. No problem, but *mo bettah* we start early."

The same afternoon, Jerry and his two guardian angels biked to Keehi carrying big empty backpacks. They returned after dark, grunting under the heavy loads of bleach on their backs. The clean water supply was assured.

The plan to start the Kailua trip at dawn had to be unexpectedly changed an hour before the mark, still in the darkness of night. Kawika's house shook with violent knocking on the door and a second later a breathless young man barged in. "Whales! Whales close to the beach!"

The dusky neighborhood suddenly resonated with banging on walls, shutting doors and excited voices. Without any apparent orders issued, the street filled with people running toward the beach, paddles in hand. Among them, Jerry could see a lot of men carrying arms as well. Handguns, shotguns, hunting rifles, assault carbines—these people were prepared for a lot more than a pig hunt.

By the time Jerry and Kawika arrived on the beach, three outriggers had already been pushed off the sand and the six-man crews were in, the barrels of their firearms barely sticking above the gunwales. The crowd—completely silent now—watched their broad backs leaning forward, paddles raised, waiting for an order. A fountain of water shot up from the dark water nearby, lit by the yellow sunrise like a limelight in a theatrical production.

"Half a mile," Kawika breathed into Jerry's ear. A blunt black shape broke the surface as a whale breached, and as if on cue, the soft-voiced command burst: "Hit!"

The canoes took off swiftly, water swirling around the paddles pulled with violent power, but as the outriggers accelerated, their movement smoothed into the quiet stealthy flight of a barracuda effortlessly cutting through the ocean. The boats split up and started approaching the large black shape resting on the surface on different paths in their effort to encircle it.

A hundred yards from the whale, the paddles were withdrawn from the water in response to a command unheard at the beach, and the firearms appeared in the crews' hands. The canoes were closing in, silently moving with the momentum, gliding without a splash. The paddlers were perfectly immobile now, pointing their arms at the black shape in the water. The crowd on the beach froze in complete silence.

The whale moved lazily, as in preparation for a dive, when the canoes were still sixty yards away. A single shot blasted the quiet morning and was followed by the multi-barrel cannonade, which carried on for at least fifteen seconds. Jerry could distinctly discern his old friend, an M249 light machine gun, raking the giant's body with a lengthy staccato.

The whale submerged the front of its body, but that was as much as it could do, its head exploded by hundreds of bullets. The ringing silence that followed was torn down by the great jubilant noise coming from the crowd on shore.

Dozens of youngsters and children of all ages flew into the water, stirring it like a school of *malolo*, flying fish, chased by a marlin. They swam to the canoes that carried their heroes and to the trophy, which was spewing a big red cloud around it.

The canoes strained the ropes attached to the humpback's tail, and slowly, with great effort, they towed the carcass to the beach, a great plume of blood extending behind it.

The size of the beast was staggering; this catch could feed a lot of people. A party, one that would draw guests from wide and far, was inevitable. Jerry knew that his trek to Kailua had to wait. A twenty-four-hour delay would be a good turn of events.

By the evening, the street in front of Kawika's house was full of happy, rowdy people. Large pieces of whale meat were roasted over a fire, boiled and smoked; nobody knew how to prepare this game properly and experimentation was the answer. One thing was certain: they would eat it, one way or another.

Long after dark, people on the beach were still butchering the unusual game. "What are you going to do with all this meat, Kawika?" Jerry asked. "It's not going to keep long."

"We'll try to smoke some, we'll try to salt some…" Kawika was unsure. "I've sent word to our people in the Leeward to come and get as much as they can use. But—in the end—you're right, most of it will go bad."

"You might send some to Honolulu … even sell it, or trade it. Maybe you could get some gas for your car."

"You don't understand, Jerry." The Hawaiian sighed. "Sure, they're as hungry in Honolulu as we are. But if we let them know we have food, they will come here by the thousands. Some may want to buy the meat, but others will just try to grab the whale and many other things that don't belong to them. It happened before and more than once. They can catch their own whale; we don't trust them."

Fires on the beach burned till the morning as the unending stream of cousins and friends from the western part of the island kept the party going. While the Leeward celebrated its big catch, east of the Koolau Mountains hungry people slept fitfully, fearing their children's hungry eyes the next morning.

Chapter 32

Jerry, January 26

Despite Jerry's fear of a long delay, they set out to Kailua the next day, as soon as the dark sky over Honolulu showed the first pink splashes.

The neighborhood was completely hushed, even the hardiest partiers cut down, paralyzed in deep sleep, while roosters and dogs, the usual early morning noise makers, had long ago been cooked and eaten.

They started on bikes, burdened like camels with big backpacks. Following Fort Weaver Road and the Farrington Highway, the expedition easily covered the flat stretch of road that never strayed far from the coast all the way to Pearl City. There Alika intended to switch to the Kamehameha Highway. Having passed this route recently, he knew that once they had hoisted their bikes and packs onto the crumpled intersection, they would have an easy ride to the H3 Highway and on, all the way to the Koolau Range.

They covered well over twenty miles before the sun broke out from behind the morning clouds and started heating up their backs and heads with some gravity. That moment coincided, however, with the point of the road's inflection, where it turned up like a hockey stick into a long steady incline, climbing up the Koolau. An hour and a half later up the broken but passable pavement, they reached the place from which they could look straight into the tunnel's mouth.

This passage would take them across, to the Windward, with ease—if only they could reach it. But the pavement ended abruptly in midair, leading a traveler into a deep precipice, like the plank of a pirate ship. A section of the highway had collapsed, leaving a wide gap between the final stub of the highway and the black hole in the mountain.

Using ropes, they lowered themselves onto the ground below and Alika, the taller guide, hid their bikes in a thicket of thorny mesquite at the foot of the mountain.

Jerry, his thighs burning from the long uphill bike ride, thought they must have reached at least the halfway point. He was wrong. The tough part was only about to start, they still had a long, steep climb to reach the summit.

As Alika led the group, frequently disappearing out of sight, Kekoa, the other guide, stayed with Jerry, making the time pass faster with his uninterrupted monolog. At least half of this heavily accented and grammatically inventive talk passed through Jerry's ears without leaving any residue of understanding, but Kekoa did not expect answers.

Very quickly, Jerry's attention became totally committed to the challenge of climbing. They trod over the unsteady gravel of eroding volcanic rock, and with every step, the slow movement up the steep slope could change into a frantic slide down, feet desperately searching for solid ground.

Jerry's backpack was filled to the top with dry food and cans from his boat supplies; his guides carried packs brimming with whale blubber, a gift from Kawika and his clan. A strong odor emanated from their burden—not the stench of spoiling meat, fortunately, but the marginally more tolerable smell of fish oil.

In the scorching heat of noon, they followed a faint

pathway between boulders up to the mountain pass. Jerry trudged in his second position, struggling to keep up with his younger companions, swaying under the mountain of canned food on his back, until they all collapsed at the summit.

Slumped in front of the big rock, they turned their faces to the cool breeze rising up along the mountain's slope from the ocean. Before them was displayed a dramatic panorama of deep green valleys separated by ragged black ridges, set against a background of the placid blue ocean. A speck, a mere rock, surrounded by millions of square miles of empty water, Jerry thought, looking out from the mountaintop. This paradise had become a prison, a place of banishment well guarded by its isolation.

Climbing downhill was no easier, he learned quickly. They slid down on their backsides as much as walked, grasping weeds, bushes and branches in desperate attempts to slow down until the slope's grade flattened at the foothill. Alika allowed a fifteen-minute rest in a grove of wild guava trees, an orchard many years ago. The small fruits packed an aromatic, pink juice that perfectly suited their cravings for energy and water. The break turned into a greedy hunt for the fruit until Alika drove them on.

He disappeared ahead, while Jerry followed the narrow pathway meandering between high, dense bushes, his eyes glued to the rocky ground. The plants were very different on the windward side. Once over the pass, the dry brown shrubs of the leeward side gave way to the exuberant green grasses, succulent bushes and leafy trees watered by the windward's clouds. The pathway took a sharp right turn around a tall rock when Jerry suddenly heard the command:

"Drop da pack!"

Jerry looked up and faced a short, thin, older man dressed in shorts, a dirty gray t-shirt and rubber flip-flops. He was holding a cut-off shotgun, but its point was not aiming at

Jerry. There was no need. His victim carried no apparent weapon, and the robber could finish the contest within a split second. His brown and weathered face was not particularly threatening; it was simply saying, I need your pack, so drop it and go away. No need to get hurt.

Jerry stopped and heard Kekoa stopping behind him ... then moving to his side.

"Eh, he wit us ... so beat it, brah!"

The mugger looked alarmed and raised his shotgun without saying a word.

"You touch him, and we hunt you down and kill like one pig," continued Kekoa, in an almost friendly tone.

This time Jerry understood every word and admired the succinct clarity of the pidgin dialect. The man stood there for another second, then suddenly jumped among the bushes and disappeared.

"You did good, brah," they heard Alika's voice from the undergrowth just behind the spot where the gunman had been standing a moment ago. He sheathed a ten-inch-long hunting knife and returned to the lead. The old man would never know how close he had been to his own end.

Kailua was completely dark by the time they entered the town. Walking between the damaged but inhabited homes, they arrived at the area the tsunami had overrun. Ruined houses, abandoned cars, old garbage—all evidence of human presence had been replaced here by the brown surface of dried mud broken into a million small patches.

Jerry was quite disoriented in this new landscape, but found Cat's home by following the canal. He recognized the once-white walls of the first floor sticking out from the mud. His heart seemed to skip a few beats—the second floor was completely gone; only the carport absurdly stuck up high above the house's remains. Stubbornly, he forced himself to examine the place more closely. Most of the contents had been taken by the water, which left behind a thick layer of sand and mud where he used to have romantic dinners with Cat.

Climbing over the fridge wedged into the kitchen doorway, Jerry saw a metallic object underneath. It was a richly ornamented samovar, an elaborate silver tea maker. Jerry recognized it at once because he had seen it many times in Cat's hands.

She did not make tea—actually didn't like the brew—this thing was her treasured heirloom of high sentimental value. She felt in touch with her parents or grandparents when she handled it. She liked to polish it, and indeed, the silver required a lot of polishing to maintain its shine in Hawaii's climate. Jerry saw Cat slowly gliding her gloved hand over the shiny curves, her eyes unfocused, as though she were talking to someone far away. He did not interfere with these moments; a few minutes later, she would put it away and return to his world.

Jerry dug it out from the mud; this could be his last evidence that once there was a woman who could touch his heart with her naked hand.

Exhausted, Jerry and his guides hobbled toward the town center. There were no lights except for candles and little lamps flickering behind broken windows, but many people scurried about. Then they disappeared from the streets, all at once.

The travelers shuffled along the dark and empty street until they were stopped by two firearm-carrying men who unceremoniously aimed their weapons at the trio and ordered them to stop. One wore a torn and dirty police uniform; the other was a civilian, but carried a double-barreled shotgun. They wanted to know what Jerry and his companions were doing out after the curfew.

"Curfew?" Jerry gasped. That would explain why people had suddenly disappeared. "We've just crossed from the leeward side. Sorry, we didn't know about the curfew."

"What's your business here? What are you looking for?" the policeman asked with suspicion, stepping back to avoid the odor drifting from the suspects.

"I'm looking for Cat, a young woman who used to live by the canal in Kaimalino."

The policeman looked at his partner who shrugged his shoulders. "Let's take them to Cat. They are in no shape to give us any trouble."

Flickering lights broke the darkness at the far end of a large hall, revealing a group of people sitting around a long table. They stopped talking and looked at the commotion at the door, raising sharp, thin faces with dark shadows around sunken eyes. From inside they could only see the outlines, as the newcomers were standing in the dark part of the room.

"These guys were walking on Kailua Street after curfew. They claim to have come from the leeside, over the mountains," the policeman reported.

Jerry saw Cat sitting in her wheelchair and felt an immense gratitude to someone … something … that had saved her. But he had to notice as well that her face, round, brown and freckled just a few weeks ago, was almost white with indrawn cheeks accentuating her impossibly high cheekbones. Her full, red lips had transformed into ribbons of pale skin, a landmark significant only in marking her mouth. Only the eyes … Cat's eyes had become a pair of big, blue windows shining with quiet power, dominating her image, cloaking in shade her emaciated body, wheelchair, matted hair and ragged clothes.

"What's that smell?" Yoshida asked, sniffing the air. "Have you guys really come over the mountains? And what for?"

"Blubber, whale blubber," said Alika. "We've got us a whale, and thought you might want some. But we come here because of him," and he pointed a finger at Jerry.

Jerry stepped forward into the lighted area and dropped his pack. He had not shaved since San Diego and had a few strenuous weeks behind him. Although he was not starving, he had lost a lot of weight and looked ten years older. He was looking at Cat, and she was looking back, not sure if this shabby man was really Jerry.

Jerry cleared his voice and found himself at a loss for words, just like when they first met. "Hello, Cat. I … I have come to be with you." His words had all the painful awkwardness of a teenager being introduced to his love's parents; his embarrassment spread to his guides, who almost cringed. But it was the truth.

"Jerry? Jerry, what the hell are you doing here?" Cat did not sound happy, rather shocked and, possibly, somewhat annoyed or embarrassed.

Kalani was looking at him with wide-open eyes, and slowly, almost inaudibly said, "It's love. It's love."

Carol started giggling and rolling her eyes, until Yoshida stopped them all saying, "I see you've brought something …"

The change of subject to the practical issue brought Jerry relief. "I thought you might be able to use some food, so I've brought a few supplies. Also, Kawika from Kalaeloa sends you pieces of the whale they have killed."

From the first moment he saw Cat, he knew he would not be able to simply take her away. She was in the middle of this crisis, and she would not quit until the drama was over. The best he could hope for was to be readmitted into her world, and that was what he planned to do.

Alika and Kekoa happily lay down on the cool marble floor, their feet elevated on the blubber packs. Jerry was also very tired, and he was not going to stay on his feet a second longer than necessary. He pulled himself a chair up to the table and sat in front of Cat.

"Yes, I've come to be with you. I see that the landscape has rearranged itself, so I would like to help until some relief arrives."

Cat recovered from her shock, and her face softened with

a smile bringing a hint of better times. "Then you may have to stay quite a while. We spoke with the governor and no relief is coming anytime soon. We are grateful for the supplies you brought, but how exactly do you propose to help us—teach us economics?"

As much as he liked to see her smiling again, the snide remark annoyed Jerry. He had made quite a few major changes in his life, and it took no small effort for him to come back, so a bit of appreciation was what he expected.

"First, I wouldn't mind a drink of water for my friends and myself. Secondly, I quit teaching economics a few weeks ago, and now I consider myself more of a sailor, a handyman, a smuggler and a pack mule. A bit of a diesel mechanic, perhaps, as well. Ah, I was offered a carpenter's job a few weeks ago as well."

Cat's face was warming up. Now, she was looking at him with pleasure and a sparkle of humor. "All that! I am sure we'll find something usable in this mountain of skills. Mike, what do you think, maybe we could use a smuggler?"

The policeman picked up on the joke. "I prefer that he fixes my squad cars so they don't need no gas." They were an easygoing bunch, even though the six of them together could not weigh much more than six hundred pounds.

"So what's in the pack?" Kalani asked. Between her orphanage, herself and Cat, the supplies that came from Rosen's home were already used up. She firmly believed she had the right to his food as Rosen never came back to change his offer, but all that was gone. She could have more had she gone back to the restaurant sooner; unfortunately, someone beat her to the food store. It was empty when she came calling with Abe and his rickshaw. The kids were again crying from hunger and she was getting desperate.

"A gallon of olive oil, a big box of cubed sugar, ten-pound sack of rice, another ten pounds of flour, vitamins and powdered milk…." Kalani's smile was getting wider and

Return to Paradise

wider. "Jerry, if Cat doesn't want you, I might consider. Just kidding—nobody tell Abe."

"Hey, sistah, how 'bout us, you consider us?" Kekoa was grinning from his spot on the floor, waiting for recognition.

"All this blubber!" Kalani enthused. "I certainly would consider, except that the good-looking guys like you must have their steady women on the Leeside."

"They don't smell too good, either," Dr. Lee sniped.

None of them did after this long day of climbing and marching. Jerry decided to cool off and wash in the ocean, a two-minute walk from the house. He hoped Cat would join him, so that they could speak privately. She agreed so willingly that he started to believe that coming to Kailua had not been in vain.

Jerry pushed her wheelchair as far as the broken asphalt allowed then picked her up, carrying her in his arms to the water's edge. She clung to him like a sleepy child and seemed to weigh just as much. Her body had lost the firmness his hands remembered.

He laid Cat on the sand and slowly helped her take her clothes off. With her full breasts shriveled, her belly sunken and her hipbones protruding, she was an icon of abandonment, his desertion. Jerry undressed himself quickly, picked her up and walked into the water.

They floated in the warm water for a moment then started swimming slowly along the beach. The moon shimmered on the black water, glittered on the small waves spilling onto the sand, and brought into relief the gray dunes stretching all the way to the motionless field of broken black ironwoods.

Cat was weak; a few minutes later they beached themselves at the water's edge. They stayed in the shallow water, holding each other just as they had in her swimming pool, a lifetime ago.

She pulled herself onto Jerry's chest, looked into his eyes and gently kissed him. "Even if you are an apparition, I will make you stay with me forever."

His hands felt her wet head, her spiky spine sharply sticking through the skin, the thin hard ribs and her tiny buttocks shining white in the moonlight. "I will stay with you forever … but I have a condition. I want a privilege. You will have to grant me the right to take care of you. To carry you, to feed you and do whatever you need—even if you don't know what it might be." For this fiercely independent person, Jerry knew, granting such a privilege would be the consent to take her.

"I do," she said, "and I want the same from you."

"I do, too," he said, and that was their proposal and marriage ceremony.

They returned to the Round House where Kalani opened a can of tuna Jerry had brought and pulled out three crackers for their wedding party. Jerry went with Cat to her office room where they slept on her narrow bed, too small for two grown people but perfect for two scarecrows in love. He felt the warmth of her body in his arms, caressed her hair and thought, "I've won her back, Pam. She is mine."

Chapter 33

Cat, Jerry, January 27–29

Surveillance transcript, restaurant conversation, Washington, D.C.

Speaker 1: What are they going to do with this Hawaii mess? It just looks worse and worse every day. Now the Navy's clamped the exclusion zone around the Islands to prevent foreign aid.
Speaker 2: Yeah, that's pretty bad. The concern is that the Chinese might take advantage of the situation and try to establish some presence. You know, an NGO relief post today, informal foreign government office tomorrow. Meanwhile, they might support local opposition, independent Hawaii movements and so on. The strategic value of Hawaii is just too high to take this kind of a risk.
Speaker 1: How about the population? There's hardly any relief effort. All our transportation assets are directed at the Middle East.
Speaker 2: Quite unfortunate, indeed. We don't have enough of the long-range transport capacity, so first things have to go first. But the prez got really pissed

about this famous governor's conversation. You have to agree it won't look good at the exhibit in his presidential library. So he ordered a few transport planes to be sent to Hawaii. They can land at the Marine base or the Air Force base—it seems that we have quite a few operational assets in Hawaii; it's only the international airport that got smashed. That should shut the press up for a few days. Then they'll come up with some other solution. Not much can be done until we can send big cargo ships, but the ports are quite damaged.

Speaker 1: You mean ... we don't have landing craft to transfer the stuff from oceangoing ships to the beaches? After all, there are beaches in Hawaii!

Speaker 2: Don't be ridiculous, of course we have amphibious craft—even in Hawaii, but they have to stay on standby, in case we need them for something else or somewhere else.

"Be quiet, mice, or Cat will get you!" Kalani threatened.

"Cat, Cat, get us! Get us!" the kids yelled happily.

Cat listened from her place beside Jerry smiling. "I should go; Kalani needs my help," she whispered, sitting up. She pulled on her t-shirt and shorts and hoisted herself into the wheelchair. She looked better that morning—some color had returned to her lips and cheeks.

Jerry came out a few minutes later to see a toddler sitting on Cat's knees while two others tried to climb her legs to get on her lap. Kalani was distributing soup into bowls. She was happy to have some real food in the pantry; it might last three or four days, but—certainly—she would not ignore the blubber. A propane stove was hissing outside the window, brewing something she called soup for lack of a better name, spewing the powerful odor of boiling fat and fish. She had thoughtfully placed the burner downwind from the house.

"Kalani, you think somebody will actually want to eat

your soup?" Jerry asked, convinced he knew the answer.

The girl smiled with mischief and declared, "First, I put ginger into the soup. That'll make it muuuch better. Second, nobody gets nothin' until they have my soup. That includes the two of you. You'll see."

Much to Jerry's surprise, the children emptied their bowls of blubber soup without a word of protest; their hunger turned out to be stronger than the blubber's smell. Only then was everyone given one guava, a multivitamin tablet from *Lady Luck*'s supplies and a spoonful of rice.

Kalani turned her eyes to Cat and said sternly, "I'm watching you." For Jerry's benefit, she added, "It's this strange situation when the mice"—she pointed at her little herd—"eat the cat," and she turned her index finger at Cat. "She gives them her food, and at some point, she'll just drop dead. But they need her; the whole *ohana* needs her more than a miserable spoonful of rice."

Cat began eating humbly.

Abe came down from the bedroom upstairs where he slept next to Kalani. Late the previous night, he had returned from the long foraging trip along the shore to the north, past Kaneohe. He had brought some guava fruit, a few coconuts and pineapples, a small heap of mussels, but the biggest prize was a foot-long fish he had killed with a stick in a tidal pool near Kaawa. He looked worn out from the lack of food and long marches.

The men shook hands and Abe sat next to Jerry. "Not much stuff to show for two days of searching," he said, half in complaint, half excuse.

"Lots of guys are looking," Jerry said.

"That's it," Abe sighed.

"Have you tried to fish? I know you're a fisherman by trade."

"Everybody tries to get fish in the bay." Abe shrugged. "There are more men in the water than fish. It's easier to get poked with a spear than see a fish. You'd have to go a few miles out to catch some real fish, but I don't think there's a boat left on the island. In any case … there's no fuel, so I'll just keep pounding dirt. God, I hate walking!"

"Abe, what would you say if I could get you a boat that can go around all the islands of Hawaii without filling her fuel tank even once?" Excited, Jerry stood up. He had never caught a fish in his life, but Abe … Abe certainly had! Deep-sea fishing! This could be their long-term solution, unlike the short-term fix of the few cans and jars still hidden in Keehi.

"I'd say that you need a doctor." Abe lay down to put his still sore legs up on a chair. "But what's the use of a doctor if there are no medicines? I told you; there are no boats on Oahu." He had found a comfortable position and would rather not move until the next foraging expedition, probably tomorrow.

"Jerry"—Cat raised her head with excited anticipation—"how did you get here from the West Coast?" With all the things to talk about, so far no one had questioned his miraculous reappearance in Hawaii.

"In a sailboat," Jerry declared, his eyes happily absorbing the impact his statement had on Cat, who held her breath and blushed.

Abe, suddenly energized, jumped to his feet.

"And the boat is sitting in Keehi Lagoon, hidden," Jerry added. "I figure …"—now he turned to the agitated man—"if we make this one last long trek to Keehi, we won't have to walk any more. What do you say?"

"I'm ready to start right now." Abe's smile had the qualities of a carved pumpkin, wide beyond nature's design and lasting till the first frost.

"You've taken a lot of risk and trouble to be with me, Jerry," Cat said softly, her blush fading.

Jerry's and Abe's sore legs had to be ignored; every day

Lady Luck spent alone in Keehi only increased the possibility of their treasure being discovered by someone else. They decided to go the same afternoon, hoping to make it to the mountain pass by nightfall, sleep in the bushes and start going down at sunrise.

Once they had the boat sailing, Abe could put to use the fishing gear stored on board, and he swore to have a few mahi-mahi or ahi on board by the time they sailed into Kailua Bay. A state of happy excitement gripped the Round House crew as though they already had all their problems solved.

That would be a lot of high-quality food … but how long does fish last without a functioning refrigerator? Jerry thought. What stuck in his memory was the mountain of meat in the form of whale carcass, destined to become a malodorous heap of waste. Fish might spoil even faster.

"Folks," he announced loudly, raising his arm to stop the happy chatter, "we need a market here. The way you function now is about thirty thousand years old. Hunter-gatherers, that's what you are." He looked at Cat, who rolled her eyes as though she was saying: Not again!

"If, indeed, we catch a few decent fish, that would be too much food for us to eat, and we can't keep it without refrigeration. We should swap the fish for something useful. We need a market."

"We could give it to the neighbors; that's what we did every time we had more than enough for ourselves," Kalani remarked.

"Giving is nice, but it doesn't encourage work," Cat remarked thoughtfully, nodding her head. She saw Jerry's point. "We have fewer volunteers now than we had at the beginning; nobody seems to be doing anything productive. Jerry's right; we need a functioning economy so everybody gets off his or her butt. But what would we sell it for? Who needs dollars? You can't eat greenbacks."

"We can start with barter." Jerry, the professor, was in

his element. "How would you like an electric lamp here or a radio? There must be an electronics repairman in town ... he could take a wind generator off a wrecked boat and fix it. Maybe he has already done it, just for himself. Now, in exchange for a tuna, he could give us a generator and inverter.

"How about starting home repairs, even your house, Cat? Building materials are everywhere—on the ground, free for the taking. Yet I wouldn't say there is a building boom around here. This better start soon, since nobody's rushing from the outside to help.

"Someone must be growing fresh vegetables as we speak. He might want to swap a few eggplants or a watermelon for a piece of our ahi. As for money," he continued, "I trust the free market. People will find something they want to keep. I'd bet that a few weeks from now gold will buy a lot of things, for example."

"Gold is good," Abe interjected. "My grandpa told me that in the thirties, when food was hard to come by, people who had a few gold coins ate well when everybody else was starving. He even got a gold piece once, when they landed a big marlin."

"What happened to it?" Kalani wanted to know.

"He bought himself a woman," Abe answered with a straight face. "But she left him after a week, because they found out that the coin was a fake. But, Grandpa said, this week was worth his marlin," and he broke into loud, boisterous laughter while Kalani pretended to be offended.

Abe knew the windward side of the Koolau Mountains even better than Alika and Kekoa, who had left Kailua the morning after their arrival. Now Abe led the way up a steeper but shorter course, which Jerry found remarkably easy without a heavy backpack. Carrying only bags with water bottles and small packets of cooked rice, they reached the pass with the last rays of sun.

The windward side was already in dark shadow, its valleys

completely black, while the western slope displayed the majestic panorama of foothills flooded with the warm glow of sunset. The golden hue of the mountaintops darkened downhill, as patches of grass, bushes and trees gradually increased in size and frequency. They saturated the slope with turquoise, peppermint, moss, lemon—all the colors of desert plants enjoying the brief winter respite, until they came to dye the strip at the ocean's edge in a dark bottle-green shade. Further out, the deep blue of the Pacific merged with the sky, overpowering the earthly palette of colors with its immense size and luminosity.

The air temperature began falling after sunset, but hot rocks, baked by the day's exposure to the full power of the sun, were slow to cool. Abe and Jerry collected dry wood during the last minutes of daylight, hid behind a big boulder and made a small fire. Abe was very much at home on the mountain. He was a confident and skillful man here, happy with his life despite its deprivations.

Jerry grew cold during the night and woke up under the black sky studded with millions of stars. Above, around and even below his mountaintop perch, the countless brilliant points congregated in swirls and patterns that fed the imagination of every race on the earth. He had seen some beautiful night skies during his cross-Pacific sail, but the sky above the Koolau Mountains was incomparable. The air clarity, and the darkness blanketing the island below, brought the heavenly lights into relief so sharp that he felt an almost religious awe.

He woke again at dawn, deeply chilled, with his limbs stiff. As he was slowly and painfully getting up, a familiar sarcastic voice asked, "Where's your backpack? You shouldn't be here by yourself."

It was him again, the old man with a shotgun. This time he was more personal and disagreeable. Perhaps he felt embarrassed about the failed ambush two days ago.

The barrel was aimed at Jerry's belly and the mugger had a threatening, cold smile on his face.

"No backpack—I'm coming back with nothing." Jerry said loudly, hoping Abe would notice that a robbery was in progress. Fortunately, the gunman did not realize he had a companion.

"Take your shoes and clothes off," the old guy commanded. Jerry sat on the ground fiddling with his shoelaces, trying to distract the scoundrel in order to give Abe the best chance for a counterattack.

The robber was getting annoyed and brutally shoved the gun's barrel into Jerry's stomach. Hit in his solar plexus, Jerry curled on the ground, missing the sudden movement behind the gunman. He raised his head only when the muffled thump of a body hit with a heavy blunt object sounded over his head.

The mugger was tumbling sideways like he'd been hit by a car. Simultaneously, his shotgun went off and the load of lead missed Jerry's chest by inches. Pellets splattered against the rock behind him, falling to the ground like lead rain, while the shooter's body rolled down the slope. His blindly clutching hands waved around, searching for something to stop his movement until one grasped a clump of dry grass. The rolling stopped, but he was hanging at the point where the steep slope became a nearly vertical cliff.

Jerry, deafened by the shotgun's blast, could not hear the words, but the lips of the mugger's brown face, distorted in a grimace of panic, seemed to say, "Help me, please!"

Abe took a few steps down the slope. "What is it, Vincent? You ate all your cocks? You ate my chicks as well? You turned to robbing people, *mokule*! Well, it's nothing new for you." He made no gesture suggesting he was going to help.

Vincent knew that his fate was sealed and said nothing, just held onto the grass, his eyes closed. As the roots started breaking out of the red dirt, slowly, one by one, he uttered a long moan then plummeted down, the dry tufts still in his hand. He disappeared over the cliff's edge, but the heavy thud of a body hitting a rock confirmed his fate.

At one point, Jerry had the reflexive urge to look for a stick, to help the old man hanging above the precipice, but Abe grabbed his arm without a word and held it.

He was right, Jerry realized—there was no other justice for people like Vincent. The basic law of the struggling town said: Take care of yourself the best you can, and we won't bother you with small stuff. But if you cross the line, we will not tolerate you among us. Vincent had crossed that line. A jail was not a facility the community could afford.

Kawika was happy to see Jerry again. Diarrhea and bellyaches had stopped troubling his people since they started using the treated water. Daily treks to Honolulu to fetch a few gallons of water had stopped. The food shortage was, at least temporarily, alleviated with the whale meat. Life in the community started to normalize.

Lady Luck waited in her hiding place, dirty and sad-looking but full of treasures. Kawika's people unloaded the remaining bleach and took it to the village, then returned to fill the boat's tanks with clean water. Perhaps fifteen gallons of diesel left, Jerry calculated. He decided to keep it in reserve. The sails were in good condition and he felt confident he could bring the boat to Kailua by the power of wind alone.

He and Abe pushed *Lady Luck* out of the mangrove cove at five the next morning, after catching a few hours of sleep. The sky was still black, but starting to turn gray and pink in the east.

They moved through the lagoon with extreme caution. Jerry did not dare to hoist any sails, though the offshore wind would help to push them out into the open ocean. The harbor was littered with dozens of submerged boats, their pathetic bows or sterns jutting out of the water, threatening any moving object. Some boats had sunk upright, with a mast projecting upwards like a tree growing from the lagoon's bottom. Coils of steel rigging hid just under the surface, the flailing arms of a zombie boat, waiting to snag the keel of a vessel that was still alive.

Jerry devised a way to move his boat based on kedging, the ancient technique of maneuvering tall ships in tight ports, used long before the motor had been invented.

First, Abe rowed the dinghy between wrecks, searching for a clear path for *Lady Luck*. In the dinghy, he carried an anchor which was attached to the sailboat. Once he had reached the end of the eighty-foot line, he dropped the hook overboard. Jerry, standing aboard his yacht, weighed the boat's second anchor at this point, and took in the line attached to Abe's anchor.

This way *Lady Luck* was pulled forward slowly but safely. When the sun's red rim touched the city towers in the east, they touched the obstacle at the channel's mouth.

At that point, Jerry raised the sails and their hard labor ended, as the wind urged the boat out into the ocean. *Lady Luck* turned her bow southeast, taking a fifteen-knot wind on her port beam. They were on their way to the Penguin Banks, where Abe was confident he would catch fish they would not be ashamed to trade.

With Jerry at the helm, Abe worked on the fishing tackle, assembling bits and pieces he found on the boat into functioning fishing gear. Soon, four lines trailed from the stern.

The first fish struck Abe's line about one, just when they had finished a can of stew from the boat supplies. Jerry had not eaten a decent meal for a few days and was hungry, but Abe … Abe had not eaten above starvation level for a few weeks! Whatever food he could find, he kept bringing to Kalani, where it disappeared almost instantly into the hungry mouths of her orphans. Abe had a feast on the canned stew but, when he was ready to relax and digest, one of the rods bowed and its float disappeared under the water.

There was nothing subtle or ambivalent about it. A big fish had taken the bait and planted the hook solidly in its mouth. The shaft bent immediately, and Abe let out some line.

High-stakes politics in action, Jerry thought, looking at the contest between Abe and the fish. Whenever the creature tried to dash for freedom, the fisherman released some line, fearing it could break off. Between the attacks, the line was relentlessly rolled in. The tired fish allowed these calm periods to last longer and longer, and finally the rainbow-colored dorsal fin of a large mahi-mahi broke the surface. Soon, a blunt head appeared next to the boat, and Jerry swiped the fish into a net on a long handle. The mahi-mahi was much too big for his net, but they pulled Abe's prey onboard by grabbing at its fins and gills. Abe hit it on the head with a beer bottle from John's cache, and the fight was over.

An interesting morality tale—Jerry thought—with conclusions relevant far beyond the field of fishing: A free meal may turn out to be bait, so don't take it. Once you taste a hook in your mouth, try to break away hard because hopeful idleness will kill you. Finally, you won't see the guy who's holding the line until you're about to get a blow on the back of your head.

Two uneventful hours later, while Abe was filleting the fish, Jerry turned the bow north. The wind increased and the boat heeled as they pressed toward Makapu'u Rock where Jerry intended to turn left and run with the easterly wind to Kailua. The rod bowed again, and before Abe had time to bring the second fish in, another floater went under the water. It was time for Jerry to try his fishing skills, leaving the steering to the wind vane. After a brief struggle, utilizing his newly developed concept of the victim's deadly idleness, he pulled in a small yellowfin tuna.

By late afternoon, while the Makapu'u lighthouse was passing leeside, they had over fifty pounds of fish on board.

Jerry started rounding the course to the west, and the ride became smooth and comfortable as the wind shifted behind the stern.

"Beats walking, eh?" Jerry grinned. He had good reasons to be happy; his new life seemed to bring many rewards.

Abe flicked a cigarette butt overboard; he had inherited John's stash of tobacco. "For sure, I forgot how good it is to be on the ocean. I was so stupid not to take old Kumashiro's boat. We both would have been so much better off." Obviously, he was referring to Kalani.

"So, what will you do now, Abe? Looks like things are good and happy between you and Kalani." Jerry encouraged Abe's reflections.

"Oh, we're fine now. You know, sometimes I have this crazy feeling that the earthquake, tsunami ... all this shit happened to bring me back to my senses. Then I feel guilty ... like other people had to pay the price for my stupidity."

"Ah!" Jerry waved dismissively. "Don't worry. Everybody had his own good reasons to have his ass kicked. Maybe young kids are innocent, but they will not remember it anyway. The rest of us, we all did enough shit to deserve it, without your help. The important thing is, we have a second chance—some folks will take it and others will screw up again."

Abe considered the idea for a moment. "You sound almost like a preacher. Cat never mentioned you were religious. I like it. We got whipped like naughty boys, but it looks like we'll survive. And if we do, we will be much better people."

"Abe, this has nothing to do with religion." Jerry felt he should clarify his position. "Don't call any shepherds on this stray sheep; I'm not religious and I like to graze by myself. It just came to my mind because they call this place Paradise. Some paradise! But again, maybe we are not holy enough to go straight to heaven. You can't have Paradise full of sinners, can you?"

They had a large heap of beautiful pink flesh lying in

the middle of the cockpit. Without refrigeration or ice, the fish would not stay this good for long. They packed it into buckets, covered it with salt water and hoped to reach Kailua in a few hours. Meantime, they enjoyed *ahi poke*, fresh tuna cut into cubes and consumed raw.

Jerry felt that Skipper Browser would have ordered him to share his beer with Abe at this point. John and Abe looked different, had unlike backgrounds, but were made from the same piece of cloth; two strong characters that confidently made their living at the perilous sea but lost their way on the shoals of domestic life. Abe had the good fortune to be knocked down and get back up to his private paradise early in life. John's chance to get a new start had been taken away from him. Jerry opened two bottles of Heineken, and he and Abe savored the beer under the sky full of stars.

Chapter 34

Rosen, January 22

The person once called Harry Rosen lowered himself slowly and carefully off the ledge to the rock's bottom. The blackness of night was turning into dark slate and he expected the sunrise within thirty or forty minutes. It was the time when even human predators were abandoning their hunt while decent folks still clung to their pillows. For exactly these reasons, Rosen has chosen this time of day to travel. He had good reason to fear the authorities; who knew how widely his unfortunate affair with Kalani had been circulated? His swollen face and off-kilter nose would easily attract unwanted attention. On the other hand, the island was full of people with swollen faces, broken body parts and worse, so maybe he was too cautious. But his incredible failure to acquire Kalani as a slave proved that there was no such thing as being too careful.

Harry could not think of it without rage. He had it all; everything was going for him, and still he had landed on the floor with his nose broken, while his prize flew away like a flushed quail. Frankly, it could have ended worse; she could have whacked him with some heavy object right then or changed him into a living torch. He would have to forgive himself and just learn from the experience. Yes, *learning experience* … it had a fine ring to it, something to drown the bad memory.

On the other hand, he was quick to remind himself, I did show remarkable foresight. There was a plan B, the contingency plan prepared and executed ahead of any need. That's why he was not very worried about the future. A small apartment in downtown Honolulu was waiting for him; there he could hide and plan for the future. His modest one-bedroom place was stocked with ample provisions, a small cache of emergency money, a never-used passport and new identity. This was his safe haven—once he got there safely.

Rosen had run out of his house in Lanikai ten minutes after having the bitter experience of watching Kalani fleeing down his driveway like she was being chased by a pack of wolves. He should easily have had thirty minutes to pack up and get out of his lair, but was not in a mood to tempt the fate. He rammed his personal treasure bag—containing most of El Diablo's assets—into the backpack, threw some food and water on top and slipped a handgun under a large foil-packed tablet of chocolate.

Just like Kalani before him, completely exposed to any chance observers, he dashed along the empty road at full speed. There was nothing he could do about these moments of vulnerability except to cut them as short as possible. He did not slow down—even when his lungs began to feel like they would burst—until he turned off Aalapapa Drive into a side street. Even then, Rosen rushed up the steeply rising lane with all the speed he could master—past a golf course, to a patch of dense bush at the foothill. He made three frantic leaps into the thicket and collapsed among the weeds, struggling to inhale enough air to keep his heart beating.

Once his power of reasoning returned, taking over from the instinct-driven mad dash away from danger, Rosen could formulate his plan in more detail. All the elements of a successful emergency evacuation were there, prepared for just such an unexpected setback. All he needed now was to put them in a coherent chain of events, avoiding all unnecessary risks.

"Fuck," he swore, touching his swollen face, which was now hurting like hell and had to be all smeared with blood.

It was not a blind coincidence that his frantic dash ended in this particular patch of tangled weeds, shrubs and gnarly trees. A trail started here, which climbed the Lanikai Ridge and led off, branching all over the Koolau Range, feeding into the network of mountain tracks. A person trekking along these pathways could walk unobtrusively like an innocent hiker to other valleys that, though located just a few miles away from Kailua, were separated by lack of gasoline like islands in their own right.

Rosen knew that because he had walked the trail, not for enjoyment of the views—although they indeed were magnificent—but for gaining familiarity with his backyard. In fact, he hated hiking—it reminded him too much of boot camp and its brain-numbing discipline—but there were things the Army got right, and one of them was scouting the terrain. Liking it or not, Rosen had passed many of these trails, just one of the hundreds of awestruck tourists, stick in his hand, water bottle and sandwich in his backpack.

Thus he knew how to get to Waimanalo, a small beach town closer to Honolulu. From there, Kaleanianaole Highway could take him to Honolulu in comfort, but it was reportedly closed be a rockslide. This obstacle could be a problem for cars, Rosen thought, but not for a reasonably fit and motivated hiker. The route to his secret shelter sorted out, he got on his still trembling legs and began the climb.

What used to take him an hour or two in daylight became a risky venture in the darkness. The narrow path seemed to end every few yards, his body bumping hard into a rock arising in the middle of the trail, or a tangle of dense thorny brush sprouting in front of him.

He made little progress until the sharp half-moon emerged from behind clouds only to disappear a minute or two later. It made sense, he eventually decided, to wait for the short periods of moonlight to make quick dashes ahead, catching his breath during the darkness. This way, slowly but safely, a few hours later, he descended from the ridge on the Waimanalo side and sprawled in the brush, resting and waiting for the final hour before the sunrise.

A dash across Bellows—the Air Force vacation resort—took him to Waimanalo's tiny commercial center, which he traversed in a few short sprints. The section of highway overrun by the black mass of rocks became visible a few hundred yards down the road. Rosen jumped the chain-link fence and found a well-protected corner behind a huge banyan tree. He had time to mull over the events of the last night now, but he fell asleep fast and sound, heartened by the good progress he'd made. Unproductive whining and self-recriminations did not belong to a master's psychological profile.

Invigorated after a two-hour snooze, Rosen returned to the road. The black, unstable rubble spread all the way from the eroded volcanic mountaintop onto the beach and into the ocean. Millions of rock fragments, ranging from a fraction of an inch to a few yards in diameter, looked ready to roll anytime someone set foot on the slope.

This was not the time to be bold, Rosen decided. He could make out a faint pathway; someone had already walked this way and more than once. This person would be back and could be used; all Harry needed to do was to wait. The ditch overgrown with leafy bushes offered a fine observation point.

The sun was harshly heating his hideout by the time two men approached the path, empty packs on their backs. Mules, Harry assumed. Will try to cross the landslide in an attempt to get some supplies in Honolulu. They would know the way and, possibly, could offer some protection from muggers. They might try to rob him themselves, of course, but not before reaching Honolulu. Why shoot a pack animal before the end of a trek? He should be safe until that moment.

Rosen left his hideout and approached the men. A soft, middle-aged man, dressed like an accountant on vacation, humbly asked if they could help him to get across the rocks, to Honolulu.

The shorter, older man, who seemed to be in charge, looked him over, his eyes lingering on the bulging backpack. His younger companion, an obnoxious-looking boy with Japanese letters tattooed on his chest and Polynesian patterns on his naked shoulders and arms, turned to the leader with a silent query. The pink-faced *haole* looked like easy prey.

"Vot's in da pack? Why you go to Honolulu?" the older man asked sharply.

Harry declared himself a tourist stranded in Kailua, trying to get to Honolulu to grab the first plane leaving the island. "The backpack? Just a few personal things ... and some food. Of course, I'd be happy to share it with you!"

The man struggled with temptation for a moment but did not reach to feel the pack; there would be lots of time for that. He shrugged and, without saying so much, agreed to let Harry tag along. The leader lightly threaded the path, followed by the youngster and Rosen, who had been commanded to stay twenty feet behind. Afraid to trigger a new landslide and distributing weight—smart, Rosen thought.

Walking uphill on the shifting mass of small rocks was hard, as they kept sliding back every few steps, and he was stiff from the fear of triggering a new avalanche. Harry had a pair of solid hiking boots, which made the climb somewhat easier, but his guides had only rubber sandals. Despite that, they were moving rapidly up like mountain goats with Rosen falling behind more and more. He lost sight of his guides when the trek turned from the loose, gravel-like pathway into an almost indistinguishable trail among large, black boulders.

Now he had to climb ledges and jump over wide fissures guided only by the faint and uncertain marks of wear on the rock's face. He pressed on with desperate determination until he came unexpectedly upon his escorts sprawled in the shade of a large boulder.

"Lunchtime. What you have to eat?" the older man asked unceremoniously. Rosen dutifully pulled out a loaf of stale, rock-hard bread, a few plastic-wrapped pieces of processed cheese and—with great celebration—a can of beer.

The guides were properly impressed, swallowed the food greedily and opened the beer. The foam of the warm and shaken beer spilled out of the can to their yells of joy. They shared it between themselves, none offered to Harry.

"Good," the boss said, "now we go. We waited for you forever."

"How much longer to Honolulu?" Harry asked. The previous night's fatigue was adding to the brisk hike of today; he was exhausted.

"Hour more over *da pohaku*, then fifteen miles to Honolulu. Way you walk, you come tomorrow." They both started laughing loudly and disrespectfully.

Harry said nothing, but it was not his plan to walk another fifteen miles that day.

The guides disappeared between towering rocks within a few minutes while Rosen followed them at a slower pace, knowing they would wait for him somewhere, probably at the end of the rockslide. The trail led him now along the exposed ocean-side aspect of the mountain. He could clearly see Rabbit Island a few hundred feet below. The threatening black finger of rubble extending from the mountain crossed the beach, pointing at the small rocky islet ringed by white surf, as though it were aiming at the target of some future assault. Beyond, the blue Pacific waters were unmarred except for the white wake of a small boat speeding south to Honolulu.

Wonder who has gas to motor to Honolulu, Rosen thought wistfully. He sat leaning against a warm rock, exposing his hot face to the ocean breeze. He was quite certain what needed to be done. Regardless of his guides' intentions—and he was sure they would try to mug him—it would be extremely imprudent to leave these two witnesses to his relocation. His broken face was easy to remember; these two men would have a story to tell to whoever might be looking for him.

As he expected, they were sitting and smoking under the first tree that had survived the landslide. The spindly acacia was sparsely covered with leaves and offered meager shade. The yellow and sickly-green grass thinly blanketed the rocky soil; they were definitely off the windward side; rain was an infrequent visitor in this neighborhood.

Harry approached the men with a tired smile, stopped six feet in front of them and took his backpack off. He reached inside and pulled out two shiny chocolate bars—soft, bent and leaking brown beads. He held the candy bars out for the hungry men to see and desire. He knew that this high-energy food would be irresistible to the starving, tired men. When they both straightened, sitting up from their slumped positions, Rosen threw the chocolate on the ground, two feet short of their extended arms. The two faces looked down and they went on their knees to snatch the bars.

Harry put his hand into the pack again and pulled out a short-barreled black revolver. Before they looked up, one shot delivered to the top of the older man's head splashed his brain onto the drying grass. A few droplets of blood and yellow fatty substance landed on Rosen's pants. The boy struggled to get to his feet, but another bullet tore into the middle of his chest while his knees were still touching the ground. Rosen looked for a moment at the two bodies; the youngster was still twitching and moving. He stepped back to avoid additional soiling of his clothes. Another crack of the gun sent a bullet into the boy's temple, stopping all movement. One can't be too cautious.

Rosen picked up his chocolate and placed the bars back in the pack. There was nothing of value in the guides' pockets. They were just the mules meant to take goods from one side of the rockslide to the other. A pack of cigarettes, found in the older man's pocket, was of no interest to Harry—a filthy and unhealthy habit. He poured the remaining water from their almost empty bottles into his own container and turned away. The long day was not over yet, even though he was dragging his feet with great effort.

There was a golf club in this area, he knew, and it would be highly unlikely for anyone to have golf on his mind these days. Rosen used his last bit of energy to reach the lodge. The handsome wooden building's interior was dark. He climbed through a broken window and sprawled his body on the cool, polished concrete floor with great relief. Things were gradually looking up.

The small apartment building on Kalakaua Avenue had a backyard entrance. The house seemed undamaged; even the windows were intact, except for the shattered corridor pane. The landlord was an old man who lived somewhere else, and this fact was just another small element of the elaborate plan of concealment that Rosen had orchestrated. Old men have bad eyesight and poor memories; therefore, his landlord would be very unlikely to recognize Rosen, whom he had met only once, when the lease had been signed. The rental checks were sent by mail, always on time. There was never any noise or disturbance; Harry Rosen was a perfect tenant, one whom the landlord would not remember.

Rosen positioned himself on the opposite side of the street in the shadow of a luscious fern tree. He sat down like a tired traveler, exhausted by walking in the noon heat. He was tired, of course, but that was not his reason for parking himself, thirsty and hungry, on the bare ground while inside his apartment, he could lie down on a comfortable bed, eat and drink.

The reason he stayed outside was to allow time and opportunity for any suspicious signs to manifest themselves. No one knew of his safe house, but being security-conscious is a mindset. He went through the proper routines every single time; otherwise—he knew—someone would surprise him sooner or later. And Rosen hated surprises.

Chapter 35

Cat, Jerry, January 28–29

The smudges of fluorescence streaked in the boat's wake like tiny unraveling strings of magic brocade, and the wind noise decreased to a whisper once the stern turned to it.

"I know my sins—stupidity, mostly." Abe was coming back to his spiritual exploration. "Do you think stupidity is even a sin?" He turned his palms up with a doubtful expression on his face. "But how did *you* get into this mess? What are you guilty of?"

Jerry was not surprised by this question because he had been asking himself for weeks, Why did I screw up so badly the first time I met Cat? To blame his posttraumatic stress syndrome would be an easy way out; it got him off the military's hook all right. But he couldn't duck the charge so easily in his own judgment; this excuse wouldn't work when he was a prosecutor himself.

The fact was that the brick-wall man, his old trouble's principal character, had ceased to exist after the first date with Cat. Whether it was Cat's magic or just the right time for his scales to drop off was irrelevant. It had happened and was not a factor anymore. So what were my biggest faults?

"Laziness and rigidity, I think," Jerry reasoned aloud. "I was so attached to my way of living and thinking, that—even though they made me unhappy—I just refused to consider anything new. I heard Cat's arguments but stuck to my old ideas like a bug to a windshield. Frankly, they were not even that wild. It's not like I'd never heard them; I did. It's pretty old stuff; every university library has some dusty volumes of Hayek and von Mises on back shelves. But I was so sold on this modern econometrics stuff that I just refused to see simple facts. I guess you could it call a form of stupidity as well. It took a disaster to kick me out of my rut and—look at me—I took quite a bit of kicking, but I am a hundred times happier."

Abe nodded his head. "Same here. I think that stupidity is a major sin, whatever the pastor says on Sunday. If you think clearly, you don't do all these bad things you are supposed to go to hell for, you know: stealing, killing and screwing around … Why should I steal if I can spend a fine day on the ocean, catch fish and make money? Killing? You must be drunk or high, otherwise it's such a stupid thing to do. Adultery? If you're smart, you pick a woman that you really, really like—then what is the point of running after another?"

Jerry agreed. "Stupidity is the root of most evil," he declared. "Not so much because people lack brains, but because they don't want to use them. The guys who are short on horsepower in their skulls are rarely a problem. They do whatever it is that they can do, and often shine in their uncomplicated ways. In fact, the decisions we make in our lives are not that hard, most of the time."

Abe watched him, sprawled on the cockpit bench where Browser used to lounge.

"No, it's the folks with good brains who have problems. They're lazy and take someone else's opinion as their own. Why should they stress out? It's easier to believe, and there is no shortage of people who seem to know so well! They

Return to Paradise

are well dressed and have great titles: politicos, market gurus, reverends—they have all the answers, so why bother thinking? It's funny to see how many holy men enjoy the good life, telling their faithful how to please God, as if it were so hard to figure out." He looked to Abe to see his response but the fisherman was snoozing cuddled behind the dodger.

The wind was picking up and clouds covered the sky, making the skipper anxious—there was no harbor anywhere close to Kailua. Jerry's plan was to pick their way through the surf break next to Flat Island, and come to the beach as close as they could, hiding behind the reef. From his kayaking, Jerry remembered the channel's approximate location, but to see the actual reef would be reassuring; unfortunately this would be impossible at night.

The second problem had no solution: the bay offered fair protection from waves, but none against the wind. Jerry had to rely on luck, hoping that no storm would catch them at the beach, where *Lady Luck* could drag her anchors and get stranded on the sand.

He planned to stay anchored for a few hours only—just enough to unpack the supplies, off-load the fish and spend a bit of time with Cat. Then they would get out of Kailua Bay onto the open water, far out into the ocean, where they would be safe from rocks, reefs and shoals—sailors' curses.

A dense layer of clouds covered the sky, reducing the dark shoreline to vaguely marked outlines. Not until midnight, when a cloud break allowed the moon to illuminate the shore, did Jerry realize his error. Mortified, he discovered that he had overshot Flat Island. They were already downwind from it. Not far, perhaps a mile or two, but for a sailboat to be downwind from its mark is no small thing.

They would have to turn far, a few miles at least, into the ocean, trying to gain the distance upwind before aiming at Flat Island again. The wind was increasing, white water swirled around the boat, and they both were very tired. They had slept only six, perhaps seven, hours over the past three days. Jerry could clearly see Flat Island now, a low-lying small black patch amidst the ocean now shining in the moonlight. He could even make out the spot inside the reef barrier where they should have dropped the anchor, but to get there was not a simple task.

Skipper Browser would say, "We turn around and tack against the wind. We come in again in an hour or two." But Jerry was not Captain Browser, the tough, old mariner with experience longer than Jerry's life. He forgot, "You don't fuck with the ocean, Jerry."

"We turn the motor on, make a turn and come in motor-sailing. We'll be there in no time," Jerry commanded. The diesel came to life and *Lady Luck* stirred, vibrating and throwing white foam behind her stern. Jerry saw Bird Shit Island on the port side, the place of his defeat that had transformed his life. He might have never met Cat if the islet had not brought him to his knees.

Jerry's romantic notions about the Rock were dead wrong. Bird Shit Rock did not care about his love life; it wanted to complete the job started a few weeks ago, finish him off. The boat turned into the wind and the bow crossed the windline, sending the headsail into an anxious flutter. Jerry would not dare this maneuver using sail power alone; the rock's proximity was too dangerous and any miscalculation could land the boat in the white boiling water. But he was running a motor, a reliable fifty-horsepower Yanmar. Jerry felt safe with the diesel to fall back on.

A sudden gust of wind leaned the boat to its right as soon as the sails caught wind and their downwind drift rapidly quickened. Jerry watched in horror as the distance between the boat and the rock was rapidly shrinking. He threw the throttle into full power. The motor roared over the noise of crashing waves and the whistle of the wind. *Lady Luck* accelerated slightly, but with the wind gust pressing even harder, a few seconds later a loud thud announced that the keel had struck bottom. Not a bone-crushing shock of running into a rock, this impact felt as though the boat had been pushed on the rocks sideways, her drifting keel prevented from moving further by a hard resistance.

The helmsman jerked the main sheet to release the sail, too slow. The wind attacked again with a great fury, but *Lady Luck* could not move aside any more; she was against the wall. A loud crack sounded above, and the sails came tumbling down. Standing behind the steering wheel, Jerry was outside the area covered by white fabric and had the full, terrifying view of his unfortunate decision's consequences.

The mast broke off six feet above the deck and, carried by the swollen sails, flew over the right railing as far as the steel rigging allowed. Its tip was submerged in the water, but not deep enough to catch on the rocks. The faithful motor kept roaring and pushing the crippled craft away from the islet. The boat straightened up once the mast fell, and in a moment the horrible thumping on the bottom stopped. They were off the rock and moving forward.

The white mass in front of the cockpit moved and Abe's head appeared from under the fabric's edge. He was not injured, just badly shaken. "What the fuck!" He looked up, no need for explanations. They tied the mast to the hull and gathered the sails the best they could.

Flat Island appeared ahead a few minutes later, and they passed the reef's breach without problems. *Lady Luck* floated gently towards the beach where they dropped two anchors in eighteen feet of water. That would have been perfect, if they still had the mast. John would not be happy with his student, but they were alive and home. Bird Shit Rock had missed Jerry again. Kalani and Cat made an official party in honor of their men, but the *Lady Luck*'s crew fell asleep with their mouths full of fish.

A bright wedge of late morning light, creeping through the shaded room, reached Jerry's head and his eyes opened. The house was quiet, its occupants gone. He remained in bed for a moment, trying to identify the substance of mental distress gnawing his unconscious mind for the past few hours. *Lady Luck*—of course.

He went to the beach and there she was, gently rocking, her broken mast sticking up, crying to the heavens about his poor seamanship. Jerry swam to her. Diving, he carefully inspected every inch of the hull—there was a nasty gash on the right side of her keel, but no puncture wounds through the wall. He climbed in and continued his inspection inside the cabin. Apart from a general mess, to be expected after their traumatic journey, there seemed to be no significant damage inside and, most importantly, the bilge was dry. *Lady Luck* was not taking water. There was a chance for him to remain a captain.

The aluminum mast had broken off six and a half feet above the deck. The stump was clearly not tall enough to serve as a mast, Jerry thought, but … were it extended by ten or twelve feet … could it provide enough power to sail a few miles out and catch some fish? This was something worth trying.

He went to Kailua town in search of Cat and the other inhabitants of the Round House. He was intrigued by a steady stream of people on Kainalu Street, all walking in one direction, toward the recreation center. He joined the procession and shortly became a part of the crowd milling about on Kailua's public tennis courts.

At least twenty people stood or sat behind tables removed from the recreation center, hawking their goods.

Jerry marveled at the variety of merchandise that this devastated and isolated town had to offer. Despite widespread hunger, many food items were available. An elderly Japanese man was showing off holdovers from better times: a few cans of sardines and tuna. A small crowd of potential customers eyed his food with lust, but he held out for a better offer. The old guy did not see anything he would swap his cans for. The concept of money hadn't entered this primitive market yet.

A Filipino family put a few bunches of bananas on the table, next to a bucket of guavas and bundles of herbs. They were in the process of haggling over an ancient manual drill, which—with no electrical power and but a tremendous need for repairs—suddenly became the object of desire. A gray-haired lady cunningly dangled the implement by its crank in front of the man, who lost his trader's cool and, despite his wife's not so subtle hints, threw in some additional guavas to close the deal.

Cat and Kalani abandoned their empty table; they were out of fish, bartered mostly for Meal-Ready-To-Eat packages. Whichever suspect way the MREs had found their way to the windward, they were now filling a garland of yellow shopping bags that Kalani hung on Cat's wheelchair. A few papayas, a bunch of bananas and a bundle of chives filled the basket resting on her knees, completing their shopping spree. Despite their spending power being completely exhausted, Cat hung about by a set of solar panels. Maybe from a future catch …

A large portion of the excited crowd were just onlookers, but the trade had been brisk since the early morning. Cat set off the cascade by sending the news about fresh fish available at the recreation center. It surged through the grapevine, bringing in hundreds of potential buyers as well as a fistful of other hopeful sellers. It turned out that many people had something they could part with, as long as an object they needed was offered in a swap. Barter was the mode of exchange, but Jerry, the economist, was sure that money—whatever its form might be—would appear soon.

Many people had no business to conduct at the market, but they lingered, drawn by the palpable excitement. The mere act of trading made them feel that common sense had returned to the confused world. Where apathy, depression and deprivation ruled, people suddenly found an outlet for their energy, a reason to make an effort. The crowd was noisy and happy; laughter, so rarely heard, broke out like a rainbow after a very long rain.

Kalani's children ran in circles through the crowd, happily adding to the din and hum of a large outdoor party. Then, one by one, they returned to their protector, crowding tightly around her, grasping onto the flowery fabric of her tattered dress. None said a word but they all looked in one direction, painful desire in their eyes. The adults followed their gaze and there, on court number three, stood the first manufacturer of post-cataclysmic Kailua. A short woman, the skin on her arms loosely hanging, held a pole crowned with a red ball. Multiple five-inch-long sticks projected out of the ball, each with a lump of colored sugar stuck to its end.

"That must be Mrs. Hewlett, the lady who owned the dry cleaning," whispered Kalani. "Hard to recognize, she's lost so much weight."

Mrs. Hewlett seductively waved the candies towards the children, who responded with a simultaneous movement of their heads, as if hypnotized. The kids, close to death from starvation a few days ago, now fell under the spell of these primitive candies, blubber soup already forgotten.

"Good morning, Mrs. Hewlett," Kalani greeted her politely. "Your candies look very tempting."

"What do you have to trade?" the older woman inspected Kalani then the rest of the group.

"The fact is," Kalani sighed, "we have nothing now. We had fish, but it's all gone."

The candy lady's shoulders dropped in disappointment. Seeing the nine kids mesmerized by her wares, she'd been ready to make a killing. She frowned but said mildly, "Well, then … maybe tomorrow.…"

"Tomorrow" has all the qualities of "never," "forget it" or "maybe some other time" in children's minds. The nine faces fell, their eyes blinking to hide tears, but even so clear drops trickled down their cheeks.

"How about a pound of fresh fish for nine candies?" They heard Abe's confident voice coming from behind. He knew Mrs. Hewlett could not refuse a few lumps of sugar for a pound of fish.

Kalani looked around. "But we're out of fish, Abe. We have none left, even for us."

"Well, a pound of fish," he insisted. "But not today … tomorrow or the day after. We will go out fishing today, right, Skipper?" And so Abe initiated the Kailua futures market in commodities.

Jerry's heart—though he did not consider himself an economist anymore—sang at this marvelous display of chaos organizing itself into the living, breathing free-market economy, in the span of one morning. Adam Smith would have been proud of the people of Kailua.

"Neighbors and friends, this is Cat again. I have some great news to share with you. We mark today as the point when our community started moving forward again. Yes, we are still in rough shape; many of us are sick, and most are still hungry. But, we've made the first step to make Kailua a thriving town again; we have restarted its economy. The market opened at the recreation center today. It has been a great success, not because so many things were sold and bought, but because we have rediscovered the reasons to work and produce.

"We need everything, and people among us will produce most of it. Today, we were selling fish, enough to put sushi on a lot of family tables tonight. We sold papayas, guavas—all these things that grow abundantly in our loving Hawaiian soil. Tomorrow, we will be selling furniture, bicycles, and wheelbarrows. The day after that, you will see electronics and you will have power in your homes. We will make it happen!

"Just remember, we have been doing it ourselves. No knights in shining armor showed up at the rec center and no one saw Santa dropping packages from the skies. You and I, and our neighbors, got off the floor like a boxer, still punch-drunk, but back on his feet. We are on our feet and fighting back! So when someone comes later, telling us how lucky we were, and what they could do for us—just ask them, 'Where were you when we were dying?'

"If there is a silver lining to this storm that shattered our lives, it must be this lesson: survival demands self-reliance. Faraway people, organizations and governments have their long lists of problems and agendas. These lists are so long, and Kailua is so low on them, that no one noticed us starving and dying. You and your neighbors are the only protectors of your lives.

"We demand the means to protect ourselves right here, within our grip, when another disaster strikes. Food warehouses in Honolulu and the uniformed men commanded from across the ocean did us no good, even though we had paid for them with our taxes. The power and resources have to remain here, where we can control them."

Cat did not feel well and wanted to finish quickly; she felt a wave of nausea coming. "That will be all for tonight, folks. Have a good rest; there will be a lot of work for you tomorrow."

Jerry stood behind the glass pane, watching her talking, gesticulating and waving her hands. She was a powerful orator and had the instincts of a leader. Cat finished and slumped in her chair. The on-air light went off and he entered the studio. Her eyes were closed and she was breathing fast and shallow.

"Are you OK, Cat? You feel warm." He was worried.

"No, no, Jerry, I'm fine. It's from excitement, and I am really worn out. Let's go home, OK?"

They traveled along the dark streets, meeting people who

greeted Cat like an old friend. Maybe it was just an illusion, but people seemed to move in a more purposeful way, their backs held straighter.

No matter how much Jerry wanted to stay with Cat, *Lady Luck* needed to go out into the ocean. They'd been lucky so far; the wind had stayed around twenty knots and the anchors were holding, but a winter gale could strike with little warning. Besides, the market was waiting for fish.

Abe spent most of the day trying to extend the mast. A pole that would be long, strong and light was not easy to find. As in the old joke, they could have any two of these features, but not all the three together. Eventually, the solution came in the form of three windsurf masts tied together with thin line and wrapped around with duct tape. Stuck into the mast's stump, the bundle— remarkably light—added ten feet of height. There was no way to know how this rig would sail to the wind, but running with it, they should have some sail power.

Jerry was looking forward to experimenting with his boat, but he was worried about Cat. She slumped in her chair whenever out of sight, feigning an energetic posture the moment he turned toward her. A sickly crimson flush colored her pale face, contrasting with her colorless lips. He worried, cradling her warm body, but staying on land was not an option they could afford.

The night was clear when *Lady Luck* passed Flat Island, her deck gently vibrated by the diesel. Starting their day so early, a few hours before the sunrise, Jerry and Abe hoped to return before the sunset, after having over twelve hours of fishing time. In view of the recent trading success, they wanted to deliver a truly commercial load of fish this time.

A mile past the reef barrier, Abe unwrapped the furiously flapping canvas from the mast and lashed its base to the boom. As Jerry turned the bow off the wind, the misshapen stubby sail filled with air—they sailed again. Their improvised flexible mast bent grotesquely, but seemed strong enough to support a headsail as well; they hauled up the jib. The boat would not tack to the wind at more than seventy degrees, but, Jerry thought, neither would Columbus's *Santa Maria*! He shut off the engine.

A tack after another long and shallow tack, they were slowly advancing to the east, into the face of the steadily blowing trade wind. This was all they needed; their fishing lines trailing behind, they were in no hurry. In the afternoon, they would turn around and, propelled by the wind blowing from behind, they would swoop into Kailua like a Spanish galleon carrying a treasure of fish.

Abe had no worries on the ocean. In town, he was a shy and withdrawn man, his personality and wit fully revealed only among friends. But on the water, Abe displayed not only amazing physical strength and agility, but also an intellectual curiosity Jerry had not suspected.

"What Cat was saying about self-reliance, you think we could actually do it?"

"Don't see why not," Jerry answered curtly. The stress of taking the crippled boat to the ocean was only slowly dissipating.

"But, you know, they will never give up on us, I mean, the Americans." Only after having said that, Abe remembered Jerry was an American. He started fumbling with a fishing rod.

Jerry shrugged. "Abe, what you are saying is that the American government would not allow that, right? I can assure you that the average American doesn't care if Hawaii has a governor, a king or a president." He remembered that waitress in San Diego. "As long as they can come to Waikiki …" he added with a sarcastic smirk.

Abe put the rod away and returned to the topic. "I don't know—they did this thing to Queen Liliuokalani … just locked her up."

Jerry didn't think Cat had Hawaii's independence on her mind when she talked about self-reliance, but the subject was interesting and the fishing lines remained undisturbed. "The question is, what is it that the American government wants from Hawaii? I don't think they are after your pineapples or fish. They want their military bases. If you try to evict them from Pearl Harbor, yeah—that looks like a major problem. They won't allow that as long as they can breathe.

"But … if you offer, say, a long-term lease … They might be open to discussion. Not willingly, mind you, but if you produce enough stink, at one point someone might say, 'To hell with it, all these problems and bad press—we can just as well keep our bases and let them run their bloody islands into muck, if that's what they want.'"

Abe smiled bitterly and asked, "You think we would run Hawaii into muck?"

"I don't know, buddy. You think you have enough people who know how to run the country?"

The fishing lines were not attracting any bites and Abe started digging in his lure box. "We could hire people. Cat, for example—she seems to know what to do and she would be willing."

"Good example, Abe!" Jerry pounced. "Hire Cat! She is a brilliant person and full of terrific ideas. But can she prepare a budget or make busses run on time? I don't think so. You need bloody bureaucrats, pencil pushers who know how to run a state, an independent state, for God's sake! Inspired activists are good to have, but they won't replace administrators."

"Well, we can hire administrators as well," Abe declared defiantly.

"Sure." Jerry shrugged. "But you still better know how things work; otherwise, how would you know if your administrators actually work for you? Or perhaps they just bamboozle you; or even worse, work for someone else."

"Perhaps, we could hire you!" Abe's white teeth glistened

in the light of the oil lamp.

"What makes you believe, Abe, that I could be hired for a government job?" Jerry sounded honestly surprised. "I've just discovered that life is better without having a boss. I'm a free spirit now, don't you see?"

Abe chuckled provocatively. "If Cat agrees to work for Hawaii, you might need a job here as well …"

He had a point, but Jerry was quite sure there had to be a more productive way to earn one's living.

The dawn colored the sky pink in the east. Now all the oceanic elements—light, wind and waves—were coming from the same direction, as though someone had ripped a hole in the great black canopy covering the earth. New and exciting things streamed through this opening into the dark, solid and static world.

Something moved at the periphery. Five torpedo-shaped creatures shot up from the water, spinning their silver bodies in the early morning light only to splash back into the dark water a moment later.

"Spinner dolphins … good luck," Abe commented and changed the subject to their previous day's discussion about personal shortcomings. "So how, you think, did Cat deserve her punishment? She's certainly not stupid."

Jerry was reluctant to admit it even to himself, but … there had to be something … Cat was just … just too perfect! Not stupid … not lazy … What was the sin she was paying for?

"Bitchy?" Abe proposed without further elaboration, looking aside.

Jerry raised his head, somewhat offended, but Abe's remark did direct his thoughts to the fact that Cat could be quite an arrogant, opinionated and unsympathetic individual. The image of the last day of his Hawaiian vacation came to his mind. Jerry smiled.

"You might be onto something, Abe … though I

would prefer to use a different word. She is … let's say, uncompromising and forceful in her opinions. And another thing: Cat has only recently learned to trust other people—not that many, as a matter of fact. Like the rest of us sinners, she's only slowly struggling toward her sainthood."

A rod suddenly bowed into the letter *U* and the float disappeared under the water. "Wow!" Abe uttered. "That's a big one!" They hoped for a large fish, and Abe had loaded rolls of hundred-pound-rated fishing line, but for this monster it might be not enough. Abe positioned himself at the stern, holding the rod. This would be a long fight with no certain outcome.

"You better haul him in," Jerry yelled. "Mrs. Hewlett is waiting for her fish."

Abe only smiled excitedly; there was no room for distractions at this moment. He did what he loved, and he did it well. Jerry thought they did not need to worry about food anymore.

The fish was running deep, taking a lot of line. Every time Abe tried to slow the reel, the rod bent sharply, so he hastily backed off. More than an hour passed and only a little line was left on the drum. Abe was desperately trying to rig an extension when the fish changed its tactics, rushing the boat repeatedly, allowing Abe to reel the line in as well as let it out.

Jerry's head snapped forward when a loud flapping noise resounded in front of the boat. The headsail had worked its way out of the improvised point fixing it to the bow and started fluttering wildly in the wind. The fabric might get shredded in no time. Jerry lashed the wheel to the pulpit and leaped to the bow. He took his position just out of the flailing sail's range, and lunged at it when the wild thrashing subsided for a moment. He brought the canvas under control weighing it down with his body and retied it.

Lady Luck was backtracking now, her bow pointing straight into the wind while her boom swung wildly from one side to another two feet short of Abe's head. Facing the stern, the fisherman was not aware of the heavy object flying behind him and could get knocked out at any moment.

The duel between Abe and the fish continued while Jerry worked to bring the boat on course. It was another hour before the fish revealed itself, jumping out of the water. A heavy, streamlined head preceded by a spear shot clean through the surface followed by a blue dorsal fin atop a submarine-like body. It kept emerging until the big fish seemed to rest for a moment, supported on its tail, before crashing back with a huge splash of white water. A thrust of the powerful tail created a water hole that could swallow a swimmer and the fish disappeared again.

"Blue marlin!" Abe groaned. "Four hundred pounds, at least!"

The fish fought fiercely for its life, charging the boat repeatedly, until Jerry shot it with his spear gun when the marlin surfaced a few feet away from the boat. The sharp point plunged behind the head, and as the harpoon's metal butterfly opened up, the fish was solidly bound to the boat by means of a heavy braided nylon line. The fight, not a sporting contest but a brutal struggle without any chivalry, was over. They won and their prize was the creature's body. Beautiful or not, noble or not—it was much-needed food. Losing this fish was not something they could afford.

The fishing trip was already a success, even if nothing else took their hook, but they continued with good results. By two o'clock, they also landed a good-size mahi-mahi and two aku. It was a good day. They were ready to return. Their bizarre sails billowed as *Lady Luck* turned her back to the wind and started her sedate journey home.

The triumphant crew filled the air with boisterous laughter as Jerry and Abe egged each other on to ever more outrageous stories and discussions. They felt like warriors coming back from an expedition successful beyond their dreams, carrying sacks of gold to prove their wisdom and power. Very shortly their women would see their prowess too.

When Flat Island came into view, Jerry confidently pointed the bow into the reef break and the boat came to rest in her previous spot. Abe went ashore to get help with the marlin, ready to start telling his story to the first person he met on the beach, while the skipper was clearing the deck. Abe returned ten minutes later, running across the sand, an anxious look on his face. "You better leave the boat, Jerry. Come home; Cat is sick."

Chapter 36

Rosen, January 23

Streets of Honolulu were much hotter than Kailua, which was cooled by the trade winds. Rosen was getting increasingly hot and uncomfortable; he was out of water. After forty-five minutes at his observation post, he got up with a groan and walked across the soft black asphalt. There were no pedestrians on the streets; anyone who could hide from the noon sun, did so.

The corridor was quite dusty, just as he remembered it, but otherwise unremarkable. The walls were moderately dirty but without graffiti; no teenagers—who might deface the walls or be nosy about their neighbors—lived in this building. The other three tenants of this quadruplex were two elderly couples and an old woman with a small dog, seemingly even older than she.

"Juan Gomez" announced the little brass plate. He had a weakness for Spanish-sounding names—sweet memories of Nicaragua, probably. The lock looked fine and his key turned twice, unlocking the door. Rosen opened the door and strode straight to the refrigerator where Gatorade had been stored. It wouldn't be cold due to lack of electricity, but he was dehydrated and craved the slightly salty drink. He reached for the refrigerator's handle.

"Señor Gomez, will you please close the door?"

A cruel, hard hand seemed to grasp Harry's guts and twisted them mercilessly. He turned his head slowly, already knowing the inevitable. In the corner next to the door sat an old man. Of all things and people on earth, there was nothing and nobody Rosen feared more than this man. Without thinking, he sank to his knees and prostrated himself before El Diablo.

"The door, Bonito, the door," reminded the voice benignly. "You kept me waiting here a long time." Rosen obediently rose to his feet and slowly closed the apartment door, which felt like the heavy steel gate of a bank vault closing on his life. The thought of bolting out did not even occur to him. El Diablo made no mistakes, except once: when he had left the hacienda in Bonito's hands. No gun to be seen, Rosen thought, but certainly, it must be there, somewhere … aimed into my belly, perhaps under the hat covering his right hand.

"The handcuffs, on the table, put them on."

Bonito took a pair of metal handcuffs, put them on his wrists and tightened the locks carefully. He knew the routine. It was a victim's duty to apply restraints. Any resistance or negligence was watched for carefully and punished extra severely to indoctrinate absolute obedience.

"Same for your legs, Bonito." Harry applied leg irons. The old man had come fully prepared. Rosen had no right to have any hope. What he had done was punishable only by death, and not just any death. He could be sure the Master had prepared something extra painful and long for him. Something that would make him hope for death, await it eagerly. But at the same time, the instinct of self-preservation would not let him rebel and invite a quick end. Rosen returned to his prostrate position.

"Bonito, your worst crime is that you have caused me

severe embarrassment. I have been ashamed watching my face while shaving whenever I thought of my negligence. Placing my trust in hands as unworthy as yours ... Unforgivable. My mental discomfort has only gotten worse as I followed you. The stupidity and clumsiness you have shown were so acute that I had to question my own judgment again and again. Having all the means you stole from me, having the benefit of my tutelage for years ... your effort to hide was the most pathetic exercise in futility."

Rosen remained on his knees waiting for the pronouncement of the verdict. Am I going to die here, or will he take me to some remote place to enjoy my cries, moans and begging for days? he wondered as his terror mixed with morbid excitement.

Carlos, the warehouse attendant on the hacienda, the stupid man who tried to steal food and escape ... he had been brought back. In fact, Bonito brought him back himself. Carlos was forced to run barefoot behind a slow-moving truck for four hours, as the vehicle grinded in low gear through the twenty miles that he managed to cover during his escape. By the time they entered the compound, Carlos's feet were leaving bloody tracks with every step. Then Bonito had him hanged by his hands from a branch of the big tree right in front of the Master's studio, close enough to be clearly seen whenever El Diablo wished to have a moment of relaxation, but far enough to avoid the smell of the decomposing body. Nobody knew exactly when he died. After a week, his body had simply fallen off, probably helped by vultures. Bonito ordered him buried in a hole dug in the jungle.

"First things first," continued the old man. "Let's start with you returning my stolen assets. They wouldn't be in this backpack, would they? That would be awfully thoughtful of you. Empty the pack!"

Rosen crawled on his knees towards the pack.

"You've really let yourself go, my former disciple."

The Master looked at him with contempt. "Just looking at you makes me sick. A fat, ugly monkey without a spark of intelligence. How could I tolerate you around me for so long? This is what bothers me, the extent of my unforgivable misjudgment. You are one of those people who can't live without a master providing structure and discipline. You are a slave, in other words, not a master's trainee. You need pain and degradation just as much as you need food and air, perhaps more."

Bonito's humiliation and fear mixed into a paralyzing cocktail. He pulled out empty water bottles and the crushed silver foil package stained with chocolate. Then, buried among plastic bags containing wads of hundred-dollar bills, the pistol handle came into his view. A sudden bolt of hope sprung him into action. He took the handle and was about to pull the gun out in a desperate attempt to win his life back, when—perhaps he moved too fast—the hat on El Diablo's hand jumped and a shot reverberated through the small room. Rosen felt as though someone had kicked him in the stomach. He fell forward, clutching his abdomen. His hand was turning red when he looked to his belly, and he couldn't move his legs.

"So, actually, in the end, you showed this tiny bit of character; you've reached for a gun," noted the old man with grudging approval. "Just as well. I had other plans for you, but you've forced my hand. Congratulations! In any case, with a belly wound, it will take you a few hours to die, so we have a bit of time to talk."

Rosen looked up from the worn-out carpet. To his surprise, the pain was not that severe. Surely, Carlos had it worse, or Consuela, he thought.

"The second reason I felt offended was Consuela. I trained that girl to become a fine instrument of pleasure, and you stole her and then thoughtlessly destroyed her. That was a dumb deed of an oafish peasant, not an act of the artist I once hoped you would become. Shame on you, Bonito! She was probably just too smart for you to control her, while not smart enough to manage you. Not like this other girl, in Hawaii! She really did a job on you, didn't she? I watched you on my hidden camera and was laughing my head off."

"You were in my house in Kailua?" Bonito asked in shock, forgetting for a moment about his wound. Intense shame and humiliation overcame his physical pain. This was the last man on earth he would have to witness his defeat. The master of the dark art of torture had observed his incompetence and laughed. Rosen used to enjoy thinking of himself as someone akin to a chess grand master, someone who planned his actions with inexorable logic and executed his moves for reasons so far ahead in the future that other humans could not possibly guess their significance. Now he suddenly became the object of ridicule. The person who truly knew the beauty of deadly intrigue, this supremely cunning mind looked down at him with contempt.

The old man chuckled happily, seeing Rosen's pride shattered in the last hours of his life. "A nice house you bought with my money … well situated, too. It's the interior decoration that was rather unfortunate. This statue of Anaïd … a beautiful piece, true, but so predictable! I thought you might want one in your bedroom, so I called around to see if any marble-sculpting studio filled a recent order for its reproduction. When I found out that such a piece—and a big one, a full-size figure—was shipped from Pietrasanta, Italy, to Hawaii, I just had to come and see it. Really impressive. And when I saw your girl dusting her … Well, old man that I am, I was more than touched. I just wish you had outfitted this apartment better. I had to wait for you here almost twenty-four hours. How barbaric!"

Harry shivered, feeling coldness spreading in his chest; now he could not feel his lower body. A pool of blood was slowly enlarging around him, dark clots forming at the edges. The Anaïd, he thought. She betrayed me, like all the other women in my life. There was no way I could keep them, even with handcuffs and leg irons. Consuela, the one who promised to remain my slave forever, escaped too, killed herself. El Diablo is right; I could never become the master, I am too weak. He let his head rest on the carpet.

"Well, Bonito, I would like to stay longer to entertain you in your last moments, but I should not repeat your mistakes. Who knows, maybe someone else is following your clumsy steps? I should go. I am going to shoot you once more in the belly, to make sure you won't survive, and I'll be on my way."

He raised the handgun and aimed between the chained man's eyes; Rosen instinctively raised his hands to protect his face. The old man dropped the barrel quickly, almost touching Harry's upper abdomen, then another shot shook the apartment.

"I told you I would shoot you in the belly, you stupid oaf." The old man chuckled again. "You don't get it even when told. Well, with your liver shot up you are as good as dead. Enjoy!" He stood up, put the safety on and slipped the gun into his pocket. Walking carefully around the bloody pool on the carpet, he took the backpack and slowly walked out. He kindly held the outside door open for an old lady coming in with a small dog and walked away with short shuffling steps, the way old men walk.

Harry felt very cold. Then darkness came over his eyes until, in the moment of terror, he saw the face of his old Master. Harry Rosen—known also as Bonito and Sergeant Adams—was dead.

Chapter 37

Cat, Jerry, January 30

Cat lay on her back, staring passively at the ceiling, but turned her eyes to the door and smiled weakly when Jerry entered the room. It was a very sad smile, a momentary happy awakening of her eyes, with hardly any movement of her sagging mouth. Jerry had seen Cat happy and he had seen her angry, but he had never experienced the dejected look of Cat vanquished. Her cheeks were flushed, glowing morbidly under her pallid forehead moistened with sweat. A thick blanket covered her body up to the chin despite the afternoon sun heating the house.

"You were right, Professor," she said, mobilizing her energy, striving to regain her swagger for at least another moment. "I must be quite sick. Nothing I can do ... can't even think. But I'm happy ... you're back. You know, Ruth was right. I can bring you back if I really, really want you. I brought you from New York and now ... from the ocean. We may not have much time together ... happy have you back." She closed her eyes, exhausted.

Jerry listened, feeling his scalp tingling. "No!" He did not mean it to sound that sharp. "We are going to have a lot of time together; I won't let you slip away again!" He turned around and bumped into Kalani hanging right behind his back. "We're going to the hospital!"

"Jerry," Kalani whispered, without moving out of his way. "Dr. Lim was already here, and she will be back in a few minutes. There is nothing they could do, she said. It's an infection and they have no antibiotics."

Dr. Lim, a pleasant older woman whom Jerry had met once before, came ten minutes later. She touched Cat's head, counted the pulse and put her gentle hand on Cat's caved-in abdomen. She exchanged a short warm smile with Cat without saying a word then stood up and took Jerry by his arm.

"Jerry, I can't tell you how sorry I am," she said, leading him out of the room. "She was our soul and our brain in the darkest hours we lived through, but now she is developing sepsis, blood poisoning. It probably started with a urinary tract infection, a common problem with paraplegics. It is usually a minor problem under normal circumstances, but these are not normal circumstances. Cat has been starving for weeks, and her body just can't fight this infection.

"Her organs will shut down soon. She will die without antibiotics and there are none here, in Kailua. I know it for sure. Believe me, I've seen a lot of people dying from infections over the past few weeks. Their families would have dug medications from under the ground, if any could be found here. There are just no drugs here anymore. They might have some in Honolulu. I've heard they unload some ships every day, but she doesn't have much time. I can't tell you exactly how much, but anything over twelve hours would be pushing her luck."

There is a chance then! Jerry's mind raced. Twelve hours ... How can I get over the mountains to Honolulu and be back in twelve hours? Even Abe couldn't do that ... How about getting Cat to Honolulu? That would halve the time ...

but can we carry her over the rockslide in this condition?

Lady Luck! I could sail with Cat to Honolulu! He rudely turned away from Dr. Lim, ready to grab Cat in his arms and run to the boat, when the terrible realization stopped him in his tracks and his body was instantaneously drenched in cold sweat. Going to Honolulu meant sailing against the trade wind, a feat simply impossible in his crippled boat. He would have to motor upwind, but only a few gallons of diesel sloshed at the bottom of the fuel tank. He froze on the spot, his mind dissecting the options desperately.

Makapu'u. That's how far I really need to motor, eight or ten miles. Once we clear the point and turn south, it's a straight downwind sail to Honolulu. Maybe … maybe we can make it. Anyway, the boat is Cat's last chance!

Fifteen minutes later, the fish was off the boat and Cat was bundled onto the cockpit bench. She did not want to go down to the cabin, wanting to stay close to Jerry. He agreed; the late afternoon was warm, the red sun bathing the world benignly. She nestled in a bed of pillows, covered with warm blankets, right beside him.

Cat's face was peaceful and she seemed to be in no pain. With a turn of the key and push of the button, the motor started and *Lady Luck* turned her bow toward Flat Island with the reassuring vibration of her deck. A group of silent well-wishers looked on from the beach as they passed the reef. Jerry kept his course parallel but close to the white breakers, hoping to shorten the distance they had to cover; the fuel gauge was trembling over "empty"; they were running on fumes.

Soon after having passed the Mokolua Islands, Jerry realized that the wind's direction was shifting. Initially blowing straight from the east, it was slowly turning to the northeast now. Even if they had a fully functioning boat, Jerry would have to tack very far into the ocean to reach the Makapu'u point, making the trip to Honolulu within twelve hours an unlikely feat. With *Lady Luck* crippled, their only chance was Iron Jenny, the motor. Give us just ten miles, he prayed, ten miles.

Abe stood at the bow, his eyes trying to penetrate the water ahead, watching out for rocks lurking under the surface, as they were skimming the reef. Cat was quiet, not complaining, not moving, following Jerry with her eyes, whenever they were open. They remained still for long periods of time, stuck to the figure at the steering wheel without any sense of understanding, as though she was asleep with her eyes open. Then she emerged, her gaze intelligent and aware again, only to sink back once more into confused apathy.

There was nothing Jerry could do but hope and keep his mind focused on sailing. With every minute, they drew closer and closer to the Makapu'u lighthouse blinking across the Waimanalo Bay. White-knuckled hands clamped on the steering wheel, he banished all thoughts except for the mantra recited with religious fervor: "Don't quit yet, don't quit yet."

It was dark when *Lady Luck*'s bow protruded beyond the tall blackness of the rock and, suddenly, the vista of the Molokai Channel opened to the south. At this point, Jerry could take a right turn and the wind, coming almost directly from the north now, would propel them to Honolulu; they had a straight shot. The old friend Yanmar was still pattering on when they rounded the point and spread their jury-rigged sails. The canvas filled with the wind, which picked up in the channel, and *Lady Luck* visibly sped up her stately pace, surrounded by hissing whitecaps.

Jerry's soul soared, even when the diesel coughed and quit a few minutes later. It had delivered, brought them as far as he had begged. Now the sails would do their part; they should be in Honolulu in a couple of hours, where, he was certain, there had to be a functioning hospital with basic supplies. The fate he kept tempting since abandoning the life of predictable safety was still smiling on him. His luck held!

The sky was overcast by feathery but dense clouds and Jerry could not see much in the darkness, but the round shape of Koko Head volcano, its blunt dome blotting out the few visible stars, was distinguishable and the irregular outline of Hawai Kai town was marked by sparse and weak lights. Then the unmistakable ridged silhouette of Diamond Head appeared, black and dominant, backlit by the faint glow of Honolulu.

Jerry kept his course close to the shore, suspecting that *Lady Luck* would maneuver poorly in the strong channel wind. Overshooting the Honolulu port, as he had done while landing at Kailua Beach, would be disastrous; there was no possible way for *Lady Luck* to sail back upwind and have another chance of entering the harbor. It was Jerry's intention to sail to the first Honolulu pier he could see, on a course as straight as possible, permits and authorizations be damned.

A few short weeks earlier, he had passed the same landmarks, holding the same steering wheel, but he was a very different person now. The city-smart New Yorker who had crossed the Pacific did not exist anymore, replaced by a man who had experienced all his life's meaningful events in Hawaii, a person remade by love and deprivation.

The crash occurred without any warning. The sudden jolt threw Jerry against the steering wheel, the wooden spikes digging into his chest the only reason he stayed on his legs. Abe, still standing on the bow, was flung overboard, but held on to the railing and managed to pull himself back in.

This impact felt very different from the drift onto Bird Shit Rock. *Lady Luck* shuddered like she'd been hit by a runaway locomotive. The explosion of the crash penetrated every fiber of their bodies, as the boat suddenly came to a standstill, listing slightly to her starboard side. She shivered as the waves—running alongside her hull—brushed her sides, and groaned when the seas crashed against her stern, but she did not budge an inch. They were stuck on a rock like a desk ornament mounted on a pedestal.

At the moment of impact, Cat slid along the bench like on a shuffleboard, but stopped on the pillows bunched up at the end. She opened her eyes and looked at Jerry, plastered against his steering wheel, without being alarmed. She even smiled, and quietly asked, "Are you OK, Jerry?" After a moment of reflection her smile grew wider. "You look funny," she added coquettishly. She was gone, not aware of the world around her.

Jerry could see the halogen lights of the Honolulu port now; they were probably unloading another ship. They had supplies while Cat was dying within reach of her salvation. In better days, on her kayak, she could have gotten there within thirty minutes.

Abe came back from the cabin. "No water's coming in."

Thank God for that; we are not sinking, but that won't save Cat. Jerry thought in desperation. What would John do? Help me, old friend, what else I can do?

His eyes fell on a dinghy lashed to the deck. Dinghy! There was no gas for the motor, of course, but maybe he could row ashore. The distance to the crashing waves that marked the harbor channel's entry was not more than a mile. On the other hand, rowing a rubber dinghy in the channel, with the wind accelerating over twenty knots, was just hopeless. Gusts punching into the boat's rubber sides would overpower the strongest man. Without a keel, his little plaything would slide like a dried leaf driven by capricious winds. But again, what other option was there—sitting and watching Cat die?

"Abe, help me put the dinghy in the water."

"Jerry, you can't make it." Abe did not move. "You'll both die."

"Put the bloody boat in the water!" Jerry yelled, already cutting the tie-downs with his knife. The rubber craft launched into the wind like a big black kite trying to take flight, but they wrestled it down onto the deck. Even forced down, the stubborn dinghy tried to turn upside down until Jerry jumped into it, taking advantage of the brief moment when the rubber bottom rested on the water.

Abe handed down the oars and lowered Cat in, who contentedly wrapped her arms around Jerry's neck. She seemed disappointed when told to let go, but snuggled against his legs on the rubber bottom without complaint.

The oars locked in place, Jerry looked up and nodded. Abe nodded back, "Good luck, *brah*," and threw the line into the dinghy. The gust seized the rubber boat immediately and yanked it away from *Lady Luck*, as though to make sure that the amusing game would have to go on.

Jerry plunged the oars in, trying to impose some direction on their movement. It would be futile to fight the wind, he knew, but he hoped to nudge the boat slowly, as she floated with the wind and waves, until they touched the shore. He would not insist on the port—anywhere along the shore would be fine, and he could carry Cat from there. They were still more than a mile upwind of the harbor and—although the dinghy moved fast with the wind—he had perhaps fifteen minutes to close the distance separating them from the land.

But his furious work produced little result. They came a bit closer when the wind slackened, only to be blown away a minute later, when a gust swirled the dingy around like a bathtub toy and pushed them away from the harbor. His heart pounding and body at its breaking point, he was not making any progress. The bright lights of the port appeared closer by now, as they were floating driven by the wind, until Jerry could look into its entrance. There was a freighter at the pier, being unloaded by a crane.

Jerry's last murderous try failed; they were again entering the darkness, this time below the port. Spun around, bounced and carelessly carried away, they were playthings without destiny. There were no lights down the shore. He was defeated. Old Man Ocean had won.

"He always does," John said. "It's just that often he doesn't mind us playing on his lap. Sometimes he feels like a grandpa; lets us take his fish and smiles when we sail our little ships. But when he gets angry, you better put your tail between your legs and get out of the way. He always wins."

I know, John, you don't fuck with the ocean. Jerry smiled sadly. He was totally spent and the game was over. He slumped next to Cat and took her in his arms. She was warm, half-conscious and seemed quite content. They lay on the soft floor, sliding on the waves—forward, backward and sideways. All they felt was the rocking movement, made gentler by the rubber craft's elastic walls. The sky above them swirled and jumped, the faint stars dancing and mixing with black clouds that shook like palm fronds during a downpour. They saw the funny Hawaiian moon, lying on its back, sometimes there and the next moment missing. The water splashing their bodies was warm, and they were protected from the wind. It did not feel like a disagreeable way to end one's existence.

Cat's alertness was fluctuating. Sometimes she tightened her arms around him or touched his face, and then she would go limp as though in a deep sleep. He knew they were passing Keehi Lagoon, where *Lady Luck* had been hiding, then Barber's Point with its single red light on a refinery chimney. After that, there was only the open ocean. Two or three thousand miles of open water to the Cook Islands, though the current would more likely float them towards Japan. Crossing the river Styx into Hades in our own rubber boat, Jerry thought.

He slept somewhat during that night, and when the first light started breaking over the horizon, he felt some energy coming back. A look over the dinghy's sides showed only water, 360 degrees around them. No land, no ships, just miles and miles of water. Surprisingly, he felt no anxiety.

What's there to complain about? I've lived through enough excitement for three lives. I have Cat in my arms; we are not in acute pain … Yes, it would be good to live with her for another fifty years, see our children and grow old together. But would I swap this moment, as it is, for a lifetime of existence as it was before Cat? No, certainly not. I've found my place. It's here, in this dinghy, because that's where Cat is.

He found a plastic bottle of water on the floor and a signaling kit. Probably, Abe threw those in at the last moment. He gave a sip to Cat every now and then. He did not drink himself; did not want to outlive her. There was no way he could throw her overboard as he had done with John and the pirates. This was a fitting way for them to go, together. In fact, although his mouth was very dry and he felt thirsty, it did not cause him great discomfort—dehydration is not a cruel death.

Once the sun was up, it beat on their heads mercilessly. Cat opened her eyes. She was not talking but appeared more aware. He gave her the last drink and filled the bottle with ocean water; soaking their heads brought relief. So many things he could tell her if she was conscious, but really, there was no need. Her blond head was resting on his lap; they felt each other's presence and it was as good as they could have it, under the circumstances.

Transcript of a conversation, Washington, D.C.

Speaker 1: This woman in Hawaii has crossed the line. What are they going to do?

Speaker 2: Well, she definitely has the nerve. There is no way to interpret her radio speech other than a call to separate Hawaii from the good old U.S. of A. Not that they will not try to spin it another way. The prez was quite irked. The last thing he needs now is to have some new trouble, a new front to fight. Much depends on what she does next. If she appears at a press conference in Washington, saying that all she wants is to fight the inefficient bureaucracy and corrupt officials, they will make her the new governor of Hawaii or something along that line. If, on the other hand, she's serious, I don't know … she better watch her back.

Speaker 1: So, did they order her arrest?

Speaker 2: Arrest, shmarrest. Why call the things ugly names? Let's say that the prez would like to speak with her personally, pronto. The Secret Service will take care of that. Meantime, the relief operation will start in ten hours, as soon as the president gets to Hawaii.

Speaker 1: You mean they have goodies on the ground and will hold off until the big man arrives?

Speaker 2: Of course. How could he miss such a photo op? They waited a month, so they can wait another ten hours. Can you imagine a Marine landing craft touching the beach in Kailua? This footage will be all over the world, and you will see it again and again until the next disaster strikes somewhere else.

Chapter 38

Abe, January 30-31

The dinghy twirled and surged out of Abe's view, disappearing into the night almost instantly. He turned his attention to *Lady Luck*, groaning and shuddering with the ocean's every blow. Big seas, born out of some fierce Alaskan storm, travelled unchecked across the open ocean until the Hawaiian Islands audaciously opposed them with their rocky coasts, constraining their flow to narrow channels. The Kaiwi Channel, a strait between the islands of Oahu and Molokai, funneled the ill-tempered ocean's energy in the form of surging waves and wind accelerating between the mountains, until these immense forces could again disperse in the vastness of Pacific, below the archipelago.

Now, a new fixed obstacle appeared in the way of the irate ocean, *Lady Luck*. Unlike a fighter rolling with the punches, she took her pounding standing and stiff, waiting for the inevitable knockout. Fully aligned with the waves and wind, the boat was hammered on her stern, punching a big foamy hole in a breaker running along the hull every few seconds. She rose and fell with a whimper of stress building in her hull, as her bow was stuck, solidly grounded.

Abe grabbed an emergency lamp from the locker, lit it in the shelter of the companionway and entered the cabin. Books, tackle and glass from a broken lamp covered the floor. Every object that was not nailed, screwed or clamped to the walls or bulkheads had flown off its place. The air was permeated with the smell of kerosene; fortunately the cabin lamp was not lit, sparing them from fire.

He pushed the junk roughly aside with his foot and removed the wood panels covering the bilge. The smell of mold, stagnant water and wet wood drifted out, competing with the stench of kerosene. This was quite normal for a sailboat that had crossed the ocean, but there was no water sloshing around, just a bit of wetness from condensation on the hull's surface. Obviously, *Lady Luck* had taken the hit entirely on her keel. With an impact of this magnitude, the thin fiberglass wall would be crushed like a cardboard box under a truck's wheel.

Abe was not particularly concerned about his personal safety. The shore seemed so close that he could not imagine himself drowning. He used to surf and was a strong swimmer; he could battle the waves for hours until he eventually reached land. Cat and Jerry, on the other hand, were most likely lost. A man in the water would not care much about the wind. A swimmer, if strong enough, could power across the waves and make it to the shore, even if the current dragged him down the coast. A dinghy, on the other hand, was a plaything for the winds. The two pitiful oars Jerry had were no match for the channel's winds and current.

His friends' destiny was to be lost in the Pacific, never to be seen again. They were *haole*, people foreign to the Hawaiian Islands, but Abe knew they would fit just fine on those travelling canoes that brought his ancestors to Hawaii. The strong men without fear, the sweet wise women ... the heroes Abe used to dream about with old Pono at the *heaiau* by the marsh.

It was friends like them that Abe always wanted, not the trash like Jose. And then these two appeared, fierce like Kane, the god of war ... Abe smiled, recalling Cat's rabid face when she was about to put a bullet into his chest. And wise like Lono ... Good loyal friends. They were the equals to his Polynesian warrior ancestors ... but now he had lost them, so soon after fate brought them together.

He took down the sails that flapped uselessly on the mast, and sat dejected on the bow, looking south, where the ocean had swallowed Jerry and Cat. The morning did not bring any apparent changes to his situation. The boat was fixed on the rock like a stuffed bird on its perch nailed to the wall. She was upright, which meant that the keel had to be wedged in the rock at a depth similar to the boat's draft, six feet. Her stern was rhythmically coming up and down with waves running from behind, but the bow seemed to be gripped in a vise. This movement must be generating a lot of tension on her hull, he thought. It was bound to crack sooner or later.

Abe lowered himself to the water surface on a line, looked into the churning water then took a big breath and dove. From the bow, he followed the bottom until his groping hand encountered a rough hard mass jammed against the boat's smooth side. He pulled himself closer and had a look as good as one might have without goggles.

The keel was stuck in a deep fissure that had almost split the brown rock. Coral! This was good news. Made of calcium-based skeletons, coral is much more fragile than volcanic basalt. This might explain why *Lady Luck* was spared instant destruction upon impact.

The coral that had caught *Lady Luck* was not even very large, a slab less than two feet in thickness, sticking out vertically from its base on top of the massive underwater boulder. The keel's leading edge had crashed through this obstacle and had been trapped in the crack, flanked by solid chunks of the reef on both sides.

In addition, Abe discovered that the good luck that let them sail all the way from Kailua was really fate's joke. The coral barrier they had run into was only six or seven feet long and could rise so high, up to a depth of six feet, only because it was sitting on top of a basalt promontory.

Pure bad luck coming on top of more bad luck, Abe thought, gasping for air at the boat's side. Had we sailed a few feet to the left or to the right, we would have missed this thing altogether. We would have never known it was hiding here. If Cat were not so sick, we could have waited after the crash till the morning, figure out something better than this hopeless dinghy dash. If gods want you to die, you die.

Abe kept diving until he assured himself that all the big screws holding the keel were intact. In fact the metal keel had come out of the collision with the rock in relatively good shape; it seemed dented and bent as far as Abe could see it in the fissure, but was still well attached to the hull.

It's crazy, he thought. If only the wind were to push the boat from either side, the soft coral might break off; it's not that thick. Either that, or the keel might get torn out. One way or the other, *Lady Luck* remained captive only because the wind blew at the stern, pushing her at a right angle to the rock vise.

The distraction of diving helped to suppress Abe's gloomy thoughts. The only thing he could do right now was to take care of the yacht and go back to Kalani who needed him. If I could only twist the boat's position a bit, he reasoned, the waves would work like a big hammer pounding on a lever every few seconds. Something would have to give—the coral or the keel. The chance had to be taken—the unceasing up-and-down motion would break her sooner or later.

He might try to tow the boat's stern to the side, or take the anchor out—as they did in Keehi—but the dinghy was gone. He tried to use the wind's power, but the trouble of reattaching the sails and winching them out proved useless.

The boat did not budge and Abe had no more ideas; he sat dejected in the cockpit.

"Eh, anyone on board?" A black curly head appeared just above the deck's edge. Abe jumped. A six-man canoe bobbed alongside *Lady Luck*. The front man stood on its bench looking inside the boat.

"Hey, *braddah, kokua*! I need some help here!"

"Got stuck on da reef, eh? You alone?"

"Yeah, my buddy tried to get ashore in a dinghy last night; must be lost."

"Could swim ashore, you never know." The paddler was not too worried. "What do you want us to do?" The outrigger crew was willing, but had no idea how to help.

"I'll throw you a line from the stern; tie it to your canoe and try to tow me that way." Abe waved his hand at a right angle, towards the coast brightly lit by the morning sun.

"Can do." A stern line tied to the canoe's last bench, the six powerful bodies threw their weight against the paddles, but the boat didn't shift even an inch. They tried a few more times with increasing frustration and anger but eventually had to admit their defeat. The helmsman waved at Abe. "Eh, *bro*—no can do. Maybe we bring some more guys later on. Have to catch some fish now."

Abe was losing his hope, too, but asked, "Once more? From a flying start? Get some speed on the left, cut across close to the boat, and stay paddling hard—until you give it a last good jerk. *Kokua;* can you do it for me?"

The paddlers talked among themselves, nodding their heads, and the outrigger slowly pulled to the left side of the boat as far as the line allowed, eighty feet. The crew positioned themselves, ready for a canoe sprint.

"Paddles up … Hit!" In one instant, the six paddles plunged into the water, sending behind big eddies, and the outrigger jumped like a spooked fish. It accelerated rapidly, whizzed three feet past the stern, propelled by powerful short quick strokes, until the line ran out. It seemed to stretch somewhat, but in a split second it brought the canoe to a sudden stop. The paddlers fell to the front of the canoe laughing and cursing, while *Lady Luck* quivered with the jolt and hesitantly exposed her left flank.

The wind filled the sail and waves started hammering the boat's side. The canoe crew picked themselves up to their seats and watched with interest the slow process of the yacht breaking out from its confinement.

Ten minutes later, Abe felt an underwater crack transmitted by the boat's fiberglass, and *Lady Luck* started drifting with the wind. He prayed that the breaking noise came from the rock rather than the boat, but did not have time to look into the bilge. The boat caught the wind and her drift was accelerating. Abe trimmed the sail and found out that she could be steered, even though she responded to the wheel with nightmarish slowness. The canoe moved along, its crew in festive mood. They forgot about fishing.

Abe pulled into the mouth of the channel, leading into the Ala Wai small boat harbor, escorted by the outrigger, and tied *Lady Luck* to the tangle of wrecks in the middle of the waterway. Held together by booms, bowsprits and masts piercing sunken hulls, and by the vines of spliced steel entangling fiberglass bodies, the jam felt as solid as a port's wharf.

The rescuers felt well appreciated when Abe pulled out the rest of the beer from the boat's storage. The brew had not been seen in this town for a few weeks. John's stash was now exhausted, but he certainly wouldn't have objected to the way it was spent.

The next order of things was to find someone who could inspect the boat for damage and fix it. Despite his recent success, Abe did not consider himself enough of a sailing expert to take on this job. He walked to a large catamaran resting on a beach, where a few men busied themselves patching its hulls with long strips of fiberglass fabric. Its mast was missing, but the deck looked intact and the rudders were undamaged.

"Not too bad, eh?" Abe remarked, by way of introducing himself.

The closest worker raised his head. "Yeah, another day and we'll put in the stick. Then she goes out to catch us some fish."

"You the boss?"

"Nah. Da boss be here in a while, go fetch mast from repair."

Abe was impressed. Things were working here; people busted their butts to get back on their feet.

The boss, a middle-aged wiry man, his skin almost black from years of working the boats, was open to new business. "Sure, will go on your boat and take a look. How much you pay?"

Abe had no money. "A bottle of tequila?"

The boat builder grimaced but had a change of heart a second later. "Yeah, a bottle of tequila will do." He was looking forward to a pleasant night on the beach with a bottle of tequila and a few well-chosen friends.

Old *Lady Luck* turned out to be tougher than the rock. The keel's front edge displayed a deep black wound of gashed metal, and its shape could no longer be described as sweeping, but it was still solidly united with the boat. The hull's blue jelco was pulverized and washed out, showing two big gray patches of fiberglass where it came in contact with the coral, but there were no apparent holes.

"She's good!" The boss waved his hand dismissively. "Solid!"

Abe was getting cocky. "How about fixing the mast?"

The repairman shrugged his shoulders. "Find yourself a half-decent mast"—he pointed toward the tangle of wrecks—"and I'll rig it."

Abe spent the balance of the day climbing dead hulls and diving to inspect submerged masts. He went to sleep with the knowledge that a fairly straight aluminum pole could be retrieved if he had a few people to help.

The mast he had chosen was shorter than the original one and had a slight bend at the top. By late afternoon of the next day, it was resting on the grass, ready to be stepped. Abe had to pay three good fishing rods for help. That's a lot, he thought, but what good is having fishing gear without a boat?

Chapter 39

Cat, January 31

Cat ... Cat ... Catherine! Listen up! It's me, Ruth. You may play dead for the whole world, but I know you can hear me. You are pushing this thing too far. To have a bit of fun and adventure is one thing, but what you are doing is extreme.

Maybe I didn't tell you, but if you knock someone off—if you kick him out of your world—you can't bring him back. You can create someone who looks the same, and has the same name, but the person inside is gone. I did it to my second husband, Erwin.

I was quite happy with him, but then I sent him off on an extramarital affair. Maybe I was a bit bored and wanted to spice things up. In any case, when I saw him banging this stupid blond—and I called her Lola—that I created for him, that pissed me off beyond my expectations. Instead of the sultry making up that I had in mind when I was planning the whole affair, I felt this urgent need to hurt him badly.

Poor Erwin was hit by a truck delivering Budweiser beer and died on the way to the hospital. I wanted him back the next day, when I realized the stupidity of my action, but guess what, I couldn't bring him back. I tried and tried, and some washed-out characters came back who looked like Erwin, but the man was gone and I never had him again.

So, I'm telling you this story because it seems to me that your Jerry is pretty close to the edge of your planet. You are very fond of him, and I am positive you will regret it very much if he dies.

The other thing: you yourself are one inch from the cliff's edge. What happens if you fall off? I don't know. I never tried it myself, and you're crazy to do things that you don't know how to control. After all, the whole game is about us controlling our worlds, right?

It crossed my mind that this whole story is actually happening, in the real world. This would be quite outrageous, and I don't think it's true, but if it were—what do I know about the outside world? You're on your own, kid.

That brings up the point we discussed in the past: how can you tell if your experience happens in the outside world or in your head? I think I'm onto something. There are some things that you just cannot dream up unless you have experienced them in real life. You have no internal image to recall it and use as a model for your own creation.

As you know, I have a bunch of kids, all of them in my head. I took care of them, washed their sweet little butts, made them breakfasts, sent them off to school and so on. But I never could put myself through an actual birth. I could imagine my big belly and an obstetrician and a screaming newborn, but I couldn't feel the pain of labor. Well, how could I? I got sick when I was in my early twenties and didn't get around to having babies. The pain of delivery was never imprinted on my brain, and I just couldn't create it from scratch. Never mind birthing, I can't even imagine anymore how it feels to have a good fart; it was such a long time ago.

OK, OK, I know you don't like it when I get vulgar, but—frankly—that's part of the living, one of the pleasures of daily existence that I am deprived of.

Cat! You are dozing off again, so I will just tell you this—snap out of it and take care of the two of you before it's too late. And if you want to check which world you are in, try to find a sensation that you never had before. Your brain couldn't make it up. If you can feel it, not see or hear, but feel it (because it's harder to fool a body than eyes), you are in the material world. And if you are in the material world, you are in deep shit.

Chapter 40

Jerry, January 31–February 6

Javelin had worked the waters between San Diego and San Francisco for the past twenty years. Her profitability had become doubtful over the past few years, as the volume of cargo between the California ports dwindled and fuel costs climbed. Finally, the decision to send her to a scrapyard had been made, but a last-minute execution stay arrived in the form of one last big voyage to crown her career. She had been chartered by a group of relief organizations to carry their mission and supplies to Hawaii.

Despite the media's general preference for the pictures filled with explosions and smoke of the Middle East, enough interest had been created by ex-Hawaiians living on the mainland to spur into action the non-governmental organizations, or NGOs. *Javelin*, loaded with drugs, instruments, generators and other necessities required to set up a field medical center, left San Diego carrying a group of volunteer medical personnel.

She was chugging south of the Hawaiian island chain, hoping to avoid the worst effects of the northern storms that can be severe in winter. The day was breezy, but since the sky was clear, most passengers preferred to stay on deck rather than huddle in the cramped quarters. Waves ran in the long, regular patterns of the open ocean, white tops here and there breaking the monotony of blue water.

Amanda stood on the lee side, hiding behind the ship's bridge from the wind. Her face already felt dry from the wind and sun and she was ready to go down to her cabin when a small orange cloud caught her eye. An orange cloud would not be unusual in the western sky, where she gazed—but not at noon. She went up to the bridge and asked the officer for binoculars. He smiled and handed her the heavy marine instrument. She definitely looked cute: a slim, blond girl seriously handling the oversized black tool.

Amanda looked where the orange cloud was a minute ago. She scanned the horizon for a moment then focused on one point. Without a word, she handed the binoculars to the officer and pointed her finger to the west. The man studied the ocean for a minute and the smile left his face.

"Course two-two-five, full power."

A rubber boat bobbed up and down, sometimes on top of a wave, more often hidden between crests. There were no occupants to be seen. Perhaps it was empty, but maybe someone was slumped on the floor. The news spread through the ship, and within a few minutes, off-duty crewmen and medical volunteers gathered on the deck. No details were available yet, but a tiny boat in the open ocean hardly ever has a happy explanation.

Twenty minutes passed before the dinghy could be inspected from the height of the ship's deck. There were two bodies slumped on its floor; they did not move even when the deep purr of the ship's diesel vibrated the dinghy's rubber walls. Four sailors slid into the lowered launch and reported a minute later, "A man and a woman, alive!"

The shaggy-looking man with a long graying beard raised his head when a rough hand shook his shoulder, looking bewildered into the wide face of master mariner Shawn Daniels. The woman, feeling the commotion, opened her eyes and mumbled something sounding like "Thank you, Ruth," although it probably was "Thank you, Lord."

The male was quite easy to help into the lunch as he was able to assist, but the woman—almost unconscious and completely limp from her waist down—had to be taken out carefully in a small cargo net hoisted directly onboard the ship.

The medical crew sprung into action as soon as the survivors touched the black metal deck of *Javelin*; both victims were severely dehydrated. Intravenous fluids pouring in through multiple lines, the medical team hung above the couple like hawks, aching for information. The man, thin and sunburned, started the stuttered account of events first, while the female—her face deflated and wrinkled like a forgotten pool toy—remained in coma.

The ship was filled to the brim with medical supplies and carried specialists in major medical fields; there was no better place within a 3,000-mile radius for Jerry and Cat to land in. They were rescued by *Javelin* as if the supreme authority had decided to end their punishment; they had suffered enough.

Jerry recovered quickly once saline filled his collapsed veins and water re-expanded his shrunken organs. As long as he didn't try to sit up, he was coherent and comfortable, reclining in an old chaise by Cat's bed in the ship's mess.

Cat had intravenous lines stuck into both arms, flooding her dried-up body, and—thanks to Jerry's input about her infection—saturating it with a broad-spectrum antibiotic. She seemed to sleep quietly for ten or fifteen minutes, deeply unaware of her surroundings, only to open her eyes with a start, her childlike hand squeezing Jerry's fingers with panic. A weak smile appeared on her thin face when she caught his anxious eyes, but a moment later it would be replaced by an expression of extreme exhaustion.

The girl who had spotted the orange cloud softly inched up to Jerry. "Professor Roberts, is that you?" she asked, looking into his face with disbelief.

Jerry looked up and refocused his eyes with effort. "What are you doing here, Amanda, in the middle of semester?" This was Miss Ambitious, the girl who was flunking his economics class, grinning under the brim of her big hat.

"I've been looking at you for a couple of hours. You looked familiar, but I couldn't believe it was really you."

Not surprising—in his new reincarnation, Jerry had a bushy beard and long, dirty hair showing a generous amount of silver at his temples. His face was sunburned and still wrinkled from dehydration; he was also a good twenty pounds lighter.

"You remember me!" Amanda was overjoyed. "You saved me from the horrors of economics. Now, I am a logistics officer for the relief group. Let me tell you, I owe you, big time. I am happy now. Come to think of it, I could still be killing myself trying to be an economist, if you hadn't told me to think for myself. Thank you, thank you, thank you!"

"Well, Amanda, you are welcome. I took the same route; I've quit the university and never looked back."

"Who is she, your friend?" Amanda could not restrain her curiosity anymore. The whole mission was going crazy about the mystery that looked incredibly romantic. She stared into the shriveled face partly covered by a tangled blond mop.

"She is my wife; her name is Cat."

"Cat? The Radio Cat?" Amanda's eyes rounded and bulged.

"You know her, Amanda?"

"Are you kidding? The whole country knows her, the whole world! Her radio speeches were transmitted by hundreds of stations."

"No, we didn't know she had such a big audience." Jerry smiled; Cat would like that.

Amanda pushed closer and touched Cat's arm. "They said in the papers that, if she wanted, she could win any election she chose. And we find her in a rubber boat in the middle of the Pacific. This is crazy! I found you, you know!" She could resist claiming credit for spotting Jerry, but to find Cat, the famous Cat—that was too much!

Cat's survival hung in the balance for twenty-four hours; only when her battered kidneys decided to resume work was she declared to be recovering.

She stayed on board *Javelin* even after the ship arrived at the Kewalo basin in Honolulu. The overcrowded hospitals of the island could not offer anything beyond the treatment she was already receiving.

Cat—still weak and on medications—recuperated quietly for two days, but could not stand her forced inactivity anymore. Jerry pushed her wheelchair down the gangplank on the morning of the third day.

Army trucks carrying supplies, construction equipment and thousands of uniformed personnel—all that she had been begging for—appeared suddenly on the streets of Honolulu and other Hawaiian cities, dominating the roads. They burst out from the Kaneohe Marine Corps base, the Army's Schofield Barracks, the Navy's Pearl Harbor and other military establishments as though the floodgates had opened and released a torrent of food, fuel, medical supplies and construction equipment.

The happy moment of breakthrough in the relief operation coincided with the arrival of the president. Prominent members of the press arrived on *Air Force One* as well, while ordinary journalists pulled in on chartered planes or hitched their rides with cargo. The whole country watched in awe as the military landing craft stormed the beaches of Kailua, carrying food, medicine and security. Many patriotic eyes became wet at this display of great American compassion, solidarity and power.

It took a week to remove the rockslide blocking Kaleanianaole Road to the windward side and stabilize the mountain. Cellular phone service went up a few days later. The island was united again even though it would be a longer while before highways H1 and H3 could be opened.

Cat missed some of these developments, as an hour after she went ashore, three man dressed in dark suits approached her not far from Aloha Tower, pushed Jerry away and grabbed her wheelchair.

She was bundled into an unmarked car with great skill and efficiency. A few hours later an extremely apologetic gentleman assured her that her civil rights and freedom were of the utmost importance, and she was a free person. However, she was requested to attend a meeting with Mr. President. The whole idea of a forceful abduction was ludicrous, as the transportation had been arranged solely for her comfort and convenience.

Transcript of a conversation, restaurant, Washington, D.C.

Speaker 1: So, how did the meeting go? I mean, Cat versus the prez.

Speaker 2: It was rather funny. The big man was so sure she was a cunning politico that it took him fifteen minutes to figure out that she was, really, a country bumpkin. So he listened to her tirade for a while, which was nothing new if you'd heard her radio talks. Then he tried to sound out what it was that she wanted out of the deal. And she would not let him in on it, which made him believe that she was a very shrewd player.

At the end, he asked her directly. She looked at him without any understanding in her eyes and—listen to this—she said that ... all she wanted was to go back to her husband.

Speaker 1: You think this is really it? Or is she playing

stupid and will spring something on us when we least suspect it?

Speaker 2: Well, what counts is what the president thinks of it. He let her go and laughed to himself for five minutes after she left.

Chapter 41

Jerry, February 6

As Jerry stood in the middle of the crowded street, a big man wearing a ridiculous black suit blocked his way while two other beefcakes hustled Cat to the car. They would not even let him say good-bye. He felt as much enraged as helpless. He kept her alive in the famine and in the dinghy lost at sea, and now these three bastards, who looked like someone fed them a few pounds of fresh meat every day, snatched her away from his hands.

He could only curse his government in action, impotently. The men had flashed their badges, and Jerry believed they were federal agents. Only the government would have a car running in Honolulu. He was not worried that Cat would disappear forever; after all, they had left him as a witness. It just made him very angry to lose control of his life again, because the price of gaining it had been so high.

He went to the Ala Wai marina, a short walk away. Someone might have heard about Abe, he hoped. A strong and resourceful man like Abe would not perish a few hundred yards from the shore, he was sure.

Jerry crossed the grassy stretch of Magic Island, the

harbor's western bank, and walked toward the wave breaker. Numerous sunken boats dotted the basin but many dinghies, propelled by oars, were busy around them. People seemed to be hard at work wherever a hull remained above the water level. With no electricity available to run power equipment, all the work was done with hammers, wrenches, pliers and whatever implements could be found in home workshops. As he approached the end of the island, where the port's channel opened into the ocean, Jerry raised his eyes to look across the water and stopped like he'd hit a glass wall, his heart pounding.

A blue-hulled boat sat twenty yards away, gracefully set off against a tangled clump of white and gray wrecks scuttled in the middle of the waterway. *Lady Luck*! And she has a real mast! Jerry rubbed his eyes. What's next? John snoozing on the cockpit bench?

But there was no one on board. Jerry sat on the shore, watching her fondly, hoping for Abe to show up. The mast was rather short for her size, he noted, and she was rigged with an unsightly mix of steel cables and braided ropes. Still … she looked like a beauty queen visiting a city dump.

At last, Jerry saw Abe, walking in the company of two much older men. A tall, heavily built dark-skinned individual, wearing a red aloha shirt, was explaining something to Abe forcefully. He grabbed the younger man by his arm and they stopped, the stranger's big intense face no more than a foot away from Abe's. His companion, a short and slim oriental-looking man dressed in a blue aloha shirt, joined this impromptu summit with some comments of his own. Abe was definitely enthralled. Unusual company for him, Jerry thought.

Abe noticed Jerry only when he stood up, blocking his way, and immediately grabbed him into a bear hug. "Where is Cat?" he asked anxiously, releasing Jerry from his embrace.

"Cat is fine. A medical mission ship rescued us. Where

she is right now, I don't know. She was snatched by the Secret Service an hour ago."

The red aloha shirt nodded his head. "To be expected. She could be worth a lot to the government, as much as to us."

"Us? And who are you?" Jerry was about to ask. Suddenly, everybody and his brother were ready to put claim on Cat. Jerry found it deeply disturbing; his rights to Cat were absolutely primary, he felt, and he would not share her with anyone, as much as he could help it. At the same time, he knew that no claims would matter much to Cat. Nobody could appropriate that anarchist. If she gave her friendship, love or dedication, it was only because she wanted to. And that applied to him as well.

"This is Roy Kaiwi"—Abe pointed to the big man—"and this is Bob Reynolds," he added, nodding at the blue aloha shirt, who, to Jerry, looked like a high school teacher. "They are both from the Executive Committee of Hawaii Freedom."

"And this is Jerry Roberts, Cat's husband," Abe completed the introductions, slapping Jerry's back.

Jerry had never heard of the Hawaii Freedom organization, but obviously much had changed since he last read the paper or set foot in Honolulu. Abe was fascinated by his companions and they in turn were very attentive to him. It looked to Jerry like Abe was getting into politics, the Hawaiian independence movement.

The blue aloha shirt wanted to explore Jerry's views on formation of a provisional government, but he was in no mood for politics. All he wanted at the moment was to hear from Cat, and once he put his hands on her, he would do his damn best to hide her away, so that no one could find them at least for a month.

"Are you coming back to Kailua now?" he asked Abe abruptly, without any regard for the aloha shirts. Cat would send a message there as soon as she could, he thought.

"Yes, of course." Abe sounded a bit upset by Jerry's snubbing of his new friends. He shook hands with both activists and promised to be in touch.

"Let us speak with Cat when she is back," the blue shirt said, turning to Jerry.

"If she wants to speak with you, I will certainly not try to stop her," Jerry declared indifferently. "But let me tell you, she is not a big fan of any government, and that would probably extend to yours."

He made a quick good-bye visit to the medical mission people on *Javelin* while Abe loaded on *Lady Luck* a few cartons of food rations that he had acquired from a government warehouse. His new connections were even good enough to get them two plastic containers of diesel fuel.

Twelve hours later, *Lady Luck*'s anchors plunged into the water off Kailua Beach, and the sailors went to the Round House. Jerry experienced déjà vu when they walked through the door. Cat was sitting in her wheelchair with a toddler on her lap and a bunch of kids hanging around her chair. Next to them, Kalani was putting breakfast into bowls.

"Hope this isn't blubber soup," Abe said from the door. "You might as well serve two more bowls."

Cat and Jerry were not ashamed of their wet faces when they lay in the high grass behind the house, locked in each other's arms, smelling the jasmine again. The cataclysm was over, and they had survived.

Chapter 42

Cat, Jerry, February 10–15

Once in Newark, Cat and Jerry had the feeling of stepping into an unheated movie theater where an old projector screened a black-and-white film. It felt so different from Hawaii where—no matter how tough life was—the masses of multihued flowers and the vibrant greenery of fresh growth pushed from all sides to cover evidence of destruction. The cold wind and gray skies were a stark contrast to the island's gentle warm air, and the smell of gasoline replaced the pervasive aromas of the never-ending Hawaiian blooming season.

His old apartment sold, Jeremy checked them into an apartment-hotel. Pam was more than displeased to hear that he would rather stay in a hotel than in her home, but eventually, she understood Cat and Jerry's need to disappear in order to enjoy each other. Selfish as it might sound, they did not want anybody else. The two of them, this was just perfect; they had a lot of catching up to do.

Cat was gaining strength rapidly since her infection had cleared, and they ate well. In fact, they ate like two bears in preparation for winter hibernation, their insatiability mixing with guilt.

"Jerry, every time I reach for another helping I feel like I'm stealing food from kids." Cat sighed, bringing the third serving spoon of rice to soak the curry sauce on her plate.

"I can check if there are any hungry youngsters around, Cat, if that would help your conscience." Jerry took the dish into his hands. "But the folks I met today mostly looked like they might use a few days on a starvation diet."

They were regaining weight fast, and Jerry started seeing the woman who once saved him at Bird Shit Rock. The pitiful, skeletal person he had taken as his wife on the beach was not only rounding out, but—to Jerry's surprise—also regaining the muscles that used to give her this particular firmness that his arms remembered. The reasons for Cat's speedy recovery of her physical vigor soon became apparent.

She was supposed to have a nap after they lunched together, while Jerry spent afternoons in the city, attending to the matters that this world of rules and regulations demanded be completed. On the third day after their arrival, he had left the hotel at one, hoping to finally sort out the formalities of terminating his employment, left hastily and in a highly irregular manner. Right at the subway station, Jerry realized he had forgotten his documents and ran back to their apartment.

He heard music in the corridor and cursed silently, thinking that a noisy neighbor might wake up Cat. Once he opened the door, it became apparent that the music was coming from their bedroom. He stepped into the open door and froze in awe.

Cat—fully nude—hung off the bed, her palms on the floor and hips pivoting on the mattress—she was doing push-ups. Her rump had plumped up nicely since the last Kailua Beach swim, Jerry observed, and projected above the straight line of her back in a pleasing counterbalance to her breasts dangling like two full grapes.

One, two, three—Jerry counted, standing silently while she kept pumping, unaware of his presence. Her shoulder and arm muscles stood out clearly under the skin, as she kept working out fast and hard. Certainly, she had been doing it for some time and was already in pretty good shape. Eventually, she stopped and, breathing heavily, wiggled up on the bed.

"How many?" Jerry asked when she looked up.

Cat was neither shocked nor embarrassed; being naked came to her most naturally. They slept nude and she did not hide when dressing. In her opinion, privacy had nothing to do with one's clothing.

They had been intimate regularly since their pledge on Kailua Beach, but … somehow, Jerry felt she was still very fragile, almost too frail for passionate lovemaking.

"Forty," she replied with a coy smile. "Do you think I'm strong enough to love this big, strong bull of a man?"

Jerry's coat, shoes, pants and shirt lay in a heap fifteen seconds later as he dove into her impatient arms. Cat rolled over and pinned him on his back like a wrestler, her blue eyes glowing inches from his face, neither smiling nor sad—just hungry.

Exhausted, they lay side by side, exhilarated beyond the satisfaction of sexual fulfillment. Strong again, they could be not only robust lovers, but also tough challengers in the battles ahead. Now—Cat and Jerry felt—they could take on any opponent head-on, without preconditions. They had fought the battle for their lives, won it and consumed the victory. And it made them stronger.

Pam was beside herself and simply refused to wait any longer. She had been patient beyond what was reasonable, tolerating Cat's seclusion on the grounds of her need to recover. Jerry had met his sister on the day of their arrival, of course, and they talked daily on the phone, but the situation of not having yet met her sister-in-law became unbearable.

Her ultimatum was to be met on Saturday night, when Cat would be formally inducted into the family.

That gave Cat two days to get ready. A trivial problem perhaps, but Cat had arrived from Hawaii without any luggage, wearing a borrowed cotton muu'muu, a long, straight, cotton dress sporting large orange flowers of hibiscus. A popular choice among Hawaiian ladies, the dress could hardly pass for formal wear in New York.

Initially, Cat refused to go shopping, saying that whatever she bought, it would not fit her in two weeks. Fair enough, Jerry thought. Their figures where changing so fast. But now, facing the formal visit with Jerry's sister, she had no way out—they went shopping.

Cat had neither the technique nor endurance that shopping required. Her deficiencies were apparent to any urban dweller and Jerry had to recognize it. An hour into their buying spree, at the second store, his wife declared, "That's it. I cannot do this anymore. I don't need any clothes. I will stay in the hotel room forever."

For the last three years, she had lived by her window overlooking the beach, working on a computer or loitering around her house, wearing a pair of shorts and a t-shirt. It was an acceptable wardrobe in Hawaii and it suited her just fine. Now, for the first time, Jerry saw Cat clueless, and she despised it heartily.

Buying from a catalog could be a solution, but time was not sufficient. However, they were in New York, the place where every need could be fulfilled, as long as suppliers were properly compensated. A few hours after Jerry's phone call, a personal shopper—armed with a pile of fashion magazines and a measuring tape—came to interview Cat who, despite initial misgivings, found the experience pleasant and exciting. Her new clothes, delivered the next day, fit surprisingly well.

As Jerry, seated in an armchair, watched an excited Cat demonstrating her new outfits, he felt that his morning call to a stockbroker was a good idea.

"Now, for a change of pace." She grinned. "Jerry, go to the kitchen and don't come back until I call."

He heard his name a few minutes later, "Jerry?"

He heard the soft clicking of castanets when he opened the door, drawing his eyes to the far corner. There, draped on the side of an armchair, sat Cat, haughty and arrogant like a dame of the royal Spanish court and seductive like a courtesan.

A long, red dress with a lacey hem, black shoes with high but sturdy heels, a proud bust barely restrained by red fabric—she was Carmen, complete with a black wig.

Cat clicked the castanets again, enjoying the effect of her appearance. She put up a token resistance when Jerry grabbed her off the armchair, but when they landed on the bed with a thud, she firmly took his head in both hands, turned it and whispered into his ear, *"Te quiero, Amor, pero ahora—no. Vamos a Pam, recuerdas?"*

The word "no" came through very clearly, while the rest of her whispering Jerry found somewhat confusing. He clearly picked up "my love" but, unfortunately, there was something about their visit with Pam as well.

It was time to start preparation and Jerry had serious worries about this evening. He knew that Pam would welcome Cat with open arms—no problem there. That his wife was eager to meet her new family and would like to be accepted was also a given. What made him uneasy was the mental image of Cat and Henry facing each other across a table.

Cat, a ferocious individualist with an anarchistic bent, and Henry, an establishment provocateur, sitting at one table did not add up to a quiet family dinner.

Pam, tormented by the long delay, prepared a full gala dinner. Silver candlesticks and elegant china had been precisely placed on the table covered with a snow-white cloth, as if presidents and prime ministers of the G20 were about to sit for their evening get-together.

Jerry had had nightmares about this kind of dining since the first time he was seated at a table without a child booster. A tiny drop of cranberry sauce could become a bloody entry wound in the corpse of such an elegant table. The hostess graciously assured the assassin that there was absolutely no problem, while the offender knew she had spent hours setting this banquet like a stage for a commercial video shoot. Jerry had dreaded formal dinners all his life and would rather eat blubber soup under a tree than pâtè de foie gras at a gala feast.

Cat, on the other hand, elegant in her navy blue suit—selected perhaps to prevent anyone gawking at her legs—exuded an air of relaxed confidence. She was sitting on a dining chair, having transferred from her wheelchair to be at the same height as the rest of the company, meeting everyone's gazes with an angelic smile.

Jerry knew, however, that Cat was tense, seeing the pinkish hue of her neck, and noting the tiny amount of food she was consuming. She just nibbled this and that … Nibbling on food was not what these two famine survivors did.

Pam's children were on their best behavior, probably intimidated by the table arrangement just as their uncle was. They kept their eyes stuck to their plates, sneaking quick looks at Cat whenever she looked away. The atmosphere was prim and proper, starched like the tablecloth under their plates. The diners were politely smiling, minding their table manners and making small talk. An intolerable, decorous, boring family gathering was in progress.

Jerry—relieved that the clash he had feared was not materializing—was quite disappointed with the coolness of this reunion. What's next? Is Henry going to suggest that they watch a game of football on his large-screen TV?

The children, certainly, needed to be excused from this dragging ritual soon, before they decided to end this fatal boredom by cutting their wrists with the silver cutlery. Pam seemed satisfied with the initial assessment of her sister-in-law, but was not cordial, which both disappointed and surprised Jerry, as she had been very emotional about Cat previously. Perhaps it's difficult to break the ice, he thought. I had it easy—all I had to do was come close to drowning so that Cat could fish me out.

"So when did you get married, exactly? And where?" Pam addressed her brother.

"Twenty-fifth … or twenty-sixth … no later than the twenty-seventh of January, on Kailua Beach," he answered hesitantly. Dates were not that important then; they measured time by their last meal.

"You aren't sure when your wedding ceremony was?" Pamela raised her eyebrows and looked at Cat.

Cat flashed her full smile at Jerry, the first this evening. "There was no ceremony. We just decided we belonged together … on the beach, one night … I think it was the twenty-sixth, in fact, when you materialized at the Round House like a ghost. We had an emergency meeting about fuel for the generators finally running out."

Pam's face fell and her mouth opened as though she wanted to say something but changed her mind.

"Free love …" A wistful whisper came from the mouth of Cecilia, the oldest child.

Cat turned to her with the same big smile and asked, "Do you think there is any other love, Cecilia?"

The girl blushed. "No, I just thought it was so cool … no priest or witness or wedding party, just the two of you on a beach."

"For the full picture, you might also imagine the full moon and gentle waves washing over our bodies; it's true though a bit too kitschy. But to remain honest, I also have to add that we were both very hungry, and your uncle Jerry smelled like a three-day-old whale carcass."

"Eeew! Uncle Jerry, you smelled like an old carcass!" The kids irreversibly broke out of their contrived proper behavior. Everyone suddenly relaxed, the aggravation of elegant manners lifted off their shoulders.

Even Pam gave up on her proper gala dinner. "Ha, you did it on a beach, without a ceremony. Kids, I think you're still living in sin, but I'm going to fix it before you have a chance to escape from New York. Have to admit, though, it sounds awfully romantic. Henry, maybe we should try it sometime, what do you think?"

"I like the idea of free love on a beach, but the notion of being very hungry in order to reach this level of delight bothers me a lot." Henry smiled coyly.

Cat looked at his portly figure. "The starvation part was an unfortunate ingredient of our romance. I think it should be optional … and I assure you that love is better with a full belly."

Cecilia was not going to let this delicious subject be switched to anything else. "Auntie, why did you choose Jerry, if he smelled so bad?"

"First of all, Cecilia, even your children will not be allowed to call me auntie. I am Cat for you as for everybody else; I won't be a part of any hierarchy. As for choosing Jerry … if someone sailed across the ocean in a tiny boat, and climbed over mountains, and did all kinds of crazy things … just to be with you—wouldn't you like him just a little bit? And if he also turned out to be the most wonderful, intelligent and brave man you ever knew, wouldn't you choose him, too?"

Pam's face filled with pride and pleasure as she listened to the list of her brother's qualifications for being the chosen one.

"My real worry," added Cat, looking at Jerry, "was that he wouldn't want me. I was not a very sexy creature. I was so thin I could have been flushed down a water spout like the itsy-bitsy spider." Now even the younger kids looked at her with admiration.

Way to go, Cat, we're making friends here, Jerry thought.

"Besides ... knowing what the smell was, I was confident I could get rid of it without killing Jerry," Cat finished.

Dessert was a much more pleasant time than the previous courses. They laughed and joked and dripped melted ice cream on the white cloth without worry or formality. The children were excused when the adults moved to a smaller table where brandy and coffee were served.

"How was your meeting with the president?" Henry asked.

Cat let the golden liquid swirl in her glass. "It was as though the two of us were in the same room, looking at each other, but speaking different languages. No interpreter. He basically had me kidnapped, so I assumed the meeting would be important.

"First, he asked me what I thought about the events in Kailua after the earthquake. I gave him what he asked for: the failure at all levels of government. I was elaborating on my criticism but had a feeling he didn't hear what I was saying. You expect the other person to respond with gestures at appropriate moments, little head movements to acknowledge a point, a sound ... something to let you know he's with you. I got none of these, as if I spoke Chinese or perhaps his hearing aid failed.

"After ten minutes or so, he became somewhat impatient and started asking about my political experience and ambitions. None on either count, and I told him so. Eventually, he looked me in the eyes and said in an awfully grave voice, 'What is it that you want?'

"What do I want? I want to go home! I want to see my husband. Have I asked for this meeting, applied for an audience with His Excellency? No, I was abducted, delivered and interrogated!

"Two minutes later, I was through one set of doors,

then another, then a golf cart took me to the helicopter that dropped me off in Kailua. I must say it was a comfy ride."

Henry chuckled softly. "You are a country lassie, Cat."

Jerry found that quite rude and opened his mouth to rebuke his brother-in-law, but Cat put her hand over his fist—let it go, it's my fight. She smiled innocently and asked, "You know much about rural life, Henry?"

"No, not at all, I was referring to your political naiveté." Henry was grinning, not at all apologetic.

Cat grinned back. "Oh, then you consider it important to be knowledgeable about politics, don't you?"

Henry shrugged and opened his hands like in a plea. "Come on, Cat. Of course the politics are important. To start with, politicians keep their hands in your pocket. They decide how much of your money to take and what to spend it for. Only a very naïve person would have no interest in this process."

The chess master was lining up his pawns for a simple, frontal assault. Henry would never overcomplicate a simple game with a known outcome. Pam was fidgeting with her glass. She hated the direction the conversation was taking. It would spoil her dinner for good.

"Henry, do you take any active interest in bank fraud, stolen property trafficking or perhaps illegal stock market manipulations?" Cat asked, not subdued after the first salvo of Henry's large-caliber reasoning.

"No." He allowed himself a patronizing smile. "I leave those things to the police and the SEC."

"But why?" Cat leaned toward Henry, fixing him with her steady, inquisitive stare. "You happily leave some of your important financial affairs to be protected by the police and SEC, but at the same time, you want to closely look at the hands of your government. Do you suspect the Congress, a body meant to keep the administration honest, is less trustworthy than the police? Or perhaps, that your duly elected representatives are more likely to steal than bankers or stockbrokers, or even perhaps thieves? Why this compulsion to supervise politicians with your own eyes?"

Henry's smile became more reflective, and he took a long time to answer, as one might expect of a chess player.

"That's a good point; perhaps I am more suspicious of politicians. Besides, the political influence is much more important and pervasive in my life than common fraud, no matter how audacious. It affects all aspects of everyone's life."

"I beg to differ." Cat was on the offensive now, and pressed her point along lines that were becoming apparent to the others. "You are quite right saying that politicians' influence is pervasive. I would add that they'd like you to believe that it's also inevitable. You know—death and taxes. But the truth is, the political class is mostly a parasitic organism living on the body of productive society. One could remove ninety percent of their activities without suffering any bad consequences. We know"—she looked toward Jerry—"because we were unwilling participants in the relevant experiment. On the contrary, the economy would flourish if liberated from the thousands of unnecessary regulations; we had a taste of it in Hawaii."

"Wow!" Henry puffed, surprised. "You had the earthquake and tsunami followed by three weeks of inaction by the federal government. You take that as a sufficient proof to argue that the government is an unnecessary nuisance?" Cat's naïveté was being exposed like a patch of black dirt under the receding spring snow.

"Who says unnecessary nuisance?" She shrugged impatiently. "The need to organize a community is real; I was a part of such a spontaneous process. But we should restrict a government to its essential functions. We don't need this all-powerful, bloodsucking political class that ties our hands with an ever-bigger mountain of regulations just to stay in power. George Washington went back to farming when his term expired, unlike those vermin who stay in Washington, D.C., for thirty or forty years. And when they leave their warm seat, a scion is ready to jump in, corrupted even before starting his career. What do you call this hereditary power regime—feudalism, nepotism-based fascism? Whatever … It's not a democracy unless you have a real choice during elections."

Pam stirred uncomfortably, leaned forward and said in a hushed voice, "Looks like you are asking for revolution, my dear. They are not going to give up all this power easily."

"You are right, Pam." Cat looked away from Henry to include Pam and Jerry. "Look at all these unconstitutional laws: The Patriot Act, Military Commissions Act … All these new tools for snooping and incarcerating without any meaningful legal oversight. A pure power grab, another arrogant step toward unchallenged power. But I am actually optimistic."

She stirred her brandy, sniffed it and took a sip as all eyes converged on her mouth in anticipation. "The sad part is that what I'm saying is nothing new. 'Men should be free from any superior power on earth, except for laws of nature'—that's Samuel Adams. Who remembers Sam Adams? Maybe for the beer. His ideas are forgotten, but I think we'll relearn them."

Cat sounded confident, like a young revolutionary addressing the crowd. "The basic truth will become obvious one day: we can do without politicians, but they will wither like your poinsettia"—she pointed to a plant on a windowsill—"if you don't water it … as soon as we cut off the money flow."

"Won't happen." Henry lost his smile, getting annoyed with Cat's adolescent idealism. "The state has ample means to ensure that the money *will* flow. Just try to 'forget' sending your tax return and wait for what will happen. They will explain it to you in a very uncomfortable way. What you propose cannot be done by peaceful means." Now he was also getting a bit worried about Cat and Jerry. She was obviously a big influence on his brother-in-law, and they both could end up in a big legal mess.

Cat was warming up and straightened up in her chair. Her glass was left on the table; she needed both hands for gesticulation. She shook her head. "I am not for any armed action. They will always have more and bigger guns. I don't want anyone killed. But there is a way to deprive the government of its magic potion.

"The change will have to start with us. We need to structure our financial affairs in such a way that the beast will starve. It will come to us, tail between legs, tongue lolling out, begging for nourishment. Only then will we be able to defang it, and set it to work on those few projects we really need a government for: protecting the borders, maintaining the legal system, and so on."

"How can you starve the beast?" Henry looked puzzled. "If you generate income you pay taxes, or you go to jail. The only other way is not to earn money—then you don't pay taxes. But I prefer to live in this house rather than in a homeless shelter."

"That's true," Cat agreed with deceptive ease. "We need income for immediate consumption. You can't deny yourself gainful work. They will get their share of that, but it's peanuts for the government. They have been spending much more than they collect even now, never mind when we put them on a diet.

"But what will happen if men like you, highly qualified experts in their fields, start moonlighting abroad in their spare time, while cutting the home activities? I know from Jerry that you do a lot of work abroad, looking after your firm's plants in China, Malaysia and wherever … What would happen if you opened a small firm, Henry Inc., in Hong Kong, and asked for your out-of-the country work to be remunerated in the form of stock, credit to Henry Inc.?"

Henry and Pam exchanged quick looks but said nothing,

awaiting Cat's conclusions.

"You wouldn't even need to be a tax cheat; you could pay your taxes on the received stock, but the capital gains would wait for you, increasing, until Henry Inc.'s boss wanted them. And they would stay out of reach of those grabby paws. Just as well you could buy some appreciating land, or gold, or buy a villa on the Mediterranean coast. All these are legal measures that would allow you to accumulate wealth without feeding the beast."

Henry nodded his head with an ambivalent smile, interested but not convinced. Go on, he invited Cat with a nod.

"The government will keep borrowing money, but at some point, they won't find any more creditors. At this point, Henry, you may need that villa in Europe. When the government really runs out of money, your wealth is going to catch someone's eye. They will come and take everything you have, legally and with full political support, because there will be millions of hungry and desperate people with no interest in preserving your private property rights. The inflation-ravaged retirees, civil servants, unemployed—a lot of them when the economy collapses—will have no second thoughts about your liberties; they will want to eat. We saw it in Kailua just a few weeks ago. They will want government assistance, and they will *demand* that your bank accounts are seized and your lovely home transformed into a ... perhaps a soup kitchen?"

"It's a scary picture you paint, Cat." Pam was visibly disturbed and looked at her husband, unspoken question in her eyes.

Henry shrugged and sighed. "It might come to it. No country ever had a debt like we do, and it's growing pretty fast. I am not as sure as Cat what will happen and when, but her scenario cannot be dismissed. Nobody can predict the future because there is no precedent."

"Well, actually there are a lot of precedents," Jerry broke in. "Bankrupt governments fall without exception—guaranteed. It's the 'how' that is not clear. Sometimes it's a gigantic bloody riot like in Russia of 1917, sometimes a miserable, seemingly endless, but fairly nonviolent depression, like in postwar England, and on occasion a new and nasty regime like the fascists taking over Germany. But there are no nice and pleasant ways out of bankruptcy."

Cat smiled again, sweet like a cupcake. "So tell me, Henry, why should I waste my time and energy at the losing game of politics? I prefer to move ahead, live in the future where the productive country lads and lassies like me will worry how to boost our crops … rather than worry about vermin."

The chess master raised his glass to Cat and smiled with respect. "Check and mate."

Pam held a napkin to her mouth, staring at him in disbelief, then turned to Cat. "So, being practical … how are you going to protect your family, if you are so sure that this catastrophe is coming?"

Cat put her hand on Jerry's arm. "First of all, I've married a blue-water captain who can take us wherever we want, without asking for anybody's permission. Then, we are producers; we can earn our living anywhere. When Jerry came to Kailua in January, nothing worked. He brought us the first fish and pushed us to start our first market. In a sense, he restarted our economy. I know he can do similar miracles somewhere else. Maybe the next time it will be a roofing company or a taxi service; it doesn't matter. He will find the need and will meet it. I feel safe with him."

Jerry's heart was melting. "And I, too, have a skill that can be used anywhere," Cat concluded.

"Aren't you going back to Hawaii?" Pamela turned to her brother.

"We are; we'll try to make our nest there. Hawaii is an exceptional place; people are warm and easygoing there. But after the experience we had, we are very changed people, not so trustful. We will always keep our ears to the ground. Cat talked about politicians and government … this is her thing."

He glanced at Cat sideways. "And I mostly agree with her," he added with a quick grin. "But for me the central question is, do you control your resources? If not—because of distance or organization or your own laziness—you will get burned, sooner or later. You can't always cover all your needs … What do I know about antibiotics, for example? But it might be good enough to have your neighbor watch your back. I would be willing to rely on Doctor Lim in medical matters. But to rely on the good will of some bored guy in Washington? Not for us. We will go to Hawaii, hoping to build our safe world there without much official interference, but if they are too intrusive …"

"The desperate people that Cat talked about a moment ago are all over Hawaii now," Henry observed. "They may not understand your and Cat's complicated ideas; all they want is food, a place to sleep and gas. Who gives a hoot where the goodies come from? They love their government now and you rebels better be careful."

The dinner ended on a pleasant note of reconciliation; Pam was relieved.

Just when Cat was ready to roll to the car, Henry asked, "How long are you folks going to stay in New York?"

Cat and Jerry looked at each other; they had no tickets and the date of return was not set. "Maybe two weeks?" Jerry offered, and Cat nodded in agreement.

"I have to inspect our plant in Malaysia in ten days." Henry winked at Cat. "Perhaps we could get together again next week?"

"Don't you have your chess tournament next week?" Pam asked with surprise.

"I might skip this one; there aren't that many opportunities for an interesting conversation," Henry answered.

"I am jealous as hell," Pam muttered in her brother's ear when she kissed him good-bye. "He has never cancelled a chess tournament in the twenty years of our marriage."

They listened to the news in the car: the price of oil went up to one hundred and thirty dollars per barrel, and gasoline supplies were spotty throughout the country. The National Guard had been called in to suppress the civil unrest in Alabama and Georgia.

"Where the heck did you get all this sociopolitical reasoning from? It can't be a part of the computer science curriculum," Jerry asked his wife.

"No, it's not part of my formal education." Cat smiled dreamily. "It's part of my growing up. It all started when I was about ten and couldn't sleep. I tossed and turned in bed, making all kinds of noises to entertain myself. My father stuck his head into my room—'Can't sleep, baby?' Rather obvious. 'I'm going to help you right away.' He was full of unorthodox fixes. He came back a minute later with one of his books. 'Read a bit and that'll put you to sleep in no time.'

"It was a book of Schweitzer's philosophical essays that my father had read recently. I was so bored that I started reading. There were some anecdotes from the author's medical practice in the African bush that I found quite interesting. In the morning, we had breakfast together.

"'So, how did you like Schweitzer? Made it through the first page?' he asked.

"I told him that I actually liked it, and we talked about Schweitzer a bit before I left for school, so he knew I wasn't just bragging. Since that day, he treated me like a partner in his philosophical adventures. I played along because I was pleased that he had such a high opinion of me. I'm sure I missed most, but some of it stuck, as you've seen."

"You never talked about your family, Cat. Maybe you should tell me a bit since we're now getting acquainted with my relatives."

"We spent very little time together, Jerry, and there was always some major crisis going. But you are right; you should know about my folks, especially that you owe them."

Jerry was puzzled but let her talk.

"The first time we met—no—I mean when you first came to see me at my home, you seemed strangely familiar. It took me a while to realize that you had a lot in common with my father. For example, take the circumstances of our first encounter. You had plunged into a potentially dangerous situation without much thought given to your safety. He was an enthusiastic canoeist. Once in Cancun, he rented a canoe and went exploring a lagoon full of alligators. He came back rather hastily when an eight-foot gator threatened him on a muddy bank."

It's true, Jerry thought. We had an amazingly easy relationship since I stepped over her threshold in Kailua. Cat treated me like an old friend or a family member right from the beginning.

Cat continued. "Then, both my parents started talking to me after you and I had that lovely swim in my pool. That was significant because I had had problems communicating with my folks for a long time."

"Where do they live? Can we meet them?" Jerry was surprised she had not invited him to meet her parents yet.

"You may think I'm crazy, Jerry, but I talk to them in my head only. They're both gone, killed in a car wreck in Ecuador during one of their crazy adventures. That was about six years ago, a year before I crashed myself. When I was a teenager, I somehow got estranged from my parents, although we had been very close in my childhood. Then I went to college, married Nick, and I never took any initiative to reconcile. And suddenly, they were both gone. I felt really rotten about it.

"After my accident, I learned to have relationships with other people in my head. Ruth taught me that—she was a woman who had progressive paralysis for many years, but lived a very rich life in her mind. I have to tell you that, sometimes, I have problems knowing which things are real in my life and which ones I've manufactured in my imagination.

"I had tried to coax my parents into a conversation, but they wouldn't come, until you entered the picture. So, I think they like you, and they encouraged me to be with you. When you came with that silver tea maker you pulled from the wreckage of my house—it was something they brought from their old country—I thought it was a sign that you were stepping right into my family. Jerry, they like you. They were not very thrilled about Nick. They never said anything negative, but I knew they thought of him as too much flash and not enough substance. Who knows, they might have been right. With you, I'm sure my father would grab you to sail on his boat, and my mother would make you model for her, naked if possible. She was a sculptor, a good one, and no human body was safe from her artistic desire."

Well, a bit of family history goes a long way to explain certain of Cat's eccentricities, Jerry thought. He wished he could meet her parents; they sounded like people he would like. They were pulling into the hotel driveway when the radio announcer delivered a news flash: an armistice had been signed in the Middle East and active hostilities had stopped.

Chapter 43

Jerry, February 28

Schumacher, Jerry's former boss, did not hold any grudge against him. Barely seen behind the stacks of journals and reams of papers cluttering his desk, the old professor waved his reading glasses like a lecture pointer.

"Jerry, I admire people who take control of their destiny. I can't tell if you took the right direction, but I respect your initiative and courage. I never had the guts to restart my life from scratch … and look where it took me," he noted with some melancholy in his voice, looking around at the walls covered with diplomas, honorable citations and awards. "Maybe not too bad …" He smirked and adjusted the position of the mahogany wood block with engraved golden letters reading "Professor Arnold Schumacher, Ph.D., Chairman, Economics Department."

"By the way, you never sent me your evaluation of Amanda Kroll. Any chance it is still resting under your coffee mug?" Schumacher asked hopefully.

"I have news for you, Arnold. Amanda escaped your clutches. The last time I saw her, she was a logistics officer in Hawaii. Looks like she has chosen the real world."

"Crap!" Schumacher actually got upset. "I'll have a phone call from Chicago, and will have to explain to her genius daddy why Amanda is not going to be a world-class economist."

Jerry chuckled. "Good luck, boss, and good-bye."

Cat and Jerry had fully recovered. Cat's face returned to its customary round shape, broken by her lush red lips habitually parting in a smile. Her figure seemed a bit fuller than normal, probably due to the lack of regular exercise, and Jerry liked it even better.

His own chronic stress and borderline unhappiness, his usual state of mind in New York, had been replaced by the somewhat irrational optimism and joy of being with Cat. The brick wall he once had built turned into dust. Fascinated with each other like high school lovers, they took full advantage of being well rested, well fed and in love.

Pam tried her best to talk them into a formal wedding while still in New York. "Cat, don't you want to have a church wedding? Pictures, memories … If you would like it, Jerry will not refuse. I am sure."

"Pam, if Jerry wants it, I won't refuse either. But we're not churchgoing people. Why make a mockery of something that's important to other people?"

"You don't believe in God? Are you an atheist?" Cecilia was horrified, and asked the question her mother didn't dare.

"I have no way of knowing if there is God," answered Cat seriously. "That would make me an agnostic rather than atheist. But, I figure, if God exists, he doesn't need all those churches, organs, 'Praise the Lord' and 'Hallelujah.' I suspect that people invented all those things to become professional middlemen between God and the faithful. Looks like it's good business."

Jerry was not sure how well that went over with Pam and Henry. To have a brother who skips a church wedding is one thing, but to have one's children led away from Mother Church could be something else.

Return to Paradise

Cat must have had a similar reflection because she added, "But I have no problems with others' beliefs. Most people I know feel better with their faith; reassurance or happiness—they gain something I don't feel a need for. In fact, sometimes I do feel like talking to someone outside this realm, and I do. But I just don't need any middlemen. So you could call me religious in some sense. But it's my own religion."

"Are there any commandments in your religion?" Henry asked with a small, enigmatic smile. It was hard to guess if his question was a joke or a serious enquiry. He possibly wanted a discussion rematch.

Cat considered his challenge for a moment. "I can think only of one: 'You shall think for yourself.'

"If you think carefully through the implications of your action, you won't need any props. The Ten Commandments, cardinal sins and similar directives passed down along generations are like brief manuals on how to behave so that life is easier for everyone. If you're willing to think, you can predict the consequences, so you don't need a cheat sheet. And if you are a scoundrel—no commandments will stop you."

Pam was uncomfortable with this discussion. The Ten Commandments being a cheat sheet—that couldn't be too healthy for her children's souls. She tried to send the kids upstairs, but Cecilia resisted and the younger ones wanted to stay if Cecilia did.

Henry did not weigh against their staying either. "You might be right on that, Cat, but mostly people are not that willing to think, particularly if you insist on careful thinking. So maybe it's not so bad if they go to church once in a while. But does it really work? Do you think churchgoing folks are more honest or better behaved?"

Cat shrugged. "You've had more time to observe our fellow men ... but I can tell you that under the conditions of extreme stress, like recently in Hawaii, we all were unrepentant sinners. We stole and lied anytime it could produce a scrap of food. Some people went further: there was a lot of mugging, robbery and even murders. I don't think there were enough atheists around to perpetrate all this mayhem; the great majority of crime had to be caused by the churchgoing, God-fearing folks."

"Someone said that if God didn't exist, he would have to be invented. Otherwise, running a civil society would be impossible." Henry was clearly egging Cat on and she was happy to oblige.

"Maybe so. It is either think or obey. Just like democracy, we could have the real thing but only if voters were willing to spend time and effort to understand the issues. Other than that—smoke and mirrors, vote buying and tap dancing every four years."

"Cecilia, go do the dishes!" Pam had had enough.

They became a real family during that month. Cat fell into the family soup like an exotic mushroom and changed the taste of the whole pot. Pam and the kids loved her, but the most remarkable relationship developed between Cat and Henry. They clearly sought each other's company and entertained the rest of the family with witty discussions that always required rematches.

Chapter 44

Cat, Jerry March 1

The broad-shouldered, sunburned men occupied most seats on the plane to Hawaii; their heads—shaved up to a small patch at the skull's top—neatly lined up, three to a row. The troops were coming back to their bases. Their raccoon-like masks of pale skin, protected from the Middle Eastern sun under government-issue goggles, clearly indicated the men's recent whereabouts. A few soft-bellied, suit-wearing individuals—journalists, insurance executives or other people with urgent business in Hawaii—sat scattered among them. But there were no tourists on the plane.

How are the Islands going to survive without tourism, Hawaii's most important cash crop? Jerry wondered. This was not an idle speculation of the unemployed economist, because the question's second portion was, how are we going to make our living there?

Cat's computer business couldn't work—even if she could find customers willing to tinker with their computer systems in the ruined economy—until broadband connections were available. This wouldn't be anyone's priority until tunnels, bridges, power lines and all other vital infrastructure have been rebuilt, many months into the future.

Their cash had been mostly spent. The first small installment of Cat's house insurance payment and the proceeds of Jerry's rather modest brokerage account paid for their New York trip. The fruit of his academic career, his New York apartment, had been swapped for *Lady Luck*. Any money from the final claim adjustment for Cat's house would be long in coming. With her property destroyed by the combination of earthquake and tsunami, Jerry smelled a protracted legal battle before they could feel any green paper in their hands.

Their life together was starting pretty close to the financial zero point, but they didn't mind. Being alive was a miracle enough. Expectations change dramatically after a close call, and they had had a lot of those.

Commentaries from Hawaii, flooding the media now, hinted that—unlike people devastated by Hurricane Katrina—Hawaiians were not taking the government's neglect with mere perfunctory bitching. The deep rumblings of a secession movement were shaking the Hawaiian Islands like the Kilauea Volcano churning explosive magma under the surface. Cat's anger-spiked radio talks still reverberated throughout the archipelago.

Grassroots Hawaiian organizations had sprung up, pushing aside the old, formally anointed and government-controlled bodies. The new activists were determined, brash and disrespectful of proper protocols, people most difficult for the authorities to deal with. But the old administration hung in, being the sole distributor of relief supplies, which were arriving from the Mainland in significant quantities now. Whatever their political ideas, citizens reported to government offices for their food rations or a few gallons of fuel, hat in hand.

Once they passed a building's security post, however ... as soon as they left the secure parking, Hawaii's residents assumed a new personality, the attitude that every administration on the planet would hate.

Hundreds, or maybe thousands—nobody knew as they were unreported—of private enterprises exploded in residential backyards, on sidewalks and on beaches, a wave of enterprise unprecedented in the Islands' history. Dozens of tiny boat-repair yards set up along the shores, blatantly ignoring zoning laws and not bothered by inspectors, who were not foolish enough to ask questions and impose fines. "A government jobber" became an epithet flung like a mud cake to insult and denigrate some poor fellow who swore that he had quit yesterday.

A fishing fleet of small crafts, defying any technical classification, scattered across the waters of the archipelago, sometimes powered by recently available fuel, more often by sails or muscles. Hawaii, once bound by red tape and innumerable restrictions accumulated during the hundred years of dependency, exploded from the Pacific waters like a humpback whale—full of confidence and unafraid.

A new fashion or, rather a new lifestyle, had emerged. Where once a large gleaming car used to be the symbol of success, now a simple bicycle had become the proof of one's worth. People of Hawaii were proud to get by with a minimum of material things. The sense of power was springing from their ability to spurn those things that demanded compliance, obedience and submission.

The airport bus stopped at the Ala Moana terminal, downtown Honolulu. Like Saigon in the sixties, Jerry thought. The broad avenue was filled with the pulsating, disorganized swarm of pedestrians and bikes. A few cars crept through the throng of muscle-powered vehicles, but they no longer owned the streets. Why bother? Jerry thought. They're slower than a rickshaw.

The last time he walked these streets, people were palpably miserable, but now laughter came from all directions, and crowds hurried along with a sense of purpose. Honolulu was not a defeated city; its inhabitants were survivors, hurt badly, but drunk on the joy of existence.

Jerry, pushing Cat's wheelchair through the crowd, was startled by the change he expected least; he realized that he could hardly understand the language around him. People who only a few weeks ago spoke perfect English now spewed words and sentences in pidgin with a speed that would make Kekoa smile.

Cat looked back to him with a grin. "Yeah, I can get it … some of it." The islanders found one more way to assert their independence; the Hawaiian pidgin united the wild mix of ethnically different people and separated them from the Mainland *haole* at the same time. And they all seemed to be quite proficient in it.

The downtown buildings still displayed their ugly gray blemishes, but many ground-floor stores had reopened. The broken windows were shuttered with rough plywood but decorated with displays of primitive art. The solid concrete structure of the central bus station at the Ala Moana Shopping Center survived the earthquake and a few buses sat in their bays. Cat and Jerry were lucky to find seats on the bus leaving for Kailua in thirty minutes, one of only two that covered this route daily.

The bus stopped on Kalaheo Street, not far from the Round House, on its way to Lanikai. The battered metal gate was open, but there was no one in the yard, still brown from the mud brought by the tsunami. The front door was locked. Kalani and her flock were gone. Jerry did not dare force his way through the plywood-covered window; the time of emergency and forgiveness was over.

He bought sandwiches at a little neighborhood market and they lay down under a tree, among tall weeds. They were tired and had no other place to go.

"What do you want to do?" Cat asked.

"Like in any wilderness." Jerry shrugged. "First find shelter then water and food. There must be someone in charge of this building; the doors are locked and someone has put the plywood in the windows. Maybe the owners have returned. They might let us stay here. If not, I'll go and find Kalani."

His patience was rewarded; he woke up from his nap when an older man appeared in the yard. Covered leather shoes and a straw hat on his head, obviously he was not a local man. The house's owner from California—Jerry assumed—checking on his property. He carefully moved sleeping Cat's head from his thigh onto the knapsack and approached the man.

Jim Crawford was indeed the owner of Round House. Jim knew Cat and had been told of her war council and orphanage operating in his building.

"Can't imagine a better use for my home," he said kindly, but a moment later added with a crooked smile, "just hope the smell of dead whale evaporates soon."

He wanted to return to his wife on the Mainland as soon as possible, so he was happy to hear that Cat and Jerry would take care of his house. Hawaii was a difficult place to live then, especially for temporary residents.

Lady Luck was not anchored at the beach, and Jerry left Cat to look for Kalani and buy some food. Kailua Road resonated with hammers banging all along. Half-naked men kneeled on roofs, stood on ladders and dug in the ground—a big push to rebuild was on. Good time to be a carpenter, Jerry chuckled—option one.

A bunch of teenage boys, sporting shirtless thin chests, sat on a concrete bench in front of the Auntie's pizzeria. They whistled at two girls walking by who pretended not to hear. The lethargy was gone—Kailua was full of life again, moving forward.

Jerry stopped at the Starbucks, which had reopened a few days ago. An honest cup of real coffee could be bought in this town again. There he picked up Kalani's tracks; the girl at the counter suggested that he try Rosen's restaurant. Since Cat told him about Kalani's grab of Rosen's food supplies, he was not surprised to hear she had commandeered the rest of his establishment as well.

The restaurant was closed, but he found the kids camping in the main room, tables and chairs neatly stored at one end. The floors were swept clean and the windows appeared spotless but, on closer inspection, he saw there simply was no glass left in the frames.

"Republic of Hawaii, Kailua Office," said a sign inscribed in red felt-tip pen on a piece of white cardboard, and pinned to the wall above the open door. Inside, Kalani was sitting behind a metal desk. Her body, which seemed to belong to a skinny teenager the last time Jerry saw her, had the voluptuous shape of a very attractive adult woman. She was still wearing the same old green dress, now definitely too tight, but there was something new about her—the air of authority.

She jumped up from the desk when Jerry knocked and wrapped her arms around his neck. "Jerry, you've come back! Is Cat with you?"

"She sure is, and she's fine. You can see her anytime at the Round House; we are the house sitters there. But look at you! You look fabulous! How is Abe?"

She let him go. "Abe is gone, fishing. He got almost religious about it; must be trying to make up for those years he bummed around. Now, he drops in sometimes to spend a night at home. Then he's gone again, usually for a few days or a week. He works your boat really hard; hope you don't mind, but he said you let him."

"Oh, that's fine," Jerry reassured her. "I hoped he would do that. I intend to become his partner."

"Are you really going to be a fisherman? You're a professor, Jerry!" Kalani eyed him incredulously.

"I *was* a professor, Kalani. Now I need to make some money, however I can. We will see what else I could do."

"You could work for us …" Kalani proudly pointed her finger at the hand-painted placard leaned against the wall, its red letters framed by the red and blue pattern of the Hawaiian flag.

"Republic of Hawaii," Jerry read aloud. "Have you separated from the USA already? I thought it would be the kingdom of Hawaii, not the republic."

Kalani would not be intimidated by mere technicalities. "The important thing is, we'll have our own government. Kingdom or republic … we can decide later."

Jerry felt a pinch of worry. "What about the old government? You know, the state of Hawaii and the federal government, the one in Washington?"

The young woman waved her hand dismissively. "We have people worrying about that in Honolulu. My job is to make sure we can run Kailua and the windward side."

"That's not a small project, Kalani. Who are you working with? Are you the boss?"

"Auntie Malia comes every morning, and she frequently brings friends with her. Other people come and go, but they would be here if I needed them. I'm here all the time, so I guess I am the boss," and she proudly raised her chin.

"I would love to help you, Kalani, but I don't think you can pay me, and I do need money. By the way, is Sergeant Yoshida still around? Does he take orders from you?"

"Mike is still at the station, but I haven't seen him in a long time. I never tried to give him any orders, so how would I know?"

Right, Jerry thought. Good thing Yoshida hadn't come to arrest her yet. Hopefully, the new republic hadn't caught the eye of the old republic so far.

Kalani pulled him down on a chair and once he was sitting, she looked directly into his eyes. "You think I'm a silly girl playing with things I don't understand, don't you?"

Jerry was embarrassed because she was right on the mark.

Kalani kept him fixed in her sight. "You know, I'm not a very educated person, but I wouldn't call myself stupid either. We have to start somewhere. I'm not going to be great help negotiating with the federal government or the governor, but I know pretty well what people in Kailua need. I've learned a lot over the past few months, when we were working with Cat, and later after you left. What I don't know, I'm going to learn, and I will try to find good people who will help, like you and Cat."

Jerry recalled the Kalani who used to clean Cat's house: a pretty but simple girl whose biggest dream was to become a nurse. The new Kalani now stood in front of him, imposing, self-confident and determined. This was not a woman to dismiss with a joke and a smile. He stood up and extended his hand.

"I will make you a deal, Kalani. I will do my best to help you with your mission whenever I can. But first I really have to earn a living for Cat and myself. Your organization needs to mature, too, before you can make use of an economist. But when you are ready, I'll do my best, as long as I agree with you, and your people, on what a proper government is. I certainly will not get involved in replicating the old system. Do we have an agreement, Kalani?"

The girl shook his hand firmly then giggled and gave him a big Hawaiian hug and kiss on the cheek. "I knew you would help us, and Cat, too. Tell her I'll come this evening to see her."

She expected Abe back in two days. He was selling his fish in Honolulu, where the market had opened and commercial freezers were available. He hired a young boy as a helper and had become a real skipper, running the boat confidently on her diesel motor. Fuel was available, though very expensive, but business was good, so he could afford it.

"Ah, Jerry—you know, they found that bastard Rosen!" Kalani stopped him in the doorway.

"Really, Rosen got arrested?"

"Nah, someone shot him."

"Abe?"

"No, they found him dead in Honolulu. Abe was with you then, thank God. I'm glad the bastard is dead. I still feel like throwing myself through a window when somebody gets behind me unexpectedly. The first thing I did when I took over his office was to smash that figurine that he kept on his desk. I couldn't stop myself until it was only dust."

Jerry decided to stop by the rec center to see the market, his personal monument to Adam Smith. The gathering of canvas tents, stalls and plywood huts spilled over from the tennis courts onto a large parking lot next to the baseball field. Jerry entered the maze.

Vegetable and fruit stands predominated, but there were a few places with simple industrial products: bicycles, rickshaws, building materials reclaimed from the ruins, construction tools—necessities. He noticed that few customers were actually buying, even though many people milled about.

He found a clue to this mystery when he checked the prices. A pound of tomatoes was offered for six dollars. He continued inspecting the prices with an increasingly tight feeling in his throat. The ten thousand dollars he and Cat still had was supposed to give them a six-month cushion, but with prices like these, they would be broke soon. They needed income as soon as possible.

Jerry came to a bicycle stand; he needed basic transportation, and a used bike would do just fine. The stall was an example of capitalism in its purest form: a steel-tubing frame covered with a large piece of blue tarp for a roof and a back wall. A metal bike-stand held upright eight or ten bicycles of different sizes. Jerry checked a rusty but solid mountain bike with good tires. The attached price tag said four hundred eighty dollars.

Four hundred eighty bucks for a used bike? That's an outrage! I can certainly do better than that! Jerry approached the bored Asian man sitting on a picnic chair in front of his merchandise. "How come your bikes are so expensive? I could get a new one for less at Wal-Mart."

The merchant looked at him scornfully. He wasn't going to engage in this pointless conversation, but after looking around and seeing no other prospective customers, he decided to chat after all.

"You went to Wal-Mart?"

"No, I didn't," Jerry admitted.

"Only rats there. The old merchandise looted long time ago; the store's closed. At Sears, you can have pots that nobody wants and maybe some clothes. But they have no bikes, no tools—nothing that people really need." Then he looked the other way.

"Why don't they sell the stuff people want to buy?" Jerry insisted. Not only did he need a bike, but he also had the strong suspicion that his financial future was threatened.

"Because they can't!" the triumphant keeper announced. "The Chinese decided not to give away their goods for close to nothing, after all. The bikes at Sears would be so expensive that people couldn't buy them anyway. Do you know what the price of an ounce of gold is?"

Jerry shook his head. The last time he knew gold's price was three months ago, and then it was about thirteen hundred.

"Sixteen hundred twenty-one this morning, and you can bet it will be more a week from now."

"Hyperinflation!" Jerry had the last piece of evidence and felt like he'd been punched in his solar plexus. No need for a professor of economics; a first-year student could tell that gold's price rising so quickly indicated horrific inflation. The hyperinflation, always a theoretical but unlikely possibility, hit us like a car running into a flock of chickens on a village road, he thought.

Schumacher, with his great computer model of inflation, didn't see it. At the end, it was Cat and her unsophisticated Internet gurus who got it right! Now, neither the Federal Reserve nor anybody else could do anything about it. The house was falling and a lot of people would be crushed. Like a tsunami, it wouldn't stop until the landscape was flattened, all traces of prosperity thoroughly erased.

The merchant watched Jerry with satisfaction. "You better buy now, before bikes get even more expensive." He seemed quite happy with the prices he could command, not understanding he would be swept into the same gutter as everyone else.

Jerry knew better. The Germans after the First World War, then the Argentineans, the Brazilians ... It happened to every nation that got seduced by the idea of prosperity achieved by playing tricks with money.

"When did it start? I mean the prices growing so fast," Jerry asked.

"All I know is," the merchant answered, now bored with the discussion, "that since I stopped trading bikes for food and started using money, I can't buy anything for the usual price. I have to pay double or triple for my merchandise. Plus my markup and—you see the prices."

Jeremy bought the bike. I was a part of this scam, he thought, riding slowly over the cracked asphalt. I taught my students the complicated theories, but never mentioned the most ancient law: If you want to consume, you have to produce. It seemed impossible to run out of goods, such was technological progress, but consumption rose even faster. The ancient truth had never been revoked.

The fat rubber wheels jumped over potholes overflowing with exuberant weeds. Jerry couldn't shake off his anxious thoughts. People came to consider prosperity a natural condition. Big mistake—nature's way is starvation, fear and an early death. Being smart and working hard can keep this natural reality away, but it will return whenever intelligence or diligence fails.

He found the living room decorated with lavender, all Cat needed to do was just a walk out to the garden. Cat was reclining on the sofa, a mango in her hand. Her body had acquired a softer shape, less athletic but definitely sweeter. Her round face glowed happily as she coaxed him with her outstretched arms. When Jerry sat beside her, she wrapped her arms around his neck and kissed him by the ear. She did not let go then but whispered, "Congratulations, Jerry, you're going to be a daddy."

Jerry's arms squeezed her body gently against his chest as if she were a fragile porcelain vase. As he lay next to her kissing her eyes and lips, Cat led his hand over her stomach.

Jerry whispered, "You know, there is nothing I wouldn't do to protect you both. A few months ago, I was a shallow boy bored to death behind his brick wall. Then you helped me to break out. You will never be alone as long as I live."

Cat's face was moist. "I feel safe with you, and this baby will have a wonderful father."

The news Jerry brought from the market concerned Cat, but did not surprise her. "Smart people kept predicting this for years. It's just … the timing is really bad. But is there ever a good time for a disaster? Still, it would only be fair for us to have an easier life for a while."

Jerry massaged her belly lightly. "Isn't it a shame the baby will come during hard times?"

"The baby always knows best." Cat shrugged. "Anyway, considering all that we went through, this is going to be one tough kid. And this coming storm … maybe it is this big rain that will clear all the foolishness and garbage that accumulated over the years. If this is what we have to endure for our child to have blue skies and a clean earth," she put her hand on her swollen abdomen, "I don't mind—so be it."

Cat thought for a moment. "Do you think, Jerry, we will

stay here? For many years, I mean. I really like Hawaii." She looked hopefully in Jerry's eyes.

"You know, Cat, I love Hawaii, too," Jerry started. "The best things in my life happened here."

She pushed her head under Jerry's arm, onto his lap, so that he could caress her hair.

"I love people like Kalani and Abe," Jerry continued. "We'll help them and make our home here, if they treat us fairly. But, if the government, even if it is Abe, Kalani and their friends, tries to turn us into its servants, I would try very hard to persuade you to move somewhere else."

Cat did not move or say anything for a while, then asked quietly, "Where, Jerry?"

"I don't know, Cat. There must be people who think like us; we would find them."

During the long hours Jerry spent in the rubber boat, holding the dying Cat's head, he thought, If I had another chance ... how would I run my life, so I wouldn't have to sit helplessly, watching my love dying?

 Never remain defenseless, was his answer. I might not have much, but what I had would be under *my* control. I would have no one in charge of my survival; no person or office would decide if I could have my ten gallons of diesel or a box of sardines.

Jerry wanted to talk about his thoughts and plans, but his wife's eyes had closed and she was breathing quietly. Cat was asleep, relaxed and trusting in his arms, at last.

Ruth, I know you can hear me; you are hiding somewhere in my head. After all, that was the only place you could move to after your pool eventually dried up. That's where you live now.

You were wrong—what has recently happened is real. Remember the reality test you told me about? Experience something I had never felt before, something my mind couldn't make up, preferably of the visceral kind.

Alex Modzelewski

Today, I felt my baby kick—how about that? Are you ready to accept it now?

And ... Ruth, thank you for that wake-up call on the dinghy. If you hadn't told me, I wouldn't have gotten up to find the flare gun on the bottom and we would have drifted away forever.

Well, we have arrived. Thank you for reading my book, hope you have enjoyed it.
Cat and Jerry's adventures certainly do not end at this point. You can meet them again in *Woman on the Moon*, my other novel (2009), where a couple of fugitives flee the long arm of their government. Later, you might encounter them in *Golden Dust*, a work still in progress.
I also invite you to my *Demon of Darien* (2010) where you can witness dangerous exploits in Panama of the man terminated as a father, husband and doctor. Can his life be rebuilt? A bit of demonic assistance might help.

Still a kid at heart, I believe that weighty issues should be considered only in context of a fast paced, exciting story.

My books are available as paperbacks at the Amazon, the Barnes & Noble online and some retailer bookstores. The e-book versions can be found at the Amazon (Kindle) and in other digital versions at the Barnes & Noble, Sribd, Smashbook, Google and other e-book retailers.

My essays and articles can be found on my websites:
    http://web.me.com/amodzelewski/Site/Welcome.html
    publishing - http://www.booksbyAlex.com
    E-publishing - Smashwords.com
Internet forum - http://www.scribd.com/Alex Modzelewski

A "WE OWE YOU NOTHING"

sign greets the marooned sailors as they approach the community of boaters drifting in the middle of the Pacific. Only the personal friendships and services provided by the floating marina hold this ocean town together, but its dwellers have one more thing in common: the deep mistrust toward any form of government.

This is exactly what makes it an ideal place for a fugitive, Doctor Paul Bronski, pursued by the military counterintelligence on suspicion of stealing the Army's drug code-named "Remorse." A pretty harbormaster, Grace, has her own reasons to avoid the authorities and when she and Paul fall in love, their problems multiply. Can determined individuals break a leash, escape from the strangling embrace of state? Or is it more like gravity and death—inevitable? As Paul and Grace feverishly search for the answer, fleeing across the ocean and the mountains of Panama pursued by a psychopathic agent, they discover something else: the magic formula for happiness.

> "Like Ayn Rand, Modzelewski uses fiction to present and discuss libertarian ideas. His characters' conversations are intelligent, interesting and philosophically sound; and they never become too long and drawn out. The story is suspenseful and exciting."
> … "The Woman on the Moon" is worth reading, especially for those who enjoy novels with a libertarian bent. And the cover art, a gold sculpture of a woman reclining languidly on a crescent moon, is exquisite."
> Jo Ann Skounsen of Liberty magazin

"Woman on the Moon" (paperback) is available at the Amazon, the Barnes & Noble online and some retailer stores. Its e-book version can be found at the Amazon (Kindle) and as e-pub at the Barnes & Noble, Ssribd, Smashbook, Google. and other e-book retailers.

DEMON OF DARIEN

Fired! Fired as a father, husband and doctor.

ALEX MODZELEWSKI

What now? Quiet philosophy reading? Alcoholism and suicide? Dr. Morrison brushes both until a weird old man lures him into a dubious intrigue. A fountain of youth, exotic woman and compassion for a child draw the doctor deeper and deeper into the Darien jungle, where his morals break one after another.

GOLDEN DUST

Not everyone cheers when people take charge of their lives. Money is lost, power dwindles and many important folks are unhappy. *Golden Dust*, the third novel in my "Spun in Hawaii" series, follows a mottled group of individuals who gave up in disgust the life as it has always been, and try to forge their future with their own hands.

A hospital ship they operate offshore Hawaii proves to be a runaway success and the medical establishment of the Islands will not take it lying on the mat. The loss of revenue and influence will be countered in ways as different as the participants' characters, but in every case supported by great financial resources, connections and tradition.

The ship's crew needs to meet the onslaught or turn their tail, if they are lucky enough to have a chance. Zbig, a surgeon and inventor, Jane, a mysterious doctor without past, and their friends have few assets on their side except for the understanding that administrators cannot function without providers. The Internet and other technological advances allow them to separate themselves from the Big Medicine and their patients love it.

This is going to be a crime thriller, medical politics drama and—I can't do without it—a love story. How it is going to end ... nobody knows yet, including me, but I promise a lot of turns, traps and blowups.

If you would like to have some insight into my current thinking, I place most of my articles on Scribd, where they can be read whenever the mood strikes.

CPSIA information can be obtained at www.ICGtesting.com
Printed in the USA
LVOW081707161111
255294LV00017B/39/P